BLEEDING MARS

Asher J. Quazar

QUAZAR PRESS

Copyright © 2024 Asher Quazar

All rights reserved.

No part of this publication may be reproduced, distributed, or transmitted in any form or by any means, including photocopying, recording, or other electronic or mechanical methods, without the prior written permission of the publisher, except as permitted by U.S. copyright law.

The story, all names, characters, and incidents portrayed in this production are fictitious. No identification with actual persons (living or deceased), places, buildings, and products is intended or should be inferred.

Cover art illustration by Sharlyn Artieda - linktr.ee/ouroridae
Formatting and other illustrations by Quazar Press
www.AsherQuazar.com

ISBN: 9798868260650
ISBN: 9798326685124 (hardcover)

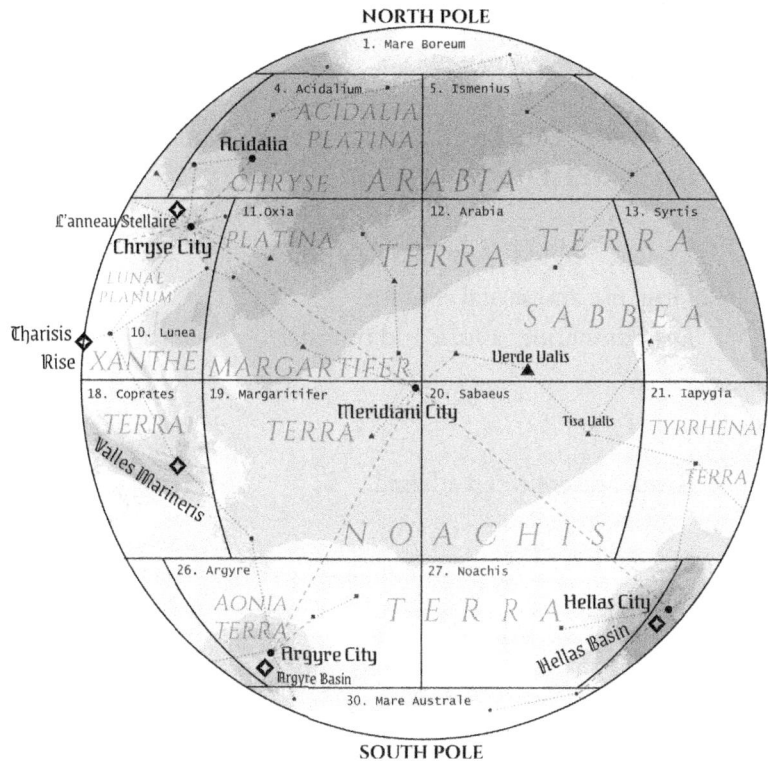

Equatorial projection of Mars

Content Warnings

This work contains mature content including but not limited to:

Violence, blood, gore, and death.
Drug use and sexual content.
Discrimination, abuse, and trauma.

Reader discretion is advised.

CHAPTER 1

Clouds

Fine red sand whipped past Dezi's visor as he rode across the boundless crater. In the morning twilight, the thin atmosphere of Mars let light from a million stars break through. The Milky Way bowed overhead like a streak of shattered opals, falling into the sunrise, and if Dezi arched his head back, he could pretend he was flying a Hadron ship instead of riding a scuffed Hadron bike.

His wrist monitor flashed red, but the rush and grind of sand drowned out its alarm. He patted the polyimide tape sealing where his helmet and stasis suit met and checked the monitor's screen. It read, *Secondary tank activated. Thirty minutes of oxygen remaining.*

He looked back at the facility's glassy, ground-hugging habitation dome a mile behind him and then eyed the ruddy clouds forming over the crater's crest half a mile ahead. *Plenty of time*, he thought.

Dezi decelerated as he crossed into the shadow cast by the mountainous ridge, stopping beside the two-meter-tall silver pipe he had followed from the facility. He threw out his kickstand and dismounted, tossing a cloud of dust under his feet. The silt sucked on his weighted boots, making every step a battle as he trudged to the water meter.

Fine as powder, colder than ice, and toxic as chlorine gas, this regolith was always piling up at the bottom of their crater. One day, the facility would end up buried in it, but he doubted Eden Natural Healing would put up the money to dig them out. All the blood and sweat they sucked out of Verde Valis, and Corporate still refused to hire an actual engineer. Now Dezi was out on the dust before sunrise, fixing something he was completely underqualified to touch.

The meter's door dangled in the low-density atmosphere, its marred screen displaying, *ERROR: 415X00.*

"Unsupported media type...?" Dezi patted his helmet and frowned.

He gave the massive pipe a sturdy kick then listened. The fluid inside slushed and grated but then glugged down the pipe, washing out the frost blockage. Although it'd be a little crunchy tomorrow, they'd have something to water the crops with. When they'd get new heating coils was a different question.

Dezi shut the meter hatch, but as he took up his bike's kickstand, a buzz ran across the dunes like an army of rotary drones taking off. So deep he felt it through his boots, the vibrations drew shimmering ripples in the dust under his feet—not good. Booming sands were moving sands, and once the sand got moving, there was no telling where it would stop. A gust shoved at Dezi as dark sienna clouds rolled over the crater's peaks. The sheets of clay-red dust piled against the ridge shifted, breaking into streams, gathering into rivers, and cascading down the crater bowl in a powdery avalanche.

A jolt of adrenaline jump-started Dezi's heart, and he leaped onto his bike, pulling the throttle before his ass was on the seat. It lurched forward as the dustslide roared behind him. Hunched down, he hit top speed in seconds, with his Hadron whining and sputtering underneath him. He didn't know if she could handle this abuse, but he couldn't let up. If he could outrace the worst of it, he had a chance. The facility was a few hundred yards away and approaching fast.

Losing ground and vision to the darkening murk, Dezi gripped his vibrating handlebars and gritted his teeth, but the front hit him like a rolling wave of bricks. It tossed him off his bike, and his vision went dark save for the dim twinkle of the twin moons, Phobos and Deimos, confirming which way was up. He landed hard and immediately scrounged for the pipe that could lead him home, but grasped nothing but sand. His heartbeat pounded in his ears, his hands shook, his throat tightened—had the dust gotten into his suit? Was he about to die exactly like Mithra had?

A gust cleared Dezi's vision, revealing a spindly column twisting in the stormglow—a newborn whirlwind making touchdown. He stumbled, head suddenly filled with helium, then felt something solid—his Hadron's handlebars—but the bike was halfway encased in sand. The storm dragged on him, sucking him closer, while the sky darkened like drying blood. His suit blared, "*Warning! Fifteen minutes of oxygen remaining.*"

Dezi collapsed to his knees. This was it; the struggle was finally over.

He choked on a sob and half-heartedly looked over his shoulder. A couple of lights switched on at the facility. Breakfast would be in an hour.

It's too far. I'm too tired. I'm so damn tired.

Something flickered in front of a light. A figure? A person holding the airlock open, trying to save Dezi.

His stomach dropped, but prickles raced up his skin. He couldn't let another person die for his mistakes, not again. He surged forward, jumped onto the fat water pipe, and hauled himself up. Staggering against the wind, he threw his weight forward, lined up each foot squarely on the pipe, and ran, ran until the specks of light grew, then dove off, crashing in front of the airlock. He groped for the handle and rattled the door, but it wouldn't budge. Every time he pulled, the screen flashed, *Entry not permitted. Dangerous atmospheric conditions detected.*

And Corporate had spoken. The tape would not hold, the dust would get in, and Dezi would ruin a good suit with his stinking corpse. At least whoever had tried to save him had the sense to turn back. He smiled, and a few of his tears were grateful ones.

"*Ten minutes of oxygen remaining,*" his suit said.

Dezi wedged himself into the corner where the pipe connected to the habitation dome, while the storm stained the facility lights the colors of rust and gore. Sand piled around him until he formed a dune himself, helmet labeled 000 sitting on top like a grave marker. Entombed, he pressed his hand against the tape on his neck seal, and the dust exerted its pressure onto him.

"*Five minutes of oxygen remaining.*"

The hot stink of his helmet, chalky taste of his tongue, and cold nylon of his suit became his world. This was how Mithra had died, taking shallow breaths alone, tangling with unfinished thoughts. Dezi recalled the last time he had kissed someone, regretting that he'd stopped it before they'd gone further. He wished he hadn't broken up with that cocky, freckled boy. It would have been nice to fall in love once, even if it never would have worked out.

"*Oxygen depleted. Emergency pressure balance initiated.*" The air valve seated over Dezi's heart halted its subtle blow. "*Life support failure imminent.*"

His breathing steadied as a hush settled over the dunes. It was quiet for a storm, though too early for one to stop. Unless it wasn't a storm at all but a sandslide so large it had kicked up a dust devil the size of a tornado.

Dezi's eyes snapped open. The door was still locked, but he shrugged off the pile of sand gathered around him and crawled, taking every second to preserve the oxygen held in his blood. He pulled the handle lightly, then again, and again. His lungs ached and his vision blurred, but when a green light flashed in the corner of his eye, he tugged, and the door hissed open.

Dezi stumbled into the airlock, slammed the pressure toggle, and threw his helmet off as the door sealed. Even though the thin air reeked of chlorine, it was better than the lung-searing carbon dioxide in his suit. He rubbed his neck and took a cooling breath, but his skin suddenly flushed.

I almost died.

Tears rose to his crusty eyelashes, but he took a few quick breaths and stuffed them down.

You've got work—worry about it after work.

He climbed out of his stasis suit and hung it with the others. 996, 997, 998, 999, 000; he touched the suits one after another, but each one but his own was dome-cold.

Beads of sweat ran down Dezi's back as he trudged to his room. He still had a full shift ahead of him, so he shut his door and stripped down. His greasy hair clung to his face as he fought to peel off his sticky thermal tights. Finally free, he wiped down with a damp towel pulled from a dispenser in the wall and let the frosty air wick the moisture off his skin.

Dezi's room was seven feet square, cluttered with tools and rusted free weights, and decorated with a single poster of a Hadron micro-class racing between the rings of Saturn. At a backcrater colony like Verde, a twenty-three-year-old man without a partner or children got the bare minimum. This single was a downgrade from his Mom's three-room suite, but he couldn't handle her constant questions about when he'd go back to college. She already knew the answer was never.

Balled up in his damp tights, Dezi's phone blared an obnoxious alarm. He groaned and got off his crinkly mattress; of course he'd hit the radiation limit on payday. He slathered himself in UV-blocker and threw back an isotope supplement, hoping to salvage his grade before extraction.

Dezi pulled a fresh pair of slate-gray coveralls, their neon-yellow label reading 000, from the drawer under his bed. His employee ID came with a matching nickname, Zero, and the responsibility of being the facility's unofficial, uncompensated engineer. The systems on Verde Valis were designed to be autonomous, but for as long as anyone could remember, it had been Zero's job to keep them running. Kick a pipe here, adjust a knob there; it was nothing a manager couldn't do themselves, but they didn't, and it took at least a day to bring a technician out from Meridiani. That was why lucky number 000 was the funniest joke on Verde—extra work for no extra pay—but Dezi had volunteered for it. It was the least he could do after the accident.

He changed into the fresh uniform, grabbed his company-issued device from its charging port on the nightstand, and laced his lead-bottomed boots, but before he left, he stopped at the speedship poster taped on the back of his door. In slick neon, it read, *Break orbit, break barriers, take your destiny.*

That had been Mithra's plan, to get the hell off this planet and actually do something with her life. She'd have made a great scientist if she'd had the money for tuition—probably have invented some life-saving discoveries along the way—but she'd gotten stuck working as the facility's Zero instead. She had been so good at it that the lights never flickered and people stopped stashing emergency oxygen tanks under their beds, but now she'd never see outside Verde.

Not that Dezi would either. He was going to die here exactly like she had; it was only a matter of time.

He tore the poster off the door and threw it on a pile of dirty socks in the corner. Giving colony kids outlandish ambitions like that was a cruel joke. No one left this place.

Dezi pressed his palm over the pain in his chest as his body tightened up, but then he exhaled harshly and pounded his fist on his forehead. *Don't be dramatic,* he told himself. *Get your ass to work before Gion docks the rest of your pay.*

The greenhouse would help him calm down. It always did.

He loaded the hydroponics monitoring tool on his tablet and left his room. Illuminated by ads for homeopathic supplements and organic juices he couldn't afford, the facility halls were dead-empty at this hour, but he liked the quiet.

When he entered the saffron greenhouse, the whisper-like hum of cyclocopters skimming the fields filled the air. Occasionally, they stopped to examine a plant and then released a burst of pesticides before drifting away on their cylindrical wing paddles. After checking the hoses for leaks and making his adjustments, Dezi took a moment to look down the thousands of rows of bulbs. For the past week, the stems sprouting from each bulb had looked like white worms reaching out of their charcoal-gray substrate, but now a swollen purple flower bud topped each stalk. There had to be a million of them ready to bloom, and turning down the water wouldn't stall them any longer.

Dezi leaned his head back to meet the Milky Way fading in the sunrise and sighed. As if this day couldn't get any worse.

Like most of the complex, the ceiling of the company cafeteria was made of transparent ceramic tile. Martian sunlight was half as bright as Earth's, and the average temperature was well below freezing, so they had to leverage every joule of energy for maximum profitability, or something like that. It made Dezi grateful that he wasn't as prone to sunburns as the average Verden.

Lined up with the other drowsy workers, he weighed his options at the food counter: tepary bean and okra chili, millet and squash mash, yuca fries, and cactus pears. As usual, the locust meal packets were untouched, and they'd remain untouched until the next global dust storm. Like their lack of a holiday bonus, storms were an inevitable, seasonal disappointment. The last one had lasted so long that the only food left was the iron supplements synthesized from the dust itself. It was funny no one ate the scorpions or centipedes; in fact, they had to feed the predators, or there wouldn't be anything to stop the jerboas from devouring their crops when the sun came back.

Dezi grabbed a serving of pears and fries and scanned his wrist-imbedded chip at the terminal. The machine played a cheery jingle and demanded he accept the terms and conditions of a twelve-hour payment plan for the one-dollar charge. It was a total ripoff, but his credit had been in the negative since he'd signed the rental agreement for his work boots. After he accepted the loan, the machine dispensed a carefully portioned unit of water into his bottle, and three chalky pills clattered out of its dispenser port. It thanked him for shopping with Eden Natural Healing, as if he had any other choice.

Dezi scanned the crowded benches, identifying 999 plastered across a wide back. Employee 999, Ajax, had hair as scant as the wispy Martian clouds, and the top of his head was red as the crater. A ginger-speckled beard covered his leather-worn face, and crow's feet etched from decades of smiling surrounded his tawny eyes. Before his eldest daughter, Mithra, he had been Verde's prior Zero, but with the build of three men stuffed into one pair of coveralls, there was no way he could fit into his stasis suit to do EVAs outside of the facility anymore.

"How're the flowers looking, Zero?" he asked.

"Purple. Too purple." Dezi placed his tray down and took a seat.

"I figured it'd be one of them days. If y'all get any blisters, I got plastaids," Ajax said.

A petite girl popped her head out from behind Ajax's mountainous shadow. "I'll need a couple, Pa. Otherwise, Ori won't give me my foot rubbing."

With number 996 on her left breast, Vesta was lanky, but her muscles flexed under her golden, sand-colored skin when she reached to take the bandages Ajax offered. Frizzy, rust-orange hair framed her sunburned cheeks and button nose. Flecked with freckles from head to toe, she'd been bullied relentlessly for looking dirty as a kid, but Dezi thought the marks were cute. Her butterscotch eyes beamed like the brightest day on a Martian summer when they darted to Dezi's prickly pears. "Can you really afford those?"

"If I skip the entrees, I can." Dezi handed her one.

"You're going to regret that." She chomped on it, sending magenta juice running down her chin.

"Why are you at the geeks' table?" Dezi asked. "Your friends are going to think you finally left for Chryse."

"I figured I could spend a morning with you and Pa. But if I'm not wanted..."

"Hold on now, girly, you keep yer butt in that seat," Ajax said.

"I was teasing." Vesta giggled. "It wouldn't kill you to hang out with my friends sometime, Dez."

"No, it definitely would." He held a finger gun to his head. "Plus, your dad's way cooler."

The old man broke into coughing, spitting laughter.

Vesta yanked her tray out of spray range. "Watch your sprinklers, Pa."

Dezi laughed. "How is Ori? Is he enjoying kindergarten?"

"Ugh, no. He can't sit still for ten minutes. They ain't sending kids headsets no more, but me and Pa are saving up to get 'em one."

"Shouldn't his adoption stipend cover school supplies?"

"You'd think it, but between rent n' food for the three of us, it's cutting it close already." Ajax let out a rattling cough, and his daughter smacked his back.

"Maybe after the merger, we'll get a couple cents' raise," Vesta said.

"More like a couple cents' cut," Ajax said.

"Wait, who are we merging with?" Dezi asked.

"Planitr. Not sure what they're gonna do with over-priced essential oils, but they've been snatching up every company they can get their teeth into." Vesta shrugged.

"Woah, that's huge," Dezi said. "So we might get a real technician?"

"Clouds don't mean rain, boy," Ajax said. "I hear at them Planitr facilities, all you got to eat is protein slurry, and they time how long you use the loo."

"Pshh, you gotta stop reading those conspiracy forums, Pa." Vesta rested on her elbow and scrolled her phone. "The stuff on there ain't true."

"We'll have'ta wait and see." Ajax sniffed and looked at Dezi. "How's the Hadron doing you? I know her software was giving you some trouble."

"Can we *please* talk about something interesting?" Vesta asked. "Did y'all hear about Aethur Charm and Beth Andronage's wedding? They rode down the aisle on real, organic elephants, from—like—Earth."

"Arther who? Naw, girl, we're talking Hadrons now. Listen and you might learn something."

Vesta groaned and sunk into her seat.

"I got caught in some sand." Dezi rolled a fruit around his tray.

"Ves, you weren't out EVA-ing this morning, were you?"

She hastily sat up. "No. I haven't touched a suit since...you know."

Ajax put his fork down with a clang. "Caught in sand or caught in a storm?"

"J-just sand," Dezi stuttered. "I'm sorry. I didn't mean to dust up your bike."

"I already told ya, she's yours so long as you keep her in shape for when Ori gets big enough to ride." Ajax slapped Dezi's back and rubbed his daughter's shoulder. "And how you'd be Zero without a bike? You can't walk yerself to them pipes."

"I don't know about that, Pa." Vesta leaned over the table to look at Dezi's behind. "Those domes can carry him pretty far."

Dezi covered his face while father and daughter hooted and laughed. Suddenly, getting back to the greenhouses didn't seem so bad.

Ring chime. Ring-ring chime.

At 6:28 A.M. the horrible jingle that marked the start of the work shift played, and by 6:33, Dezi and the other harvesters had filed into the greenhouse, clippers in hand, where a sea of pale purple flowers swayed in the ventilation draft.

The floral scent was sticky and sweet at first, like sun-baked dates, but that gave way to something muskier and bold; it coated Dezi's tongue like a kiss after a heated argument. The last note was acrid, like burning flower petals—or maybe that was the dust. Checking the air filters would have to wait, because the saffron lost potency by the minute, so the harvest couldn't stop until every open bud had been gathered.

The AI operators tried to stagger the blooming times, but organic systems were difficult to forecast even with quantum models, so the junk Verde was running didn't have a chance. Eden Natural Healing had spent billions trying to automate the harvest, but it took a human touch to pluck the flowers without bruising their stigmas, which was essential to producing quality safranal. The facility manager, Mr. Gion, loved to remind them their safranal was the one thing of value in this crater, but he forgot that every human body here contained ten units of vitamin-D-rich blood.

After hours of weaving up and down the hydroponics rows, the pollen had stained the tips of Dezi's fingers orange. He grabbed a crop of flowers, clipped the stigma's scarlet tri-tips, and dropped them into the port of his saffron receptacle. He raised the clear canister slung by his hip and measured the mess of red threads inside, then noticed Vesta sitting nearby on a metallic hydroponic basin with her phone held high in the air.

"You're getting rust stains on your uniform," Dezi said.

"Then that's the cost of fame." She lifted her leg onto the basin lip and took another picture.

"And how many followers do you have again?"

"Hey! I have a ton. You stop bellyaching about my side hustle or I won't let you keep sucking up my satellite data. You think it pays for itself?"

"I'm not judging, but how do you always meet your quota messing around like that?"

"Eating my vegetables helps." She bobbed her head.

"Nice." Dezi rolled his eyes and grinned.

"Have you thought about leaving yet? Elay says he can get us into Chryse if I take out a lil' bit of a loan."

"You're going to trust the guy who smuggles pirated movies and cheap liquor into town?"

"Not trust, hire. And he hasn't lost a shipment yet."

"Getting two live humans past border control is a lot harder than sneaking through a pillowcase full of hard drives. And there's no way you have enough credit for a MagnaLoop ticket."

"That's the trick." Vesta hopped to Dezi's side of the basin and whispered, "He says we won't need a ticket, 'cause if we can get on the train, he can sneak us off. Think about it. You and me in Chryse City. The Darklight Domes—The City of Sharp Smiles! From there, we could get better jobs and make our way off-planet."

"College taught me one thing, Ves: Don't take a loan you can't pay off."

"Ugh! Dez—" She threw a fistful of petals at him. "How else are we gonna get outta here? You said it yourself, we'll never afford a Magna ticket, and picking flowers all day ain't gonna get you closer to being an astronaut."

"An astronaut flies freighters and fixes asteroid miners. I was studying to be an exonaut." He swung his receptacle over his back.

"Wait up, rocket man." She chased after him. "You see any ships 'round here?"

"No, but we have a ton of cool rocks." He shrugged as he walked to the deposit chute.

"I got a plan B, if loans are a no-go." Vesta bounced on her toes and wiggled her eyebrows. "You wanna hear?"

"Probably not..." Dezi lined his receptacle up with the chute and jerked it a quarter turn, causing the vacuum to suck out the tangled threads.

"Lookie here." She bounded to a door marked *Restricted Access* and cracked it open.

"Stop." He slammed the door shut.

"I'm not gonna go in, I wanted to show ya. Pa told me the key scanner broke, so they had to turn it to fail-open mode. I figured that means it ain't locked."

"That's what it means, but why are you telling me? I'm not qualified to fix it."

"They make the safranal in there. If we got a bit, I could sell it to Elay, easy."

"That's a terrible plan." Dezi walked to the greenhouse. "They track exactly how much safranal is produced."

"Can't you fudge the sensors or something?"

"Do I look like a criminal?" He balked. "And if I can't fix a scanner, how could I hack a billion-dollar facility?"

Vesta dropped her shoulders and lost her silly grin.

Dezi's lips tightened. "I can help you save money for your ticket, but I think it's better if I stay."

"On what world? You been itching to ditch this rust bubble since you got here." She kicked a basin.

"I don't *want* to stay, but"—he knelt to tighten a loose bolt beside the scuff mark Vesta had left—"who will keep this place running if I go?"

"It ain't your fault Verde's always a sneeze away from breaking down."

"But it is."

She knelt beside him, touching his arm. "It isn't."

He couldn't hear that from her, of all people, not when it was his fault her sister was gone. Every breakdown Mirtha could have prevented was his fault. If Verde failed, it would be his fault.

Dezi quickly stood, but static rushed to his head, and he teetered back.

Vesta leaped to steady him. "Are you okay?"

"Y-yeah." He forced a smile. "Got up too fast."

"You need to eat more." She squeezed his shoulder. "You better not be skipping meals to save money for me."

"No—I wasn't hungry. I'm fine, really." He picked quickly to prove it to her. "I need to concentrate or I'll miss my quota."

"Your mom's gonna chew you up again..." Vesta's sun-speckled cheeks puffed up when she frowned, but she went back to work.

By 8:07 P.M. Dezi's shoulders were satisfyingly sore, and greenhouse three was a graveyard of pale worms and skeleton fingers again. Seated on the edge of a hydroponic basin, he examined a petal pinched between his fingertips, wondering how many subsidies it took to keep Verde profitable. Sure, there was flooding and fallout on Earth, but at least they had air.

Smaller than a saffron bulb, a jerboa dug its way out of the substrate and shook the volcanic gravel off of its sail-like ears. It hopped on its tall back legs, searching saffron stalks for dew drops. Dezi glanced over his shoulder as he took a yuca fry out of his pocket. If he got caught feeding a pest, Mr. Gion would slap him with a fine. Food was for useful livestock—scorpions, centipedes, and humans—but Dezi always admired the mice. Those first few adventurous pets had escaped their owners centuries ago, and now their descendants inhabited every habitation dome from Verde to the planet's capital. From traps to poison to laser-equipped drones, they had survived every extermination tactic Corporate threw at them. Did jerboa in the city have it better? Dezi imagined there was more food in Chryse, but more predators, too.

"I guess I'm more like the flowers than you, huh?" He tossed the fry.

The jerboa lunged for the morsel and then burrowed into the substrate, its fluff-tipped tail worming under the pebbles without a speck of gratitude. Dezi frowned before he noticed what had made the mouse so flighty—Mr. Gion was pacing up the rows. He shouted, "Zero, get a move on!"

"Yes, sir." He jogged to the end of the queue of laborers at the greenhouse exit, and as he got in line, his dried-out manager began lecturing him on Eden Natural Healing Business Brand Etiquette.

Dezi nodded and mumbled in agreement as he absently scanned the new ads playing on the poster-sized screens dotting the facility corridor. In one, a porcelain-skinned woman with lips as red as the sucker she popped out of her mouth winked and whispered, *Donate. You're my type.*

It was corny but still stole a chuckle from Dezi. The next screen stole his breath. It was an image of Mr. Everest Eden himself, surrounded by young men and women, all with the same brilliant crimson hair and luminous amber eyes. A head taller than all of his family members, Mr. Eden was a tremendously muscular man in a Mars-red suit with waves of glossy hair tumbling down his chest, a courtly closed smile, and a jawline you could pop open a bottle on. The text read, *We live because you give. From our family to yours, thank you.*

Even when they had gotten half a day off work to celebrate Mr. Eden's centennial anniversary, they hadn't been shown a picture of him, yet his visage was undeniable—preternatural. He didn't look a day over thirty-five, though Dezi didn't bother to check for airbrushing. The Edens were a perennial family and, thus, functionally immortal. Dezi frowned at the toddler in Mr. Eden's arms; surely that perennial was too young to take hemoglobin treatments.

"Are you listening?" Gion looked back.

"Oh—sorry." Dezi caught up with the line. "So that new ad... I thought the Edens kept a low profile."

"They did, but Planitr puts a face to their brands. On that note, this quarter's numbers *must* be perfect. We *need* Planitr to pick Verde for a 9999 facility upgrade."

"They're refurbishing facilities? I didn't see that in the newsletter." Dezi reached the end of the line leading to the medical center, and as he stepped through the plastic slit of the dust-blocking membrane, the smell of latex and cleaner fluid hit him.

"I'm trusting you with this information because you aren't any other employee. We're a family here, and we depend on you."

The doctor cleared her throat. "*We* are a family?"

"It's a turn of phrase, Renata." Gion smiled at her too hard. Dezi had never liked how Gion smiled at her.

He sat in the chair and clenched his fist as the doctor looked for a good vein. With bronze skin only beginning to gather wrinkles and deep, hazel eyes, she was an uncharacteristically beautiful woman for a town like Verde. Her genes came from curated stock, and she had the Earth-Latin accent to prove her off-world heritage.

"You're going to watch?" Dezi asked Gion. "Don't you have to check the saffron?"

"I'm ensuring we hit *both* harvest numbers."

The doctor inspected Dezi's tear ducts and frowned.

Gion groaned. "Not this again."

"He's anemic," she said.

"Zero, you're letting the team down!"

"It's a medical condition," she snapped.

"Renata, if you were going to bring your thin-blooded kid here, you should have put him through college instead of sticking me with him. Isn't there something you can prescribe him?"

Dezi's mother—the facility doctor—met her son's eyes, then raised her head like she didn't remember fights with Gion always ended in threats of termination. "Will you cover the cost of his prescription?"

"What? Of course not," Gion said. "Just take the blood."

His mom opened her mouth, but Dezi interjected. "I'll donate. I can't afford the fine."

"That's the team spirit." Gion grinned. "Extract what you can and bring me the numbers."

Dezi's mother watched their manager leave, but when he shut the door, she rolled up her sleeve.

"Stop," Dezi whispered.

"Dezi..." She looked older than he remembered, but her eyes still blazed.

"Let me give at least half of it."

She smiled weakly. "You don't have to fight me every time I help you."

"Then who else would I fight with?" He rolled up his coverall sleeve.

His mom shook her head. "*Meu coracao batendo...*"

It was a bit of language from the Old World that her father had left her, broken from aged memory and blended with Earth-Latin. She said he used to call her, his youngest of many children, his beating heart. Perennial families liked to keep those ancient dialects alive, and Dezi's grandfather had been the last immortal of the Merlo line, before he had died.

Dezi closed his eyes and tried not to shake too much when she swabbed his arm. He was still waiting to grow out of his fear of needles.

After Dezi had donated as much as his mom would let him, and she gave as much as her body allowed, he helped her to her suite. Her home smelled like citrus disinfectant spray, and it brought back memories of his childhood birthday parties. Mom had a habit of stopping mid-party to clean, and she always hosted because being the facility doctor entitled her to a spacious suite, though his father's career in sales had certainly helped.

Dad and Ajax used to sit in those synth-leather recliners, discussing the newest contract he was working on, while Ajax's wife made sweet nut-butter bites for the kids. Dezi hid under the blankets with Mithra and Vesta, staying up late to watch space science videos that put poor baby Vesta, five years their junior, to sleep. In the morning, Mom had their necks for sneaking in meteorites Ajax had found on the dunes, but if Dad wasn't on a business trip, he would talk her into letting him keep them.

The kid with the biggest house and nicest toys, with an Earthling accent to boot, Dezi didn't blame the other children for treating him differently. But, somehow, he'd become best friends with the two wildest girls in Verde. He smiled as he helped his mom into a recliner, but the cozy feeling didn't last. Now his father was gone, Ajax's wife and Mithra were dead, and his mother's suite was as silent and sterile as the medical center.

"I'm sorry," his mom mumbled.

"For what?" Dezi almost laughed. "Giving birth to me?"

"I should have helped you through school… I tried…"

Dezi's joke soured on his tongue. "You apologize too much. I was the one dumb enough to miss my final."

"Dezi." His mom sat up with sudden vigor. "You are not unintelligent, and what happened was not your fault. You finished early college at eighteen. Who else here graduated any college?"

"You. And I did a two-year program; that's not a real degree."

"But you got into Argyre University."

"The online program. The acceptance rate for the actual campus is different." Dezi shut his eyes. "And I spent the money you saved without even passing the first year."

"I'm sorry… If I hadn't chased your father off, we'd have—"

"No!" Dezi startled himself with how loudly he said it. "I mean—he left. And I won't abandon you too."

"I don't want you to spend the rest of your life as a harvester to be with me." She smiled at him in the knowing way of a mother. "Something is on your mind, son. Talk to me."

"I don't know." He sunk into a chair. "I don't know what I'm doing anymore."

"What do you want to do?"

"Does it matter? The odds of me starting an actual career are as good as Mr. Eden calling me up and asking me to replace him as CEO. I guess I'll work here until I drop dead like everyone else does. I nearly did this morning."

"What do you mean? What happened?"

"Work. Mars. You know." He shook his head, but he'd said too much. "I'm too tired to talk about it."

"Yes, Mars...we should have never brought you here." She took her tablet from the end table and offered it. "I want you to take this and go to Chryse with Vesta."

"I can't take your retirement money." Dezi shrugged, but even that was difficult. "I'll just end up back here anyway."

She pressed the tablet towards him. "No, you'll leave Mars."

"You know I won't!"

The room went silent.

He stared at the floor. "I'm sorry."

"It's late. Why don't you stay?"

"No. I get up early. It'll bother you." He retreated to the hall. "I'll let you rest."

He shut her door before she could press and then ambled to his room, ignoring the promises of late-night companionship whispered by the glowing ads along the walls. When he got to his room, he picked up the crumpled rocket poster from the floor and spread it face-down on his desk, smoothing out the wrinkles. There was a message scrawled on its bottom corner.

I heard this program of yours is pretty tough, but don't forget to enjoy college! So long as you know where you're headed, you'll get there in your own time.

-M

Dezi re-taped the poster to his door and collapsed onto his bed without changing or washing. It stunk like mechanical lubricant, sweat, and saffron.

CHAPTER 2

FLOWERS

Magnetized drones rolled up and down the outer dome, discharging static dust from the late-autumn storms. Mithra stepped out of the battery silo, joining the parents and children in the courtyard to enjoy her first taste of sun in a week. Under the copper sunshine, Vesta sprawled out on the rubber walk tiles while Dezi tinkered with a rover in his lap.

Mithra squatted beside him, resting her forearms over her thighs. "You got her suspension balanced yet?"

Dezi poked his temple with his screwdriver. "Yeah. You were right about the rocker joint; the angle was too low."

"She ready for her maiden voyage?"

"Maybe, but I don't want to risk it in this weather."

Vesta rolled onto her stomach. "I still think you should have sent her into the storm. A video of that woulda scared the tights off them city-goer classmates of yours."

"You'd have a hell of a time getting the airlock open." Mithra examined the overcast, apricot sky. "But looks like it's clearing up. You want to give her a shot?"

"I'm not sure." Dezi snapped the rover's back panel shut. "The forecast this morning was pretty bleak, so I asked my professor for another extension."

"Can she even give you one?" Mithra put out her hand. "Your final's tomorrow."

"Probably not." He sighed and handed over his rover.

"Then it's settled." She popped onto her feet. "Let's tear up some dunes!"

Vesta rolled her eyes. "You're always looking for an excuse to get out of the hab."

"Damn right. You won't catch me dead in this fishbowl. I'm just waiting for you to finish up secondary school so we can all get out of here." Mithra poked Vesta's forehead. "You couldn't have done me a favor and graduated early like Dezi?"

"Hey, you didn't even graduate! And trigonometry's not gonna make a lick of difference when I'm struttin' down the red carpet."

"Every superstar needs a little math, like every rocket scientist needs a little of the arts. It'll round you out, get you into a good college." Mithra plucked the shreds of rubber out of her sister's frizzy curls and smoothed them down. "So, until you make it big, study for the both of us, because I'm not sending Pa back to the fields for my sake. And that goes double for math. No more Ds, unless you plan on becoming a glorified farmdrone."

Vesta puffed up her cheeks and pouted. "That's big talk coming from a farmdrone."

"Your sister is an engineer, whether or not it's her job title." Dezi picked up his laptop and stood. "Be careful. This is thirty percent of my grade."

"You can't get between an explorer and the wide open, Dez. Freedom's calling!" Mithra lifted the little rover into the air. "Let's go find your daddy some alien life."

She bounded to the airlock and slid into her stasis suit. It was chill and sweat-tacky from her maintenance run that morning, but it'd warm up. She tightened her bootstraps and rotated her shoulder joints to knock the sand out, then took her helmet off the rack and gave the visor a kiss for good luck, but when she screwed it on, it didn't click right. The hundred-year-old thing had been gunking up worse and worse, but the new gaskets were on backorder since Pa had first shown her how to fit them, so she blew into the groove and gave the helmet a hard twist.

Click.

She hit the pressure toggle, opened the door, and set the drone in the sand. They needed it to make one hundred meters for full points, so Mithra kept a foot in the doorway and an eye on the rover's path. Dezi, Vesta, and every kid in the courtyard pressed up to the dome glass and watched the rover's six wheels make tracks in the pristine sand. It pushed up a small hill, with Dezi's new suspension handling it smooth as sub-butter spread, but then its back wheel snagged on a jagged rock seventy meters out. Seventy—a single point above a D. Mithra looked at Dezi, and while the whole town was watching the rover spin out, he was looking at her.

She stepped a foot out of the airlock. This would only take a second.

Ring chime. Ring-ring chime.

Dezi woke, clawing at his throat, gasping for air. He rolled onto his side and caught his breath, but his heart drained out—that alarm wasn't his.

In a stupor, he tossed off his damp blankets, flew out of bed, grabbed his tablet, and ran out the door without relacing his boots. He had to make it to the greenhouses in five minutes. If he didn't, the late fee would blow away the credit he'd saved for Ori's school headset. Rounding the corner full-tilt, he spotted Vesta peering out the greenhouse doors. The clock above read 6:32 with seven seconds to spare.

"Vesta! Catch!" He hurled his tablet like a frisbee. It tumbled through the air, straight at Vesta's chest. She slammed it between her hands and landed square on her butt, flashing her snaggletooth with a massive grin. Clocked-in meant having their company device pass through the door scanner, so as far as Eden Natural Healing knew, Dezi wasn't late.

He jogged over, about to make a joke about Vesta's hard landing, but a glimpse of the greenhouse gagged him like a face full of methane from a leaky fertilizer tank. If yesterday had been a gentle sea of flowers, today was a maelstrom; blossoms crowded the planters so densely that they smothered every inch of substrate. Their cloying perfume was dizzying.

"So I'm guessing you slept in?" Vesta asked.

Dezi's cold sweats ignited into a swelter. Too much water stressed the saffron, and stressed bulbs bloom, desperate for their chance to reproduce. Every Zero knew that, so they always adjusted the auto-irrigator each morning during a harvest. His coworkers wouldn't know how he had screwed up, but they'd be up all night picking because of him. Their legs would ache, they wouldn't eat dinner with their families, and they'd finally realize he was a garbage-tier substitute for Mithra.

"It'll be alright." Vesta wrapped her arms around Dezi's ribcage and pressed her chest into his, forcing the air out of his lungs along with some of the strain from his heart. "We gotta get to picking, but we'll get it done."

Mithra used to do this for him whenever she had caught him in a panic attack. It was embarrassing, and he'd made her promise to keep it secret, but she'd told Vesta. She had known Dezi needed someone to keep him grounded, and Mars was the type of planet where any day could be her last. She was wise like that, and Dezi was grateful she had broken that promise.

He hugged Vesta back. "Thanks, Ves."

"Let's get to it." She passed him his tablet, and they each grabbed a handful of petals.

Dezi didn't think about much; at least, he tried not to. He did his best to ignore the lack of friendly chatter between the hydroponics rows or imagine what Gion would say when this was over. He tried hard not to think about kicking down the airlock door and walking, just walking until his limbs were too cold to keep going.

For a moment, he looked out at the dust devils whipping over the dunes; then the woman he shared his planter row with shot him a glare and murmured under her breath, so he put his head down and kept picking.

As the sun sank into the crater's jaws, the mustard gas sky turned to arsenic-orange, blood-red, before a ghostly blue-gray. At least Gion wasn't screaming at them to pick faster. Actually, his absence was concerning.

"Dezi." Vesta bounded down the aisle. "Pa and Mr. Gion are looking for you."

Dezi swallowed his raspy tongue. "Am I fired?"

"No, I think something's broken in the labs." She grabbed his arm and rushed him past the rows of laborers steaming with sweat. Most limply picked on, but a few had collapsed against the basins and were pressing fistfuls of damp substrate to their foreheads.

In the back, workers gathered around deposit chutes stuffed with saffron, bickering about where to put their harvest. Most dumped their crop on the floor before turning back to meticulously gather another. A trail of yellow footsteps led to the door labeled *Restricted Access*, with Gion's distinct wailing coming from the other side.

"When you get in there, remember our plan B," Vesta whispered as she opened the door for Dezi.

Stealing was not high on his priority list when he entered the sweltering lab. Crusty steel tubes crisscrossed the walls, shooting jets of steam or dripping golden oil, and the air was dense with the sweet, earthy scent of refined safranal. Massive stills lined both sides of the room, radiating heat and frothing with bright yellow foam, while the cisterns on the upper levels beeped and blinked with error codes.

Sweat drenched Gion's normally pristine button-down shirt, and yellow stains blotted his hands and face. "Marsdamn you, Zero! What in the blood and dust did you do?"

Ajax heaved himself off a stool. "I keep telling ya to look in the logs. He didn't touch a thing. This mess is what you get for putting off them maintenance orders."

"You think this is my mess? *My mess*? Do you know what happens when auditors get called to a gutter-dust facility like this? They retire it and ship the staff off to recoup losses, so don't tell me this is my mess." Gion pointed at Dezi. "And you! You and your liar mother owe a bond's worth of blood. I've been letting you two off easy, and this is how you repay me?"

Dezi balked. "K-keep my mom out of this."

"You want me to keep her out of debtor's prison too? I'll be lucky if I don't get sent to the same asteroid! We can't get a technician until tomorrow, so you're going to use those damn manuals to fix this."

"You made your point, Gion. We'll see what we can do," Ajax said. "You tell 'em to take that there saffron out the chutes and put it somewhere cold 'til we're ready for it."

"You damn well better, because either Verde gets refurbished, or it gets retired." Gion adjusted his collar, leaving fingerprints on it, then turned for the door with all the poise he could muster. "I'll handle the harvest. The lab is in your hands, Ajax."

"Picked a cosmic time to let us in on that, didn't ya?" Ajax mumbled as he lumbered to the intake valve, but then he stumbled on a small ledge.

"Ajax—" Dezi rushed to steady him.

He coughed and waved Dezi off. "I'm tired is all, but looks like you're gonna have'ta climb them ladders for me." He turned the valve and the glugging in the pipes quieted.

Dezi looked from the churning chaos of the lab to Ajax. The old man expected him, the guy who couldn't even remember to turn down a stupid water valve, to fix a billion-dollar facility. "I don't think I can help. A-ask Vesta."

"You know diodes and grease never interested her. You been Zero coming on five years now. That's about as long as Mithra was."

"I've never worked with equipment like this. I'm not even supposed to be in here."

"Remember when we first taught you to solder a pipe? You didn't think you could handle that either. Couldn't even remember the password to the dang tool store. First time's always tough, but you won't learn nothing without giving it a try."

"But I've been trying—so, so hard—and all I do is make things worse. I want to help, but I just can't. I'm not Mithra."

Ajax chewed on his cheek for a second, then leaned in like he was sharing a secret. "I saw the Hadron buried out there. A storm caught ya, didn't it?"

Dezi nodded.

"And you saw her."

"Her?"

"Mithra. I see her in the dryfog too. She's watching over us. Now I'm gonna tell you what I told her when she couldn't add up the ounces to half a gallon of pesticide and poisoned every crawler in town. What if the problem ain't you, but this place?"

The tears Dezi had worked so hard to lock up leaked out. He couldn't hold them back if he spoke, so he shook his head.

"There's an awful lot of stars out there, son. If you ain't shining here, why don't you try another? Now, you get stuck, come down and tell me whatcha saw. You'll be my hands for me." Ajax gave him a rough pat and turned him towards the first ladder. "Get to it, and we can have mashed jicama for dinner."

Too numb to fight the old man, Dezi climbed the ladder. When he reached the top, he realized why Mr. Gion was so yellow; the byproducts and pre-products of safranal synthesis stuck to every surface.

He edged over the catwalk to the first cistern, a tank twice the size of his room. Dezi hadn't realized there was this much water in all of Verde, yet here it was, used to rinse the stigmas.

"You found the holdup?" Ajax shouted.

"N-not yet!"

Dezi crept to the next vat containing a soupy red mixture with yellow foam sticking to its walls. He turned on the control panel, and the Self-Clearing Industrial Liquidizer flashed through three eye-gratingly bright diagnostic screens. Once it loaded its archaic UI, Dezi tapped the mixer-start pictogram, and then something at the bottom of the vat clicked repeatedly, sending up volleys of steaming juice in the center of the pool.

Before he could check the error, a cartoon test tube bounced onto the screen and said, *Hello, I'm Drippy. Would you like to submit a bug report?*

Dezi clicked no, but Drippy cartwheeled across the UI. *Connecting you to customer support...*

A little red light blinked next to—was that a webcam? Corporate would not respond well to a harvester tampering with their equipment, and Dezi wasn't naive enough to believe honesty would change their minds, so he smashed the close button. The damned thing put him through anyway, but before the bespectacled support engineer could start his canned greeting, Dezi ducked and flipped the kill switch on the underside of the console. As it shut down, he stood and wiped the sweat from his brow, smearing floral goop on his forehead. "Bleeding Mars, give me the error code already."

He interrupted the system startup to keep the console in diagnostics mode and loaded the raw logs. Error messages in the wall of text mentioned the rotor overheating and intake overloading, so he referenced the codes in his manuals, and they brought him to the machine's troubleshooting guide. The steps read, *Stop blending, drain tank, check blades for obstruction.*

Dezi entered the commands into the console, and the tank's water level drained, leaving behind a stringy mass of saffron wrapped around six four-foot-long mixer blades. He checked the toolset mounted by the panel for something to clear the blockage and selected a telescoping hook, then he aimed it down the bowl and pulled the spring-deploy pin. The staff slid from its sheath and flopped down the side of the bowl like a limp noodle, which was not how it looked in the troubleshooting diagram.

Dezi tossed the floppy pole aside. "Okay, let's try something else..."

He pulled down the safety harness suspended over the console, but the brittle plastic crumbled in his hands, forcing a single, broken laugh out of him. Sure, the thing was probably older than Ajax, but it could have stuck around to do its job at least once.

Dezi circled the cistern, flexing his hands as he looked for a spare—for anything to clear out the clog—but the ancient tools were rusted and useless. The refinery was supposed to be fully automated; it was never designed to be fixed. The rickety grating creaked and the factory floor swam under Dezi's feet. He grabbed the handrails, but they warped under his weight.

"The tools giving you trouble?" Ajax shouted. "Why don't you come down and take a break?"

"You heard what Gion said! If I don't fix this tonight, everyone will lose their jobs because of me."

"We got time, son. Take a breath and tell me what you see."

Dezi slowly exhaled. "The mixer blades are tangled with saffron."

"I betcha they need a sharpening, but we can leave that 'till tomorrow. You think you can get 'em cleared out?"

He spotted a sturdy-looking ladder mounted beside the mixer. "I can try."

The blade tips stuck out of the saffron lump like shark fins circling carrion-filled water while Dezi shakily lowered the ladder into the bowl. The first rung creaked softly when he tested it, but it held his weight. He stepped on the second, then the third, but as he took the fourth, his heel slipped and his knee buckled. The ladder shuddered, then twisted sideways when one rail popped out of its socket.

Dezi clung to the rungs with all his strength, but his palms were slick with saffron juice. He slipped off it and slid down the side of the bowl, hurtling towards the massive blades. In a breathless panic, he threw his arms up to shield his face.

Thud.

His lead-bottomed boots bored through the damp mass and stopped hard. His torso lurched forward, and his left hand, searching for something to slow his momentum, found the blade. Dezi's scream echoed in the steel bowl like a bell.

"Zero? Zero!" Ajax stomped below the cisterns.

Dezi's blood poured down his arm, but the saffron wad had slowed his collision well enough that his hand wasn't severed. He was alive. He hastily wrapped some plumber's tape around the gash on his palm and then tore the strip off with his teeth. The waterproof adhesive stuck despite the blood. Both the cut and his face were numb, but when he gingerly tested his fingertips, they still had sensation. Thank Eden the blades really were that dull.

Ajax rattled the ladder. "Dezi!"

"I slipped, but I'm okay!" He jerked his boots free from the blades.

"Woo-e! You about gave me a heart attack, boy!"

Dezi cautiously pulled the gooey chunks out of the mixer blades and hucked them over the bowl. He re-secured the ladder into its slots and climbed out at glacial speed, cradling his cut, then checked the errors on the console and followed the instructions to flush the pipes by sending the half-mixed material back to be blended again. Dripping red and yellow, he followed the processing chain and taped up pipes that had burst from the material overload, though his one-handed technique wasn't ideal.

Finally, he waved down at Ajax. "I think I got it! Can you turn the intake on?"

Ajax turned the valve, and the saffron began to flow. "Ain't no Zero fixed 'er like this before! Mithra would be damn proud!"

A dark vortex formed in the center of the mixer as it swirled, staring back at Dezi like the pupil of a crimson eye, but it eventually processed into a creamy fluid. There'd be a little blood in the next batch, but no more than Mr. Eden typically drank. Normal people couldn't afford safranal anyway.

While the lab hummed away, Dezi climbed down the ladder to Ajax, with his left hand hidden in his pocket.

Gion rushed through the door and gave Dezi a sticky, bleary-eyed hug. "I always knew you were a bright one." When he spotted the blood on Dezi's sleeve, his nose twitched, and he yanked Dezi's hand out of his pocket, shooting pain up his arm. In his usual slimy tone, he said, "I won't be able to explain where you got this cut without sharing more than upper management needs to know, so can we call off the next blood draw and call it even?"

Dezi winced and nodded. If he pressed for workplace injury compensation, he'd end up in arbitration, and nobody won arbitration.

"Let's take you to see yer mom." Ajax patted Dezi's back.

His boots sloshed and slapped on the concrete as they walked to the greenhouse. Verdans' busy hands picked the remaining wisps of lavender petals under the midnight moons, and their praises greeted Dezi as Ajax led him down the aisles.

"So y'all really fixed it?"

"Yellow looks good on you, Zero."

"You're gonna smell like saffron 'til you're sixty."

Dezi blushed at his boots, smiled back, and nodded. Whatever Verde's fate would be, he'd done his best to save it. He only hoped it would be enough to prove to the Planitrs that this resilient little town was worth keeping around.

Tack, tack, tack.
Three staples drove into the fleshy part of Dezi's palm.
Tack, tack, tack.
Three more down his wrist.
"Don't move. Silver nitrate."
"W-wait!" Dezi flinched when his mother pressed a black matchstick into his wound, cauterizing the sections still oozing blood.
"I cannot believe you let Ajax convince you to crawl into a blender. I thought you were past these risky behaviors." His mother's face flushed redder than the skin around his wound. "You are lucky it missed your ID chip. Lucky, lucky child..."
The last time his mom had been this upset was when Dezi had snipped a bit off his forefinger with the saffron snipper—and that other time he'd sliced his thumb open with a pair of wire cutters—but if she knew how yesterday's dustslide had led him to sleep in and cause the system to get overloaded, she'd try to rope him into therapy again, so he kept his motives to himself.
His mom rinsed the wound, patted it dry, and wrapped it in silicone film. "Tomorrow, we are having dinner with Ajax and his family. I'm sure he spent too much on it, so you *will* be there."
"I know." Dezi flexed his painful fingers.
"You have approval to use the medical shower, and you are exempt from work tomorrow; that fool Gion isn't completely heartless." His mother paced to the door, but then lingered before shutting it. "Clean up and rest well, Son."
"Thanks, Mom. You too." He gave her a small smile, and she returned it before shutting the door.
Dezi peeled off his syrup-stiff uniform and saffron-infused boots, opened the glass door to the wet shower, and stepped in. When the device sensed his weight, the monitor displayed a countdown, and with a hiss, the shower head sent out streams of liquid

foam. He worked quickly to scrub the gritty foam mixture into the stains on his skin. The stream switched to water and, although it was cold, Dezi let out a gratified sigh; it had been years since his last wet shower. Before he had fully savored it, the water stopped and warm air jets spun up. He let them dry him off and then exited the shower while the water recollection process continued to whirl and buzz.

From the corner of his eye, Dezi caught his reflection in a tall mirror, and it startled him as if it were a naked stranger. He had covered the mirror in his own room years ago, so he hardly recognized himself. The man standing before him had a broad frame and bleak eyes that had looked down death twice this week alone. With a rigid jaw and strong brow, he wasn't a lanky teen anymore, and it scared him. He was a twenty-three-year-old man, going nowhere.

Dezi's melancholy broke with a chuckle when he noticed the stains on his feet looked like bright yellow socks. He picked up the spare uniform his mom had laid out for him and pulled it on. Luckily, the saffron hadn't affected the color of his brow-length hair, cut in the eternally trendy style Vesta had recommended out of the ten Verde's auto-cutter could do. His dark green eyes appeared gray in the artificial light but were still striking against the brown skin he had inherited from his mother. He touched a mole on his neck he didn't remember having, hopefully not a cancerous one, then felt the stubble under his jaw. If he moved to Chryse, he'd have to remember to shave.

Deciding whether to leave would be easier if he had earned that degree, but as it stood now, was there anything out there for him? Verde was his home, and Chryse had a bloodthirsty reputation. Even courageous Vesta wasn't brave enough to go alone; she had planned to leave with Mithra.

He turned for the door, but he couldn't walk away. He looked back at the boy—the man– in the mirror, and a Zero returned his stare. One in a chain of other Zeros who'd poked through the sand to kick water pipes until they died, and half a dozen people remembered their name until they died too. If he kicked the pipe hard enough, he might leave a mark on this world, but eventually they'd replace the pipe. It was a meaningless, forgettable life he was leading.

Dezi squeezed his fist, then clutched his injured hand as a trickle of blood escaped from underneath the silicone. This worthless job was shredding him alive. The dust was caking his lungs and the radiation was corroding his cells. Mom, Vesta, Ajax—everyone in Verde was slowly dying for these stupid flowers. Mithra would have been the one to find some meaning in it all. Mithra and Vesta would have escaped to Chryse and done something with their lives, but Dezi had stolen that from them.

Despite the pain, he clenched his fist until his shaking steadied. He had done a good thing today, but he could do better: what Mithra had planned to do. He would take Vesta to Chryse, because if Mithra really was watching, he wanted her to see Vesta make it out of here for the both of them.

Chapter 3

Tracks

Dezi woke sometime after sunrise. With his mind as blank as the concrete ceiling, he lay in bed and enjoyed the silence. It felt good, but there was work to do. Whether Verde would be upgraded or retired was in Mr. Eden's hands now, but it was still Dezi's job to ensure the systems ran until a new tech arrived. He'd need to get his equipment in order before leaving, too, which started with his Hadron.

He rolled out of bed and picked one of his few non-coverall outfits: jeans and an itchy sweater he hadn't worn since Christmas. After he shaved and brushed his hair, he removed the pillowcase covering his room's mirror. His reflection was still unfamiliar, but he liked how it looked.

Dezi grabbed his tool bag and stopped by Ajax's locker to borrow a shovel before suiting up in the airlock. As it depressurized, he hopped from side to side and repeatedly checked the tape on his helmet seal. Then, with a hiss, the door released him to the serene expanse.

His boots sank into the gritty powder with a hushed fizzle as he trod to his Hadron. The bike was buried nose-first like a jerboa stuck mid-dive in the sand, and when he gave it a shove, it didn't budge. Dezi groaned and unfolded his compact shovel.

"Exercise. It's not like I do enough of that already." He sassed the sand as he dug. His left hand was totally numb from whatever his mom had wrapped it in, so he was lucky the shovel was small enough to use with one hand.

After an hour of shoveling, with dust backfilling every scoop, he found himself at the bottom of a wide and shallow hole. The sand filtered through his bike's mesh tires as he lifted it free. He tapped the screen between the handlebars, but it was dead. Dezi threw his head back, sighed dramatically, and collapsed. As he lay on the cold sand, he panted at the teal sky. Martians called days like this Earth weather. Dezi hardly remembered the color of Earth's sky, so he called it Earth weather too.

He got up, tied some utility cord around the Hadron's handlebars, scrambled out of the hole, and looped his cord through the airlock door handle. He heaved the rope over his shoulder and dragged his bike out. Luckily the gyroscope wasn't dusted, so the Hadron kept itself upright and wheeled out easy. Even with a busted screen, Hadron engineering didn't let him down. Dezi guided his bike into the airlock and used the hose mounted on the wall to clean it, blowing out the wire mesh of the nitinol tires before moving to the body. The paint was scuffed from decades of abuse, but he admired what was left of the iridescent purple-green shimmer on its angular body plates. He ran his hand over the amorphous alloy bars of the frame; no matter how old the bike got, the dark metal still sparkled like stars on a black night.

Other than his meteorite collection, this bike was one of the few objects he actually owned, since his possessions down to his undertights were leased from Eden Natural Healing and liable for repossession if he hit his credit limit. Even the blood in his veins was on loan, sold as part of his work contract to pay off the prior year's debts. Unless he and Vesta planned to arrive in Chryse butt-naked, they'd need to square what they owed to Corporate, somehow.

Dezi tried the screen again, and the green LEDs Mithra had installed under the chassis flashed, but then flickered off. The bike was in bad shape, no doubt, but repairing it was child's play compared to handling the lab. He returned his stasis suit and pushed his Hadron to the facility courtyard, blushing and nodding when he bumped into anyone who had heard yesterday's big story, which was everyone. The slower a colony's internet signal was, the faster their gossip traveled.

The exterior doors slid open, and Dezi rolled his Hadron over the knobby concrete to the plastic grass near the dome's edge. Under the warm sun, kids chased each other around the courtyard while grandparents attempted to corral them. Retired Verdans worked on pet projects such as growing cacti and carving stones, which attracted small audiences of curious children.

Using his good hand, Dezi pulled out a chunky laptop with a cracked screen and plugged its retractable cable into the diagnostic port on his Hadron.

"Dezi!" A bootless boy leaped over his head and tumbled to the crunchy grass.

"Ori! Where are your weights?" Dezi checked the five-year-old for damage.

He grinned and waved his tablet in its thick rubber case. "Take me on a bike ride."

"You're supposed to be in class."

"But it's boring!" Ori stomped and pouted like his sister often did. "I wanna help with the heist."

"The heist?" Dezi asked.

"Yeah, Sis said after she did her top-secret plan, you and her were going to Chryse. And I want in!"

Dezi knelt. "I don't know anything about a secret plan, but do you want to help me fix your dad's bike?"

"Yeah! Yeah!" Ori bounced over.

Dezi loaded the Hadron's diagnostics window on his laptop, which displayed the blue screen of doom. "This error means we have to try a hard reboot." He winced and clicked enter.

The screen played a fifty-year-old version of Hadron's animated logo, two indigo stars flying upward to form a ring and smashing into each other at the top, then displayed a simple message: *Inter-*

planetary law requires anti-collision AI version 3050:1:1 or later. Update firmware to proceed.

"You look sad." Ori pulled Dezi's sleeve. "Do you need a hug?"

Before Dezi could explain that he'd never get a strong enough satellite signal to update the bike, a murmur swept the courtyard. Everyone stopped and pointed to the sky, where a passenger rotorcraft flew overhead, its four sets of stacked blades spinning furiously. Bearing Eden Natural Healing's stigma-shaped logo, it passed silently over the courtyard on its way to the facility landing pads.

Children pointed and shouted, demanding someone explain what that flying thing was, but Ori clung to Dezi's leg. "Why did a rotor-motor come? Did someone die?"

He rubbed Ori's back. "I'm sure it's an engineer here to work on the lab, but I'll check."

"I'll go too."

"No, I need you to keep our Hadron safe. I'll be back in five minutes—promise." Dezi bolted to the greenhouse without giving Ori a chance to argue.

He jogged down the planter rows, but before he could find Vesta or Ajax, Gion noticed him. "Zero! What are you doing here?"

"Who was in that craft?"

"It's none of your concern. You need to stay in your room—out of sight."

Dezi frowned. "But it's my day off."

"For—ugh." Gion pinched his brows. "You don't understand the delicate situation we're in. I'll comp you another day if you head back now. Deal?"

"Okay...Thank you, sir."

Getting another day off was unexpected, but based on Gion's secrecy, those visitors weren't a simple maintenance crew. It seemed Mr. Eden's decision would come sooner than expected, and either outcome would make the role of Zero obsolete. The thought was terrifying, but at the same time, it gave Dezi the urge to ask his mom if she still had his old suitcase.

The greenhouse was swimming with chatter about that rotorcraft, but Vesta was more interested in speaking to Dezi. Visitors meant the lab would be unsupervised, and that spud hadn't remembered their plan B when he was busy saving the town. She vaulted over a hydroponics basin, but then quickly shuffled back when Mr. Gion approached Dezi.

It probably wasn't a good idea to get chewed up for "stealing company time" right after she had been busted for wearing earbuds at work again. She wished Pa would let her get one of those DIY cochlear chip kits. Fia had gotten one done last week, and it hadn't scrambled her noodle. In the thirty-first century, it was every eighteen-year-old girl's market-granted right to load up on silicon if she wanted. Whatever. It looked like she was on her own. If Mr. Gion was going to accuse her of stealing, she might as well take something. They wouldn't miss one little bottle of safranal after yesterday's fiasco.

"Fia, hold down the beds for me." Vesta tossed the girl her stigma receptacle.

Fia caught it and tapped her ear, silencing her super-deadly chip. "You leavin' for Chryse?"

"Just about. You wanna come with?"

Fia's wire nest of auburn hair bounced as she shook her head. "There ain't nothing but trouble in the cities."

"Trouble's better than picking flowers dusk 'till dawn. You gonna spend the rest of your life in a rust bubble like this?"

"That's what my momma did, and Gran before her. Those flatlands get storms ten times what we see." Fia paused her picking to give Vesta a wishful pout. "It ain't glamorous, but the Edens take care of us."

"Oh no, you can't convince me to stay."

"I know." Fia sighed. "You watch your neck out there, alright? And don't forget me when you're a superstar."

"She's taking *another* break?" Eythor walked up from the next row and rested a muscular arm on the basin's edge. "Looking for your next boyfriend? I hear the ones in Chryse bite."

"How many times you gotta make that joke before you realize it ain't funny?" Vesta cocked her hip.

"Naw, it's still funny." Fia held Eythor's arm and laughed, brushing her curls on his stubble and snuggling him.

"Get a pod." Graycion came up the other side of the planter, saying exactly what Vesta was thinking.

The fair-haired boy kept his head down and picked furiously, but his eye roll wasn't subtle enough. Quick as a scorpion sting, Eythor snatched a blossom from Graycion's hand. "Feeling lonely? I think I found your next man, Ves. He's been dry as the dunes since—"

"Shut it, Eythor!" Vesta stomped for emphasis.

"Alright, alright." Eythor waved his palms in unapologetic defeat. "If we're covering for you, at least tell us how Dezi fucked the glove yesterday."

"Ew, don't be gross." Fia slapped his arm.

"I want to know if the loner actually fixed the lab." Eythor bumped Fia's hip.

"He fixes everything. But you already know that." Graycion stole a chilly glare at Eythor but kept his eyes off Vesta.

"I heard he got cut messin' with some giant blades. That's pretty orgo." Fia offered a sympathetic smile, as if it was her job to clean up Eythor's mess. At this rate, she'd be stuck steaming his undertights and reheating his dinners, too, since his momma never taught him.

"He saved all our behinds—yours included. Now can I go?" Vesta made a show of plucking and clipping the last blossoms on her row.

"Vesta." Graycion held his forearm like he was hiding a tender bruise and gave her an equally guarded look. "How's he doing?"

"Good." Vesta struggled to meet his copper eyes. "Pa said he was smiling more yesterday than he'd done all year."

"So once, right?" Brick-headed as ever, Eythor took a sip from his canteen and held the flask to his forehead. "Try to get back before lunch this time."

"Fia, your boyfriend's a butthole." Vesta flipped her poofy hair on her way out.

Maybe Dezi was right to blow off her offers to reintroduce him to her friends. They weren't bad people, but when you were tired, sweaty, and achy, you had no energy for subtlety. Verdans said what was on their mind.

Still, when Mithra had been around, she and Dezi could bounce jokes so sharp they left even Eythor dumb quiet. But that was then. Now they'd let that hole Mithra left sit for so long it had grown as wide as the sky. Everything left unsaid was like sand in a blister; without airing it out, it'd never heal. That's what she and Pa had done. Screaming, crying, shouting. They popped that blister the night they took Mithra's body away and picked it bloody till there was nothing left to say. The scar would always be there, but it was healing.

Dezi wasn't like that. Vesta had asked him about Mithra once, and he gave her a look, like, *Mithra who?* But she knew he thought about her. Some mornings, she'd watch him looking out the dome glass like he remembered the exact spot where she fell, but he wouldn't talk about it, not even to a professional. That was why getting him out of Verde was double-important. He'd always been an outsider, but the town made him into a pariah when Mithra died. Didn't matter that it'd been an accident; Verdans wanted someone to blame. But the squinty eyes switched to raised eyebrows when he walked into Gion's office and demanded to be made Verde's next Zero. Dealt a real blow to Pa's ego, arguing that an old man forced out of retirement couldn't handle the job, but he wasn't wrong. Verde was lucky someone like Dezi was around. He'd always been good with screens and wires, too good to be stuck in Verde doing it for free.

He could try to baby her all he liked, but Vesta knew he'd thank her for swiping this safranal when she used it to pay her city connection to get them into Chryse.

She jogged out of greenhouse four and wrapped around to number three. It reeked of petals, but the rows were empty except for a drone scanning the spent bulbs and a couple of scorpions snipping at each other. She crept towards her little opportunity, the unlocked lab door, and when the handle turned for her, she squealed with excitement.

The lab was brightly lit, its pipes and steel kegs shockingly clean. She snickered; Mr. Gion must have been up all night scrubbing it. Served him right.

Vesta meandered between the cisterns, dodging jets of steam until the sound of clinking bottles piqued her ears. She jogged to the end of the lab, where whizzing conveyor belts carried perfume-style bottles and glossy display boxes. In a precisely choreographed dance of machinery, needle-like nozzles squirted safranal into the glittering bottles, and the second their flashy packages were sealed, they zipped into a dark chute in the wall. Vesta figured it was a security protocol to hide the finished product, but who cared about the cardboard? She only needed the bottle. Though at this speed, if she stuck her hand into the belt all willy-nilly, it'd set off a nasty chain reaction that'd bring Mr. Gion running.

Vesta cursed her luck as she examined the liquid gold just outside her reach. Each decanter held the work of a full day of picking condensed into a few drops of oil. The bottles wasted so much glass to justify their out-of-orbit price tag that she could probably huck one from four stories without breaking it. A grin snuck across her face, and she grabbed a wrench. Vesta felt the tool's weight, then wound back and chucked it dead-on at the line of bottles.

WHAP!

The wrench connected with a darting bottle. The bottle teetered, missed its box, and flew into the chute, taking the wrench with it. Vesta cringed when the next bottle missed its box, and the one after that, but after a few more, the line stabilized. Plenty of cardboard had fallen off the belt, but every heavy bottle had gone straight for the chute. Stellar.

She picked up a gold-and-purple package off the floor. "Marsdang it! Why didn't Pa bring me in here with Dezi? We could have figured something out together."

She tossed the box and backtracked, searching for something heavier to fling. Some type of hook or lasso might do it. Right as she opened a cabinet filled with boxes of hair nets and gloves, the lab door clicked, easing open.

Vesta dove into the cabinet, shoving boxes to make space and curling up like a chilly viper. Crossing her toes for luck, she peeked out to check whether she'd been spotted.

"As you can see, all operations are in normal order..." Mr. Gion entered the lab, rattling off percentages with lots of decimals and fast-talking like he was trying to sell air to an Earthling. Behind him came the outsiders.

The first two wore dark armor plates and masks made of a polarized lens that covered their faces. Various tools hung off their belts, but the batons and stun guns put cold sweat on Vesta's palms. Behind the guards followed a man and woman, dressed in overalls and blue rubber gloves, with pale, almost translucent skin. A woman in a pink blazer came next, and her heels clicked on the lab's steel tiles as she took notes on her tablet.

The last visitor was different. Her slow strides took her further than the quick steps of the ants ahead of her. The android-like woman wore glossy, latex-white gloves that seamlessly connected to the sleeves of her dress, and her tall boots covered the length of her legs. Under her glittering eyeshadow, her amber eyes swam with bursts of sunlight and flecks of garnet. Ruby-red locks cradled her pearly face, and a clear plastic collar cupped her neck, protecting and presenting a scar shaped like a saffron stigma. The plastic goddess was a real-life perennial—an Eden.

Her voice rang out, loud and clear as a speaker. "If I wanted your general status, I would have called. Tell me about the incident."

Mr. Gion stumbled. "Yes. That. The automated systems may have a few bugs that need addressing..."

Ms. Eden raised a manicured eyebrow.

"Our harvest yield has outpaced our processing capacity."

"Wasn't this issue remedied several cycles ago?"

Mr. Gion forced a wide smile. "We had a workaround, but if we were granted an on-staff engineer—"

"Stop. 999 facilities do not get engineers." Ms. Eden adjusted the snowy fur shawl lying over her shoulders, and her dagger-shaped nails glinted like fiery chrome. "We lost—how much did we lose, Yessica?"

The assistant checked her tablet. "Two million, Sire."

"Your facility was on track for an upgrade, but with this, we'll be lucky if Planitr doesn't liquidate my entire division."

"Well, the systems—"

"Are utter garbage. And what do you think the Planitrs will do with a crater full of garbage?" She grabbed his tie. "They will throw you out. We must convince them this was caused by human error. The question is, which human will be our sacrifice?"

Mr. Gion massaged his hands. "What exactly will happen to this particular employee?"

"They will be handed over to the Planitrs to deal with as they see fit, obviously."

"Madam, with all due respect, I'm not sure they will believe a single harvester caused this."

She shook her head slowly. "You are disappointing the family, Gion. Are you concerned for the cattle?"

He nodded like a kid caught running the faucet.

"After all my mentorship, you still think like them. Planitr has asked our patriarch to consolidate forty plants, managers included.

Do you want to return to being livestock?" Ms. Eden's nose bridge crinkled into a pretty snarl. "If you plan to wear my family's brand, you will *speak*."

Her scornful tone made Vesta's blood rush into her heart to hide, and her face blanched so hard she went dizzy.

Mr. Gion's knees buckled and he blabbered, "Z—Zero—worker 000. We have security footage of him in the labs."

"Continue..." Ms. Eden examined her knife-like nails.

"With some judicious footage selection, we can paint a picture for our leadership." Mr. Gion climbed off the ground.

Son of a scorpion, Vesta mouthed.

"I'll need that prepared before the first quarter update, and—" Ms. Eden lifted her nose, sniffing. "Do you have a rat problem? Something smells dreadful."

"We have a few jerboas, but it's under control."

She surveyed the room, her eyes lingering on Vesta's cabinet. Vesta pulled it shut and tried to stop sweating so hard.

"Sire," Ms. Eden's assistant said, "I think the rats have disturbed the packaging equipment."

"Gion!" Ms. Eden rang out, and their footsteps traveled to the far end of the lab.

Vesta took her chance to creep out of the cabinet and escape. They were going to fire Dezi—or worse! Dust muffins, this was bad.

When Dezi opened the door to Ajax's suite, the smell of buttery jicama and roasted desert hare greeted him.

"Dezi!" Vesta threw her arms around his shoulders, then checked down each side of the hallway. "Did anyone follow you?"

"I don't think so. Why?" He stumbled as she yanked him into the party and slammed the door.

"There's the town hero." Ajax lumbered over, his thick arms opening to demand a hug. "C'mere, boy! Ain't we practically family?"

Dezi awkwardly relented, and his mother, who had been sitting quietly at the dinner table, broke into a giggle.

"So that's what it takes to make you smile, Renata." Ajax released Dezi and belly laughed. "Get you a plate and dig in, sonny."

Dezi prepared a full serving and sat beside Ori.

The boy climbed up onto his knees and whispered into Dezi's ear, "Sis cut me out of her heist, so I'm planning my own."

"Oh yeah?" Dezi laid a napkin on his lap. "What are you stealing?"

"Nuclear fuel rods. You have to take me to Chryse to get 'em, and Sis ain't invited."

"What are you two scheming over there?" Vesta squinted.

"It's top secret." Ori dropped onto his butt. "And big dummies who show up without the loot don't need to know."

"You lil' nipper." Vesta reached over with her spork and stole some of Ori's rabbit.

"Settle down." Ajax pointed at his kids and rebalanced the meat. "What in the blasted dune's gotten into you two?"

Ori's small face twisted into tears. "Sis has been sneaking around and stealing without me, and she's gonna take Dezi away to the city and leave me all alone!"

"I ain't done nothing, and I told you to keep your rock-eating mouth shut," Vesta snapped.

"Woah now." Ajax patted his son's head. "What's your brother on about?"

Vesta's cheeks went pink, but then her lips quivered and turned downward. "Alright, I'm coming clean. I snuck into the lab, but y'all better thank your lucky stars I did, because I overheard Mr. Gion talking to the outsiders."

Dezi covered his mouth, finding that his hand was shaking. "Are they retiring the facility?"

"Even better. They're pinning the refinery mess on you so they can build Verde's upgrade on your broken back."

His face went numb. "You're kidding."

"I cannot believe this!" his mother exclaimed. "After all we have done for this place, that *desgraçado* Gion plans to scapegoat my son. Why I ever let your father convince me the Eden bloodline was worth anything—" She rattled off a string of curses under her breath.

"Of course it had to be me." Dezi's numbness prickled into panic. "Am I going to prison? Debtors' work camp?"

Shiney tears dropped down Ori's cheeks. "Dezi's going to asteroid jail?"

Vesta pulled her chair closer to his. "We'll get you a lawyer and take Mr. Eden for all he's worth."

Ajax shook his head. "Those parasites got legal teams that can run circles 'round whatever we'd scrounge up."

"But the Planitrs are buying out the Edens, right?" Dezi asked. "Maybe I can talk to them. Maybe they'll be reasonable."

His family didn't reply; they just watched him pitifully. As the largest conglomerate in the system, the Planitrs were known for two things: using the cheapest human labor, and applying the maximum penalty to employee transgressions, without compromise. If they got their hands on Dezi, he'd never see natural sunlight again.

"I have to run." He looked at Vesta. "I have to leave Verde tonight."

"Okay." She nodded. "My guy can get our papers together, but we still need a way out of here. Ms. Merlo, could you pack us onto the Magna with the medical supplies?"

"I have the code for the refrigerated car," Dezi's mom said, "but the unloading crew will catch you."

"My guy can handle that. Problem is, he don't come cheap, and I didn't swipe nothing to pay him with."

"Well." Ajax leaned back in his seat, pulling something out of his sweater pocket. "I should be bleeding mad with you, girl, but I guess the fruit don't fall far from the tree."

He planted a crystal safranal vial on the table. "If the Edens ain't going to take care of their people, I'll damn well make 'em."

"You crazy old man." Vesta's face lit up. "How the heck did you get one of those?"

"I heard through the drip line that you needed a little money to help you on your way out, so I picked it up when the lab was shut off. Figured it would be payment for all the work us Zeros did."

"You're leaving with me?" Dezi asked Vesta. "But your contract isn't up."

"It'll cost the Edens more to track me down than what's left on the darn bonds." Vesta planted her fist on the table. "They can pound sand trying to catch me."

"Alright." Dezi took a slow breath and picked up the weighty safranal. "Pack your bedsheets; it'll be a cold ride."

Phobos hung low in the sky, bloated like the lump in Dezi's throat, as he and Vesta stealthily carried their bags down the dim hallways. They reached the loading bay where Dezi's mom and Ajax waited by the open MagnaLoop door. Mom tightly crossed her arms to preserve warmth, while Ajax's red nose dripped as much as his eyes.

"We're ready." Vesta fidgeted like she was resisting the urge to dance.

Mom did a poor job hiding her frown and handed Dezi a cloth bag packed with bandages, water bottles, and metallic locust meal packs. She slipped a medical package into his hand and embraced him, whispering, "This is your next testosterone implant. You may need someone to help you install it."

He slid it into his pocket. "I can handle it." It wasn't that he didn't trust Vesta, but people saw you differently when they knew you were trans. At this stage in his life, it wasn't a conversation he needed to have anymore.

"Don't worry 'bout us." Ajax choked up. "I'll keep an eye on yer mom for you, Zero."

"Ajax, please call me Dezi."

"Dezi...you got to take care of Vesta, you hear? She's a wild one, same as her sister." He broke into a sob.

"I'll do my best." Dezi touched his arm.

Mom gave Vesta a serious look. "Watch over Dezi. I know you will."

"Darn straight!" Vesta raised her fists.

"Cool your toast, hunny bug, and give yer old man a hug. You promise to call home, you hear?"

"I do. I do." They both cried and grinned in each other's arms.

Dezi asked his mom, "Can you say goodbye to Ori for me? Tell him he can have my poster and all of my meteorites."

The train buzzed at the humans delaying its departure.

Dezi's mom clasped his shoulders. "Swear to me that you won't give up. Promise you will get off of this planet and do—see—live the life you want." Her grip trembled and her eyes welled. She hadn't wept when Dad left or when Mithra had died; her face was always calm as still water, but now tears clouded her eyes. "I want you to stand under the blue skies of Earth again, and—send me a picture?"

"I-I will." Dezi wiped his rolling tears with both hands.

She smiled, briefly embraced him, then pushed him through the train door after Vesta.

"Keep yer heads up, you two!" Ajax clutched a rag to his eye.

"I love you, Pa! I'll make you and Ori proud!" Vesta waved and cheered, revealing her snaggletooth.

Dezi sniffled and waved at his mom. She let the tears run down her cheeks, smiling with a glimmer of pride he hadn't seen since his college acceptance letter.

The gunmetal door slid shut, and the train jerked forward, throwing the two of them against the racks of hanging blood bags. This was it: them and a delivery of fresh blood to the City of Sharp Smiles.

CHAPTER 4
Specters

Crisp light shot down the MagnaLoop's walls as its portholes passed under the flood lamps in the facility tunnel. When the rays hit any of the hundred hanging blood bags, crimson glare scattered across the poly-steel interior. Dezi and Vesta sat shoulder-to-shoulder in the space of one removed shelf as the train's acceleration pressed Dezi's tongue into the back of his mouth. Vesta's voice jiggled when she whispered, "I'll bet you this is how lift-off feels."

KA-CHUNK.

Past the threshold, the cabin went dark, and magnetic whirring replaced the clattering of the low-speed wheels. Dezi's inner ear ached from the drop in pressure and the icy grate bit into his legs, but the MagnaLoop's speed stabilized.

"I think we're out of Verde now. There won't be any lights until we pass a station," he said.

Vesta raised her phone, illuminating the pint-sized bags of blood hanging from racks all around them. Alongside a row of aluminum kegs, three cryocaskets were stacked alongside the row of aluminum kegs gathering frosty condensation on their fake gold handles. She brazenly shone her light into the window of one. "More bags. No one's died since the last train, so I doubt there're any stiffs in here with us."

A low hiss from sand brushing the underside of the MagnaLoop made Dezi shiver. "I can't imagine what they need this much blood for…"

"Immortality treatments, duh." Vesta explored the cabin, blinding him with the flash of her camera. "I hate how our earwig of a manager did you, but at least Verde will finally get those repairs. Knowing you, you wouldn't have set foot on this train until you personally tightened every bolt in town."

Dezi tucked up his knees and sighed. "Gion has a responsibility to everyone in Verde. I wouldn't want him to sacrifice their jobs for my sake."

"He didn't give a green 'tater about the town. Him and that Eden lady were covering their own behinds."

"So you really saw a perennial?" Dezi perked up. Although his grandfather had been one, Dezi had never met him; all his knowledge about the elusive immortals who occupied the system's seats of power was secondhand. "What was she like?"

"Beautiful." Vesta's eyes glimmered in her phone's light. "She had a figure like a doll, all slim and round at once. Her face was so smooth it shined, and her hair was glossy as glass. Even the way she moved—I never seen someone so prim and posh. But why are you asking me? Isn't your dad a perennial?"

"No—or, I don't think so."

"How can you not know if your own pop is immortal?"

"We haven't talked in years."

"He stopped calling?"

Dezi crossed his arms and shrugged. "I stopped picking up. But Mom thinks he'll be back any day now."

"Will he?"

"No." He had left sixteen years ago, and while inconsistent orbital signal explained why the calls were infrequent, it didn't excuse the lack of visits or how the checks had gotten smaller until they'd stopped entirely. Either Dad was already dead or he would never die, but it made no difference to Dezi. He and Mom had clearly been dead to his father for a while.

The silence festered, coarse and barren like the tunnel walls, until Vesta huddled next to Dezi, warming him with the touch of her shoulder. "I got a sperm donor out there too, but he don't mean nothing to me like Pa does. Not half what you, me, and Mithra made. That's family. I wish she could see us now."

Dezi nodded. "Ves, do you believe in ghosts?"

She snorted. "I ain't a colony bumpkin."

"I guess I *ain't one neither*."

Vesta's cheeks turned peachy pink. "I don't sound like that! You better watch it, 'cause one of these days I'll be a planet-hopping perennial, and you'll be begging to come with."

Dezi turned. "You want to be one of them?"

"Uh, who doesn't?"

"We don't even know how they're made. Or what they *really* are." He glanced at the caskets.

"So that's why you brought up specters. I can't believe someone like you would buy into Pa's leaky-lock stories about perennials being undead."

"Someone like me?"

"You know, educated. Earth-born."

"Vesta, on Earth they're called vampires."

Her entire face flushed. "That's a strong word."

He nodded; the term could get you suspended for a month on a Planitr-owned colony. "You're going to hear it in Chryse. You want to be a *vampire*? To drink blood?"

She crossed her arms and pouted. "I'm gonna be young forever and have the money to set Pa and Ori up somewhere nice. I can't believe you wouldn't want that, too."

"I—" Dezi paused, studying the void-filled porthole on the ceiling for a moment, then surrendered with a sigh. "I don't know what I want, but there's no point in stressing about something that will never happen."

"It can if you dream it. Once we get to Chryse, I might find me a Venusian boyfriend to show me the stars. You can come too. I won't forget the little people in my life." Vesta victoriously booped Dezi's nose.

He snorted. "I'm just glad you didn't forget me back in Verde..."

Her laughter fell off. "I couldn't ditch you in that crater. I feel bad enough leaving Pa and Ori."

"Thanks, Ves. I know I can be a dry toothbrush sometimes, but...thanks."

"That's what family's for." She wrapped her arms around him and shook him left and right. "Now, help me with these blankets and I'll set us up a movie. It took me darn near a week to download this new romance flick."

Dezi tugged the sheets out of their pack and groaned. "The one where an immortal billionaire whisks a barista away to Venus?"

"What, you can't appreciate a Romeo and Juliet story?"

"Romeo and Juliet were three years apart in age, not three hundred."

"I've seen your watch history. You love that sappy stuff."

"N-no I don't!"

"Well, I love it. Plus, the guy's only seventy!" Vesta tossed the blanket over their heads and hit play.

The movie sucked, but the actor was pretty hot; dark chocolate hair and maroon eyes were a combo that just did something for Dezi.

Metallic squealing pierced through Vesta's sleep as the Magna suddenly jiggled on its tracks.

Dezi lifted his head, wiping the drool off his chin. "Are we in Chryse?"

Vesta rubbed the bone-deep chill out of her arms and checked her phone. "It's been three hours; we're not even halfway."

The train swerved to the side, rolling Vesta against the wall. She cried out, but Dezi took her into his arms, cradling her head, as the brakes slammed down. They both tumbled forward, clinging to each other as the car crunched and whined. The blood sloshed around them, bags falling from racks and slapping down on Vesta's back. The cabin was going to pop open and flash-freeze them any second—barely a foot out of Verde and it was already over. Vesta buried her face in Dezi's chest and cussed her lungs out until she could hear her own voice again.

"Taint-diddlin'—" She raised her head. "We're slowing down." The Magna limped to a halt, and Dezi shakily let her go. "I think that was an emergency stop."

Once the cabin had settled, Vesta clambered up a rack and pressed her face to the porthole on the ceiling. They were in a round, concrete tunnel wide enough for a dozen trains, but the window's angle made it impossible to see anything at ground level. White and yellow pipes ran along the cavernous ceiling, and every sixty feet, an industrial lamp with a dreary orange light hung from a wire.

She checked the tiny window in the door, but it was five feet from the tunnel wall. "You think we're refueling?"

"No," Dezi said. "Lev trains get induction power from the tracks. There must have been a mechanical failure; maybe the wind carried debris into the tunnel. I'm sure drones are inspecting the train now."

They waited, listening to the Magna shift and groan, while Vesta tapped her toes on the grate until she couldn't take it anymore. It had been over an hour, and she hadn't heard anything that sounded like a repair drone.

"I'm gonna get a look around," she said.

"What?" Dezi jerked his head off his knees. "We don't know if there's air out there."

"Those plastic pipes couldn't hold up to surface pressure."

"But it could be dangerous. What if someone catches us?"

"If we stay here too long, we'll run out of oxygen." She yanked the sliding door. It hissed like opening a can of soda, and musty air entered the cabin.

She gave Dezi her *told-ya-so* grin, then crept onto the clay-red gravel. He followed behind as she used a ladder mounted on the

Magna to climb over it. On the other side, they found eight sets of tracks, a rusty train, and a squat building with cracked walls tucked against the far side, but there wasn't a single repair drone to be seen.

"The front car," Dezi whispered. "The propulsion engine is gone."

"Lean beans! We're gonna be stuck here. Unless—" Vesta pointed at the rusty train. "You think we can ride that one?"

"We don't know where it's going. Our train has blood on it, so they have to move it eventually."

"How long before blood goes bad?"

"A day or two?" Dezi rubbed his neck. "I don't know..."

"We can't stay here *a day or two*. Gion will be on our tails the second the sun rises." Vesta checked her phone, but it didn't have signal. "You can't use your big noggin' to figure out where that train is bound for?"

He grimaced. "I guess I can try."

They snuck over to the other train and climbed the boxy car. Dezi turned the wheel on the hatch top and lifted it to reveal a pile of minerals, with plenty of room for sitting. Vesta shone her light in, and he examined the rough crystals. They were fist-sized, scab-colored, and textured like bundles of dry spaghetti.

"It's rutile, titanium ore." Dezi's muscles bulged as he put the massive lid down quietly. "This train is going to a refinery."

"Chryse has plenty of those, right?" Vesta clapped once. "Let's hop in."

"Shhh—this car isn't insulated, and it doesn't have much air space."

"Then we need stasis suits. They'd have at least two in there." She pointed at the building across the tracks. "Extra scrubbers and tanks, too."

"We can't steal. And what if someone catches us?"

"Have you seen anybody? Plus, it's a little late to get high and mighty about stealing."

"Ore can sit here forever, but they won't let blood spoil." Dezi blinked his sad eyes and used that soft, heartfelt voice of his. "Please, let's be patient."

The sugar cookie of a man knew how to tug a girl's heartstrings, but Vesta couldn't let her ticket to Chryse slip away, and she'd be damned before she let any corporate deadbeat slap a pair of handcuffs on her best friend. "You've been through a lot, Dez, so let me handle this one. Keep an eye on the Magna for me, and I'll be back with two suits in the shake of a tail."

Vesta hopped off the ore car and scuttled across the gravel to the train station. She snuck alongside the building, but paused when she noticed the cracks in the cement wall were stuffed with pebbles and glue. The bulging veins on the gray face of the building resembled some type of grungy installation art, but she questioned who had the free time to waste on something so ugly. She took a creepy selfie with it.

Vesta peeked through the nearby windows and slid up to the door. She tried to wipe her feet on the doormat as she entered, but the bristles were worn to rubber. The glow from the tunnel lamps cast a dim light on the checkered floor and retro-futurist decor of the lobby. The tables were urine-yellow petroleum plastic, their corners crumbling away like stale bread, and a dead sweeping drone sat in the corner of the dustless room beside an empty trashcan lined with a crisp, white bag.

Vesta's stomach made a gloomy rumble as she wandered to the ancient vending machine, but it was powered off and picked clean. She turned to a display of pamphlets and examined one. It read, *Start your new life on the Martian frontier by taking advantage of reduced fares to any Planitr-partnered facility on the new MT-Ultra. Marztran and Planitr: a partnership built for the eons!*

The pamphlets advertised Chryse City in faded colors on real wood-pulp paper, but the map had three habitation domes, and if she remembered Ori's homework right, the city had at least twenty now. This was bad news for her search because if this station had been built during the first wave, its life-support gear could be equally ancient.

She returned the brochure and slunk down the halls, uncovering maintenance closets and restrooms, but no signs of life, not even roaches. At the end of the hall, she spotted a person-sized panel embedded in the wall painted emergency orange. Jackpot! She tugged the handle, but the door was jammed, so she jogged up the hall in search of something to pry it open with.

When Vesta rounded the corner, a chugging and hissing sound made her jump worse than bumping into Mr. Gion. Through the station windows, she saw the Magna sliding forward. She bolted outside, but the train was picking up speed faster than she could match—with Dezi's head peeking over the ladder. Was he leaving without her? There was no way he'd jump, but he wasn't even inside the cabin.

She held her breath as Dezi crawled on top of the car. Flat like a lizard and quivering like a stalk, when he brought his eyes to hers, those frightened saucers found focus. He threw their bags off the train and tumbled after them, rolling onto the gravel.

Vesta shouted, "Dezi!"

He was too still. Didn't even raise his head.

She took two bounds, but a voice crackled behind her. "Where the hell do you think you're going?"

A monster with a face wrinkled like gray sackcloth grabbed Vesta's arm and dragged her back. She shrieked and struggled, but his grip was lead-heavy and just as cold. His torso was round as a melon, though his arms were pure bone, muscle, and purple veins.

Vesta shouted, "Stop! Stop! Let me go!"

He leered at her with coal-black eyes. "Never been caught? You're going back to whatever dust bowl you came from."

"What?" Vesta caught her breath. "Wait—I can pay you. I promise I ain't worth the trouble."

"Marztrans don't take bribes." He turned his cheek, flashing the puncture scars on his neck.

Vesta's jaw dropped. "You're a perennial?" She didn't want to say it, but the man looked like a skinned apple rotting from the inside out.

"Obviously. And nobody gets a free ride at my station."

"Where are your employees? And your passengers? You can't even afford to keep the lights on."

"You don't see the lights?" He pointed to an unlit bulb hanging above them. "Or do you think because Ambrose Industries announced those new magnetic trains that Marztran is out of business? They'll have to lay those tracks over my dead body!"

He belly laughed, and Vesta's knees gave out. "You're crazy," she blubbered, and her feet scrabbled on the floor as he dragged her down the hallway.

He entered his office, tossed her onto a plastic stool, and sat in his desiccated leather armchair. "Which town did you ride in from?"

Vesta adjusted herself in the seat. "Verde Valis."

"Verde...? Are you making up names?" He sneered at the laminated map on his desk.

"I mean this in the kindest of ways, but you've lost every bean in your bag. Sir, you've got dementia."

He furrowed his brows like a gorilla ready to bear his fangs. "Are you trying to make me angry, girl?"

She balled her fists and bunched up her nose. "I don't give a hoot either way, but there was a Magna on your tracks a minute ago, ya rot-brained fart!"

He stared at her, then at his map. "What year is it?"

She simmered down as she saw the old man for what he was: a prisoner of this dilapidated station, trapped by his own decrepit mind. "3076."

He rubbed his bald head, pressing oily warts out of the way. He didn't have a scrap of hair, not even eyebrows or eyelashes. "3076...?"

Vesta shakily stood. "If you don't mind, I got places to be."

"I don't care what year it is. No free rides." His snarl exposed his pus-colored teeth. "Sit down."

She stood firm. "You don't even know what year it is, so how're you gonna accuse me of anything?"

"I've been at this for two centuries. I know a hopper when I see one." He picked up the wired phone on his table and dialed.

"Wait—let's make a deal. My credit's good, I swear!"

"Sure it is, bloodbag."

Vesta hesitated. "I got blood."

He stopped dialing.

"I'll trade blood—a cup of blood—if you get me on a train to Chryse."

"I can buy blood." He pressed another number.

She gritted her teeth. "Then why're you wasting my time?"

"I'll do it for skin." He grinned, revealing his cracked canines. The enamel-white veneer on his left one was worn down to a bare metallic spine.

"A bite? No way."

He dialed again, each click sending spider legs running across Vesta's skin. She couldn't go home yet. Dezi couldn't go home ever, or they'd have him smashing asteroids until he was sixty. For all she knew, he was bleeding out on the tracks while she waffled.

Steadying her shallow breaths, Vesta rolled her sleeve up to her bicep. "You can bite here for ten seconds."

They glared at each other in silence, but the monster finally nodded.

She held out her arm. He snatched it in his bony mitts, cracked open his jaw, and held her to his wet teeth. The spines in his canines shot out, driving themselves into her flesh. It stung like a vaccination, but this time, the needles wouldn't come out and the injection was his stinking saliva.

Vesta gripped the edge of his desk and focused on the pain in her knuckles instead of her arm, forcing herself to stand through waves of nausea. She counted aloud while he sloppily siphoned her blood. "—Eight. Nine. Ten!"

He didn't let go. Vesta tugged, screamed, but he wouldn't let go. She kicked his legs and beat his head while his cold slug of a tongue stuck to her skin. When she dug her thumbs into his eyes, he gurgled and unlatched. Still gripping her arm, he stared into the distance, foggy-eyed and murmuring incoherently. She pried herself free and ran.

Slamming into doors and walls, she found a bathroom and rinsed the wound. She grabbed a fistful of paper towels and pressed it against her arm, but her blood seeped through, forming lacey curls in the wet sink. An icy hand touched her shoulder—she shrieked.

The bloody-mouthed monster jolted, then handed her an ancient bandage. "Shut up and take this."

Vesta snatched it, then wrapped her wound and pulled her sleeve over it. "You're gonna—"

He grabbed her wrist. "Don't tell anyone about this."

Used, degraded, and quivering all over, she glared him down. "Get your hands off me or I'll call the cops right now."

He licked his slimy lips and, slowly, let her go. "Look for the set of cars by the front of the tunnel. The first cabin will be unlocked for five minutes."

Vesta backed away, then sprinted out of the building.

She ran across the tracks to where she had seen Dezi fall, but there was nothing there. Where could he have gone in a state like that, or was there another monster lurking somewhere out here? She whirled around, counting every precious second she had, then spotted him. With his jeans torn and bloody, he lay slouched against the rusted train.

"Dezi, Dezi—" She ran to him and grasped his cheeks. "Wake up, please!"

"Ves?" He opened his eyes like he'd been napping. "The Magna left, and you were gone."

"Thank my stars." She embraced him. "Can you walk?"

"I think so..." He stood, steadying himself on the car. "But we're stranded."

Vesta's arm was agonizingly hot, but she rubbed away her tears and picked up both their packs. "I did it, Dez. I found us a ride."

He winced as he hobbled after her, but they needed to get out of sight before that creature smelled his blood. "Are you alright?"

She met his stormy eyes, saw them grappling with what they had left in Verde. And now he'd been thrown from a moving train because she had wanted to be the hero. She couldn't burden him with this, make it his fault. No, this was her shame, and she'd take it to the grave.

"Ves?"

"It's okay. But we need to get in this cabin, now." She ran ahead to a Magna car down the tracks and tugged the door.

Dezi came up behind and pulled with her, sliding it open. "It's unlocked. How did you know?"

"Schedules." Vesta climbed into the crate-filled car and sat on a box of produce. "I don't think any human has been in that station for decades."

He shut the door and sat with her. "That sounds spooky..."

Shivering, she scooted closer. "I shouldn't have left the Magna. You were right. I shouldn'ta left."

He rubbed her shoulder. "Are you sure you're alright?"

"I'm fantastic." She couldn't stop the tears. "I know it was hard for you to leave your mom, and you were scared, 'cause it is scary, but I couldn't have left without you."

"You're going to make me cry too..." Dezi gave her the bashful smile that he always did when she complimented him. "I'm sorry I held you back as long as I did."

"That's in the past now, all of it." She leaned on him. "From here on, we stick together no matter what. Nothing back there matters, 'cause this is the start of our new lives."

Dezi bundled her up in the blankets, and eventually, the Magna jostled. It slid forward, leaving that nightmare in the dark where it belonged.

CHAPTER 5
NEEDLES

EVENING SUNSHINE STROBED THROUGH the MagnaLoop as its brakes squealed. The train slid to a halt with a hiss, blasting the cabin with warm air that popped Dezi's ears. Vesta opened her eyes and shifted against his shoulder, then the two quietly gathered their sheets. Vesta had sent her contact a message to inform him they wouldn't be on the correct train, but there was no telling whether he had gotten it or even cared. They were fugitives now, but they had made it to Chryse, a city swimming in criminals and bond skippers, so with any luck, they'd get lost in the noise with the millions of other runaways.

They paused at every creak and whine in the steel until several sets of footsteps approached alongside their car. Was it the unloading crew? Dezi could handle drones, but he wasn't confident he could talk his way past live people. Huddled on the floor like mice, he and Vesta held their breath as the heavy thuds slowed. The door rattled, then screeched when a man with a spider tattooed on his shaved head forced it open. Beside him stood another man in jean overalls with insect tattoos creeping down his arms. The thugs' taut skin made their faces look like skulls, but their arms were pure, grainy muscle. Shaded under a black umbrella, a thinner man stood behind them, wearing baggy streetwear and bearing a snake-like scar on his jugular.

He lowered his mirrored sunglasses, and his fanged grill crowded his mouth as he said, "Vesta, honey eyes, you're late."

"Elay! Son of a biscuit, you could have said something." She threw her balled-up sheets on the ground and stood.

"We've been over this. It's *L-A*, not *E-lay*." He held up a hand adorned with chunky rings and long nails. "Now, where's the product?"

"We can't get out of the Magna first, *Elay*?" She playfully cocked her hip and fought her accent to pronounce it.

"I can't go soft in front of the guys." His gilded smile caught the daylight, blinding Dezi.

"Ugh, whatever." Vesta pulled the decanter from her back pocket. "This thing was bruising my rear all night."

Elay took it, flashing the red head of the giant centipede tattooed on the back of his hand, and passed Vesta two envelopes. "You know what to do with these?"

"We'll manage." She cupped them to her chest.

"I'ght. Appreciate the business." He stuffed the safranal into his coat and turned.

"Wait, we ain't done." Vesta jumped over the gap between the train and platform.

Elay swiveled on his heel, bobbing a finger. "Oh yeah, I almost forgot. There's a bounty out on a Verdan runaway." He lowered his shades and locked his rust-brown eyes on Dezi. "Two mill for the young man who sabotaged a Planitr facility."

"He—we—" Vesta's limbs tensed. She eyed Dezi and then glanced down the tracks.

Elay laughed so hard his umbrella teetered, unshading himself. "Ice it, kids. I'm no shark. I don't care if you're bond skippers or serial killers, snitching is bad for my brand. Most of my customers are one or the other, after all."

Dezi went lightheaded from relief, but it was short-lived. "T-two million dollars?"

Elay nodded. "When they got money to burn on bounties that fat, you see why people think twice before crossing the Planitrs. Fly low, kid. Don't touch anything in their orbit, you get me?"

Dezi looked at Vesta, but she shrugged.

"Fresh as fruit off the shuttle, huh?" Elay raised an eyebrow and whistled, but his grill made it a whiney hiss. "No Eden boutiques, no MacroDose vending machines, and watch your traffic violations in Planitr Simulo. Every time you touch something they own, that's a blip on their radar. Stack up enough, and a bounty hunter might show up at your place. Lucky for you, the tolls are run by Luminair, and they're on the Ambrose side of the feud, so they won't care even if you nuked a Planitr satellite. Hell, they might even give you a discount. Most importantly, no cops. Debt sharks gotta follow laws—confirm your identity and all that, which won't be easy with fresh chips—but the blue will bag and tag you before their stun lances wear off."

"If Mr. Gion already reported Dezi, how are we going to make it past border control?" Vesta asked.

Elay checked his watch, tapping its touch screen. "The bounty order just came in, so if you rub some dirt on your face and hurry, you'll be fine—probably."

"Thank you." Dezi studied Elay; he seemed friendly for a criminal, but they were in no position to judge.

"Make this worth my time and don't get collared. I got work for a face that pretty." Elay smiled at Vesta in a way that Dezi decided was, indeed, too friendly.

She crossed her arms and puffed her lips out. "Where's our cut for the safranal?"

"This was your cut, honey. If you're smart, you'll scram before someone comes looking for the unloading crew." Elay sauntered to a shiny SUV parked by the tracks. "You got a five-mile walk to the checkpoint."

Vesta stomped after the men. "You were supposed to give us three hundred bucks!"

"Consider your tab closed and your credit revoked." He winked and stepped into his ride. "Welcome to Chryse City, baby! Call me if you make it."

"Eat my boots, ya roundworm!" she shouted, but their off-roader kicked a cloud of dust in her face as it pulled off. After coughing up a fit, she sulked back to gather her blankets. "Heck, Dez, what are we gonna do?"

He looked around. Dozens of rusted tracks striped the ground, and bipedal forklifts removed crate after crate from trains both new and centuries old. Bales of millet, pallets of pistons, frosty cryocaskets—a megacity's worth of supplies. The MagnaLoop ran so far in each direction that its lead and last car disappeared into the dryfog, and a dome bigger than all of Verde Valis arched over them. He pointed at the glow of neon in the distant smog. "We get to the checkpoint, then we find a place to stay."

Vesta groaned, heaving her bag over her shoulder. "Step one to building our new lives: a five-mile hike."

After a few hours, Dezi and Vesta reached the front of the MagnaLoop and the passenger cars it had picked up during its stops between Meridiani and Chryse. Beyond rows of industrial fans blowing back the dust, patrons in fur coats and stylish particle masks queued up for taxi services.

Vesta headed towards the line of glossy cabs, but Dezi grabbed her hand and said, "Those look expensive."

"We can afford one ride. I've been saving up, and you gotta have some credit."

"Planitr can track us through our company accounts, assuming they haven't closed them already."

"Butter my buttcheeks." Vesta rubbed her palm on her brow. "I got some money on my social account we can use. Should be enough for at least a night."

"Huh. I never thought I'd be grateful for how much time you waste on social media."

"It's not wasted. It's my career." She huffed. "If we're hoofing it, we gotta make it through Clearair. That's the dust buffer between here and city proper."

They approached the dizzyingly tall edge of the UV-yellowed dome and then pushed through the layers of tacky plastic membranes that made up the barrier between this habitation zone and the next. Dezi took a deep breath of Clearair; it was frigid, astringent, and perfumed with sewage.

"Woo-wee, it stinks!" Vesta raised her arms, earning herself side-eye from the locals.

The residents of Clearair squatted on curbs or sat on overturned buckets, moving only when taxis threw up sand by racing down the wide road. The whirring of electric engines gave way to soft talking, coughing, and the occasional spitting. Even here, the residents wore masks, though they were made of simple cloth and as dust-stained as their tattered clothing. Many of the migrants were old-stock Martians, chatting in their unique colony dialects, but some were interplanetary immigrants speaking Earth-Latin or rarer Old-World languages.

Dezi and Vesta walked the trodden dirt that formed a patchy layer over Clearair's gray tile. The flimsy dome overhead was a ribbed archway instead of a proper semi-circle and so low that it brushed against the shanties constructed of shipping crates haphazardly welded together. The peeling flakes of the shacks' red and yellow enamel lay scattered on the ground or stuck to children's bare feet as they laughed and danced between broken bottles.

Dezi passed a young man and woman huddled under a strung-up tarp. With his face covered in scab-like moles, the man attempted to light his partner's tin foil pipe, though the lighter only tossed useless sparks. Dezi threw his blanket over his shoulders, but Clearair's chill still burrowed into his chest. Why were these people living in a giant airlock, and more pressingly, how would Dezi ensure he and Vesta didn't suffer the same fate?

While he was distracted, Vesta stumbled.

Dezi dropped to his knees to catch her. "Ves! Are you alright?"

"I need a break." She puffed.

He guided her by her clammy shoulders to a shack she could slump against. "You're burning up..."

"Do we have any water?"

He hurriedly offered the supplies his mom had packed. "Here."

She took a bottle, tore open a locust meal bag, and crunched on the pellets inside, panting but still smiling. "We need to eat these before the checkpoint at Old Chryse."

Dezi opened his bag, forced down the powdery crickets, and chased it with half-frozen water. "Old Chryse? Aren't we in Chryse?"

"Chryse City's got a bunch of bubbles all stuck together now, but Old Chryse was the first one they ever built. That's probably where we'll be living, since I hear rent's the cheapest."

Their phones blared a metallic alarm, and Dezi checked the notification. "We hit our radiation limit. We should get to the border."

"Sand in my syrup. We better get these new chips installed." She handed him an envelope marked with his initials.

Dezi opened the package to find a note containing a ten-digit number, a disposable syringe, and one trapezoidal razor blade. Vesta held the tip of her blade to her wrist, but her shaking fingers made the steel slick with sweat.

"Wait." He touched her arm. "Let me do it."

She wrinkled her nose, but then glanced at the huge microchip-delivering needle. "Okay, but make it quick."

He nodded, took her utility razor, and held her small, calloused hand in his. He gently probed her wrist until he found the rice-grain-sized chip capsule beneath her skin. She shut her eyes as he pressed the blade in and drew a controlled line. Darkness crept into the corners of his vision, but he pushed the knife tip in and gingerly pried her implant out.

"Screaming stars—you looking for buried treasure in there?"

He flinched, and Vesta's bloody chip fell into the dirt. She jerked her wrist back and pressed the cut to her tongue; Mom would yank her ear for doing something so unsanitary, but Martians didn't waste blood. "Thanks. You need me to get yours?"

"No, my wrist's already cut open." Dezi peeled back the silicone film on his swollen gash. He had to dig around the mushy tissue, but it was pretty numb, so the chip came out easily. He pushed the stalk-sized needle into his wound and pressed the plunger, though the chip went in at a weird angle. "It's crooked...great."

"Mine too." Vesta chuckled goofily and heaved herself up, still way too cheerful considering the bags under her eyes. Dezi could tell she was hiding her exhaustion to avoid putting extra stress on him. Although she was more knowledgeable about the city than he was, Dezi would need to step up, or she would run herself into the ground by trying to take responsibility for both of them.

As he gathered their trash, he saw that the symbol Elay had scarred on his neck was spray-painted on a corrugated steel wall. This detailed version had a black squiggle for its body, yellow lines radiating off it for legs, and a red dot serving as its head. The gang tag confirmed Dezi's suspicion that Vesta's city connection belonged to a perennial crime family.

He asked her, "Do you trust these new IDs?"

She scanned the shanties and then stuck a spare bandage to her wrist. "As much as I trust a dermafilm condom, but we ain't got much of a choice."

He nodded. "If someone recognizes me, you need to run. Try to get through without me."

"You know there ain't a two-moon chance of me leaving you behind."

Dezi examined his dirty razor for a moment and then, on impulse, began sawing his bangs short.

"Uh, Dez. You feeling alright?"

He put on a medical mask. "Then I can't be recognized."

Past the packed alleys of Clearair, Dezi and Vesta reached the checkpoint guarding the entrance to another grand dome. They entered the queue leading up to a line of border agents and body scanners. Vesta sat on the ground every chance she got, but Dezi studied the hopeful travelers who were turned away, searching for patterns.

A man in a polo shirt shook his phone at an agent. "But my credit limit is seven thousand dollars. You're supposed to let me in."

"The credit minimum is ten thousand," the agent said. "If you can't meet that, you either need a tier-one passport or active employment in the city."

"C'mon, aren't you in the middle of a blood shortage? I'm healthy, I can work; cut me a break, man."

When the dead-eyed agent lifted his radio to his ear warningly, the man dropped his shoulders and wandered back into the dust.

Dezi advanced one step in line. "There's a blood shortage?"

"The city's got more perennials than young people to donate, so I bet the ugly weather slowing down the trains made 'em a little short," Vesta said. "But that means our blood will be worth more when we get in."

He looked at his numbered scrap of paper. "And this is going to help us?"

"Elay got us fake employee numbers, so this should be a smooth landing." Fidgeting, she checked over her shoulder.

Dezi gripped the note they had bought from a known scammer and fussed over Vesta's blankets, even though she insisted she wasn't cold.

After a mind-and-toe-numbing wait, a border agent waved them over. They shuffled up and placed their load of bags onto the scanner's conveyor. The agent, who had tightly pulled-back hair that gave her a no-nonsense style, looked up from her terminal. "Scan your implants."

Dezi and Vesta held their arms to the RF block mounted on her desk, and after a moment of held breath, it flashed green. The agent observed the bandages on their wrists. "That's a funny coincidence, you two getting injured in the same spot."

Dezi immediately peeled back his bandage, revealing the top of his very grisly, very authentic gash. "Wild, right? You should see the color of pus on Vesta's. She got tagged by a pipe viper on her last day of work. J-just our luck."

"Cover that." The agent winced and typed into her terminal. "Vesta Dunne, do you have work in the city?"

"Yes, ma'am." She handed over her slip.

"You don't know where you work?"

"I ain't got a clue." She cocked her hip. "Do you know how to do your job?"

The agent frowned and checked her terminal. "Enter the body scanner."

They both took a step, but the agent held up her hand to stop Dezi. "Not you. What was your name again?"

Sweating like he was kissing a solar flare, he lowered his paper mask. "D-Dezi."

"Is that short for something?"

He swore his parents had changed his legal name over a decade ago, but could it still be his birth name? No, then his gender marker wouldn't be updated either, and surely the agent would have commented on that to ensure she set the body scanner to the appropriate sex, so this was a trick question, right? He needed to answer. Every second he wasted increased his chances of getting caught.

"Is your full name Desmond Merlo Marrow?" the agent asked.

It was absolutely not, but Dezi smiled and offered his paper scrap. "Y-yes. And this is my employee number."

She took it. "You can step through the scanner. You didn't pack anything you shouldn't have, did you?"

"I hope not," he said meekly, pulling up his mask.

"We'll see." The agent chuckled as if Dezi had been joking.

Dezi walked into the scanner and raised his arms before exiting on the other end. Vesta stood by her bags while another agent prodded its contents with his baton.

"You figure out my pants size yet? Why ain't anyone else getting searched?" Vesta planted her palms on her hips, and the agent rolled his eyes.

The no-nonsense agent picked up Dezi's bags and gestured for him to follow her to a steel table.

When he passed Vesta, the male agent caught his shoulder. "Take off that mask. You look familiar..."

Dezi shut his eyes, and his guts twisted up into the perfect blend of humiliation and horror.

"You!" the no-nonsense agent shouted. "You're under arrest—stop!"

Dezi flinched, but the male agent released him and ran with his coworker back to the body scanners. The low-credit guy they had turned away earlier had climbed over one of the concrete dividers and was making a break for the road. The no-nonsense agent took out her stun gun, the male agent shouted into his radio, and Dezi grabbed Vesta's arm.

"Let's get out of here," he said.

She snatched her bag, and they sprinted toward the line of travelers meeting their family members at the edge of the checkpoint. The onlookers formed a wall, watching the agents chasing and tackling each newly inspired runner. Every time they cuffed someone, another person hopped the dividers and took off. Panting and missing half their luggage, Dezi and Vesta pushed past the crowd and approached the dry showers that formed the last barrier to Old Chryse.

"I think we made it." He took Vesta's bag, and she was too tired to protest, which was a bad sign.

"Good thinking back there." She gave the shower door a tug. "Ugh—open."

"I don't think these are free." Dezi studied the payment terminal mounted beside the door.

"Shoot. Nothin' is." Vesta leaned against the door, offering Dezi her phone. "Can you figure this thing out? My head hurts too much to deal with tolls and junk fees."

He offered the scanner her phone, and the system returned an approving chime. He pulled Vesta into the pod with him. "We'll save money if we go together."

They forced themselves and their bags inside, and the door slid shut. Chest-to-chest, Dezi focused on the top of Vesta's head, but he swore she was staring directly at his face.

"*Hold for cleansing,*" the system's AI said, then the shower pelted them with vibrating air from multi-directional jets as its screen played an ad for packaged starch granules.

"*Tired of those pesky surge energy rates at lunchtime? Try new Nutrosia self-heating nutrient blends, powered by healthy gut bacteria—just add pH-neutral fluid. Choose between fruit-ish, cheese-like, or spicy Earth-style flavors; available where Ambrose Industries products are sold. Thank you for using the Luminair SonicAir System, and welcome to Old Chryse.*"

The exit opened, and Dezi took his first step into the capital of Mars.

The dome of Old Chryse was constructed of millions of clear triangles with opaque metal borders. The UV-blocking film pasted over the panels was worn on the eastern, wind-facing side, and cast an uneven shade over the city like a permanent cloud cover. Three hundred years ago, when the plating had made the bubble look like solid gold in the immigration ads, they nicknamed Chryse *Nueva El Dorado*.

Swathes of stone skyscrapers crowded Old Chryse's historical downtown, but its center was reserved for the exotically shaped skyneedles that glistened like ice in the sunset's teal glare. One tower, a twisted ribbon made of black diamonds, touched the peak of the dome: The Hadron Mars Headquarters marked the heart of the city it had been built to found. But Dezi didn't have time for sightseeing; night was approaching, and they still didn't have a place to stay.

"Do you need another break?" he asked Vesta.

She took a deep breath. "It's warmer here. Better air pressure, too. Let's keep going."

They passed the squat consignment stores and credit lenders that filled the outer edge of Old Chryse. Boarded-up restaurants shared the streets with dollar stores brimming with goods, though the local graffiti artists had eagerly tagged both.

"Cratered Mars!" Dezi jogged to the next block, where several Stax cranes were printing a new building. They rapidly ejected line by line of gritty foam that expanded and hardened in seconds before another crane wrapped around to deposit the next layer. Windows and staircases formed before his eyes as drone arms hammered in rebar and smoothed the new building's corners.

"C'mon." Vesta tugged his arm. "You're making us look like tourists."

"Right—let's decide where we'll stay tonight. Did you research our options when you were planning this trip?"

"Yeah, I was hoping to get into a hostel, but since our social credit standings got wiped, GigCrib's gonna be our best bet."

"Got it." Dezi unlocked his phone and opened the home-sharing app. The prices on the vacation rentals that first appeared made his toes curl, but when he sorted the list by price, the options got more doable. "The cheapest one is eighty dollars a night."

"It has running water for only eighty dollars? That's too cheap. Bet it's a kidnapping racket."

Dezi studied the posted images of a cramped kid's room, trying to stay optimistic. "The bio says it's owned by an older woman renting out her spare room. Maybe she enjoys the company?"

"Alright, but if anything feels off, we leave."

Dezi nodded. They couldn't afford to be too picky, though, since the next-best rental was three times the price.

The dome overhead was black and starless by the time Dezi and Vesta reached their destination, though the skyneedles behind them danced with violet, magenta, and acid-green light like a vivid aurora.

Dezi climbed the stairs of a brick building and rang the buzzer.

"Hello—"

A metallic voice interrupted him. "Room number."

He checked the app. "1807."

The door clicked, and he helped Vesta into the dingy building. The barred windows cast long shadows in the narrow stairwell, ancient security cameras glared down at them, and crushed cig cartridges sprinkled the floor like confetti. After winding up the stairs, with Dezi supporting Vesta's back for fear she'd tumble down, they found the door to unit 1807 decorated with a wreath of purple, plastic globe flowers.

"Garlic flowers," Dezi remarked as he knocked on the door.

"I guess our host ain't a you-know-what," Vesta said.

The door's several bolts unlocked, and a stout Martian woman with salt-and-ginger hair buzzed down to her scalp and chunky yellow glasses opened it. Her smile caressed her tired eyes, and her kitten-covered pajamas looked equally warm.

"Vesta Dunne?" she asked.

"That's me." Vesta pushed aside Dezi and coughed.

"Well, get outta'da cold sweetie. I'm Nikita. Your room's on the left and the washroom's at the end of the hall." She shimmied to her bathroom. "I'm on the night shift, so we'll have'ta save introductions for the morning."

"Thank you." Dezi lugged their bags in and shut the door. He had never heard an accent quite like their host's, but it reminded him of the movies set in gritty American mega-cities that his dad had once enjoyed.

Family photos and symbols from multiple different religions lined the tight hallway. Dezi took the left turn to their room, where a child-sized bed with an old teddy bear sitting on top was situated. He pulled back the thin curtains to find their view of the street blocked by an intricate rig of antique solar panels feeding into various herb terrariums hanging from the ceiling. The setup looked like a fire hazard and smelled like a spice rack. Bafflingly, an open tube of deodorant rested on the windowsill beside a note that read, *Do not touch*.

Dezi dropped his pack in the corner. "I'll sleep on the floor."

"We can share the bed." Vesta watched her toes, flushed from her fever. "It'll be cold on that rug."

"I'd rather not." He'd hate to make the girl he saw as his little sister feel too uncomfortable to sleep well.

"Oh. Well. At least take the comforter." She pulled the thickest blanket off the bed and pushed it into his arms.

"All righty, you two, the spare keys are on the coat hanga. Be sure to lock up if you go out," their host shouted before leaving through the front door.

"Rest up. Second day of our new lives and all..." Vesta walked to the bathroom, cradling her arm.

Dezi spread the comforter on the floor, kicked his shoes off, and lay down. It was cold. He rolled himself up like a burrito and shut his eyes. The ventilators clanged and sirens wailed in the distance, but when he heard Vesta get into bed, the sounds faded.

This could work.

CHAPTER 6

STARS

VESTA OPENED HER EYES when Dezi brushed the damp curls back from her forehead. "Are you awake?" he whispered.

She groaned. "I don't think I caught a wink of sleep."

Kneeling beside her bed, Dezi was so close that she could smell the saffron lingering on his skin. It reminded her of home.

"How do you feel?" he asked.

She cleared her throat and sat up, pushing her sweat-drenched pillow aside. "Like I'm dying."

His sea-green eyes widened. "R-really?"

"No, but I ain't in any shape to go job hunting, and we're real low on funds."

"That's alright, I can start looking." He folded up her blanket and helped her out of bed.

Their host knocked on the bedroom door. "Breakfast's ready."

"We'll be out in a minute." Vesta adjusted her stretchy bra and zipped up her coveralls. She wished she could take the sticky things off, but she couldn't let Dezi see the bandage on her arm.

Nikita cracked open the door and then gasped. "You left the window open?"

"I was hot," Vesta said.

Nikita dashed for the window. "You can't! You're inviting 'em in."

"What in the lean beans and tambourines are you talking about?" Vesta stumbled back.

Nikita slammed it shut and turned. "*Vampiyahs.*"

Vesta laughed hoarsely. "If a perennial wanted in, they'd use the door."

"They can climb straight up walls and ceilings. Look!" Nikita pointed to the windowsill. "They took my deodorant!"

"That was probably a rat or something." Vesta coughed and punched her chest, but she couldn't clear the gunk rattling in her lungs. She kept coughing, gasping between bouts, and then swooned to the side.

Dezi caught her waist, holding up her limp body. He was shouting, but it was so hard to hear him. "Are you alright? Can you breathe?"

"She might need oxygen." Nikita rushed over. "I'll call the emergency line."

Vesta shook her head frantically, covering her mouth and wheezing. There was no telling whether their fake IDs would hold up to close inspection, and the stakes for Dezi were too high to risk. She swallowed the goop in her mouth and breathed in through her nose. "I got bad lungs. Always have."

"Must have been the chill that worked it up. Well, I'm sure some breakfast will get you right as sky light." Nikita waved her wrinkled hand for them to follow her down the hall. "Don't take too long or it'll get cold on you."

Dezi stroked Vesta's shoulder. "We need to take you to a clinic."

"We can't afford a clinic." Vesta tied her hair back with one of the frayed elastics from her wrist. "I'm fine, really."

She walked down the hall to Nikita's dining nook, where a modest spread of sausage biscuits drizzled with blueberry syrup waited for them. The dried herbs and tinfoil medallions hanging over the windows gave the place a witchy vibe, but it was still homely. It must have been rent-controlled for the little old lady to afford so much space this close to downtown.

Vesta heaved herself onto a stool. "So they do got orgo meat in Chryse."

"Oh no, sweetie. I can't afford the real stuff." Nikita mixed herself a cup of instant coffee with a heaping spoon of powdered dairy. "Are you kids here for the sights? Sorry to say, but you missed the lights dropping on the Hadron Tower for New Year's."

"We're here for work." Dezi held his biscuit in both hands and took a polite bite.

"We're here to make a name for ourselves." Vesta punched her spork into a patty.

"Well, you stay out of those blood clubs. I've seen too many bright-eyed youngsters get sucked to the marrow. Here." Nikita rummaged in her handbag and handed Dezi another stick of deodorant. "This'll keep the suckahs off."

"Uh—thanks." He took it and gave the stick a whiff.

"Don't listen to her superstitions." Vesta snatched it and planted it on the table. "It's supposed to be garlic that scares 'em, anyway."

"Maybe you country folk have fresh garlic, but in Chryse, we got Ancient Spice deodorant." Nikita opened the tube and rubbed a little behind her ears, making the table reek of oranges and musky grandpa.

"You know a perennial owns the company that sells that." Vesta pointed with her spork.

She frowned. "I'm only watching out for you. No matter what they offer, don't let them bite'cha. That's how the *change* starts."

Vesta touched her arm as the wound throbbed to the pound of her heartbeat. "Becoming a perennial is a medical treatment. Biting's got nothing to do with it."

"Then why do vamps have scars on their necks? Biting's the first step. Then, they juice you up with chemicals and embalm your immortal soul so you can never remigrate to celestial unity." Nikita clasped her hands and murmured an unorthodox prayer.

"Maybe religion is too heavy of a topic for breakfast?" Dezi nodded politely and took the deodorant.

Vesta rolled her eyes, then broke into a coughing fit.

"Poor thing, you need a check-up." Nikita brought out a thermometer and stethoscope from her handbag.

"Where'd you get all that?" Vesta raised her hands, ready to karate chop her if she got too close.

"I'm a practical nurse in the psych ward down at Chryse Correctional. Let me get a listen."

Vesta warily took the thermometer and let Nikita listen to her lungs.

"You might have caught a city bug." Nikita put her tools away. "A lot of colony kids get one the first time outta their bubble."

"What if it's something serious?" Vesta rubbed her biceps. Its achy tingle seemed to creep up her veins, worming through her whole body.

"Then we'll get you on antibiotics."

"Can we get some now? So I get better faster?"

"All you need is fluids and rest, missy."

"I could buy some flu medicine for you," Dezi said. "I need to find a job anyway."

"Maybe Hadron's hiring." Vesta took out her phone. "I'll give you access to my credit account, so you have some money."

Nikita whipped her head around. "Keep your neck covered around that tower. An Ambrose vamp is still a vamp."

"I'll be careful, but I don't think they're hiring college dropouts. Thank you for breakfast." Dezi pulled on his boots and eyed Vesta. "We're *both* extremely grateful you opened your home to us."

Vesta stuck her tongue out at him, but the suck-up just smiled at her and took the spare key fob on his way out.

"What a nice boy." Nikita gathered up their paper plates and put them in her composter. "How long have you two been together?"

Vesta choked on her water. "You got us all wrong. Dezi and me are besties. Best besties through and through."

"Oh, well, let's get you washed up and outta those nasty overalls."

Dizzier than a lizard stuck in a solar cell, she let Nikita lead her to the bathroom.

"You said you're a nurse?" she asked.

"I'm a practical nurse, so I know a thing or two." She set Vesta on the toilet lid. "I work with vamp leftovers. Real sad stuff, but that's how I know so much about the bloodsuckahs."

"Vamp leftovers?" Vesta peeled off her old uniform, careful not to disturb her bandage.

"People who've had close-up encounters with vamps, the older ones especially. Those leeches chew people up and, when they get bored of toying with them, dump them like last week's dusty air filter." Nikita wiped Vesta's back with a refreshingly damp towel. "My patients have advanced cases of vamp brain."

Vesta wrinkled her nose. "Vamp brain? That ain't a real diagnosis."

"It sure is. Vampiyahs have soul powers, like mind reading. They get into people's heads, and in serious cases, victims get visions and dreams. Some even stalk their vamp."

"That's not magic. Crazy people have always stalked celebrities."

"This is different. It's how they feed. People with vamp brain beg to get sucked on—think they're in love—but in the end, their vamp finds someone tastier and trades them in. Their old victims never take it well. Some even get put on suicide watch." Nikita wiped around Vesta's wrinkly bandage. "How old is this, sweetie? We need to change it."

"No. I got it." She scooted away, but the combination of sweat and expired adhesive let the bandage slide down her arm.

Nikita's eyes bugged out. "They got you..."

"No! This—it's a snake bite." Vesta hid the gooey red holes.

Nikita pushed her hand aside and dabbed the irritated flesh with her washcloth. "Can you call your friend? Is he hurt too?"

"No—no, you can't tell Dezi. Please—"

"I understand." Nikita nodded solemnly. "I won't say anything, but you need prophylactics and a BTD test."

Vesta grimaced and held back her tears. She didn't have a damn reason to trust this woman. She wanted Mithra—wanted her to squeeze her tight and tell her it'd be okay. But, short of her sister, a stranger was the only one she could bear to share this filthy secret with.

"It'll be alright." Nikita pulled her into a soft hug. "Cry if you need to, but I promise you'll survive this."

Vesta hugged her back, but she didn't cry. She would not let that monster have her tears again.

Along the streets of Old Chryse, young men loitered under the shade of rusted artificial trees, smoking and chatting. Occasionally, they shot Dezi a nod as he passed, and old ladies laden with plastic bags gave him toothless smiles. As Dezi made his way downtown, the soft-cornered printed buildings were replaced with skyscrapers constructed of metallic glass and carved stone. Their moldings reminded him of the ancient cathedrals and pastel apartments of the Old-World cities he had once called home, yet their scale was mind-bending: Three times taller than anything on Earth, each building spanned an entire block. He soon approached the mile-high skyneedles that set the dome aglow in acidic neon.

Dezi's phone rang, and he hurriedly answered.

"Ves? How are you feeling?"

"Still breathing. Could you pick up some antibiotics?"

He checked her bank app. "Do you know how much they cost? We only have a few dollars of credit left."

"More—" She broke into a coughing fit.

"Don't worry, I'll look for somewhere to sell blood. You focus on resting."

She caught her breath. "Thanks, Dez. I don't know what I'd do without you..."

He laughed, scratching the back of his head. "Wow, the last time you said that was when I helped you fix Mithra's telescope. You cried your eyes out when—"

"It ain't my fault she left leggy tools out where a twelve-year-old girl practices her dancing."

"You didn't have to practice in your room."

"Ugh, you sound just like her."

Dezi's heart twinged. "Sorry."

"It's a good thing. But don't go big sis'n me. I ain't been a tot in awhile."

"I'll try not to," he said, knowing he was lying. "See you soon."

Dezi raised his eyes to the Hadron Tower's ring-shaped logo glowing ultraviolet against the mustard-yellow clouds. Its onyx glass scattered shards of light onto the sun-bleached buildings around it as it spiraled into the sky. He traced from the tower's dome-kissing peak to the metal bars between the bubble's triangular glass panels until he hit the horizon. The shadows cast by those bars striped the ground like a jigsaw puzzle, marking every inch of the city Ambrose Industries had made possible. Dezi had dreamed of seeing the view from the top of that tower since childhood, but now it felt further than ever. Hadron wasn't known for hiring college dropouts, and yet, on rare occasions, they did.

He cupped his hands over the tower's glass to block the glare, studying the building's interior. He spotted a model of Fujin, Jupiter's first trans-atmospheric drone, and Nesaku, one of the earliest laser-amp satellites, hanging from the ceiling. A titanic statue of an angel without a face stood before the stairwell at the far end of the room, poised with ultra-modern grace as the rings of the solar system floated above the palm of its hand.

An ice-cold glove touched Dezi's shoulder, slicing his investigation short. "Remove your hands from the glass."

Dezi pulled back. The stranger looming over him wore a solid black suit, but his blue, shoulder-length hair beamed as brightly as plasma exhaust. Narrow sunglasses shaded his eyes, a sleek particle mask covered his face, and a blank ID badge hung from his breast pocket. Dezi's joints locked when he noticed the scar on the man's jugular, the mark from a bite bearing a dozen fangs. Each dimple shined like a little pearl on his quartz-white skin.

The perennial rolled his head back and sighed. "Martian, *move.*"

His command hit Dezi like jerking his Hadron up a harsh slope. His stomach rolled up his body, and his feet ended up above his head, but before he slammed onto the pavement, a slender arm caught him. A smaller perennial dusted the knee of his star-silver suit on the sidewalk as he knelt beside Dezi, supporting his head with a gentle hand.

"Seiyo, please. They are fragile." The brilliant perennial helped Dezi up. "Are you injured, young one?"

"N-no." Dezi held the stranger's arm tightly as he recovered his footing.

With a mirrored visor covering his entire face, the immortal looked like a high-end android. His limbs were similarly strong and cold, but his movements were impossibly fluid, and his voice was like velvet, embossed with a luscious Old-World accent.

As he stepped back, straightening his crisp Panama hat, he oozed class. "Apologies if my associate frightened you. Jetlag rarely complements his mood."

With his coat sleeve, the gloomy perennial buffed off the smear Dezi had left on the glass. "Indeed, that was unnecessary. You have my apology."

"Oh, Mars—I'm so sorry." Dezi backed away, delayed panic creeping up his neck and flushing his face. He'd never been this close to an actual blood-drinking immortal, much less fallen into one's arms.

"It's perfectly alright." The blood drinker touched a silk-gloved hand to his shirt and laughed with musical grace. "Did you want to go inside?"

Dezi shook his head, stammering, "N—No. I was—I—"

"We don't have time for this." The gloomy perennial lifted his glasses, and the pupils of his jet-black eyes caught a crimson glare like a nighttime predator's. "What are you here for?"

"A job," Dezi blurted out.

He raised a dark blue eyebrow. "What are your qualifications?"

"Well—I came to Chryse for a job. I-I'm not really qualified for anything."

Holding his arm at his elbow and pinching the bottom of his mask, the brilliant perennial examined Dezi for a moment, considering his different angles. "No, you don't quite suit my needs."

That was obvious, but it still hit Dezi in the chest. What was he thinking, stomping up to the Hadron Tower with his ragged hair and off-season Christmas sweater? Hell, if he couldn't clean himself up, he wasn't even fit to be a janitor.

"Chin up, dear. I'm sure you'll find an appropriate match elsewhere." The perennial pointed down the street. "In fact, if you are still building your resume, why not try the temp agency a few blocks down?"

"O-oh. That's a good idea. Thank you." Dezi dipped his head; Martians rarely bowed, but it felt like the polite thing to do.

The brilliant perennial removed his pocket square and reached for Dezi's face with it. Dezi flinched, causing the immortal to pause. He placed the lavender cloth in Dezi's hand instead. "A tidy appearance will improve your appraisal."

"I'll remember that." Dezi wiped his cheek with the soft linen. It smelled amazing, like a caramel macchiato on an autumn evening. That was probably how he smelled. Dezi's heart thumped, and as if in reply, the kind immortal tilted his head like a cat perking its ears.

His associate cleared his throat, taking the handle of the vintage limo waiting for them on the curb. Sleek as a Hadron cruiser and accented with a silver hood, the vehicle looked slighted by the indignity of sitting on such a pedestrian street.

"*Oups.*" The brilliant perennial laughed lightly and headed for his car. "You will have to excuse us. I am terminally late wherever I go."

"Wait, your handkerchief." Dezi followed, offering it back.

"*C'est pas grave.*" He waved his fingers and stepped into his ride. "Best of luck on the job search. And remember, young one, we all start somewhere."

"But"—Dezi leaned down, halfway to climbing in himself—"what's your name?"

The gloomy perennial shut the door in Dezi's face, shooting him a withering glare. He climbed into the driver's seat and the car pulled off, leaving Dezi holding an exceptionally expensive linen monogrammed with two star-shaped initials. He couldn't bear to get any more dust on it, so he folded it into his pocket and stopped in a convenience store restroom to fix his appearance.

The door chimed when Dezi entered the brightly lit temp agency. Behind life-size cutouts of smiling construction workers lay a line of booths with red curtains, where a queue of people lined up to use the donation terminals held within. Many of them looked similar to the migrants trapped in Clearair, but in his damaged work boots and fraying jeans, Dezi realized he matched the demographic too. For the first time in his life, he faded into the background, and he wasn't sure how to feel about it.

"Hey, man." Speaking Earth-Latin, a guy by the door waved Dezi down. "*There's a stellar contract out. Eight dollars and I'll give you a ride there.*"

"*I don't have any money. Sorry,*" Dezi replied in his out-of-practice mother tongue. He surprised himself with how much came back to him, though he still couldn't read or write it.

"*No problem, sell some blood.*" He gestured at the terminals. "*I'll be here until the van's full.*"

Dezi waited in line for the booths, then sat down when it was his turn.

The touch-screen terminal greeted him with an oddly sultry, synthetic voice. "*Welcome to the Express Labor Chryse Interview Experience, a subsidiary of Ambrose Bond Acquisitions. Please scan your implant.*"

He offered the RF block his wrist, and the machine flashed a light at him, snapping his picture. "*As this is your first time using our services, would you like to hear about the additional streams of revenue available to you?*"

He shrugged. "It can't hurt."

"*Are you interested in selling any of the following?*" It switched to a recording of a tired-sounding man. "*Kidney, lung, bone marrow.*"

"No, thank you."

"*Do you possess functioning ovaries and/or a uterus?*"

"No."

"*Would you like to learn about full-anatomy reverse mortgages? Get up to five thousand dollars today and retain ownership of your tissues for the term of your mortal life.*"

"Can I give blood already?"

"*Calculating response...*" A hatch opened below the screen. "*Insert your arm to begin blood quality analysis.*"

Dezi slid his forearm into the dark hole, flinching when a rubber grabber locked him in place.

"*Hold for sampling...*" The machine pricked his arm and displayed an animation of a blood vial filling. "*Based on our analysis, we assign your blood grade C. The rate for grade C is five dollars a milliliter. How many milliliters would you like to contribute?*"

Eden Natural Healing paid him in company credit, and half of it had come upfront when he'd signed his five-year bond—which he technically owed back, along with two million dollars—so he wasn't sure whether this price was fair. Either way, he didn't have the luxury of shopping for better offers until Vesta had her medicine. "I'd like to sell one hundred milliliters."

"*Hold for collection.*" The terminal stabbed him with a needle and presented an ad for candy-colored silicone patches as it chugged his blood. "*Need a pick-me-up to plug through those all-nighters? A downer to put you out at dawn? A shot of dopamine after a rough breakup? MacroDose Dermalz deliver the pseudomines you need for on-demand energy, sleep, or emotion. Side effects may include anxiety, suicidal thoughts, catatonia, and constipation.*"

The machine clicked, loudly swallowing its last gulp. It released his arm and spat out a complimentary bandage with an angel-shaped logo below the screen. "*You are now registered with Express Labor Chryse. Please allow twenty-four hours for your funds to settle into your new Ambrose Solar and Interplanetary Banking account.*"

"You're kidding. I need money now." Dezi snatched his bandage.

"*Would you like to browse available contracts in your area?*"

"Sure," he grumbled.

The screen flipped to a list of jobs, displaying their employer rating, pay, and how many slots were left. With no reviews himself, whatever contract that driver was talking about wasn't available to Dezi. All he saw was a smattering of odd jobs that barely covered the cost of an auto-taxi there. To qualify for any real shifts, he'd have to get some reviews or improve his social credit standing. Dezi didn't like returning empty-handed, but he needed to regroup with Vesta.

He stepped out of the booth, and the driver quickly approached him. "*You want that ride to Simulo?*"

"I couldn't get the contract."

"No problem. No ID, no problem. If you're ready to work, these guys will pay."

Dezi eyed the other temps, who were meeting up with their preferred drivers and loading into their vans. Whatever was going on here was apparently routine for people looking to keep a low profile. "*Is this work legitimate or under the table?*"

He laughed and patted Dezi's shoulder like they were buddies. "*Alright, six dollars and I'll take you. Money in your hands tonight.*"

Conveniently, that was within Dezi's budget. "*Deal.*"

For all the chatter in the temp agency, Dezi was surprised by how silent the ride to Planitr Simulo was. Packed into a beat-up white van with the seats torn out, everybody bumped against one another as the driver aggressively wove through the autonomous traffic. At least Dezi was next to a window. Up and down endless overpasses, he couldn't see the sky past the layers of storage crates dangling from rails that connected the different micro-manufacturers. An algae breeding plant fed into a rubber synthesizer, to a tire manufacturer, to a drone assembler—Simulo was a factory of factories. The habitation dome was sponsored by Planitr, making this job a calculated risk on Dezi's end, but he'd leave that part out when he came back with Vesta's medicine.

They passed under a set of glacier-white flood lamps as the driver brought them to a windowless factory near the edge of the dome. As soon as the van stopped, the other men slid the door open and rushed out. Dezi briskly rubbed his arms as he followed them to the facility dock. Past a hangar door and between two refrigerated trucks, a crowd listened to a man in a lab coat explain the job using posters that displayed pictures of people, ice, and eyeballs.

"Temps here for job A, you're clearing carbon dioxide ice. Put on the gloves, boot covers, hairnets, and insulated coveralls, then pass the sanitizing gate. Workers for job B, you've been here before, so you know what to do."

Dezi followed group A and changed into his uniform while maintaining the antisocial silence of his co-workers. Suited up like a surgeon, he closed his eyes and stepped through the sanitizing station's astringent mist, wishing he had asked for a job description before jumping into that van.

When he stepped into the building, the taste of ice and iron slid down the back of his throat. He opened his eyes, and his knees weakened at the sight of vacuum-packed livers flying down suspended conveyor belts. Fat camera lenses scanned the packaged organs and either sent them down a fork in the sorting array or beeped and dumped them down a level. *Beep, beep, beep,* to the metallic tempo—the lower it fell, the grayer the meat.

A man elbowed Dezi out of his way, sending him skidding on the ice that encrusted every surface. He landed on his stomach, and his lungs burned as if he'd taken a breath full of dust. Realizing that the fog pooling at their feet was pure carbon dioxide, he clambered up using a steel rack. He caught his breath and adjusted the trays he had disturbed—plastic boxes containing pairs of bright human eyes.

Dezi gagged and turned, bumping into another man.

He caught Dezi. "Woah, slow down."

"I-I'm sorry."

"You new?" The man laughed and knocked the icicles off the eye rack. "Pretend the plant makes sex robots and the bits are all silicone."

"What? That's—" Dezi shook his head.

"Or don't. Just keep breaking ice." The man shrugged. "How about you take that broom and brush it into the drains?"

Dezi wiped his nose in his paper mask and nodded. He took the plastic broom and concentrated on the ground, trying not to listen to the buzzing of lasers and saws. He pretended the organs were from slaughtered animals for a while, but then felt bad for the imaginary animals.

"You," a haggard-looking man called to Dezi. "You're sweeping crumbs. Come with us to the next section."

"O-okay." Dezi followed the three men deeper into the facility, where the icicles formed blood-tinged pillars.

"This your first time working a collections center?" one man asked.

"Yeah." Dezi kept his head lowered.

"I give him two days," the second murmured.

"Twenty says he doesn't last the shift." The third snickered.

"Here." The first handed Dezi his hammer and heat gun. "I'm taking a piss break. Try some real work."

"T-thanks." He accepted the gear.

When Dezi looked up, he was greeted by a marching line of skinless human torsos. His eyes shot to the start of the production chain, where anemic corpses bearing the same tan lines as the Verdans he'd grown up with slid out of cryocaskets like ashen sausages. Under giant mechanical arrays, green lasers flashed across their flesh, blades penetrated their bodies, and spidery rubber grabbers extracted their organs. Every inch of skin, gram of fat, and lock of hair was peeled back and packaged.

Dezi shook harder than a jackhammer pressed to the ice, but he could not stop staring. He could not tear his eyes from the tiny corpse hanging from a hook threaded through her headless spine as probes dug through the slit in her stomach.

The men roared with laughter. "Hand over that twenty! I think he's gonna piss himself."

Sour spit climbed up Dezi's throat, and shadowy mites swam over his vision, but before he could drop, a thick arm propped him against the wall. "*Hey, are you alright?*"

"Oh, shit. It's Pearl."

"*Perla*, not Pearl!" Taller than Dezi and built like a freighter ship, the woman glowered at the men. "Wasting time and harassing your comrades? *Idiotas...*" She asked Dezi in Earth-Latin, "*Do you need medical attention?*"

Dezi shook his head. "I'm fine."

"You speak English? Come with me." She guided him through the maze of dark machinery.

"Wait—I can't leave. I need this job."

"Then I can show you job B." Perla led him to the end of the production line. "We sort off-color eyes. If you pretend they are silicone—"

"What do I need to do?" Dezi approached the belt carrying boxes of glassy eyes. Each pair was pinned to a fleshy backing and threaded through with red tubes and green wires.

She handed him a laminated sheet with various color swatches. "We grade the irises when the machines can't decide. Pull them off the belt and put them on the color-grade rack."

Dezi studied the card; his eyes would be a G4-B1. "Where are the brown ones?"

"Lighter irises turn a brighter red."

He balked at the parade of eyeballs. "These are for perennials?"

"Everything here is, besides the reclaimed protein. A person can live for five hundred years, but the same liver can't, not on a diet of Adderall and cocaine." Perla chuckled and reached for a pair of fog-blue eyes. "Live forever, they say, but no care for the body."

He glanced back at a truck being loaded with a colony's worth of hearts. "All these people...never mind. I'm sorry."

"It's not normally this many. A storm pierced the dome of Indus Valis."

"Indus? That's an Eden facility. I can't believe they all sold their bodies premortem."

"If you die with an active bond, they *liquidate* your assets." She sighed. "Not even death frees you from termination fees, eh?"

"So this is how Planitr will get their money out of me...?" Dezi asked, mostly to himself.

"That depends on how much you owe. They have worse ways." Perla plucked a pair of honey-yellow eyes off the belt. They were the exact color of Vesta's.

Chapter 7

Friends

Vesta turned on the faucet, closed her eyes, and let the water wash over her scabs.

Her BTD test had reported she'd contracted a case of strep, but after three days of antibiotics, her fever had finally passed. Nikita told her she'd dodged the real hairy infections and, with proper care, this injury would fade to an unremarkable scar. She promised the memory would fade too, but with that bloated corpse still haunting Vesta's nightmares, she couldn't imagine a future where she didn't wake up in the middle of the night kicking and thrashing. Whenever Dezi would catch her, he'd kneel by the side of her bed, dab the sweat off her brow, and whisper her back to sleep. She told him she was dreaming of breakdancing. He didn't believe her, but he didn't press either. Sometimes she wished he would.

As Vesta smoothed a fresh bandage over her arm, her phone jingled. It had been blowing up day and night, since the only thing she could do while sick was network. Through the wonders of the web, she had connected with local influencers, fresh-start agents, and kids of real-deal producers. No ancient perennials yet, but if she could break into the right social circles and get a few references, she'd be on the lev-train to fame. She might even find Dezi a job as a stage tech or something geeky. She hated that he was out working two full shifts a day to cover her rent.

Vesta checked her phone and found that Dezi had messaged her, *Come outside. I have something to show you.*

She pulled an oversized sweatshirt over her head, slipped on her boots, and swung around the stairwell.

Dezi was waiting for her on the sidewalk with a massive grin on his face and his hands on his Hadron's handlebars. "Mom shipped my bike."

Vesta bounced on her tippy toes. "Paint me red and call me a fire drone! Things are finally turning our way."

"Yeah, looks like you're feeling better too." Dezi rolled his bike to the door. "Can you help me carry this up the stairs?"

Her phone jingled again, and she whipped it out on instinct, catching the exact message she had been waiting for.

"Oh. My. Stars."

Dezi lugged his bike up the first few steps to the apartment complex's door. "Gravity's lighter and all, but I could still use some help."

"Listen to this." Vesta read the message out loud. "*You should come party with me and my friends in the Disk sometime. I know a club with no credit minimum. We just got invited to hit the town!*"

"*You* got invited out." Dezi popped his kickstand. "And I'd like to know by whom."

Vesta clicked on the guy's social profile, where the twenty-something posted pictures of himself sharing drinks in Diskos bars with minor celebs, all dressed to kill. "His name is Jaxon, and he sure knows how to network..."

"You're not going out to meet some strange man alone."

She pouted. "Well, I was gonna ask if you would come with. Don't you want to meet people our age? Find yourself a cutie to take home?"

He rested his elbow on his bike seat and shrugged, but Vesta had hit his weak spot: his romantic's heart. "That sounds nice in theory, but isn't it a little early to relax? Money is still pretty tight."

"Dez, we're in the cultural capital of Mars! Perennials from all over come to scout out overlooked talent. If I met the right influencer and set up a collab, it would be the boost my career needs. Then, I could help you pay for school tuition, and then you could get a real-deal tech job to pay down your debt, and then—"

"Okay, okay, you win." He patted her shoulders. "My contract at the collections center expired today, so I don't have anything to do until a new one comes in."

She embraced him and squealed.

Laughing, he wiggled free and took his bike's handlebars. "If you want a ride anytime soon, we better get this firmware update started."

"That'll give me time to rustle up something for us to wear. And you'll need a new cut before I take you anywhere." Vesta ruffled his hair, giggling.

"Don't remind me..." He groaned.

She held the door open for him. "Diskos, here we come!"

Vesta attacked Dezi with her powder brush, and he coughed in the cloud of glitter.

"What is that?" he asked.

"Illuminator." She shooed his hands away to get at his face. "Everybody wears it."

"I'm good. You already have me in this crazy outfit." He buttoned his knockoff Systématique shirt up to his collar.

"You're not supposed to wear it like that," Vesta whined. "And those aren't the right pants. You can't hit the club in blue jeans."

"The ones you got are too tight."

"They're supposed to fit like that." She took down his shirt buttons and poked between his pecs. "I'll lay off the glitter if you wear the pants."

While Dezi grumbled and switched pants, Vesta tore the tags off her skirt, sending a few of its sequins twinkling to the floor. She adjusted her neon-yellow bandeau, pulled on her faux fur coat, and smoothed down its shaggy white fur. Mashing together an outfit from charity store racks hadn't been easy, but she had nailed the throwback look from this week's trend cycle.

Nikita shimmied into the living room. "Is it date night? Hold still and let me get a picture."

"No photos, please." Dezi blocked his face and grabbed his boots.

"Sorry, Nikita, we've got people to meet." Vesta strapped on her heels.

"Have fun, you two. And don't forget the warding sigils I taught you."

"Yes ma'am, we'll show them draculas what for."

Before Nikita got wise to their clubbing plans, Vesta grabbed Dezi's hand and hauled him down the never-ending stairwell next to the always-busted elevator.

When they got to his Hadron, Dezi flipped up the seat and pulled out two slim vests studded with deployable balloons. Vesta put on one of the full-body airbags, pulled the straps tight, and hopped onto his bike. The steep, sporty seat pushed her against Dezi, and she eagerly wrapped her arms around his ribs.

He flipped the ignition switch cap and scanned his thumb on it, then Mithra's acid-green LEDs pulsed under the chassis.

"Where to?" he asked.

"Anubis Club and Lounge."

He twisted the throttle and sent them surging into the night. They whizzed past tangled power lines and rusted satellite dishes on their way north until they hit the toll between Old Chryse and Diskos. The car-sized dry shower played an ad for cosmetic rib removal as it pelted them with air, ruining all the work Vesta had put into gelling Dezi's new spikey do.

When Dezi eased out of the gate, Vesta took a deep breath of the warm Diskos air; it smelled like morning dew, epoxy, and synth-egg stir fry. The buildings glimmered like bioluminescent stalagmites in a city-sized cave, where bat-like rotorcraft glided between private landing pads. Roads interlaced the towers, forming rivers of starlight headlights and lava brake lights, and logos twinkled like constellations on the blacked-out dome.

Dezi turned onto an on-ramp, plunging them into the neon streets. The bike growled, rumbling Vesta's entire body, as he took them up a steep overpass leading to the skyscraper-level roadway. They sped around a building sheathed in a billboard advertising male genital augmentation, and she pointed at the planter-bed-sized cyber-sausages, laughing as loud as she could, but the roaring wind swallowed her squeals.

Dezi didn't waste a second on traffic—Vesta gasped when he cut between the curb and a semi-truck. "Where the heck did you get your license?"

"Where everyone does: online!" He glanced back. "We're taking this underpass. Hold on!"

Vesta's heart leaped to her throat, and she screamed all the way down. She squeezed Dezi, leaned her cheek on his back, and let the city engulf her. Neochrome-wrapped convertibles, holo-ads the size of titans, perennials lounging on the balconies of blood bars—an endless rave of beautiful, ageless faces flickered by. Tonight, she would be one of them.

Dezi slowed the bike, stopping between the curb and a sidewalk-sweeper charging station. "We're here."

"What?" Vesta lifted her head.

"Did you take a nap back there?" He tossed his windswept hair and shot her a rugged smile over his shoulder. She could hardly believe this was the same boy who had been too timid to leave Verde a week ago.

"With the way you drive, I was holding on for dear life." She hopped off the bike and checked down an alley, scoping out the couples nuzzling necks and the trippers slumped under walls with creepy-crawling gang tags. "Welp. I don't see any parking."

"Hadrons are tough to steal, but I'll disconnect the battery from the motor to be safe." Dezi took a multi-tool from under his bike seat and popped open a body panel.

While he undid the bolts and slipped them into his pocket, the eerie pounding from Club Anubis drew Vesta in. She wandered down the sidewalk to where party people wearing luminescent tattoos and disco-ball bikinis shared drinks and cigs. Under the club's neon sign, a golden jackal's head, they filed down the concrete stairs before disappearing into the gloom.

Dezi met Vesta at the end of the queue, straightening his shirt. "Not much of a tourist spot, is it?"

"You got to be in the know to hear about this place." She smoothed her ponytail. "They don't ID, but they'll turn you away if you don't match the vibe."

He huddled close behind as they approached the bouncer. Muscular and mean with glassy implants studding his scalp, he raised his chin at them, revealing a squiggly scar on his neck.

Dezi smiled warmly, but Vesta elbowed him, then he switched to the same aloof look everyone else was sporting.

The bouncer stretched his hands, and the metal nodes embedded in his knuckles squeaked. "You're good."

Vesta leaned in, asking, "Ain't there a cover?"

"Mortals get in free 'till dawn." He pointed his thumb at the door. "Keep moving."

As Vesta descended into the dingy passageway, she let the beaded curtain hanging over the doorway tickle her face. Past a throng of grinding, glistening bodies and towards the thud of morbid drums, the cavity of Club Anubis opened wide. Two levels of balconies surrounded a dance pit packed with clubbers worshiping the bass like cultists. Buffeting her like a storm and tittering like gunfire, the industrial music grabbed her heart and threw it against her ribcage. Cocktails met fanged smiles, organic skin pressed against ageless, and reflective eyes watched her. It was a real-deal, underground blood club, and Nikita would crack her dome if she knew what Vesta was up to.

She and Dezi wormed through the crowd to reach the second-story balcony, and he pulled her to a corner with some breathing space. "It's pretty intense."

Vesta peeked over his shoulder to the third-story balconies, where figures in elegant gowns sipped red wine. "You think the VIP section's up there?"

A group of VIPs with bright gray eyes seemed to stare right at them, and Dezi's hand got sweaty in hers. "M-maybe."

She snagged an empty barstool for him. "Here, I'll bring us some drinks."

"Water, please." Dezi sat and watched the dancers writhing through the fog and lasers below.

Vesta bounced down the stairs and ordered an overpriced alcosynth and cola for herself along with bottled water for Dezi. A soft hand touched her shoulder, and her heart did a triple tuck as she turned, coming face-to-face with her first Diskos connection.

"Jaxon? You're stealthy as a whiptail."

With a crisp blazer, several thin chains, and a sharply groomed beard, Jaxon didn't fit in with the crowd, but he was handsome all the same. He laughed and flashed a set of candy-apple-red fangs that gave him a slight lisp. "You don't put on that accent for your socials, huh?"

She quietly gagged on her cola; those teeth weren't in the dating profile. "Did you bring your friends?"

"They'll be here in a few." Jaxon flagged down the bartender and ordered a beer. "Where's yours?"

"Lemme show you where I planted him." She took her drinks and brought Jaxon up the stairs. Shockingly, Dezi had two elegant women at his table, both watching him like thirsty scorpions sipping dew.

"Stick me in substrate and call me a tuber." Vesta giggled. "Who are your friends?"

He shrugged, adorably unaware of his stormy emerald eyes and lost-puppy pout that could make a coven of sirens throw themselves off their shoals.

"Excuse me, ladies." Jaxon slid past Vesta. "Would you mind if we take these seats? Our friend was saving them."

The women masked their disappointment with blindingly white smiles. "Of course. It was lovely talking to you, young one. Join us in the private lounge anytime..."

They both tried to brush Dezi's arm as they left, making him dissolve deeper into his seat.

"I'd steer clear." Jaxon pulled up a chair. "They're hunting for young guys with low credit, if you catch my signal."

"They were vampires?" Dezi asked.

"*Perennials*." Vesta sat.

"You can tell by the nails; they're too glossy. I'm Jaxon, by the way."

Dezi jumped at the sight of his fang implants.

Vesta elbowed him. "It's a mod. Chill out."

"O-oh. That's cool." He smiled unconvincingly.

"I'm still a fledgling, but I had a ton of cavities, so I decided to pull the trigger and start my second life early." Jaxon pressed his thumb to the sharp tip of one tooth.

"But you're so young. How can you afford mods like that?" Vesta chased her drink straw without taking her eyes off him.

"My night job is in sales, but I do some head-hunting on the side."

"You're a talent agent?" Dezi asked.

"Not quite." Jaxon checked his phone. "Looks like the others are here."

Vesta bolted up. "C'mon, Dez."

She followed Jaxon, swaying to the synthetic voices and buzz-saw beats. They met two twin girls by the door, one with acid-green hair and the other with hers dyed highlighter orange.

Jaxon hugged them. "Lenn, Lela, this is Dezi and Vesta."

The girls each held out one hand to Dezi and the other hand to Vesta, and all four of them giggled at the complexity of figuring out how to get them all shaken.

Lenn's smile squinted her puffy eyes, and Lela stood an inch behind her sister. They simultaneously said, "The pleasure is ours."

"Aren't we missing someone?" Jaxon arched his neck, revealing a mark the same as the bouncer's behind his popped collar.

A man barreled through the crowd and gave Jaxon a bear hug.

"Woah! Koji." Jaxon caught him.

Koji laughed, throwing his long, black hair out of his face. Wearing a band shirt torn into a V-neck and a smudge of eyeliner, he owned the bad-boy look outright, which made him Vesta's exact type.

"Hey! Two fresh faces?" Koji grabbed Dezi's arm and shook his hand firmly, jangling his silver earrings.

"H-hi." Dezi smiled. "I like your tattoo. Is that a chrysanthemum?"

"This thing?" Koji touched the magenta flower that started below his jaw. "Yeah, I got it a few years back in Tokyo."

"Tokyo, on Earth?" Dezi still hadn't stopped shaking his hand.

"Is there a Tokyo anywhere else?" Jaxon yanked Dezi's sleeve.

"That's the one that got you dumped on this sandball, right?" Lenn asked. "*Great placement.*"

"You're one to talk, suck junky. You bring extra hot sauce this time?" Koji grinned.

Lela pulled a packaged wet wipe from her purse and offered it, but Lenn snatched it. "He wasn't serious."

Vesta asked, "Hot sauce?"

"Spicy skin encourages salivation." Jaxon shook his head in a theatrical display of disappointment. "They're complete bite addicts."

Vesta gasped. "You season yourselves?"

"What is this, an intervention?" Lenn mumbled as she fished a pill case out of her bra. "Half these Martians don't even pack juice."

"I bet Venusians had a wicked hit. Too bad your sire noticed the extra scars. Now you're on his shit list and stuck here with us." Koji patted Dezi's back like they were both exiled fledglings. "But at least Chryse has a great nightlife!"

Like Koji, the twins had distinct branding marks on their necks, but while his was tatted over, theirs were crossed out with X-shaped scars. Lela dreamily offered Dezi a spice wipe. "If you want to try, I know a Luminair who's *incredible*."

Red-faced and glued to Koji's side, he laughed politely. "No thank you."

"Well, you've *got* to buy us a few drinks." Lenn grabbed Dezi's arm and dragged him to the bar. Dezi looked back at Vesta, begging for rescue.

Koji shot Vesta a crooked smile. "I didn't catch your name."

"Vester—" It fumbled over her tongue, so she cleared her throat to try it again with less accent. "I'm Vesta."

"Care to dance, Vesta?" He held out his hand, too gentleman-like for a club, but too charming for her to resist. Dezi could survive one song without her. She took Koji's hand, and he led her to the dance floor.

Rocking her hips with the music, she wrapped her arms through her hair and smiled at Koji. He smiled back, and they danced inches from each other, song after song, getting a millimeter closer each minute—until Jaxon tapped Koji's shoulder and whispered in his ear. He nodded, bent down to Vesta's level, and shouted over the music. "Can I get you a drink?"

No boy had ever offered to buy her anything. Heck, there weren't even any bars in Verde. "Yes! Totally!"

She followed Koji to the bar, meeting up with Dezi and the twins.

"Coke and rum for the colony girl." Jaxon put a glass in her hand. "And a pint of Asahi for the wanna-be system traveler." He placed a frothing glass of imported beer in front of Dezi.

"This must have cost a fortune. I can't." Dezi showed his palms.

"Think of it as an investment in our friendship." Koji winked and raised his own glass. "*Kampai*."

Dezi timidly raised his beer and took a drink, and then another one. "Wow, this is great. Thank you."

"Finally, you're loosening up. Here." Lenn fished around her purse and pulled out a hot-pink device that looked like a mini blowtorch. "Hit this."

"No," Dezi said flatly as he sipped his beer. "I have no idea what's in that."

"It's only nos." Lenn scoffed. "You don't trip, you don't dance"—she looked at Vesta—"I hope you're not a complete downer, too."

"No, I'm cool." Vesta quickly put out her hand. "Downright cryogenic."

"You're not taking anything these girls give you." Dezi sat up straight, engaging the stick up his butt.

Lela took the device from her sister and puffed it like an inhaler. "Jeez, guy. If we wanted to drug you, it'd be *waaay* easier to slip it into your drink."

Dezi gave the twins a look like they were a pair of centipedes crawling out of his toothpaste tube and pushed his beer away. "Okay, we're leaving."

"But we just got here," Vesta said.

"I'm getting a bad feeling." He leaned closer, speaking under his breath. "They were discussing gang activities while you were gone."

"They were probably talking about their dealer," Vesta whispered. "You don't have to be their friend, but we're here to make connections—scout out opportunities."

"Are you seriously talking about us when we're right here?" Lenn asked. "You hicks have no class. Why *don't* you just leave?"

"Here she goes again." Koji sighed.

"No, I'm tired of pretending to be friends with these tourists. They're always posers and we never have any fun."

Vesta grabbed the inhaler and brought the metal tip to her mouth. Dezi's eyes widened bigger than when she had confessed her plans to become immortal, but she wasn't about to let him ruin her first shot at networking with real perennials. She pulled the trigger, filling her lungs with sweet, sizzling gas.

"Ves!" He snatched it away. "Are you kidding me?"

Her head swam, and her whole body tingled as she burst into a bout of giggling. "Mars, Dez, it's laughing gas. But if you wanna go, you can go. You're clashing with the wavelength."

His expression tightened, and he got up from his barstool, head held high, and made for the exit.

"Shit," Jaxon said. "Koji, talk him down."

"Got it." Koji hopped out of his seat and jogged into the crowd.

"You always have to fuck these up, don't you, Lenn?" Jaxon asked. "Go apologize or I'm cutting you out."

"You can't be serious. It's not my fault that colony dork doesn't know what nos is."

"Catch him, or don't bother coming back. Same for you, Lela. I don't care if you know how to dose, you both suck at this." Jaxon put another drink in Vesta's hand.

As her senses came back, a heavy feeling settled in her gut. She shouldn't have done that, but why did Dezi have to be so judgmental? He wasn't above alcohol, and it wasn't like nos was illegal.

"I'm sorry about that." Jaxon threw up a hand. "Those two always pull this type of shit."

Vesta downed half her glass in one go, trying to think about the tingles instead of Dezi's expression when she had laughed in his face. She really shouldn't have done that.

Jaxon stirred his drink. "So, Dezi's your...?"

"Good friend." She sighed and finished the other half of her drink.

"Yeah, he didn't seem like your type."

She giggled. "And you know *my* type?"

"Koji; he's everyone's type." His smile twitched. "It drives me fucking nuts, but it makes him useful."

"Ushful?" She slid off the barstool, but Jaxon caught her.

"You've had enough of that." Koji suddenly plucked her drink away.

She scrunched her face and flexed her hands. "I cabn't feel my finbgers."

"You're blasted." Koji helped Jaxon lift her under her other arm. "Hold tight."

She clumsily put one foot in front of the other, praying they were leading her to a toilet she could puke in. Her ears were full of water and everything was a blur of shapes, but her legs kept moving until car sounds replaced the banging music.

"What happened to the other one?" Jaxon asked.

Koji rolled his eyes. "I tried to reel him back in, but he wouldn't talk to me after I grabbed his ass. Jumped onto his busted old dune rider and pulled off."

"Dude, learn to soften your pitch. If he gets into a wreck, it's your fault."

"Shit, Lela got his drink too? Shouldn't we do something?"

Jaxon shrugged. "Too late now."

"No, man, I don't feel right about this. I can't get a manslaughter charge on my record." Koji shoved Vesta into Jaxon's arms and dipped back into the crowd.

"I'm keeping your cut, asshole!" Jaxon shouted after him. He pulled out his phone as he carelessly hauled her to the curb. "I could have gotten a grand for both of you runaways, but you had to be a bitch."

She tried to shrug him off, but her shoulder didn't move. Panic seeded its roots into her—she was a passenger in her own body.

"Still, your bounty's easy money. You credit-dry hicks are too gullible." He opened the door to an auto-taxi and lowered her into the seat, lifting her knees and tucking them in like she was a life-sized doll. "I can't turn you in to Planitr this fucked up, so maybe we'll stop at my place and—"

A hand tattooed with the red head of a centipede slammed Jaxon against the cab by the back of his head, and a familiar voice growled, "The fuck are you doing?"

"E-Elay!" Jaxon blubbered with his face smeared against the window.

When Elay saw Vesta, his grip loosened. "You got to be fuckin' kidding me..."

"Relax." Jaxon backed up. "I was only taking her home—I mean helping her home."

Elay's eyes narrowed at Vesta. She tried to say something, begged her body to move, but all she got was half a tear to run into her mascara.

Elay shook his head. "You're sharking again. You remember what happened last time people started getting picked up at the family's clubs?"

"Me? A bounty hunter?" Jaxon scoffed. "What kind of blood brother throws accusations like—"

Elay grabbed Jaxon's shirt and screamed in his face, "They stopped fucking coming!"

He launched Jaxon over the cab. The grown man soared like a sack of flower petals and landed in the gutter with a cloud of dust.

"I should peel that brand off your neck, but your uncle would kill me." Elay leaned into the car and tapped Vesta's cheek. "He got you good, huh?"

He shut the cab door, got in on the other side, and buckled her in. "I watch out for you, and you come to one of my clubs without even saying hello? Damn ungrateful."

Vesta screamed at her limbs to smack him, but it was useless. She couldn't even tell if her lips moved.

"Too late to cry about it. I'll take care of you, honey eyes." He groped her coat pockets and stole her phone, while all she could do was stare at his gilded scowl.

Chapter 8

Breaks

"Fantastic," Dezi grumbled as he wheeled his bike away from two drunk guys making out against the drone charging station.

"That wasn't a complete waste of time; look at all the friends you made." He pulled out his multi-tool and screwed his Hadron's bolts back into place. "It's not like you had a million more important things to do than try to fit in with those jerks." He mounted it and hit the ignition. "Like it wasn't obvious you didn't belong."

Dezi rode aimlessly, weaving up and down Disko's endless layers of luxury storefronts. There was no point going far, since he'd have to pick up Vesta when she was done. Why did she even want to impress those fledgling rejects? If they had any clout, they wouldn't have been exiled here. Mars, he hated them. He hated them more than he had a right to, but he knew why; he saw himself in them. All of them had fucked up somewhere in their past, but unlike Dezi, they had safety nets to land in. He was a bit too poor for that, and it made him blindingly jealous. Why did he deserve to fall through the cracks while they partied every night, burning money on drugs? It was bullshit. Why was everything always so bullshit?

He palmed his brow as the wind pulled the cold sweat off his arms. Where was he even going?

Running away again. That's what he always did. Even when he had tried to fix his mistake back in Verde, the Planitrs chased him out anyway. Now he'd be on the run from this debt forever. Hunted, forever.

Faster, he swerved, catching air on a curb. The neon lights blurred together, and his stomach churned with panic.

He couldn't live like this, not with a two-million-dollar weight dragging on his neck. Maybe Mithra could have, but not him. She had been the one who was supposed to bring Vesta to Chryse. She could have talked her into leaving the club. If Dezi had died instead—

From the corner of his eye, something whipped into his lane, and his arms went stiff. The front wheel of his bike connected with a red-and-white-checkered drone. Dezi lurched forward, but then the airbag between his handlebars exploded into his chest. Launched backward, he watched his Hadron crumple into the pizza delivery drone; the flexible frame curled in on itself and the brittle drone shattered, flinging cheese and bread everywhere. His vest deployed, rapidly encasing him in compound balloons. He hit the ground and bounced as shrapnel metal jetted over his head.

BANG!

Inches from his left ear, air roared and hissed, and the back of his head smacked the pavement. Dizzy, he rolled over and tried to prop himself up, but his arm wouldn't move. His ribs were sticky, too. He looked down at a plastic shard embedded in his bloody biceps. Funny, he didn't feel a thing. A pizza slapped onto his bike's cracked battery, and it smoked for a moment before catching fire.

Dezi lay back and bled.

I'm tired.

The drone's engine whirred uselessly, shooting sparks that clattered against the pavement, and blue fog leaked out of his Hadron, pooling on the asphalt. Cars formed a clearing, maneuvering around the scene as their navigators drew green lasers across the wreck and Dezi's sprawled-out body. Past their tinted windows, the passengers didn't look up. The auto-cleaners would be here soon. And police with them, to take Dezi to Planitr.

Run.

The ringing in his ears was unbearable. Or was that screaming? No—children laughing. Amongst the wreckage, a girl and boy chased each other, playing laser tag. The boy pointed his gun at Dezi, blinding him with the laser point. Dezi squinted, but he couldn't focus on the child's face; it shimmered like fog, though his eyes were piercingly green. The girl ran to the boy and lowered his gun. She had Mithra's stormglow eyes.

Dezi, run, she mouthed.

He rolled over using his other arm and stumbled onto the sidewalk, but the pressure between his temples swelled and his knees hit the pavement. There was no laughter or children, only the shuffling of Diskos oxfords.

"I can stand," Vesta murmured.

"Yeah, but you don't need to." Elay held her under his shoulder and banged on Nikita's door.

Dezi opened it, pale as a ghost. "Ves—"

"Hey, asshole." Elay shoved him. "You ditched Vesta?"

"Please stop..." she mumbled.

"Are you okay?" Dezi recovered his footing and helped her in.

"Elay bought me pancakes and gave me a ride." She held Dezi's arms, fighting the urge to fall into them. Something was off about him; he had a fresh welt on his jaw, and his clothes were torn.

"That's what you're telling him? She got drugged—because you left an eighteen-year-old girl alone at a vamp club." Elay jabbed his finger in Dezi's chest.

Dezi's eyes widened. "The drinks?"

Vesta nodded, and Dezi looked like he wanted to puke. He had spotted the red flags from a light year away, but she had been too selfish to listen.

"I'd teach you a lesson about manning the fuck up if it didn't look like someone else got to you first." Elay huffed and then nodded at Vesta. "Rest up. And respond to my messages. I got work for a girl like you."

"Thanks…" She pulled her coat closed and leaned on the wall.

When Elay stepped out, Dezi gingerly locked the door.

With her stomach and inner ear locked in a backflip competition, Vesta held the wall and walked herself to bed.

Dezi helped her down and shakily unstrapped her heels. "I shouldn't have left you. I'm so sorry."

"Your gut was right. Jaxon was a bounty hunter, and I nearly got us both turned in." She tugged his shirt until he gave up on her shoes and sat next to her. "And I was a down-right butthole to my best friend. Can you forgive me?"

"Always." He squeezed her hand.

She touched a scrape on his cheek. "What happened? Did you get into a fight?"

With his lips pressed tight, he showed the motor-oil-smeared bandage on his arm.

She covered her mouth. "Can you move it?"

"Yeah…" He shrugged and winced. "But the Hadron is totaled. I-I don't know if someone will come after us. I just left it there."

"Oh, Dez…" Hot tears beaded in Vesta's eyes. "We can't keep doing this, barely scraping by. Something's gotta break."

He stared on at her like he hadn't heard a word. She'd seen that dead look on him before—when Mithra had passed, and he'd slid right into the dark. If she let him slip away again, he might never come back.

Vesta hugged him, wrapping her fingers in his grimy hair and squeezing like it was goodbye already. "I messed up. I wasn't taking this seriously—I didn't realize how difficult it would be—but I need to grow up. I need to listen and think."

Dezi embraced her back, choking down a sob. "He could have hurt you. I'm so sorry."

"And I let him hurt you. But I'll make this right."

He gently pulled back. "How?"

"I'm going to get us jobs." She said it with a smile, but she was about to call in a favor she didn't have with a man she didn't trust.

Vesta took out her phone, swallowed her pride, and messaged Elay.

You said you had work?

Elay gave Vesta until lunch to rest before sending her the address for somewhere in EastDome. She pressed a kiss to sleepy Dezi's forehead, caught a ride to the suburbs, and met Elay waiting by a hole-in-the-wall fast-food joint.

He sat at one of the two tables outside the food terminal, blowing fat clouds on his peppermint cig. "You want a burrito?"

"Sure." She sat across from him.

He plugged their order into the terminal of the truck-sized vending machine. Past its plexiglass window, it squirted layers of paste onto a starchy disk and wrapped it in foil. He pulled out two hot burritos and two frosty cans, brought them to a table, and cut into a hot sauce packet with his fangs.

Vesta reached for the red soda can printed with an appetizing picture of cherries.

"You don't want that." Elay pushed the blue one to her.

"Why?" She snatched the red can. "Hemo? I never seen this one in Verde."

He shrugged and cracked open the blue can. "I warned ya."

She opened the red can and took an ice-cold gulp, but it was thick like sweet and sour sauce and too salty to be cherries. "Ugh!"

Elay laughed and took a picture of her with his phone.

When she smeared her lips, she found blood on her fingers and retched. "What in Eden's name did you feed me?"

"It's fake; artificial blood. Sit down and eat your burrito, honey."

She spat on the ground, then cleared her palate with a bite of beany goodness. "Nasty. Why don't they make it clear, and less salty?"

"That'd be Hemo-lite." Elay struggled to down the metallic drink, but then snatched her soda and gargled it. "You ain't a real vamp if you can't drink blood. I been trying to work up to it since it's supposed to be better for you, more natural and all."

"Weird..." Vesta watched him take out his grill and eat the same bean burrito she had.

"If you wanna be a vamp, you get used to it."

"I want to be a *perennial*; living between the stars, not stuck here like you. No offense."

"Yeah?" Elay cracked a harsh smile. "Where's your buddy Desmond fit into that plan?"

"He can come with. They gotta have humans working up there."

"They got humans, honey, but you don't want to be one of them. Star vamps treat 'em like chew toys." Elay took a slow drag from his cig and watched the sky. It was a sunny saffron-yellow day, and Phobos hung faded just past the darkened Diskos dome, but beside it shone the unmistakable twinkle of a satellite city approaching near-orbit. Elay pointed his cig at it. "And that's the finest of them all: AZURE. They say Azurian vamps hunt their own kind for a taste of something that fights back."

She scoffed. "That's not what it's like. AZURE is run by the Ambroses. Maybe the Planitrs and Edens see us like juice boxes, but the Ambroses build orphanages and stuff."

"I never been myself, but I wouldn't trust the PR. Big shots gotta keep up appearances." He shrugged. "So, you wanna hear about the dancing job I got for you? It's at Stellaire, the big-ass casino outside Egress."

"Ain't that a five-star resort?" She pursed her lips and narrowed her eyes. "How'd you get an in at such a swanky place? And what's the catch?"

"I have my connections." He put his fangs back in and winked. "This is a gentleman's apology for what my blood cousin tried to pull."

"You ain't no gentleman. You ripped me off the first day I got here."

"I'ght, point taken. You want the job or nah?"

"I need it, but I need a favor too."

He shook his head and grinned. "Favor?"

"Dezi needs a job."

He rolled his eyes. "He ain't up for the type of work my guys do."

"A job at Stellaire. They have bussers, right?"

"They ain't hiring bussers. They're always looking for hosts, but you need serious charisma for that work."

Vesta touched his arm. "Please, an interview's all I'm asking for."

He raised his chin. "I'ght, but you owe me a big favor, 'cause I'm pulling strings here."

Elay was the last guy she wanted to owe anything, but he wasn't going to help Dezi for free. She wiped her hands on her pants and sighed. "You got a deal. And thanks for taking me home last night. You could have looked the other way, but you didn't. I won't forget that."

He took another drag from his cig and nodded. "I told Jaxon to lay off, but if he figures out the type of bounty your buddy's got, he'll be back. Remember, the kid gets one shot at this interview. Chryse ain't known for second chances."

Vesta rocked Dezi's shoulder. "Time to get cleaned up. You got an interview to prep for."

He sat up on her bed. "What do you mean?"

She helped him out of his torn shirt. "There's a resort hiring handsome, charismatic guys to work their bar."

He looked at her skeptically. "We don't know any of those."

"Dez, this is legitimate, full-time, and pays real good. The top hosts can make three thousand a night in tips."

"No resort is paying people that much to bring drinks. What is a host, exactly?" He winced when she removed his bandage and wiped his wound.

"You ever played a dating sim? It's like that, but perennials can afford flesh-and-blood hosts to tickle up to 'em instead of AIs."

"Entertaining perennials?" His eyes widened. "You know there's no way I'm getting this job."

"Who wouldn't want to hire a tall, polite, well-spoken guy like you? You put these local boys to shame, and you already know which spork's for the salad and which is for the soup."

"Well, one's a fork and the other is a spoon..." Dezi blushed as he buttoned up the fresh shirt she had picked for him.

"Spoken like a class act." Vesta teased his hair into shape. "I know Chryse ain't all we hoped it'd be, but going home ain't an option. Remember what we promised Pa and your mom?"

"I promised to take care of you, and I failed."

"I'm a big girl, Dez. I shoulda took care of you."

He locked his sad green eyes on hers, looking at her like she was still a little nipper running between flower beds with her fists full of substrate. "I'll go, but I'm afraid of disappointing you."

"Then we better practice." She booped his nose with her washcloth. "Look me in the eyes and smile with those teeth your mama paid to straighten—yup, like that. Woo-wee, with that face, you'll knock 'em twice dead."

He tried to frown, but she had cheered him up too much. "Looking you in the eyes is easy. It's other people that are the problem."

"Nikita!" She shouted. "Dezi needs your help with an interview!"

"No!" He tried to cover her mouth, but she fought him off, giggling the entire time.

Gambling wasn't legal in Chryse, but the Casino de l'Anneau Stellaire had its own exodome outside the city. Tucked in the Kasei canyons, it was sheltered from the worst of the storms, but still close enough to receive mined ice and nuclear power from Chryse. A few minutes' drive from Diskos and a few hours' shuttle from the tallest mountain and deepest canyon in the system, Stellaire was the ideal vacation destination for anyone rich enough to honeymoon on another planet. Dezi would never get a job at this place, but he had promised to try.

He checked in at the gate at Egress, using the complimentary ticket the resort had provided him, and stepped up to the dome's edge to enter a gondola. With an eight-person limit, it was the least efficient way to bring guests miles into the westward valleys, but very flashy. A family of seven loaded in behind him, with children in tiny designer labels and parents discussing which off-planet boarding school to send them to. Held by her nanny, their infant screeched and waved her arms in protest at the swinging of the gondola, while the other three children ran in tight circles and squealed with joy.

Dezi sat in the corner and gazed at the expanse of shallow dunes and craggy ice sands below. He would have loved to ride his Hadron over those. Ajax's irreplaceable, vintage Hadron. Mithra's Hadron, which he had wrecked and abandoned. His chest tightened, but he pulled out the pocket square a kind perennial had once given him and pressed it to his mouth for a moment. It smelled faintly sweet, and the silly memory of receiving it got his mind off things. It reminded him that everyone started somewhere. Maybe the service industry could be Dezi's start.

When the gondola slid into its dock, he folded the lavender cloth into the pocket of his rented blazer and followed the perennial family into Stellaire.

Images of plush clouds drifted before one bright moon on the dome above, while flames from brass street lamps illuminated the soft grass, and the smell of a cool, dewy night filled the air. As Dezi lingered by the entrance, he was struck by how Earth-like the illusion was; it tickled nostalgia he hadn't realized he had. Down the walkway, the limestone-white resort boasted rows of palm trees whose tops brushed a neon sign that spelled *Casino de l'Anneau Stellaire* in graceful script. Hulking, armored limos orbited the massive fountain out front as they dropped off perennials and their entourages of handlers. Onlookers snapped photos, and valets opened black umbrellas to protect their guest's privacy, though Dezi didn't recognize any celebrities. He dodged the sharply dressed bellhops to slip into one of the revolving doors—though it took him two tries spinning around to make it through to the building.

If the exterior was a tropical resort, the interior was a chateau, complete with crystal chandeliers and gold-leaf moldings. Dezi's steps echoed against the marble tile as he approached an attendant at the counter.

"I have an interview. Dezi Merlo Marrow—but the first name might be under Desmond."

"Follow me, Mr. Marrow." Smiling a bit too much for comfort, the attendant stepped out from the reception desk and led Dezi into the neon-lit casino.

The massive complex was adorned with red carpets, wood-veneered game tables, and chattering slot machines. Dezi thought he saw a room-sized chandelier hanging in the distance, but there were people on it, sitting at a bar that glistened like carved ice. The attendant brought Dezi to a one-hundred-foot-long bar with an equally long chandelier composed of delicate crystal rods dangling above the countertop like fiery drops of blood.

"Please take a seat, and Ms. Mai will be out shortly." The attendant indicated a table tucked away from the spattering of guests.

Dezi sat, hands on his knees and knees jittering against each other as he mentally rehearsed his unimpressive curriculum vitae. He watched the bartenders in their silver vests flip, flambé, and juggle mixed drinks. A cheaper place would have hired robots, but ancient perennials had a reputation for preferring traditional aesthetics. One of the bartenders reached below the counter and brought up a glass of dark wine that stuck to the side of the cup a little too much.

A thin woman sashayed out from behind the bar, rattling the pine-green sequins of her dress. Her straight black hair was pulled into a tight ponytail, and her dark red lips were striking against her pale skin. With a narrow nose and thin lines around her large eyes, she had the threatening beauty of a viper.

"Mr. Marrow?"

"Please call me Dezi." He stood and dipped his head.

Ms. Mai took her seat while examining her tablet. "I see you have a recommendation from—" Her lips pinched and she laid the tablet facedown. "Let's make this quick."

Dezi hadn't expected Elay's referral to help much, but he had foolishly assumed it wouldn't make this any harder. He sat and did his best to smile, even though he was sweating through the three layers of Ancient Spice deodorant he had on.

Ms. Mai intertwined her fingers. "Tell me about your family lineage."

"Yes, ma'am. My mother is a Merlo."

"Merlo? I'm not familiar with that bloodline."

"My grandfather, Dr. Eduardo Merlo, was the last immortal of their name."

"So, a defunct line. The name is useless, but what of your genestock?"

"My mother is Earthborn Brazilian, and my father is Earthborn American. They had me using combinatorial genetic tailoring, but I-I didn't bring the certificates." They didn't match his forged ID.

"Exotic, aren't you?" She noted something on her tablet.

Dezi ignored the racial connotations of that compliment and continued smiling. "As an Earthling, I'm familiar with the Old-World customs and terminology your customers might expect."

"Guests."

"Excuse me, ma'am?"

"We do not have customers, we have guests."

"I'm so sorry. I promise I'll remember that."

"Dezi." Ms. Mai crossed her arms over the table. "How do you differentiate a cola from a rum and Coke?"

"I'm not sure."

"A lime. How many units of blood can a human offer a patron before they die?"

He swallowed. "I don't know."

"Greater than three is a risk, while six leads to certain death. Why do you want to work here?"

"I'm looking for the opportunity to—um—work my way up to—"

"We aren't hiring future managers; we're hiring servers and hosts. How old are you?"

"Twenty-three."

"Twenty-three." Ms. Mai examined him languidly. "Most of my staff are women, especially the hosts, but we do need more men. The issue with men is they think this job involves drinking for free while being entertained by rich women. What do you think this job is about?"

"Doing what you tell me to?" Dezi managed a polite laugh.

"That's not the worst answer I've heard, but no." Her smile exposed too many of her bleached teeth. "*You* are the product here. And looks matter, but attitude is everything. It does not require skill to take drink orders. What takes skill is building relationships. I want hosts so magnetic that if they quit for another resort, their clientele leaves with them. You do not have the attitude."

Dezi pressed his palms on his knees and lowered his head. At least he had tried; that's what he'd promised Vesta he'd do. He recalled her face when she sent him off: speckled cheeks tucked into a dumb grin and butterscotch eyes brimming with hope. He had been hopeful too, but he didn't just want this job, he needed it. He couldn't go back to that corpse factory, go back to working harder for less than the Edens had ever paid him. This interview was his one shot at breaking out of that soul-sucking temp work, and he wouldn't let it slip away without a fight.

"The turnover has been ridiculous, but is this the best we can find?" Ms. Mai muttered as she picked up her tablet and pushed her chair in.

"Wait—" Dezi stood. "I know I'm not the most charismatic, but I swear I can learn the attitude if you give me a chance. I want to work here. Even if it's sweeping up, I want to work."

"Humble, aren't you?" She snatched Dezi's chin and turned his face to each side, as if checking a fruit for bruises. "I have some guests who might enjoy you, but if I put you in front of them, what's my guarantee you won't embarrass yourself and damage Stellaire's brand?"

He met her eyes with a steadfast stare. "Tell me what you want me to do. I'll do it."

A smile slowly split her lips, and she tapped her tablet. "Thank your parents for making you so handsome. You won't host, but I'll let you serve the dead man's shift. We'll see if you learn anything. Now, do you have any questions?"

"Really?" He beamed. "How soon can I start?"

Chapter 9

Guests

Dezi woke at the dip of sunset for the first shift of his new nocturnal life. Before seeing him off, Nikita insisted he put on another layer of her ancient deodorant and warned him not to look any star vampires in the eye, what with their unholy telepathic powers. Vesta reminded him that *Satelliter* was the polite term, and since biting people was illegal, he shouldn't worry. Unfortunately, that was just one of a hundred things he had to worry about. At least Vesta's shift started at the same time, so they shared the auto-taxi that brought them through the subterranean tunnel from Chryse to Stellaire.

When their ride slowed to the curb of the underground entrance, Vesta hopped out and opened the car door for him. "I don't wanna stress you, but we need to make four hundred bucks by Friday to pay Nikita the back rent we owe her."

Dezi followed her to the resort's glass doors, jittering like he was late, even though they were right on time. "I'm not sure I can make that much; this is my first day of training."

"Dez, the interview was the hard part. You got the job. I got a job dancing at the ritziest resort on the planet! The perennials here have got money falling out of their pointy ears, so between the two of us, we'll be riding easy in no time." She slapped his back.

"Still, at twenty percent gratuity, that's two thousand dollars' worth of drinks."

"Then we better get started. I gotta go to the dancers' dressing room, but your locker's down there." She shimmied her knees, faintly blushing. "Before you go, promise to check out my show if you get a chance? This is my stage debut and all..."

"Of course. My shift ends before your last show. Look for me in the crowd." He rubbed a smudge of dust off her ear, which made her crinkle her nose.

"Just remember, no flash photography."

Vesta turned, and her fiery curls bounced against her back as she skipped down the hallway, disappearing behind staff pushing carts piled high with scrubbers and hydrogen peroxide. Dezi took a deep breath, exhaled slowly, and flexed his sore arm. This wasn't his dream job, but it was a good job. He might even enjoy serving the interplanetary travelers here; in fact, he could listen to an immortal talk about their life all night. What had Mars been like a hundred years ago? What had Earth been like a thousand years ago? Stellaire was one of the few places on the planet where a mortal could sit down with someone centuries old.

Dezi entered the locker room, where a line of well-groomed hosts stood before Ms. Mai.

She adjusted the blonde curls tickling the smallest girl's shoulders before dismissing them all with a nod. "Dezi, you'll find your uniform and server book in your locker, and your designated trainer, Ms. Monika Sae-Ueng, will show you how to clock in."

Short and plump with a subtly square jaw, Monika had lively eyes and a vibrant smile. Her smooth hair, black with caramel tips, fell to her hips, and dazzling turquoise eyeshadow marked her tan skin. She wore the same royal blue vest and pearly button-down that Dezi found in his locker.

"Monika is my work name, but my friends call me Non. I'll turn around so you can change." Non playfully covered her eyes.

"Yes, ma'am." Dezi pulled on his slippery shirt and velvet vest. They were tighter than he liked, but Martian-made clothes were always either too small or way too big.

"I look like a ma'am already? I better get into management soon, huh?" Non peeked over her shoulder, caught Dezi struggling with his tie, then lifted onto the toes of her kitten heels to tie it for him.

"So, which resort did you come from?"

"This is my first service job."

"Really? I assume you have experience with formal etiquette from somewhere else then." She buttoned Dezi's French cuffs for him, humming along to the smooth jazz that drifted from the hallway.

"I did the online training, but I might have exaggerated my skills at the interview." He cringe-smiled.

"A complete freshie." She sighed. "You don't need to do anything special for Martian guests, but Satelliters love their etiquette. They and the Venusians won't tell you what they're thinking like Earthlings will; you have to watch their body language."

"Wow—um—how do I tell where a particular guest is from?"

"Experience. For now, focus on the basics: Don't speak out of turn, no eye contact, say sir and ma'am, and don't shake anyone's hand. Actually, don't let them touch you at all; they can be pretty strong. Combine that with alcohol and...we don't want any accidents. Most importantly, don't use the V-word. *Perennial* can get you funny looks from off-worlders, so I usually go with *immortal*."

He nodded eagerly. "What about building a clientele?"

She gave him a strange smile. "If a guest asks you for host services, tell them all you can offer is what's on the menu."

"O-okay." He rubbed his neck.

Non walked him out of the basement, past the lobby, and to the main entrance. She waved to the windows, inviting Dezi to admire the marble statues, designer boutiques, and celebrity restaurants scattered in the outdoor plaza. "We do one thing at Stellaire and we do it well: opulence. Our indoor beach has real sand, our restaurants serve real meat, and our spas put real cucumbers on your eyes. Everything here is the real deal—except the sky, grass, and the strippers' asses, but they're still the best fakes money can buy."

"It's a lot bigger than I realized. I might need a map..."

"No you won't. You'll be stuck in the dungeon with me." She swiftly paced back into the building towards the brilliant, blinking casino archway. "Say goodbye star-shine and hello neon."

Dezi followed her past the aisles of slot machines and digital poker tables as she explained the layout of attached bars, stages, and clubs. Stellaire had an odd mix of cutting-edge and vintage tech. The table-side menus were the latest hologlass displays, but the players exchanged physical poker chips with human dealers. Despite the antique decor, none of the guests looked particularly ancient; well-dressed and wealthy, for sure, but they could have been mistaken for mortals.

"All of our guests are perennials, right?" Dezi asked.

"Mostly, but the VIP lounges are where you get the real old bloods." She pointed to the crystal platform hanging from the ceiling; part-bar, part-chandelier, it was the center diamond on Stellaire's crown of casino camp. "You've got to be a top earner to be assigned there."

He eyed the twinkling glass staircase that spiraled up to it. "I bet VIPs tip pretty well."

"I've seen hosts take home six figures in a single night."

"Woah." If Dezi could find a reliable way to make tips like that, he might be able to pay off his bounty himself. "How do you become a host?"

"You're nowhere near ready to entertain VIPs. For the next month, all you're doing is looking pretty and carrying drinks." Non stopped to adjust the drawn curtain of an empty dining booth, ensuring the maroon velvet draped appropriately. "Speaking of, part of your job is dropping off hosts' orders to these privacy booths."

He helped her with the other curtain. "Where do I pick the drinks up?"

"The main bar, of course." She took him to the bar beneath its chandelier of crimson lights and then pointed to the colorful bottles on the top shelf. "And that's what you're trying to sell. The only drinks worth more are in there." She pointed at a row of black coolers installed with chrome scanners and heavy-duty locks.

"You mean—?"

"That's what they bleed us for every second Friday." A bow-tied bartender slid over. "Don't eat anything weird the night before, because the guests can taste it, and they *will* complain."

"I was getting to that." Non rolled her eyes. "Dezi, meet Stellaire's worst bartender, Cormac."

"Ouch." Cormac clutched his chest, but his smile was so wide it lifted his ears. He wore a stylish goatee, and his bright teeth and silver earrings shone against his deeply brown skin. "You working my section, freshie?"

"Ms. Mai's got us on the markets for Q-ten," Non said.

"Damn! I'm jealous. Let me know if anything blows up."

She shook her head. "You are the *definition* of a problem gambler."

"It's pronounced *investor*."

"What's a Q-ten?" Dezi asked.

"It's only the biggest financial showdown four times a year. Stellaire's the largest all-hours stock broker on Mars, and high rollers shuttle in from all over to watch their bets play out live." Cormac shot Dezi a thumbs up and a crooked smile. "Hit me up if you want to talk investment strategy sometime. I'll make you a millionaire."

"No soliciting the freshies." Non pulled her server book out of the pocket in her waist apron. "Looks like the tour is over. It's time to make some money."

Over the blaring of slot machines and bar blenders, Dezi struggled to copy down the orders Non took from guests. Despite her short legs and pinpoint heels, she wove through the bustling floor with ease, carrying trays of rainbow cocktails in each hand while instructing Dezi to ferry the drinks into guest's hands.

"We're running behind." She pushed a tray with four glasses of blood and four of water into his arms. "Take this order to booth twelve-A for me."

"Where?" Dezi balanced the tray on his shoulder and good arm while opening his server book, but Non had already disappeared into the crowd. At least his order pad had a map.

Amidst the flickering lights of game machines, he squinted at the tiny gold numbers on the walls between the private booths. As he searched down the rows, he noticed the occasional host chatting with a client. Always in pairs, they sat close to their guests and lavished them with eye contact. Dezi's neck itched when he saw an immortal with fog-colored skin trace his pointed nail over a young host's cheekbone. She was surely earning a hundred dollars tonight; Dezi hadn't made a dime yet.

He approached booth twelve-A, kicked out his server stand, and lowered his tray onto it, but hesitated to open the closed curtain. It felt improper, though the guest had ordered drinks, so they should be expecting him. He peeked past the heavy velvet. "I brought your order...?"

Illuminated by the holographic flame of a single candle, the booth held a lone host facing the wall and a gorgeous woman kissing her neck. The woman's eyes snapped open, piercing as shards of ice, and she pulled her teeth from the host's flesh.

Blood dripped from her lips onto the host's scarlet collar as she smiled. "Excuse me, young one, but would you mind closing the curtain? Unless you came to join us..."

The host whipped her head around and covered the bite with her hand, glaring at him. Dezi jerked the curtain closed and stumbled back. He touched the back of his neck and then covered his mouth, fighting off a swell of nausea.

Non came around the corner. "You're letting the drinks coagulate. You—you're pale as a sugar cube."

"I-I think a host is being assaulted." Dezi pointed at the curtain, realizing the order was for the booth on the right, not the left.

Non sighed and picked up his tray. "We need to get these remade."

"S-she was—"

"You see that?" Non pointed to a black dome mounted on the wall. "And that one there? Cameras. If a guest does something a host has a problem with, they're not getting out of Stellaire."

"But morstitution is illegal..."

"We aren't in Chryse, and we don't use that word here." Non pointed at him sternly. "Guests pay for hosts' time and drinks. Their private activities are private, and you never pull back a closed curtain."

"Is that what hosts do? Why they're paid so much?"

"Not all of us, but there aren't a lot of hosts who can keep an immortal entertained with their personality alone. I mean, I can because I've been working here so long, but you..." She sighed. "You have no experience whatsoever. There's only one reason Ms. Mai would consider making you a host."

Dezi's face flushed. "For guests to drink."

"Assuming you have grade A in your veins, but I could be off. Just make sure you know *what* you're selling before taking a promotion."

He laughed weakly. "My blood's grade C, so I don't think you have to worry."

She chewed on her bottom lip.

"Non?"

"Yeah." She nodded. "We need to get back to work."

After they had the drinks remade, Non let Dezi complete an order for a group of AstraTrust fledglings she hosted on weekends. They tipped him fifty dollars. He stared at the signed check on his screen; a whole fifty dollars for thirty minutes of work.

"You'll never forget that feeling." Non peeked over his shoulder. "The Q-ten reports come out in a few minutes. Why don't you take your break by the market section and watch the show while I sort some schedules?"

"Do you think I could take some more orders?"

"Those gambling degenerates will be too busy to think about drinks, but we can do a few more when I get back." She took his tray and sent him to the section of the casino packed with big screens.

Finely dressed guests filled the air with their murmurs and smoke as they settled into their seats. The armchairs were grouped in loose semi-circles around a wall of depth screens displaying financial charts in high-dimension 3D fidelity. The immortals sorted themselves, with those wearing silks and diamonds filling the front rows, and the ones with orange dust on their synth-leather loafers seated in the back. Dezi picked a spot behind the chairs to stand and listen in on the immortals' discussions of wealth management.

A guest with stone-gray eyes locked on the candlestick graphs nudged the man sitting next to him. "You're sure your information is good?"

The second guest tapped at the trading app on his phone. "Come on, the Ambroses landed a shuttle on another star system. It's a sure bet their stock is launching tonight, but if you want something less risky, go long on Planitr. They acquired, what was it again? Eden Essentials or something?"

"Eden Natural Healing, and no thanks; Everest Eden's a dud."

Unabashedly eavesdropping, Dezi nodded along. Mr. Eden had nearly run Verde into the ground, and Planitr's buyout hadn't improved much.

"You're talking like this is a done deal," the gray-eyed guest continued, "but I'm not sure I can stomach the risk."

"Can you afford not to?" his friend countered.

"I don't know." The gray-eyed guest took a shot of liquor and shakily wiped his sleeve across his forehead. "I can't afford to lose."

"Ah, well..." His friend took a pull off his glitzy cig and blew the smoke out of the side of his mouth. "Guess you don't have it in you."

The clock ticked to midnight, the stock charts flipped to green, and the gray-eyed guest's glass dropped from his hand. He showed his phone to his friend. "Holy shit—look."

"You went in?" His friend leaned over, and then his eyes bugged out. "Suck my fucking spine out! How leveraged are you?"

"Shh—they're reporting." He pointed to the massive screens, where a super-sized image of a newswoman walked into view.

She beckoned several graphs to the foreground. "Good evening, Chryse, and I bid you all a profitable second quarter. While Planitr missed its earnings projection last cycle, Ambrose Industries showed strong growth due to rising demand for extraplanetary housing developments. The conglomerate's subsidiaries—"

The roars and whoops from the crowd drowned her out when the stock price for Ambrose Industries soared, its chart forming a smooth, green arc.

"I'm up twenty-X!" The gray-eyed guest stood and brandished his phone to anyone who would look. He had made forty million in less than a minute, and Dezi couldn't help but crack a smile at the ludicrousness of it. With each swing of the chart, millions of dollars appeared and evaporated like they were numbers in a video game.

"Don't sell—don't you dare!" His friend climbed onto his chair and shouted, "I'm going to buy a fucking space yacht!"

While the perennials cheered, absorbed in their spontaneous fortunes, red numbers flickered onto the screens behind them; one by one, the losses gathered momentum until Ambrose Industries was the only ticker clinging to green.

The room hushed, and the gray-eyed guest finally turned around, his smile dropping faster than his net worth. He fell back into his seat, wide eyes watching the Ambrose Industry's graph stumble and stutter. A few steps down, then a few more up, it fought between short red and green bars, slowly climbing back to its peak.

"...despite Hadron's recent landing," the newscaster continued, "skeptics wonder how practical exospace travel is..."

All at once, a sell order for a billion shares appeared on the on-screen table, the crowd broke into hysteria, and Ambrose Industries crashed through every hard-earned inch of green. Immortals knocked over drinks, flung their phones, and fell to their knees wailing. The gray-eyed guest was silent, his stony eyes staring past the screens. When his friend tried to touch his shoulder, he shot him a few curt words, and the second perennial retreated, leaving the gray-eyed guest to mourn in solitude.

Dezi, too, felt the urge to reach out to the man, but it wasn't his place. The whole display left him questioning who in their right mind found entertainment in these charts when the consequences for playing them were so devastating. He didn't know much about investing, but he thought it was better left as a boring thing rather than made into a blood sport.

Like a flurry of gold glitter, laughter floated above the somber room, originating from a guest dressed head to toe in velvety black. The pitiless immortal's silken particle mask, large sunglasses, and wide-brimmed hat left only their powder-white brow exposed. The living shadow caught Dezi's eye, then beckoned him with a curl of their fingers, and as if caught in the gravity of a black hole, Dezi found himself drawn in against his will.

When he arrived at the table, he hastily pulled his server book from his waist apron and awaited the guest's order, praying it didn't include his blood.

The shadow lounged back in their seat, gracefully shifting their posture as they pointed to the gray-eyed guest. "Two Hangman's Bloods. One for me, and one for that gentleman."

Their voice was as rich as the low strings of a grand harp, yet its softness begged Dezi to place his ear by their lips. He wanted to know where their accent was from, what they were laughing about, anything they might say simply for the pleasure of listening.

He ought to ask what honorific they preferred, but—the shadow tapped the table expectantly.

Dezi hastily opened his server book, dazing himself with its bright screen. "W-would you like Yolet's silver gin with that?"

"Platinum." The immortal bobbed a glossy heel as they surveyed the other guests.

"For the brandy, would you like the Remi decade?"

"Century."

"For the port—"

"You're new, no?" The shadow faced Dezi, measuring him through their tinted lenses. "I don't recognize you…"

Their scrutiny hit him like a gust of hot air, and he immediately dropped his gaze to the floor. "I am."

"Hm. Write top-shelf on the ticket. The bar should handle it."

Dezi struggled to find that option in the endless menus of his server book's UI.

They sighed, put a gloved hand on the edge of his notebook, and pulled him in. "Scroll to the bottom."

When the shadow looked down to complete the ticket themselves, Dezi caught a glimpse over their sunglasses. The red on the bottom of their boots was nothing compared to their eyes. They were deep, glossy, fresh-out-of-the-body, blood red, and as Dezi fell headfirst into those sticky pools, their warmth oozed into his every crevice, steeping into his heart and lungs, until he was drowning in them.

Pulling him up for a gasp of air, the shadow snapped the book closed and fixed their shades. "Get on with it. I may be immortal, but I don't have all night."

"T-two Hangman's Bloods. Right away."

Dezi raced to the bar, weaving through the commotion and forcing himself between guests when there was no clear path.

Cormac leaned out of the server station window. "This is a storm of an order. You sure you got it right?"

Dezi gripped the bar top. "I am one hundred percent sure. Hurry!"

"Sheesh." Cormac moved his ticket to the front of his on-screen queue. "You met a high roller, didn't-chu?"

"I don't know what I saw," Dezi mumbled as the ghostly afterimages of the shadow's eyes swam in his vision.

Cormac poured the honey-toned spirits and ice into his shaker. "This fool ain't gonna tell the difference between ten or a thousand dollars' worth of liquor when he's ordering five spirits with a splash of champagne, but at least we're making money." He laughed as he rattled the shaker by his head. "Hey, my uncle died last week because the doctors couldn't figure out his blood type."

"What?" Dezi asked.

"At least Dad was supportive; he kept yelling *be positive!*" Cormac placed two skinny glasses on the bar, poured the liquor with flourish, and topped them off with sparkling wine. "Here are your Bloods. Don't drop them, and remember to smile."

Dezi snorted at Cormac's awful joke and took the drinks onto his tray. "Thanks, man. I needed that."

When he returned to the market section, the guests were back to betting and chatting, but a few sat alone with their faces buried in their arms. Dezi gingerly placed one drink in front of the shadow and skittered away to bring the other to the gray-eyed guest.

As still and silent as a piece of furniture, the pitiful shape was crumpled over in his seat. "I can't afford that," he said without looking up.

"It was ordered for you by that guest." Dezi stiffly gestured to the shadow.

The immortal took a messy swig of his drink and heaved himself up, heading for the shadow's table. "Bet he fucking wants something too..."

Dezi fell back against the wall and finally exhaled. He had managed not to drop the drinks, but—crap—had he remembered to smile?

Non jogged across the section and to his side. "Cormac said you sent him a stella expensive ticket. Who ordered it?"

He pointed, but she pushed his finger down. "The one with the big hat?"

"Yes. Why are they disguised like that?"

"Some immortals are sensitive to light, since UV's bad for your telomeres, but some don't want to be recognized."

The shadow turned their cheek towards Dezi and tapped the table twice.

"They want their friend's drink refilled," Non said. "Don't make them wait."

Non left to do her closing duties while Dezi brought his guests several more rounds. Whatever the shadow had said to the gray-eyed guest, it'd had a mending effect on his posture. They may have been flirting, but Dezi didn't risk getting close enough to listen in. Eventually, the shadow exchanged contact information with their new friend, sent him stumbling out of the casino, and watched Dezi expectantly.

His smile cracked and quivered as he approached. "Was there anything else I could get you?"

"I'll have the check." The shadow stirred their untouched drink. "You had no other guests?"

"Well, I'm actually in training." Dezi pulled his server book from his apron. "I'm sorry if staring was rude."

The shadow stood, snatched the book, and briskly signed the bill with a set of star-shaped initials that Dezi recognized from the pocket square that had become his good luck charm. He took it from his apron and checked the silver embroidery, confirming that this high roller was indeed the kind perennial who had helped him get his first temp job.

The shadow lowered his stylus and frigidly asked, "Where did you get that?"

"You gave it to me. Outside the Hadron Tower?" Dezi's voice squeaked on the half-formed question.

"Did I?" He dismissed the tension with a surprised laugh. "My mistake. I thought you were preparing to deliver some form of threat."

"Oh no, I'm sorry. I should have realized you wouldn't remember me."

"I recall the encounter, though I did not recognize you. How could I? You clean up handsomely." The shadow removed his sunglasses, subtly looking Dezi up and down. "What was your name again?"

"Dezi." He lowered his head and awkwardly offered the pocket square. "I guess I should return this."

The shadow took it, but he lingered on Dezi's hand. "What a wound you have here." He ran his silk glove up Dezi's palm, tracing his scar, and then delicately massaged his wrist. "And your chip is crooked. How odd. Did this injury force you to reinstall it?"

He nodded vigorously. "Yes. That's what happened."

"With a cut like this, you'll be mistaken for a runaway." Eye-to-eye, the shadow regarded him smugly as he noted something in the server book. "You ought to cover it. It would be a shame for this new career of yours to end over an unfortunate assumption."

Dezi's heart rate kicked up a level; he hadn't realized he could lose his new job that easily. "I will, sir."

"*Dezi.*" He said it as if to savor the feeling it imparted on his tongue. "You have a name that crawls its way into my mind."

The sound of his name spoken by that voice sent a shiver dribbling down Dezi's spine to the bottom of his heels. His shoulders reactively flexed, and his gaze snuck back to the shadow's. He needed to say something—the silence was extending—but all he could think of was to beg the immortal to do it again.

"I am afraid I have dinner plans tonight, but I might have you entertain me on another occasion." The shadow put on his sunglasses, and his icy fingers brushed Dezi's shoulder in the warmest way as he slipped away. "*Au revoir, Dezi.*"

He shut his eyes and braced against another shudder and, when he felt the shadow's presence was gone, gingerly opened his server book. It held the immortal's sharp initials above a one-thousand-dollar tip.

Dezi's knees nearly gave out. He read the screen over and over, then brought it to Non to confirm this wasn't a mistake.

Her jaw dropped. "Did the guest say anything?"

"He said I could be his server again."

"As long as you tell them to stick to the menu." She waggled a finger. "Hey, let's catch the last stage show."

"Vesta's show?" Dezi's chest warmed.

Non took him to Stellaire's smaller theater, where a jazzy reinterpretation of a pop song played for the sparse crowd. Showgirls lifted their arms and shimmied their hips as they filed on stage, and Dezi spotted Vesta's freckles in the back row. Like the other dancers, she was dusted with pearlescent powder and bedazzled with rhinestones and lace. Deep-scoop backs framed the dancers' shoulder blades as their feathered skirts swayed like the foamy crests of ocean waves. Vesta pirouetted her narrow hips and projected a sultry face with every move, keeping eye contact with the audience, but never staring at anyone in particular. She smiled at them all and flourished every bend and twist with a passion the other dancers didn't capture. In an ocean of weary waves, she was an unexpected whirlpool making every inch of sea she claimed sparkle.

Non elbowed Dezi. "Did she keep you up all night stomping out that routine?"

"I'm used to it. She's always practicing—it drove her little brother nuts—but it's great to see her dancing professionally. I don't want to say I never thought she'd do it, but..." He pressed his sleeves to his eyes. "S-she went through a lot to get here."

"A lot of people want to work here. But remember, immortals aren't known for being charitable. When they tip that much, it's because they expect something in return."

"I understand." Dezi squeezed his server book, clutching the money that would keep him going for the next two months as if it might not be there when he next opened his hands. He didn't have much to offer yet, but there was at least one guest who saw something in him. Dezi just hoped it was potential for conversation, and not as a potential snack.

CHAPTER 10

Toasts

Vesta pinched the shoulders of her costume for backup dancer number eighteen and gave it a hard shake.

"If it's dusty, you can get a dry-cleaning voucher from Castel." Leaning in towards her locker mirror, Non applied her mascara.

"I'd rather be musky than pay for extra cleanings." She rustled the sequins with another shake. "Could you put in a good word for me with him? He keeps giving me matinee shifts, but I'm plenty ready for the main stage."

"That's not how it works. It's one girl in, one girl out. If you can't wait for someone to quit, you'll have to tell Castel who to demote."

Vesta puckered her lips. "Won't the other girls have an issue with me stealing their spot?"

"How do you think they got their shifts? But..." Non tilted her head side-to-side. "You *just* started, and every girl with a serious spot has made Stellaire serious money."

"I get it. Seniority and all." Vesta sighed dramatically, loosening the knot in her chest a little. "So, did Dez ever top that first tip?"

"Not yet, but the guests love him."

"No kidding?"

"Yeah, but in the way a kid likes a toy no one else has played with yet. If he's not careful, they might break him." Non coated her lips with coral lipstick and smacked them.

"I hope not. Dezi's not great at sticking up for himself..." Vesta watched a host peel a bandage off of her windpipe and grimace at the scab she found under it.

"I've never let one of my trainees get in over their heads." Non shut her locker. "I'm not starting with him."

Vesta performed her first show of the night flawlessly, so it was a shame the audience was stuffed with parents and tots playing on their phones. She hopped over the beetle-shaped drones re-waxing the floors and caught up with the dance manager backstage. While he fussed over three missing rhinestones on a girl's tights, Vesta raised her head and strutted up.

"Castel, I need a weekend shift. I've covered four shifts for London this month and—and I'm a better dancer. Half the time she doesn't even smile. You should give me her shift."

Castel put his arm around her shoulder and pointed to a slender dancer with milky pale skin. "You see Lyra there? She graduated top of her class at Chryse Performing Arts. And you know Bethany, right? Her mother is Elizabeth Zenimount."

"The reality star?" Vesta straightened her back. "That's swell and all, but what's it got to do with me?"

"I'm illustrating the fact that you are a nobody." With a smile, he clapped his hands. "You got this position because I owed some unsavory lenders a debt, but if you keep wasting my time, you won't have it for much longer."

Her stomach clenched. "But what about London? What's she got that I don't?"

He sighed. "The assload of revenue she generates on the pole. I'll admit you're good, but not *that* good."

"So it comes down to money. How do I make more? I want this shift."

"Well, that's something I can work with. Are you familiar with the art of exotic dance?"

Her nose twitched. "I can become familiar."

"Splendid. I'll get you on the schedule. Best of luck, and remember, it's not about how well you dance." He looked down at her breasts, then winked.

"Butthole..." Vesta whispered under her breath.

She shut her heart, pushed through the curtains, and mechanically performed her remaining acts. She always seemed to hit the same wall, even in her social media career: connections were queen. It didn't matter if she had all the talent and spunk in the world if she had to share the audition bench with the producer's side piece. Whatever. She'd do a couple lap dances if it got her on the big stage. She had promised to take life more seriously, so she couldn't expect to be handed a headline act. But once she had one on her resume, she could start selling online dancing lessons and slowly build her entertainment empire.

She could see the pieces falling into place; she'd help Dezi pay off his debt, send Ori to a good school, and set Pa up in a mansion in Platinum Plateaus. After she was immortal, nobody would care whether she'd made her first million in jazz shoes or stripper heels.

With a renewed bounce in her step, Vesta pranced to her bench in the changing room with the other backup dancers. She peeled off her false lashes and buried her face in a towel to sop up the sweat and glitter.

From behind, a too-cool voice asked, "Are you Vesta?"

She swiveled her seat, facing a set of huge boobs stuck with snowflake pasties that screamed, *this is where my nipples are.* London stood tall in her chrome pumps and black fishnets, with holographic glitter sprinkling her sunrise-brown skin.

"What can I do you for?" Vesta returned a substrate-eating grin.

"You've been talking shit, and I'm here to set a few things straight." London threw back her tinsel-woven braids, twisting her curvy torso into fine folds. Her figure didn't have the perfect cushions from the bio-boutique ads, but she looked nice to hold.

Vesta rolled her eyes and returned to her mirror. "Don't you know how things work around here?"

London yanked the back of her stool, sending her to the floor. "Honey, *you* don't know how things work."

The back of Vesta's head hit the checkered floor. Dizzy, she rolled around, rising to her feet. "You wanna tussle? You picked the wrong girl."

She took an earring off, but London held her palm in her face. "I don't need to fight you, beanpole. You don't even know why Elay got you this job."

"I got it 'cause I'm five times the dancer you are."

"You think he gives a shit about cabaret? You're here because that's where he wants you."

"What are you talking about? He owed me a favor."

"That's what he told you?" She snorted. "Let me save you some time, leg bone. You don't have the figure for the tease bar. Flat ass, no tits, plain face—you look like boiled chicken."

Vesta glanced at the skinny girl in the mirror, with her sinewy limbs and gross, bumpy abs.

"You will never take my shift, so get settled dancing for the day crowd, *darlin'*." London strutted out of the room, lining her pumps one after another to sway her luscious hips.

The other girls snickered and whispered while Vesta picked up her stool and scattered make-up.

"Yeah, well, I didn't come here to make friends. You'll remember me when I'm a star, and I won't remember none of you." She tried to sneer, but her tears got in the way.

When Dezi arrived for his shift, Vesta wasn't waiting to greet him like usual.

"Non." He caught her speedily switching her white shirt for a red one. "Did Vesta leave already?"

"Thank Nova you're finally here." Non grabbed his arm and dragged him down the hallway. "Raphael told me to take you off the floor."

"Who?"

"The hospitality manager." She tugged him into a jog. "He handles hosts, VIP services—that stuff. You need to tell him that you won't do it."

"Do what? Wait—" He stumbled after her into the back office.

"Dezi, I presume." Raphael, a tall man with no hair but a magnificently groomed beard stood from his desk and offered his hand. "We don't have much time. Let's get you into uniform."

Dezi returned a firm handshake. "I left my vest in the locker room, sir."

"You won't need that one." Raphael offered him a host's scarlet button-up.

"No way. Am I getting promoted?" He looked at Non.

"No, you aren't," she said exasperatedly. "This has to be a mistake."

Raphael adjusted his tortoise-shell glasses. "The guest requested him by name."

"He can't host yet," Non said. "He'll embarrass himself."

"I'm aware of his lack of experience, but Mai told me to put him on."

Dezi butted in before they went into more detail about how badly he sucked at his job. "I can do it. I've been here for four weeks and I've learned how to handle myself." He could also use the opportunity to make another big tip.

"Good man. Wait." Raphael pointed at the light pink scar on Dezi's palm. "What is *that*?"

"Oh." He hid his hand. "I had a glove in my bag..."

Raphael scrounged in an overhead cabinet. "It's indecent. Do not enter the premises with *mastications* like that uncovered."

Dezi flushed. "Mastication? This wasn't from a v—guest."

"It's still unsightly." Raphael gave him a tan glove and a host's menu with a burgundy leather case.

Dezi changed his shirt and slipped on the glove, even though it didn't match his skin tone; rather, he didn't match it or any of the expectations set for a host.

"I could use a quick primer before I go in," he said.

"Of course." Raphael undid the first four buttons on Dezi's shirt and ran a comb through his hair. "Keep the conversation going, but don't pry for personal details; this particular guest is private. If they smoke traditional media, light it for them. You don't have to smoke, but you are expected to drink. And do keep in mind that alcohol is an anticoagulant."

"This is ridiculous." Non snatched Dezi's host book. "He's not ready. And hosts don't work alone."

"He won't be alone." Raphael handed Dezi a new menu and an ice bucket containing a champagne bottle. "You'll be going with him. The guest requested every host on staff."

"They—what?" Non blinked.

"You know how VIPs can be." Raphael patted her shoulder and then shoved another ice bucket into her arms. "They're in the red room. It might be a tight squeeze."

She pressed her lips together, massaging her lipstick. "A VIP. Of course. Let's go, Dezi."

Dezi followed her, carrying the bucket in two hands with his server's book and host's menu wedged under his armpits.

Non stopped at the door to the private room, but her hands shook so hard it rattled the ice in her champagne bucket. "This guest is nothing like the ones we've worked with. Keep your head down, and we'll make it out in one piece."

Before Dezi could reply, she pasted on a grin and swung open the door. "I brought more *champaaagne*."

Twelve hosts and hostesses filled the crescent-shaped couch, teeming around the dark figure occupying the center seat. As Dezi's eyes adjusted to the magenta mood lighting, he recognized the shadow in his elegant disguise and high-heeled boots. A tall-collared coat shimmering with metallic green and purple embroidery sat on his shoulders, and silver crosses dangled from his pointed ears. The locks of crystal-white hair sneaking out from under his wide-brimmed hat gleamed like prisms, scattering multi-colored shards of light onto his sunglasses and mask.

He flourished a pale hand welcomingly. "Our final attendee arrives. I hope you don't plan to keep us waiting, *Dezi*."

He stumbled at the entryway, spilling ice all over the floor. Non caught his bucket and helped him place it next to the others, but the damage was done. This was not how he had imagined meeting this VIP again—searching for a broom while every host in the building stared at him like he was an idiot.

"I am so sorry about that."

"Someone may have snuck into the wine early." The shadow laughed quietly. "Why don't you sit down before you break something?"

"Of course. Yes, sir." Dezi tried to plant half a butt cheek on the edge of the couch, but the host beside him bumped him off. Non cut the line by sitting on the table directly in front of the shadow, so Dezi hastily copied her.

"I hope you don't mind if I remove these." The shadow handed his sunglasses to Non. "It's a tad dim to get a good look at you all."

"No, sir." She took them, politely avoiding eye contact.

"Now that we have everyone." He raised his champagne glass, and the hosts filled their own. "To fresh starts and fresh blood."

Either the hosts found his toast hilarious, or they were spectacular actors, because they laughed like old friends and downed their glasses. Dezi took a sip, but the dry carbonation bit his tongue and forced itself into his sinuses. When he stifled a cough, the shadow's amused gaze wandered to him.

"Mmm..." Playfully rubbing his pointer finger on his mask, he examined each host in turn. Some flinched when his focus landed on them, but others met it full force by returning their own hungry stares.

He set down his full glass and brushed a loose lock of Non's hair behind her ear. "I haven't seen you in red before. It's curious, because you are astonishingly beautiful."

"I—" She blushed and glanced up. "I usually only host my regulars."

"Perhaps I may become one of them. As for each of you." One at a time, the shadow pointed out seven hosts. "I'm done with you. Leave."

The room hushed, but the VIP's eyes never stopped smiling.

"Now, a toast to the survivors," he said.

The veteran hosts stared at Dezi incredulously as they left, but those remaining rushed to fill their glasses.

Keeping his movements slow and intentional, the shadow put his arms around the women beside him. They nestled against him like a pair of remoras shadowing a shark, blindly self-assured he wouldn't snap one of them up.

"I'd like to know something about each of you," he said. "Your hometowns, previous employment, whatever you believe makes you the most remarkable host here."

Non scooched onto the edge of the table so her knees almost touched the shadow's. "I was born in Thailand, on Earth."

"Dear, I know what planet Thailand is on." He laughed loftily. "If I recall, didn't King Rama the Eternal recently welcome another child to our system?"

"Yes, they call her *Mai-daow*—new star. She was born the same day Hadron reported that mission landing on..." Her face reddened as she waffled.

Alpha Centauri, Dezi mouthed. The shadow's gaze drifted to him, only to dart away again when he met it.

"That is quite adorable. I regret rejecting the invitation to visit." The shadow turned to the blonde on his left. "And how about you?"

She returned a hot-pink smile. "Clover. My last job was as an actress."

"There aren't many of those anymore." He twisted a finger in her bleached waves. "Might I recognize you from anything?"

She brought her lips to his ear and whispered.

He chuckled and faced her, very close. "I don't doubt it, love."

"It's stuffy in here." She touched a finger to his coat. "Do you really need all seven of us?"

"I do not." He arched an eyebrow, then turned to the woman on his right. "Where are you from, dear?"

Host after host described their colorful home country or a wild story from the last resort they had worked at. They battled to monopolize the VIP's attention, attempting to extend their time or interrupt others, but he decided most were only worth a single sentence before silencing them with a judgmental blink.

"Dezi, what brought you to Chryse?" he finally asked.

"Um—work." He laughed awkwardly and shrank into his seat.

"Is that all there is to you? *Tell me* what brought you to Chryse."

"A MagnaLoop," he blurted out.

"Oh. Did you finance your ticket, or is there another patron in the picture?"

"No, of course not. I just kind of snuck on."

Damn it. He shouldn't have said that either, but every time the shadow asked a question, Dezi's lips went numb and the truth seemed to fall out.

The shadow leaned in, making it even harder for Dezi to focus. "So you are a rugged outlaw hailing from the Martian wilds."

Dezi shrugged. He didn't consider himself a particularly tough guy, but if the VIP was into that, he wouldn't hurt his chances by denying it. "I've seen a storm or two."

"Excellent…" The shadow's charm seemed to melt away, leaving only a predator's unflinching stare. "I do so love a runaway."

Needles raced up Dezi's fingertips, and he quickly lowered his head. The VIP knew he was a bond skipper, and now everyone in the room did too.

Suddenly, the shadow sat upright and pointed. "You four, you may leave. One last toast to...opportunity? No, why don't each of you give me a toast instead?"

Dezi, Non, and Clover glanced between one another. Were they the winners, or the finalists?

Clover fluidly stood, raising her drink. "To your longevity and good looks."

The four of them clinked glasses, and the shadow lowered his mask to sip his champagne.

Non eagerly stood. "To your generosity and good company."

They clinked glasses, drank, and then all eyes turned to Dezi. He was last, again. He searched for an idea, but the obvious ones had already been taken. What was left to say?

"Well?" The stunning blonde smiled, her unnaturally bright green eyes twinkling.

Dezi squinted back at her. Maybe it was the champagne, but he decided to toast something actually worth celebrating.

He raised his glass. "To Hadron's successful landing on Alpha Centauri. Someone once told me that we all start somewhere. Maybe this will be humanity's first step to conquering the galaxy."

He beamed at his cleverness, until he caught Non's befuddled expression and cringed at himself. That was unprofessional—geeky.

"I am afraid it is we immortals who claim that victory, but we cannot forget the mortals who paved our way." The shadow reached over to dash his glass against Dezi's. "Thank you for your company, ladies, but you are dismissed."

Non stood. "Are you sure? You need at least two of us."

He fluttered his eyelashes, unused to being questioned and apparently not enjoying it. "Only he interests me. Leave."

They looked so shocked that Dezi couldn't help but smirk. Who'd have thought he was more charming than a room full of professional hosts? The champagne was getting to him again. He exhaled, and when the door shut, he found himself alone with an immortal.

Chapter II
Games

The shadow's pupils dilated when they locked onto his captured prey.

"Dezi. I am so glad to finally have you alone."

Like an insect hopelessly entangled in black widow's web, Dezi found himself immobilized. "W-what do you want with me?"

"What I want?" He moved closer, and his irises seemed to glow like coils of magma under the shade of his brimmed hat. "To see where the night takes us."

Dezi couldn't stop another shudder from cascading down his spine, but neither could he look away. Maybe it was the way the VIP sat as if every seat was a throne, or how his movements were too controlled, like he was liable to break anything he touched, but his mere presence made the air heavy.

The immortal turned his face and held up a hand to cover his eyes. Although his features were obscured, he appeared to be on the younger side of Stellaire's clientele. "You're quite new to this. Shall I put the glasses back on?"

Dezi's shivering softened. "No, it's okay. But you keep staring."

He peeked above his fingers, slowly raising his feathery lashes. "My apologies. Your eye color robs me of my manners."

Dezi's breath hitched into a laugh. "I can't believe you remembered my name. I never caught yours."

"You may call me Umbra." He lifted one of the many open champagne bottles. "Care for a drink?"

"I still have some." Dezi pointed at his glass, though it was far too dry for him to finish.

"Hm." Umbra lowered his bottle into the ice. "Would you tell me about the train again? Where were you coming from?"

Dezi grimaced; a VIP probably had better things to do than chase the few hundred dollars a bond skipper could net, but a two-million-dollar reward was worth even an immortal's time. "I can't say."

"That's not very hospitable..." Umbra tilted his head and furrowed his brows. "Say, do you gamble?"

"Nope. I guess that's ironic since I work at a casino." Dezi pushed out a laugh.

"We must amend that." Umbra clicked a pen in his coat pocket, scribbled something onto a drink napkin, then folded it. "Give me a number; if we match, odds or evens, I'll purchase ten more bottles of champagne."

Ten one-hundred-dollar bottles would make for a big tip. If Dezi secured this VIP as a regular, there'd be a lot of big tips in his future, but he had a sinking feeling that he was digging his own grave.

"What if I lose?" he asked.

"If you pick the exact number, I will buy one hundred. *Choose.*"

The tone of the immortal's command made a threat directly to the lizard part of Dezi's brain—*choose or die* was its implication, and his survival instinct answered.

"Zero." Dezi covered his mouth.

Umbra unfolded the napkin to reveal the number seven. "So sorry, *cher*. Now what is my prize?"

Dezi steadied his breathing and lowered his hand. *Don't be dramatic*, he reminded himself. *Umbra is only a person; rich and powerful, but not magical.*

The immortal's pupils caught a blood-light glint. "How about a drink?"

"What?" Dezi stood.

"That's what I've won; finish your glass of champagne." Umbra pulled his boots onto the couch in a childish position and turned his chin. "Or did you think I meant something else?"

Dezi sat and stiffly finished his glass.

"You are terribly suspicious of *vampires*." Umbra accentuated his accent, lavishing the word to ensure Dezi knew he loved the feeling of it against his fangs. "You Martians think yourselves so enlightened, but your distance from the Old World has made you naive."

"I'm not Martian, sir, and we aren't allowed to use that term."

"Well, don't dare call me a perennial." He sipped his champagne, flashing his extended fangs before replacing his mask.

The blood drained from Dezi's face; the vampire was so hungry his teeth were already out.

"And that is precisely the ignorance I refer to." He poked Dezi's chest. "Do not presume I'm fantasizing about making a meal of you; I do not wear deployable canines, as I have no desire to hide my true nature."

"Oh, your teeth always look like that?" Dezi buried his hands in his lap. "You must bite your tongue a lot..."

"I cannot recall doing it once." He produced an antique coin and rolled it over the back of his fingers. "In the spirit of cross-species friendship, I propose another game: we flip coins, and for each win, you may ask a question about my kind. For the losses, you drink."

Several curiosities floated to Dezi's mind, but his recent loss had reminded him why he hated gambling. "What if I take one drink for every question instead? Like a trade." He could manage two or three.

"He's a negotiator..." Umbra returned the coin to his breast pocket. "You have a deal."

"Nice. So, when did you become one?"

He snorted his champagne. "Excuse you—questions about *vampires*, not me."

"Then, are you really immortal?"

"Immortal with maintenance, yes. Many of our first generation still walk." Umbra filled Dezi's glass. "Imagine that, surviving a millennium."

"They must have some pretty neat stories." He drank.

"One would think, though we are a forgetful lot. It makes us quite sentimental." Umbra offered his old coin. It was marked *2 Euro*, with a portrait of Copernicus on the back. "This memento is from my grandfather."

"Wow, is it gold?"

He laughed quietly. "I assume they made it of copper. It's hardly one thousand years old."

"He gave you an old-millennium coin? Your family line must trace back to the first generation..."

"Whatever gave you that idea?" Umbra quickly pocketed his coin. "I remind you to restrict your questions to the topic of my kind."

"Sorry, I got carried away." Dezi smiled sheepishly, though he wasn't ashamed of sneaking that bit of information out. He had a million questions, but since they weren't free, he had to prioritize the juiciest ones, and there was one mystery that had been sizzling on the back of his tongue ever since the immortal had first suggested this game. It was the secret he had asked his father countless times, never to receive a clear answer.

"How do you become a vampire?"

"That is a contested topic; it's my opinion that one makes themselves a vampire."

"That's not possible. There's medication. You need replacement organs, too."

"But is that all a vampire is? A sufficiently aged person? Not every elder will live forever, and many of the young have resolved to never die. In fact, you are perfectly capable of biting a human's neck and draining them of life. No surgery can give you that conviction, nor can it give you the determination to persist—to thrive when entropy wants you dead." Umbra fought the cork of a fresh bottle, inadvertently snapping its neck and tearing away a fistful of glass.

Dezi clasped his guest's hands as wine frothed over them. "Hold still. I'll call the medical team."

"What a kind nature you have..." He opened his hand, revealing his stone-smooth palm. Where the champagne had landed, it'd washed away his powdery concealer to reveal that his exposed skin shimmered like starlight and labradorite.

He curled his fingers to hide it. "Vampirism is more a mindset than a medical state. As for your question regarding what they call *perennial treatment*, the process may vary, but it begins with an exchange of ichor from sire to scion."

"Can I ask"—working up the nerve, Dezi leaned in—"who made the first?"

"Isn't it obvious? I created them." Umbra opened his arms, flashing his palm's otherworldly glimmer. "And to this day, there un-lives only one true vampire."

"You? No—you wouldn't tell me that if it were true." Dezi frowned. "I guess you don't know where they come from either."

"I would have your tongue for that, if I were not in such a permissive mood." Umbra rested his crossed ankles on the table beside Dezi while the champagne worked its way to the pink tips of his ears. "Let me be more charitable still; ask a free question."

Dezi searched his fuzzy head, then smiled when he remembered what he had wondered on the MagnaLoop.

"They sell synthetic blood, right? So why collect so much from humans?"

"I'd challenge you to drink that slop. Blood is an acquired taste, I'll admit, but the flavor and texture of the synthetics is all wrong. Let me pose my own question: If I presented you with a block of soy and a wagyu steak, which would you choose?"

Dezi snorted. "Meat actually tastes good. I won't drink again if you keep lying."

"But blood cannot? Come now, consider it: the velvety mouthfeel and delicate balance of metals; the symphony of breath and thrust of a heartbeat. You can't convince me cherry syrup is comparable."

Dezi's legs clenched. "You're talking about b-biting people?"

"Of course. Each individual has a unique flavor that cannot be experienced via needle. Because panicked mortals yield a sour taste, most prefer calm blood, but passion is truly the most elusive and decadent of all flavors. Nothing compares to the direct union of vampire and victim—their pulse entering and heating you as your tides of blood become one and you savor an embrace rapturous to every sense." Lost in a daydream, Umbra's eyes briefly shut before opening on Dezi. "With an experienced partner, the mortal shares in our pleasure."

Dezi covered his mouth and swallowed the saliva flooding his tongue.

That was a proposition. To do *that*. With this vampire. And—oh Mars—he wasn't actually desperate enough to consider it, was he?

"Seems I'm explaining steak to a vegetarian." Umbra winked and reached for a pitcher. "I think you'll need some water."

"Th-thank you."

The room was silent save for the clink of ice as Umbra slowly filled his glass. Despite his failed advances, the vampire looked quite pleased with himself.

"I'm curious, what was your profession before Stellaire?"

"I did temp work for a while." Dezi took the water and sipped it.

"And before that?"

"I worked a crap job at a nowhere colony." His wine glass was full, too, so he took a deep drink. This last bottle was something sweeter and not half bad.

"When we first met, you were struggling with employment. Do you find this work suits you?"

"Honestly, I'm still trying to figure that out. I have no clue why you picked me over the more polished hosts."

"How could I choose another dull cosmopolitan when presented with a rough-jawed man with a sordid past?" Umbra playfully tapped his fingers over his masked lips. "Those scars of yours are daring, and I have been dying to learn how you earned them."

He scratched his palm; it was always itchy, and flaky, and gross. "It's not something I like to talk about."

Umbra's gaze hardened, but then he raised his glass and winked. "Well, whatever ills befell you in the past, they led you to Stellaire, where—I must say—the uniform fits you splendidly."

Dezi blushed and filled his own. He was pretty sure it was his job to stroke his guest's ego and not the other way around, but maybe hosting was easier than he had realized. Umbra was eccentric, sure, but it made him fun to drink with.

Dezi struggled not to slur his speech. "Stop telling me you can turn into a bat if you won't show me."

"Did I not explain it must be a full moon?" Umbra unsteadily balanced a half-full champagne flute on the tip of his glassy nail.

"Demios is full tonight."

"Then clearly your Martian moons are too lumpy for me to draw my magic." He shrugged, causing him to drop his glass and laugh.

"Are you seriously going to spend all night trying to convince me your heart doesn't beat?" Dezi rolled his eyes. "Tell me about what planet you were born on or what year."

"Those are off limits, darling. I'm here for your story. What is your nationality? Who are your parents? What colony did you call home?"

"Woah, one question at a time. My vallis was like any other Martian crater. Your life is way more interesting."

"Dodging yet again. Aren't I the guest? You're supposed to do as I say." Umbra crossed his arms, definitely pouting under that mask. "What must I do to unravel your mystery?"

Dezi poked his own chin. "If you tell me your family name, and I like the answer, then *maybe* I can share more—but you better tip me, too."

"If you like my family name..." Umbra's eyes narrowed. "You're on the run from some bloodline. Which?"

He looked so deadly serious, pink-faced and drunk, that Dezi had to laugh.

"I can't tell you. What if you're them?"

"Then you should return to us. Someone is going hungry without your blood tonight."

"Yeah? Let 'em." Dezi swallowed a gulp of fancy wine.

Umbra groaned and leaned back in his seat. "Would you at least tell me your blood type?"

"Nope." It wasn't secret; Dezi just liked being obstinate.

Umbra took a swig straight from the bottle and then sloppily filled Dezi's glass. "I'd wager you're an O. O is my favorite..."

Dezi shifted in his seat, reminded that it was on a blood drinker's dinner table. "Is that why I won your competition?"

"He thinks he won..." Umbra tapped the napkin with a seven drawn on it, spun it one hundred and eighty degrees, and the curly digit became a two.

He broke into loud laughter, and Dezi crumpled the napkin. "You cheated me!"

"There was never any contest; each outcome was my design." He snatched the tip of Dezi's glove, slipping it off. "As much as I enjoyed your elaborate explanations of desert mice and yam farming, I've been waiting all night to hear the story behind that scar of yours. Why don't you do your job and tell me?"

"And you can keep waiting! My suffering isn't your entertainment." Dezi grabbed for his glove, but Umbra tauntingly lifted it out of reach.

"Oh, but Dezi, it is incredibly entertaining."

"You—you're an asshole!" He pushed the table back and stood.

"Really, now?" Umbra's wild laughter bounced off the walls, resonating in Dezi's skull like a symphony of brass bells. His vision swam, and his balance toppled, but Umbra caught his arm, pulling him to the couch. The vampire's strength was too much for Dezi, and he stumbled over his feet into his lap, igniting more arrogant chuckling.

"Careful, dear. I am not done with you quite yet, the *asshole* that I am. However, if I can't hear your story, what other use do I have for you, hm?" He pinched Dezi's chin, stealing his breath and sinking a frightful thrill to his core.

His grip was weak enough to break, but some foolish part of Dezi wanted to be held. This was another game between them—that or a lurid nightmare, because with the room spinning so hard, nothing felt real but hunger in this man's eyes, his savage desire for Dezi.

He pulled down his mask and pressed his fangs against his lower lip; he had six, lethally beautiful and sharper than sin.

"Don't think me indecent, but I have been wondering how you taste. You smell so delectable, irresistible. Dezi..." he murmured, low and rough, "you should stop me."

Dezi's heart lurched to a frightful hammering, but he did not move. Adrenaline raced through his limbs, yet he neither resisted the vampire's icy hand sliding up his nape nor his steely arm tightening around his waist. He was too strong; he could hurt Dezi—that was his intention—but he sought Dezi's hand and entwined their fingers, promising to be careful. Promising, *you'll enjoy this*. Dezi wondered what it would feel like to have a vampire's lips and teeth against his skin. They said it was better than sex, but he had never done such a thing with a stranger.

He nodded, surprising and sickening himself all at once. This was a mistake—he couldn't justify it—but he wanted to feel this dreadfully gorgeous man's mouth on his neck.

Umbra's breath became heavy, laced with honey and wine, as he leaned his victim's head back. He widened his shark-like bite and drew Dezi up. Fear spiked through Dezi's heart, but he gripped Umbra's hand, pressing his scar to the vampire's cool palm, and braced against it.

Umbra abruptly froze, holding his parted lips a breath away from Dezi's. Eyes wide, he studied Dezi's face, and in the dimness, Dezi stared back. Their limbs were carelessly mingled, and the young vampire's cheeks sparkled with blush, yet his fangs dripped with saliva.

What the hell were they doing? And why had it stopped?

Umbra pulled his mask up, laughing uncomfortably. "We'll have to call it for tonight; I have a bit of a headache."

"What?" Dezi fell back on the bench.

"No, that was profoundly inappropriate—reprehensible." Umbra rubbed his temples, stumbling past the couch. "I don't know what came over me, but you'll be compensated appropriately."

Dezi was torn between begging him to wait or diving under the table for fear he might come back. He settled on more stammering. "C-compensated?"

"You have my word." Umbra fled for the door. "And when you see Mai, tell her I wish to speak."

"O-okay. I hope it was—your stay was stuper." He fumbled his lines for an empty room.

Dezi steadied himself on the staff corridor wall as the realization of what he'd done sobered him. He hadn't just forgotten to smile; he'd shouted the VIP down. He'd offered himself to a hungry vampire and then been tossed aside like day-old instant noodles. It hurt, getting rejected like that, but with this much alcohol in his system, would he have bled out? What had he been thinking?

With the amount of champagne in Umbra's system, he could have missed his mark and torn out Dezi's windpipe.

"There you are." Raphael came down the hallway. "Are there other hosts with the VIP?"

"I was the last one."

"Oh." Raphael tugged his beard. "How did it go?"

He remained silent.

"*Fantastic.*" Raphael exhaled through his teeth. "I warned Mai this was inadvisable. You better report to her."

Dezi ambled to her office. When he entered, she placed her phone face-down on her glossy desk and intertwined her fingers. "Aren't you pleased with yourself?"

"No, ma'am," he mumbled. Fired already; Vesta was going to kill him.

Ms. Mai paced up and pulled his collar open. "You had him put it somewhere discreet, too? You *are* a quick learner."

Dezi's posture crumpled, and every inch of skin his uniform exposed felt twice as cold. *Blood whore. She thinks you're a blood whore. Was it worth the attention he gave you?*

She pushed his lips back to check the color of his gums. "Wait—he didn't feed from you?"

That sent the nausea gurgling up Dezi's throat. He swallowed it and shook his head.

"Then why did he order this favor?" She opened a velvet box on her desk, revealing a strand of one hundred gleaming emeralds.

"That has to be for someone else. I-I yelled at him."

"He prefers humans that bite back." She let the string of gems tumble between her fingertips. "Still, I can't imagine why he chose a gift like this."

"Isn't neckwear against the dress code?"

"Typically. My hosts call them mosquito repellent—don't repeat that phrase on the floor—but they discourage certain guests from requesting your services." Ms. Mai adjusted her lace neck corset. "You'll find a twenty percent gratuity in your next paycheck, and you must wear his favor whenever he visits. You can pick it up from the hosts' safe, but it cannot leave Stellaire."

"Twenty percent of that?" Dezi gawked.

"This is how we compensate hosts. The gratuity for drinks is thirty percent, garments are twenty, roses and select organics are five. That may sound low, but getting fresh flowers on Mars costs a fortune." She pulled a tablet and gold-plated stylus from her drawer. "You must sign this NDA before you host him next."

Dezi couldn't get his eyes to focus on the screen. "He wants to see me again?"

"He's your client now." She bobbed her head disdainfully, jiggling her chunky emerald earrings.

Dezi didn't come to Chryse to end up pockmarked by strangers' teeth; his mother would never look him in the eyes again. He should not have agreed to be bitten, or drank as much as he had, but would the VIP have taken no for an answer? Dezi couldn't say. He didn't know why Umbra had stopped when he did.

"I don't want to be...forced."

Ms. Mai's scowl softened. "Then don't go anywhere there isn't a camera. It's easier to get away with murder than *that* on Mars."

"Refusing is allowed?"

"Of course, but you won't keep his attention with conversation alone. Not for long." Eyes narrowed, she looked him up and down. "I'll be honest, his tastes are unconventional. Set your boundaries, collect your favors, and I'm sure he'll move on from you quickly. So, are you ready to sign?"

"I'm not sure." He rubbed his pounding forehead. "But he wants to speak with you."

"Me?" Ms. Mai dropped her stylus. "We can talk about this tomorrow. I need to go."

She rushed out, leaving Dezi with a choice. The last contract he'd signed, his work bond with the Edens, hadn't ended in his favor, but it also hadn't come with a promotion and a giant check. This was too much. He needed a glass of water and a long nap before he considered seeing that asshole again.

Chapter 12
Tips

"Here, Ves, you can hold it." Dezi handed her his weighty emerald necklace.

The gradient of crystals, from forest green to mint to diamond white, created the illusion of lights racing down the string. It was the most beautiful thing Vesta had ever seen, and it was giving her a headache. She handed it back. "There's nothing you need to tell me, right?"

"Why do you keep asking that?" Dezi laid the gems over his collar and fastened the platinum clasp.

"Non told me you were alone with that VIP. What happened?"

"We talked for hours, but I can't remember much of it." He rubbed the back of his neck and laughed. "I drank too much."

"Do you think he did something while you were drunk?" The mere thought of it made Vesta want to punch somebody important.

"No, no." He waved his palms. "I checked myself for cuts to be sure, and I'm completely clean."

"But there's no way he gave you them jewels for nothing in return. I've heard of girls trading a whole pint of heart juice for less."

"It's hard to believe, right?" Dezi lifted the gems from his neck, throwing little rainbows against his locker door. "He wants to be my regular client too, but I haven't signed anything yet."

"Sounds like you're already decided."

"Non said guests who spend this much without receiving a *direct donation* are basically unicorns, and she'd take a second shot at him if I didn't, but something about him feels off. It's irrational, but what if he's a Planitr? Or some type of mega debt shark? He asked a lot of questions... What do you think?"

Vesta crossed her arms and bit the tip of her acrylic nail. "He wants your blood and our snake of a manager is juicing you for him."

"Well—he could have picked a different host if that was all he wanted."

"Ugh, so he likes you 'cause you got straight teeth and a round butt. I guess people pay to sit with someone like you..."

"Ves..." He stopped buttoning his vest and walked over to her.

"Go away. I'm putting on my powder."

Dezi's stupid, pretty face met her in the mirror. "You're beautiful, and you're going to do great tonight."

"You're only saying that." She stuck her bottom lip out, frowning at her reflection. She had paid good credit to get professionally made up, with her neon-pink lips, glued-back ponytail, and beetle-shell glitter sprinkling her eyes, but the type of work she really needed was out of her price range. "I'm even uglier with no clothes on..."

Dezi's expression got muddled, and he took his time to reply. "You're a very talented performer, but I don't want you to feel forced to do erotic entertainment."

"I knew you'd say that. I gotta put in my dues, Dez. This stripping gig is a stepping stone to better things."

"If I take this promotion, I can cover our rent while you apply for more showgirl shifts."

"I don't want you taking care of me like I can't earn my own way. I'm a grown, working woman. And maybe I like what I do."

"As long as you enjoy it, I support you." He patted the top of her head. "I just want you to understand you have options."

"What if I pay your rent so you don't gotta sign your neck away hosting?"

"I'm not signing my neck away, but I am taking the promotion." He closed his locker and fixed his cuffs. "Remember, you have options."

"Giving up ain't an option." She pulled at the straps of her plasticky, clear bikini top and made sure the glow-in-the-dark stars printed on it covered the goods. "See you after work."

To the pounding base of grisly beats, Vesta swung into her work. The blinking acrylic pole stuck to her thighs as she slid twelve feet toward the mirrored floor, whipping her hair in low-grav arcs. Guests gathered around the edges of her countertop platform, grubby faces dappled with neon and mitts clutching poker chips like there was any better time to fork them over than now.

Vesta kicked off a slow spin and leaped up the pole, grabbing it with both hands. She walked her legs through the air like she was swimming, and men whistled at her gravity-defying talent. She had underestimated the creative potential in pole dancing—that, and how many people visited a strip club on a Tuesday night—but the real money was in private dances.

She gathered the chips tossed at her feet before the other girls could snatch them and then ducked backstage. After stashing them in her locker, she rubbed her sore biceps and slipped off her candy-colored heels; break time.

Her hair tickled her bare back as she pranced to the main bar in search of a free drink. Tugging the bottom of her purple shorts, she set her heels on the counter. "Cormac, can you spare a little something?"

"If you get those nasty things off my bar." He hung a freshly dried martini glass on the rack overhead.

She pouted and dropped her shoes to the floor. "Rude."

"We keep it classy out here." Cormac's grin shifted his moles up his cheeks. "What can I get you?"

"An extra-Long-Island iced tea, please?"

He mixed her liquor and topped it off with cola while keeping an eye out for managers who might catch him serving freebies. "Rough night?"

"My neck's been stiff since London knocked me on my ass. I shoulda given that tank-headed hussy one for the road while I had the chance..."

"She wasn't always like that." Cormac took his time selecting the next glass to polish. "She fell in with a bad crowd."

"You mean the other dancers? They're a pit full of pebble vipers if I ever saw one." Vesta laid her head on the cool bar top. "Ugh, guess it's time to woman up and do some lap dances."

"You done one yet?"

"A couple, but it was too weird. Why's anyone paying forty bucks for me to rub my sweaty hams on them for three minutes?" She sat up and sucked on her straw. "Life been treating you good?"

"Hell no. I dumped the seven K I made last quarter on this currency where every coin cryptographically minted defined a potential phenotype of the species *Felis catus*."

"You mean kitty-cat genes? Never mind—skip to the part where you tell me if you made any money."

"Lost it all. The founders got sued by the Fancier family, and the corpses running the courts decided you can't copyright phenotypes if someone else already owns the genotypes."

"Well, duh. How'd you feel if someone snatched your genes out from under you and made a bunch of Cormac clones? Or a seven-foot-tall Cormac 2.0?"

He stroked his goatee thoughtfully. "If someone stole my jeans, then I guess I'd be pantsless."

"Barf! That's why you and Dez get along, couple of cornballs. You know you shouldn't gamble. How many people you seen ruin their lives in here?"

"You're a skeptic now, but someday you'll be putting your retirement funds in the Cormac ETF."

"I ain't got a retirement or any idea what an ETF is."

"You don't know what an index fund is? Seriously?"

"Uh—no. You're talking to a future perennial superstar, not a finance geek." Vesta finished her drink with a noisy suck under the ice.

Cormac shook his head. "You won't get anywhere without understanding capital appreciation."

She scrunched her face. "The heck does a celebrity need to appreciate math for?"

"Alright." Cormac wiped his hands and rested his arms on the counter. "See our esteemed patrons?"

She puffed up her lips and surveyed the bar, spying a party of Venusians in their patterned silks and some Earthlings in fur-trimmed coats. The Venusians didn't talk to anyone outside their own, always expected someone to fill their glass for them, and took a lot of pictures—but that figured, counting for how far they flew to get here. The Earthlings were so outgoing it gave Vesta the creeps, what with them toasting and chatting up strangers. They ordered a lot of pickles and little cheeses too; she heard that was a European thing. Of the types of Earthlings Stellaire usually got, this set was pretty rare. They were so sharp-faced, smooth-skinned, and straight-toothed that Vesta wanted to find a nice tablecloth to hide under and never show her mug again.

"What about 'em?" she asked.

Cormac pointed at his face. "How many look like me?"

He was black—blacker than anybody she'd known in Verde, since everyone in Verde was, well, Verdan. Beside Mr. Gion, who was pale as wheat paste, and Dezi and his mom, they were all this kind of round-faced, rusty-haired, gangly limbed colony people covered in spots and splotches. Not quite dark, not quite light, when people like her got written into TV shows, they were typecast as hard workers who spoke an old-timey type of English instead of proper Earth-Latin. Off-worlders assumed every Martian looked one type of way, despite the fact that plenty of people here looked like Cormac and Non.

Vesta offered her freckle-smeared arm. "Well—how many look like me?"

"Not many; that's my point. Don't get me wrong, we ain't in the same boat, but neither of us is in a superyacht, and I'm here trying to show you how to use a paddle."

Vesta played with her straw in her empty drink. "I didn't mean to nip at you... I been feeling down in the dunes about my—ugh—phenotypes."

"The genetic lottery ain't fun when your parents could only afford one ticket." Cormac frowned and rubbed at a mole by his nose. "But that's why we've got to hustle ten times harder."

"I been trying to save up for a little skin lasering, but between rent, auto-taxis, and getting done-up, there's hardly a tenth of a cent left over at the end of the month."

He pulled out his phone. "I have this five-week grind-set course on the billionaire mindset you could sign up for—you get a discount if you use my code."

Vesta stuck her tongue out at him.

"Or..." Cormac scratched the back of his head. "You said you wanted to help your dad retire, right? I could help you set up an IRA account for him, so you could save a little each month."

"As long as that ABC thing ain't code for some pyramid scheme." She giggled and slipped her pumps on. "I gotta get back to the poles."

"Remember to spin ten times faster than the other girls." He winked. "And if you see London, tell her I got a Cosmic Taser with her name on it."

"I think I'll do her liver a favor and not." Vesta slid off the barstool. "And I'll ask the first guest who comes up if they want a dance."

Vesta lifted a leg and hooked her toe behind the pole, gracefully twisting through the fog as she scouted out someone to offer her services to. She could try her luck dancing for a woman this time; maybe they'd tip better.

A man walked straight up to Vesta's spot on the stage and raised a gleaming one-thousand-dollar chip above the crowd—Elay. Of course he'd be the type of guy to come here.

Vesta strode to the platform edge and squatted to his level.

He rested his arm on the counter. "Long time no see. How's Stellaire?"

She mounted the ledge and hopped off. "The usual bleed."

"Can't believe you're in the strip pit. I thought you'd be center stage by now."

She shook out her curls. "I go where the fans are."

"If you say so..." He checked her up and down, thinking he was slick. "Can I get a dance?"

"Yup." She tensed her smile. If Elay wanted to hurt her, he would have done it while she was drugged, so he wasn't *not* trustworthy, but he was still a man, and she had learned a lot about men in the last few days.

Vesta walked him to the nearest private booth, and when he sat, pulled into a handstand and flipped herself onto his lap.

"Damn! Who've you been practicing those moves on?" Elay held his tattooed hands up. "I hope it isn't that Desmond kid."

"Dezi, and no." She mechanically rubbed up on him. "What are you even doing here?"

"Handling business. I heard you got bad blood with one of my girls, so I told her to back off."

"Thanks, but I was looking forward to pulling a chunk of her weave out."

"Nah, honey, you'd like London. You gotta chill with us sometime." He stuffed cold poker chips one after another into her bra.

She wrinkled her nose. "You ain't supposed to touch."

"You don't want 'em?" He grinned, flashing the starburst engravings on his grill that were supposed to look like little diamonds but probably just trapped bits of food.

Vesta turned around so she didn't have to see his smug face; they both knew she wanted that shiny chip.

"You making good money here?"

"It's stellar. Everything's stellar."

"Then why are you on my lap instead of on stage?" He inserted a chip into her butt crack.

"No touching!" She stood. "I'll get you tossed out on the dunes."

"You gonna tell on yourself too? You been letting me touch as long as it came with one of these." He threw a chip, and it bounced off her bare midriff.

She glared at him.

"That's what I thought. This'll be our little secret." He got up. "Talk to London. She wants to apologize for being a bitch."

"I don't care." Vesta yanked the curtain back.

Elay snatched her arm. "You still owe me one. *Talk to London.*"

"Fine." She jerked her arm free.

On his way out, he held up the one-thousand-dollar chip and winked. "Remember, honey, if you want to get paid, you gotta earn it."

"Friggen' pee hole…" Vesta shook the small-dollar chips out from her bra and shorts and counted them up—not worth it.

When she left her booth, London caught her eye from the bar, dripping in glitter down to her ten-inch heels. Vesta tried to fast-walk to the exit, but the load of ass and hips cut her off.

"We need to talk," London said.

"I'm heading out. *So sorry.*"

London crossed her arms and raised an eyebrow that had Elay's type of ego all over it.

"Fine." Vesta followed her to a booth.

"Elay asked me to show you something." London closed the curtain and pointed at the seat.

"He said you were gonna apologize."

"The hell he did. Sit down. I'm showing you the reason he got you this job."

Vesta cautiously sat, and London settled onto her lap and slipped something into her hand. "We sell it like this, one roll for sixty. Extract cartridges are two hundred. You can pick it up from the bartender with the heavy eyeliner when you drop off the chips."

"Drugs. I figured. Tell Elay I ain't interested in getting fired."

"You too good for smoke? I know you've been smelling it all night. Management understands that VIPs expect a place like this to have the good stuff. They let hosts sell trips down the Milky Way."

"I bet the cops expect so, too."

"This dome isn't in Chryse; it's corpo country, leased by Ambrose Industries. No pigs get in without a warrant signed out to Mr. Ambrose himself."

"I ain't a drug dealer."

London smirked and pinched Vesta's cheek. "You eat, don't you?"

She slapped her hand away. "Are you high?"

"I wish. Look, when an immortal can't afford blood, they die. If you can't afford enough of those smelly-ass burritos you stuff your locker with, you die. Eat or die. I don't know about you, but I don't plan on dying—ever. So, do you want to keep making pennies on lap dances, or are you ready for a promotion?"

"You sell one roll for sixty? That's batty. Elay never charged me that much..." Vesta fluffed her hair. "What's your cut?"

"Twenty."

A few dozen of those a night, and she could make as much as Dezi with his fancy necklace.

She sighed. "I'll think about it. But get off. Your dump-truck ass is crushing me."

"Sure thing, leg bone." London rose. "Find me when you're ready to eat at the big kids' table."

Chapter 13

Favors

"Have you been well?" Umbra clasped Dezi's cheeks and kissed the air to each side of his face. "You're a touch pale, *mon hôte*."

Dezi shrank from his sudden touch. Umbra's velvet gloves were incredibly warm and soft, and Dezi wasn't sure what to do with his own hands with someone else so close. "I donated this morning."

"Then I arrived a night too late." He brushed the back of his fingers across Dezi's necklace and laughed.

Blood rushed to Dezi's cheeks, scalding them as he fought a shudder. This was not how a host should react, but Umbra had arrived so suddenly that Dezi hadn't had time to fix his hair before Ms. Mai dumped him in front of the VIP, and now his chest was too tight to draw breath to form an apology.

"Oh dear." He withdrew. "Did I overstep again? It was meant in jest."

"J-jest?" Dezi croaked.

"I partook before my arrival, so I'm not even peckish, I promise." He drew a cross over his heart like an Old-World priest and then removed two stacks of chips from his pockets. "In fact, I happened to be in orbit and thought I might stop by to play a few games. I hope you'll humor me."

Dezi balked at the tower of golden, hundred-dollar chips Umbra deposited into his hand. "Of course, sir."

He led Dezi to the bar and ordered two whisky sours from a bartender wearing a fresh orchid clipped to his shirt. All the staff in this VIP gaming room wore the same royal purple, excluding the hosts, who remained in red. What separated an elite host from a regular one was the wealth of their patrons and the extravagance of their favors. Few wore as many crystals as Dezi had on, and none had gotten over the shock of losing this guest to him. Dezi hadn't quite come to terms with it himself. He had tried hosting a few other clients in the month since he last saw Umbra, but they never came back.

"You're a contemplative thing, content to spend your time locked up in there, hm?" With a cherry-and-orange-topped cocktail in hand, Umbra poked Dezi's forehead. "Come, entertain me with those quaint stories from your home colony."

"They aren't very interesting..." Dezi rubbed his head and nibbled on the boozy skewered cherry in his drink.

"Then tell me something that is." As Umbra strode towards the game tables, the fiber-optic lightning embroidered on his Venusian robes swayed behind his heels. With two albino peacock feathers wrapped around the band of his hat and platinum gaskets on his particle mask, his outfit was worth nearly as much as Dezi's bounty. He peered over his shoulder. "How about the story of that scar?"

Dezi washed down the lump in his throat with a smokey, tangy swallow of dumb courage. "I'd rather talk about gambling. If you don't want me to lose all your money, you'll have to teach me to play."

"Well then, my student, shall we begin with games of chance or dive straight into cards?"

Dezi approached the roulette wheel, watching a white marble spin around its lacquered numbers. "This one looks fun. How do you play?"

"It's quite simple." Umbra lowered a stack of chips onto the table, letting them fall with a string of satisfying clicks. "Let's start you off with a thousand."

Dezi cupped his cards to his chest: a ten of hearts and an ace of spades. He wasn't sure whether they were any good, but he was feeling lucky.

Seated on his left, Umbra tapped his shoulder. "Keep your cards on the table, face down."

"Oh—" He put them down. "When I have to spend a hundred dollars to play, it makes me second-guess every hand."

While hiding his face behind his hand, Umbra lowered his mask and took a shot. "Nothing risked, nothing won."

Not wanting to appear impotent, Dezi doubled his bet. Then came what Umbra called the flop, where the dealer laid out three cards. He placed a ten, a jack, and an eight onto the green felt. Dezi's eyes widened, but he bit his tongue to keep his face still while the other players decided whether to bet or fold. With these cards, Dezi had a pair of tens and a chance at a straight. His fingers twitched as he added up the probabilities of all the different hands his opponents could construct.

"Sir," the dealer asked, "your bet?"

"Oh—um, I check." Dezi pushed another two one-hundred-dollar chips out.

"Hm. Raise," Umbra said. Unlike the other stone-faced players, he appeared pleased with every outcome.

The man to the right of Dezi clicked his tongue and tossed his cards. "You've got something, don't you, kid?"

"Me?" Dezi shrugged. "I think my guest might. I call." He glanced at Umbra, searching for a tell, but the vampire was composed as ever.

The dealer gathered up their chips and turned another card onto the table: the queen of clubs, which completed Dezi's straight.

He gave it a moment so he didn't seem too eager, then pushed in ten chips. "Raise. One thousand."

"Call," Umbra said without hesitation. He must have something pretty good; a seven would give him the lower straight, or he could have a set of high pairs.

The dealer revealed the last card, a seven of diamonds. This was it; Dezi had the best straight possible. He pushed in twenty chips, though his hands jittered as he watched his stack shrink by enough money to pay his rent for four months. "Raise."

Umbra shuffled his mountain of chips for a moment, considering his play. Frick, Dezi had gotten greedy with that raise and scared him off. Umbra had warned him poker was as much about psychology as statistics.

"You play a good game." He pushed in all of his chips. "Let's make this memory a lasting one."

Dezi covered his mouth. Umbra had gone all in; he had gone all in when a third diamond was placed on the table, and he had bet when the first two came out as well. All signs pointed to a flush. Dezi glanced down at his puny pile of chips. He had risked so many already, but he'd lose everything if he played this hand.

"I fold." He sighed, pushing his cards away. "How are you always so lucky? That was my best hand."

"Oh, darling, luck has nothing to do with it." Smirking, Umbra tossed out a pair of clubs.

"You had nothing." Dezi dropped his head to the table with a bonk. "You're kidding..."

Umbra took Dezi's shoulders and pushed him side to side, laughing merrily. "You timid boy, my intention was to give you that money."

Dezi groaned, limply falling against him. "That makes it worse."

Umbra pulled him a little tighter. "What if I split my stack with you, hm? Then will you smile for me?"

When the vampire's breath tickled his ear, Dezi's posture turned to jelly. "I-If you keep dealing me in, I'll have to buy you a vending machine dinner—because, you know, we'll both be poor."

"That sounds delightful. Shall we go now?"

"You're not joking?" He looked up into Umbra's eyes. Outings and shopping trips with regulars were part of the job, but the guests always paid, and it was never cheap. If Dezi took his guest out, it would be like an actual date.

Umbra's phone buzzed. He sighed and checked it. "We'll have to hold off on dinner. Seems I'm needed elsewhere."

"Oh...well, better cash out your chips."

"Keep them; I'm afraid I'm too pressed to cash them myself. How time escapes me in your company..." Umbra blinked at him languidly, and Dezi would have risked all his winnings to know what that look meant. "Would you be a gentleman and walk me to my car?" Umbra asked.

"Yes-sir." Dezi wanted to add something gentlemanly, but the feather twirling in his ribcage made putting one foot in front of the other an Olympic challenge.

"This way." Umbra tugged the bottom of Dezi's sleeve, pulling him to the stairwell and keeping hold as they descended. "My assistant sent my car to the tunnel."

Dezi opened the door to a face full of frosty, dust-dry air. Lit by sparse orange lamps and the headlights of the occasional limo racing down one of the six lanes, the tunnel was not a place VIPs frequented.

"Are you going to Diskos?" he asked.

"Oh no, I'm heading directly to my shuttle." Umbra stepped up and over the dust gutter to where an armored limo waited. "Off to Venus to put out another fire. *Joy.*"

Dezi pulled the limo's handle, using both hands to get the foot-thick door open for his guest. "But didn't you land on Mars a few hours ago?"

"*Oui, cher.* Is it difficult to believe I visited solely for you?"

Dezi laughed, tugging his tie. "You must have spent more time on the shuttle than you did with me."

"Not at all. The two million miles flew by like a breeze on my Class-P."

"You own an antimatter jet?" Short of personally knowing an Ambrose, the only way to get a hold of a Hadron pion rocket was at a multi-million-dollar auction. "Sometimes I forget how rich you are, but it's still a long way to come just for me."

"Indeed it is, though I doubt Stellaire would be willing to send you to me. I don't suppose you'd be interested in meeting outside of work hours." Umbra pushed a loose curl behind his ear, then fussed with the loops of his mask. "No, that would be unprofessional. There I go again, being far too forward..."

"Is it? I mean, I would have to check the employee handbook."

Umbra's gaze darted up. "You'd consider it? I would provide shuttle and lodging."

"L-lodging?" Other hosts whispered about luxury overnight trips with their VIPs, but never off-planet, and never novices like Dezi. But Umbra could take him anywhere in the system, maybe even far enough to escape Planitrs. He suddenly couldn't get enough air. His fingers fumbled at his chokingly tight collar.

Umbra stepped closer and took Dezi's tie, slowly loosening it. "Dinner on Venus, dessert on Earth, *mignardise* on Luna. If all goes well, I might even take you—"

CLANG.

"Fuck—open!" A man in a python-pleather trench coat kicked one of the doors to the resort and promptly fell on his ass from the force of his boot smashing against the chip scanner.

The crumpled scanner whined, "*Insufficient credit.*"

Umbra's eyes narrowed to ruby slits, glowering at the creditless jerk. "What is that imbecile doing?"

Further down, Vesta and another dancer exited the staff doors together, and the jerk ran to the dancer, lisping, "London, badge me in."

She laughed, shaking her large chest in her Argyre U hoodie. "Not happening. If you don't have money to play, what do you need to get in for?"

"I know Elay's in there and I want to talk to him. I don't like how he's running this operation."

"Yeah, we don't give a fuck. Call your daddy for some fresh credit."

Vesta scooted behind London, but the guy snatched her arm. "Wait—I know you!"

And Dezi knew him too. He sprinted towards Vesta, grabbed the bastard's shoulders, and yanked him back.

"You!" Jaxon lifted his lip in a triumphant grin, revealing the length of his pepper-red fangs. "And here I thought the trail went cold."

"What the heck do you want, you marsdamned sewer snake?" Vesta stepped beside Dezi.

"I'd like to get a look at that bike of yours. You keep it around here somewhere, right?" Jaxon dropped his head to the side in an eerie tilt. "Call it up."

"No." Dezi squared his shoulders; he didn't do this often, but some men only understood a physical language, and he wasn't afraid to use it on this human carcinoma. "You need to leave Vesta alone. She *never* wants to see you again."

Jaxon snorted and giggled. "It's batty. The same night we met, someone crashed a vintage Hadron Akira with a registration from Verde Valis, and a couple weeks earlier, one Dezi Merlo Marrow skipped bond from the same facility after sabotaging two million dollars' worth of product." He grinned like a toddler who'd been caught pissing in the water aerator. "Public records are a bounty hunter's best friend."

"So what? Gonna call the cops? They'll love the free tip—if Stellaire gives them tunnel access. Either way, you ain't getting a cent!" Vesta balled her fists, but Dezi held her hand before she took the first swing at a would-be guest. So long as they were in Stellaire, this punk couldn't touch them.

"You should leave before someone calls security," Dezi said calmly.

Jaxon squinted and slid his hand into his pocket, finding something weighty.

"Elay said they're off limits." With an expression cool as iced champagne, London stepped in. "And if you make a scene at his best retail location, you're done."

"What?" Jaxon threw his hand out of his pockets. "Do you know how much this guy's bounty is?"

"Don't know. Don't care." London leaned back on her platform heels and looked him down. "If you stopped turning in your customers, you'd still have some sales."

"This kid doesn't buy shit!" Jaxon traded between lisping and stomping his banana-yellow boot. "This is bullshit!"

"Go cry about it to daddy. Oh wait—he doesn't give a fuck about you either." London shooed him with her bedazzled nails. "Buh-bye, now baby boy."

Dezi put his arm around Vesta while she gave Jaxon a vicious glare.

"We aren't done. Watch your fucking necks, because we aren't done." Jaxon shoved his hands deep into his pockets and stomped down the tunnel, too credit-dry to afford a ride.

"Did Elay really say that?" Vesta asked London.

"If it pisses Jaxon off, he might. But no promises Jaxon will listen; you don't want him tracking down where you two live."

"Heck, that's easy to say, but he's a blood-sucking sleuth."

Dezi's stomach went a little gray. "I think he had a gun. We can't get Nikita involved in this, Ves. I can't keep putting you in danger."

"But it's my fault he's on your tail. We stick together, no matter what."

"When me and Cormac were running from bad bonds, we did pods," London said. "Two hundred stories and a thousand pods per floor—you could give him your building number and he'd have better luck sucking sand through a straw than finding yours."

Vesta nibbled on her thumbnail. "They finished up some pod hostels in Nikita's building we could move in to, but will that be enough?"

London shoved her hands in her hoodie and shrugged. "It will stump Jaxon's dumb bounty-hunting ass, but not the shark that sent him. All that stops debt buyers is paying them off; maybe skipping the planet, depending on who you owe."

"Thank you, London. We appreciate it." Dezi nodded and nudged Vesta.

She puffed her lips out. "Thanks, but don't go thinking we owe you one."

"I'm protecting Elay's investment." London sauntered to the curb. "You better get back to your guest. Vamps don't like being ignored."

"Crap." Dezi whipped his head around.

From across the sidewalk, Umbra pointed at his watch, then waved and entered his limo. Had he waited that whole time just to say goodbye? A warm, cottony sensation filled Dezi up to his cheeks. Umbra had been watching to make sure he was okay.

"He didn't look ruffled." Vesta swung her handbag over her shoulder.

"He isn't stuck up about etiquette. He's actually easier to talk to than the other guests." Dezi took out the two handfuls of chips Umbra had given him. "Do you think this is enough for us to rent pods?"

Dezi was surprised that Vesta had found a pair of pods so quickly, because he hadn't seen a single vacancy in the dorm, but with all the discussions of bid prices between neighbors, it didn't take long to realize she had won theirs by paying one dollar more than the people who had lived here before them. Having his own bed was a stellar upgrade—he'd forgotten it wasn't normal to wake up with a sore throat and aching back every morning—but the sheer number of pods packed into the floor made him feel like a battery hen, and the free gym was not as well-equipped as advertised. Not to mention, one slob leaving out their Carb Crisps was all it took to bring in the local wildlife. Dezi might have made friends with the cockroaches if they didn't have a habit of running for the warmth of his boots as soon as he put them up.

He slid his boots into the locker next to his bottom bunk and hastily shut it. With the capsule door open on her top bunk and a ring light mounted on her tripod, Vesta smeared gray cream around her eyes as she spoke to her camera. "For another money-saving hack, conditioner works great to clean mascara..."

Dezi climbed into his pod with its freshly sanitized sheets smelling like chlorine. He cracked the heat seal on a liquid meal and shook it before beginning his nightly ritual of tucking into an audiobook. Although it was blowing up on every planet, this one wasn't distributed on Mars. He felt daring, listening to a piece of contraband, but the truth was he'd gotten embarrassingly hooked on vampire romances.

Right as the heroine embraced her immortal prince, and his newly awakened hunger embraced her, Vesta hung her head over the side of the bunk, tickling Dezi's face with her copper curls. He took his earbuds out.

"Did you get Non's message?" she asked.

"No."

"You check your phone?" She raised an eyebrow, her face turning pink from hanging upside down.

"No..."

"There's a sending-off party for Clover." She crawled into Dezi's bunk and sat on his shins.

He tucked in his knees to make space for her. "The host with the green eye augments? She doesn't like me."

"She wants to rub it in your face, but she's paying, courtesy of her special client. He sponsored her work visa on SPECK Orbital."

Dezi's jaw dropped. "She's moving to a satellite city?"

"Yup. Her guest liked her so much that he couldn't wait for the satellite to come back 'round every half-season."

"No way. They're *together*?"

Vesta laughed loudly. "Heck no, he's got a wife. He hired her to be a nanny."

Dezi grimaced. "So, adultery?"

"I seen 'em both visit Clover, and she looks real pale after they stop by."

"Huh. At least it's consensual, even if it's unconventional."

"It's more than conventional, it's contractual. She signed a lifetime blood bond, so she's a *bonded human*, which is legal speak for full-time bloodbag."

Dezi's already uneasy stomach clenched. "Why would anyone do that?"

"Are you kidding? It's basically every host's retirement plan to get set up in a cushy mansion with the nicest perennial that bites. No more rad meters, dry fleas, or foot rust for the cost of getting sucked once a month? It'd be a good deal if it didn't mean you signed away your shot at becoming immortal yourself."

"I'm sure they made her plenty of promises, but giving someone that much control over your life sounds like a recipe for abuse. I can't believe something like that is legal."

"Planet-side, it ain't. But with shuttle prices like they are, I can't say I blame her for taking the deal, 'cause that's looking like the one way for a girl to get off this rock."

"Not necessarily. I've been looking into it, and if Hadron's new class-P shuttles get approved for commercial flight, it could cut interplanetary transit cost by ten times."

"You know it takes darn near three generations for those gonzos to pass anything. But once my new stream takes off, I'll have the money for both our tickets." Vesta slapped his knees. "So, you coming?"

Dezi tilted his phone away from her. "I'd rather stay here..."

She wrinkled her nose mischievously and then tickled his ribs. "Fine, but when I get back, you tell me if your goopy romance book has got anything steamy, you hear?"

He covered his warming face. "Talk to you later…"

She giggled and hopped out of his pod. "I'll bring back leftovers."

Dezi switched to a technology podcast about neural chips, since hearing about Clover made his romance novel feel…too real. The billionaire hottie's possessiveness wasn't as sexy when Dezi realized there were perennials out there who wanted to, essentially, purchase humans. Though, after experiencing how his guests had treated him, he shouldn't have been surprised. Umbra was the only immortal who addressed him like a person instead of a servant.

He lay back, closed his eyes, and ran his thumb over his scar. He hadn't even seen Umbra's face, and yet he could tell something about the VIP was different. If he was willing to eat a vending machine dinner, he might be down for a walk in Delta Park. Next time he visited, Dezi should ask. Going off-planet with the guy was a little much, but he looked forward to deepening their relationship—in a strictly professional manner, of course.

Chapter 14

Masks

"Attention, everyone." Ms. Mai stepped up to the employee metrics display and addressed the staff room, causing Dezi to look up from lacing his shoes. "The gondolas will be closed due to inclement weather, so I need greeting staff in the traffic tunnel to welcome guests arriving for the Blue Nova Resorts shareholders' conference. These are our owners, and as such, I expect peak performance for the length of their stay. Remember, at Stellaire we are...?"

The crowd responded robotically, "Stellar."

Vesta bounded to Dezi, rustling the sleeves of her new puffer jacket. "What type of blackmail does Ms. Mai got on you to be working mornings again?"

He knotted his tie and shrugged. "She asked."

"Ugh, stop being such a suck-up. You know praises don't pay the bills."

"The employee of the month award includes a bonus, Vesta." Ms. Mai made her jump when she approached from behind.

"And how much was that again?" Vesta twisted her hips, bowing her skinny legs. "A twenty-dollar gift card?"

Ms. Mai's drawn-in eyebrow twitched. "You would do well to learn the satisfaction of a hard night's work from Dezi. He's trained for three different roles now, and I expect he'll make a fine assistant manager one day."

"I don't mean this sideways, miss, but I know what spending twelve hours picking flowers feels like, and it ain't satisfying. I'll stick to shaking my ass six hours on Sunday."

Ms. Mai sighed. "Dezi, why are you wearing that necklace? I didn't mention that your VIP was here."

Vesta bumped her butt on his. "You never noticed he wears them jewels darn near every night? It keeps the bats off 'em better than a garlic wreath."

Ms. Mai pressed her hand to the chains of platinum and gold running down the neck of her dress. "Dezi, have you been avoiding other clients?"

"No. This favor—uh—matches my eyes." He offered a frail grin, mentally cursing Vesta.

Ms. Mai laughed. "Considering the key clientele you serve, we can make an exception for you. And I appreciate you taking that extra shift in the café. There was an outrageous number of last-minute call outs."

"Must be the murky skies making everyone so un-satisfaction-full," Vesta said.

"I would expect the opposite; guests flock to these valley-shielded resorts when a storm approaches." Ms. Mai smiled, exposing her bone-white teeth. "Are you sure you wouldn't like an extra shift?"

"We ain't due for a storm, ma'am. It's only a couple of clouds." Vesta picked up her pack and hugged Dezi. "Enjoy minimum wage, Dez."

Ms. Mai's weird tone had worked up his anxiety, so he gave Vesta an extra squeeze, just in case. "Stay safe."

He returned to his locker mirror, tossed his bangs, and practiced a few different smiles, but he couldn't figure out how to make his eyes brighter. Where his eyelids pinched, the more he forced it, the more they angled downward. He sighed, adjusted his necklace, and polished his new platinum cufflinks. The client who had gifted Dezi his favors hated fake smiles, anyway. Thanks to Umbra, Dezi was making the equivalent of a six-figure salary and saving every penny.

He had tried to call one of Planitr's offices to ask about how one might, hypothetically, set up installments to pay off a criminal debt, but they'd laughed him off the phone. He assumed that meant it was an all-or-nothing-type deal. Two million dollars: the sum he owed was enough for a consultation at an immortality clinic. Humans didn't have that type of money.

Despite the hopelessness that kept him up some nights, he was still grateful for this job. If Planitr wouldn't take his money, he could use it for classes at Chryse Community College and work towards a technical career. What field that would be in, he wasn't sure, but he had time to figure it out. As much as he appreciated Umbra's generosity, he'd prefer to make his own money someday. He wanted to be respected for his skills and remembered for his accomplishments—once he had a few.

He smiled again, and finally realized that he needed to relax his eyebrows.

The aroma of coffee and pastries filled the café as Dezi made drinks for the swarm of perennials sipping their iced lattes in the shade of palm ferns. This was the busiest morning he'd seen at Stellaire, though he was surprised by how few off-worlders had come to attend the conference. He would have thought at least a few non-Martians would have been interested in bumping elbows with the apex of Chryse's elite. But, then again, the wealthiest city on Mars was still on Mars.

Dezi dumped a fresh load of beans into the grinder and reached below the counter for a shot of stabilized blood, but the dispenser only dribbled a few drops. He scanned his wrist at the blood cooler beside it and, upon opening it, found that, of the few bags left, none were of the correct grade. He hoped the guests wouldn't mind, because there wasn't much he could do when the delivery was late again.

Dezi's skin crawled as he gave the gallon bag a sloshing shake, then he inserted it into the dispenser hatch and poured his shot.

He placed his cup under the expresso machine's nozzle and, while it hummed and brewed, yawned and slapped his cheeks awake. Once the mahogany-colored cappuccino had its foam topping, he scooped the order onto his tray and stepped out from behind the counter. This morning, the faux sky was bright, the temperature was cozy, and the café jazz was delightful.

With his tray held high and a linen draped over his arm, Dezi approached the guest's table. The immortal sat by the windows, twisting the end of his silk scarf between his fingers as he read from his tablet. With rays of sunlight beaming through his dove-white curls, he was heart-stoppingly gorgeous. The edges of his face were wolfishly sharp, yet his lips and eyes were round and innocent. His heavy eyelids and arched eyebrows would make him look haughty if his smile wasn't always so sanguine. Like a cherub burgeoning into manhood, blessed with the deepest crimson eyes, Umbra was simply too lovely for mortal terms.

And he was just sitting there. Was Dezi supposed to pretend he didn't recognize him? He wasn't a skilled enough liar to pull that off. No, this was his opportunity to finally take a peek past the VIP's mask.

Dezi set the cappuccino au sang on the vampire's table, mustering all the formality he could while trying not to grin like a fool.

"Umbra, I didn't expect to see you again so soon. How are you enjoying your stay?"

"Dezi?" He adjusted his scarf. "I thought you worked the Casino—at night?"

"Normally, but Ms. Mai has me pulling double duty for the shareholder's dinner. Are you going to it?"

"I—" He scoffed. "You recognized me just like that...?"

Dezi laughed and pushed his bangs to the side, hoping they weren't too messy. "You didn't hide your eyes. I mean, they're pretty remarkable."

"Fair enough. I admit, I planned to attend the shareholder's dinner and request your services in the later hours, but you've thrown a wrench into those plans." Umbra flourished a hand in surrender, wafting his ruffled sleeves. It was uncanny how he flickered between the appearance of a beautiful man or a handsome woman based on a slight difference in angle. He showed Dezi his cheek, a social gesture he had never used on him before, though Dezi was technically breaking etiquette by making eye contact with a Satelliter.

"You have something more to say?" Umbra asked.

Dezi held his tray behind his back. "I didn't realize how young you were."

His carnivorous eyes darted to Dezi's. "Is my appearance an issue for you?"

"No, not at all, sir." It was certainly a little intimidating, but Dezi was mainly fascinated by how inorganic his features were. His hair was like fibers of diamond and his nails were polished glass.

"Of course not. Why should it be?" Umbra raised his head, striking a noble pose. "You understand our discussions were in confidence, correct?"

"That's what the NDA is for." Dezi promptly nodded.

"You don't realize how much I appreciate that." Umbra returned a weak laugh and sipped his cappuccino.

"Well, if you need anything, I'll be here, grinding beans." Dezi stumbled while backing up, died inside a little, then rushed to the kitchen. He peeked over the bar as a taller guest with Neptune-blue hair sat at Umbra's table. From across the café, Umbra spotted Dezi staring and then pointed him out to his friend. Dezi ducked.

"Dezi!" Ms. Mai stomped through the door connecting the café to the restaurant. "What are you doing down there?"

He stood. "I—uh—dropped a fork."

"Raya called out. I need you in the ballroom tonight."

"Straight through? That's a sixteen-hour shift."

"Was that a *no*?"

"No—I mean, I can do it."

"That's my assistant manager material. We're taking note of your loyalty, and it will be rewarded." With her creepy corporate smile, she left to go squeeze more work out of someone else.

Dezi sulked to the bar and picked up a round of Bloody Marys.

Cormac set the drinks on his tray. "Who sneezed on your quantum amplifiers?"

"I'm working a triple."

"I told you to call out today. They work the pretty ones to death when the board's in town."

"Are the tips good at least?"

"Hell no. And watch yourself, 'cause the grannies get thirsty too."

"Shut up." Dezi tossed his dirty cups into the dish pit, and the auto-cleaner's grabbers chased them as they bounced around the conveyor.

"I'm serious. When the board is in town, accidents happen." Cormac impaled a mini pickle with a toothpick for emphasis and dropped it into a cocktail.

"Alright, I hear you." Dezi peeked over the bar, wondering how long Umbra planned on staying.

Arms stacked with trays, Dezi paced the one-hundred-seat ballroom table in a room where the odor of blood hung in the air like fog. With their pupils glinting in the candlelight, the shareholders looked ready for a fashion runway in their ostrich leather bralettes, unbuttoned silk shirts, and catsuits embedded with bioluminescent beads. Extravagance was the dress code, down to the intricate crystal chokers that accentuated the unique scars on their jugulars.

With his boyish curls immaculately gelled, Umbra wore a turtleneck that obscured his scar. He'd look underdressed in his slim-cut, navy suit if it wasn't for everything above his neckline and past his wrists. His eyes were stab-wound red compared to the others' plastic-colored irises, and while their gray skin was dusted with the same glitter Vesta used, Umbra's emanated a ghostly light from within. Without the concealer he had used to disguise it, his pores glimmered like a billion finer-than-sand moonstone crystals. Most striking of all, he was the youngest immortal at the table; he could have been Vesta's age, and yet he occupied the head seat. The other majority shareholders watched him closely, whispering to one another, but he didn't seem to care that they excluded him from their conversations.

A woman draped in tropical feathers asked him, "Are you holding that seat for your sire, youngling?"

"I am not," Umbra said without looking her way.

Her orange lips formed a snooty frown. "But where are you from? Your etiquette is…aberrant."

"Off planet." He smiled sweetly at her, cutting his grilled fish into smaller and smaller pieces. As far as Dezi could tell, his cutlery usage wasn't the problem. It must have been his apparent youth, since he had been concerned about it in the café.

"That much is obvious," said the man taking the second-most-eminent position at the table. "But you can't sit there without introducing yourself. You must be a Nova, although the matriarch would never blood someone so…" He cleared his throat.

Umbra's smile slipped away, revealing a dead-cold expression. "Finish your thought."

"I'm afraid I lost it." He laughed and raised his bourbon glass. "I drink too much at these things. Apologies, sir."

Umbra sighed quietly and lifted his hand to call for service.

Dezi stepped up to his side. "Yes, sir."

He raised the menu. "Five ounces of…hmm."

Dezi bent down and whispered, "By the way, you look stunning tonight."

Umbra stared at him for a moment, then his expression softened. "May I have a glass of O negative?"

"My pleasure, sir." Dezi lightly touched his back and turned for the kitchen, but before he made it far, the woman in the feathered gown flitted her hand at him.

"Waiter." Her smile exaggerated her many fine wrinkles, and her chunky amber jewelry encased priceless fossilized insects.

Dezi reluctantly stopped and gave her a short bow. "What can I get you, ma'am?"

"Are *you* on the menu?" She laughed with the thin women beside her, then reached around to pinch Dezi's butt cheek.

He jumped. "Ow! Please—"

"Where did you get that gorgeous strand of emeralds, young one?" She reached her pink claws for it.

He stepped back. "It was a favor, ma'am."

"Won't you sit and tell us how you earned it?"

"I'm so sorry, but—"

"Clumsy me." She knocked her wine glass onto the floor. The blood smacked the carpet, and she kicked the cup under the table. "Would you be a dear and fetch that?"

"Let me get you a fresh glass." Dezi's tray rattled in his hand. "Please..."

"You dare refuse me? Do you know who I am? Take off that neckwear and *crawl*."

As if a weight fell onto his back, Dezi's palms dropped to the sticky carpet.

"Enough." Umbra's humorless voice rose above their rancorous giggling.

The woman sniffed the air and tittered. "I thought I smelled you on this plaything." She reached for Dezi's necklace, wrapping her wiry fingers around his neck. "It's a lovely favor you gifted him. I'd get him a tiara to match, but you can't bear to share your hors d'oeuvre?"

"*Tu moule à merde*, I do not share." Umbra stood, and his nails bit into the tablecloth, cutting ten small holes.

The woman and her posse bristled like cats. "You mean to threaten me, you little abomination?"

Umbra cracked a smile. "How original. You think you are the first to call me that?"

"Don't make a joke of this. Tell us, what loathsome family blooded a child?"

"It's fairly obvious. You simply lack the class to know." Umbra tilted his head, observing her scar. "A Marztran. No wonder you share the pallor of a corpse. How is dear Nicholas? Fairing no better than you, I'm sure."

"Keep my sire's name out of your mouth," she hissed.

"But I think he would be interested in how his spawn are carrying on—with whom they are seeking feuds. Tell me, is he still playing pretend in abandoned train stations, or have you finally chained him up in a nursing home?"

"He—" She went rigid. "No one knows about that. Where the hell did you get that information?"

"Wish that I had no need to bother with terrestrial scum of your ilk." Umbra stepped forward, and with him rolled a pressure that made the hairs on Dezi's neck stand. "Your paltry sire would exsanguinate you for an audience with a fledgling from my line. Address me again, dust-blooded wretch, and I will ensure he does."

She glared at him, venom pooling on her tongue, spine hunching as if to leap, but her brows faltered. She looked to the rest of the table, though they had long since hung their heads after realizing what was now dawning on her. Umbra was a lion among street cats at this affair, and his patience with their yowling had hit its limit.

Her color drained, and she lowered her head, leering at Dezi. "Be careful with that one, boy. His kind has a kiss you will never recover from."

Umbra rolled his eyes and took Dezi's arm. "Dinner is well spoiled. Escort me to my room."

As Dezi led him away, every ounce of angst the stakeholders had for Umbra bored into his back, but his outrage at how cruelly they had treated his guest was his armor. He wished he could have said something. Mars, he wished he was half as clever and brave as Umbra.

When they exited the dining room and entered the warm light of the lobby, Umbra's skin shimmered with a surface iridescence like that of a pixie's wing. He was too pretty. Dezi was getting sweaty. And Umbra was holding his arm. And—oh Mars—everyone was staring.

Umbra released him, smiling politely. "My apologies for entangling you in social politics. These Martian perennials fight over status like a gaggle of pigeons thrown a slice of bread."

"I think I set her off by whispering to you. I'm really sorry."

Umbra's next step was stilted, and his jaw clenched. "I'm glad you saw that—how they treat me."

"I can't believe they ostracize you for how you look. That's terrible."

"Not all of them; many are more curious than anything. It is forbidden to halt one's aging before twenty-five, though I am older than I appear. It's something I struggled with even before I was blooded."

Appearing much younger was an issue Dezi himself would have faced if he hadn't gotten transitional care as early as he did. He had suspected Umbra was trans for a while now, and he badly wanted to ask about it, but announcing he'd clocked him felt extremely rude; Dezi would be mortified if someone did that to him, though Umbra's presentation was more fluid than his own.

"Do you mind if I ask about your gender?" he asked.

"Oh no, I find those conversations painfully dull. Call me what you like. He, she, they; these words are the perceptions of others. They don't define me. The same goes for the insults of small-minded terrestrials and their archaic laws. I feel so fortunate to have found a host who is above those preconceptions, one with which I can be myself." He took Dezi's arm again, leaning into his shoulder as a tuxedoed security guard lifted the velvet rope to the

VIP wing of the hotel for them. "You must agree to stay with me awhile longer. I find myself missing your company so terribly after we part."

"I'd love to host you this evening. Would you, um—" Dezi tried to catch his breath and not sound too squeaky. "Would you like to visit the park with me?"

"Don't be ridiculous; I couldn't fathom going to Chryse with these foreboding weather reports. I'd much prefer to show you my room."

"Your room? I couldn't—I'm not allowed." Dezi's knees were so weak that Umbra was the only thing keeping him up. The vampire was practically dragging him down the mural-lined hallway.

"Nonsense. I have to give you a tour of the Jupiter Suite. We're already here."

At the end of the hall, two oak doors inlaid with stained glass panels depicting their namesake planet waited for them. Umbra opened them to a short foyer with plush carpets and marble columns. Past that lay a grand living space, equipped with floor-to-ceiling windows and a private bar, where several hosts lounged on the ivory couches. A butler attempted to greet Umbra with a bow, but he snapped twice and pointed at the exit. The butler, hosts, and bartender rushed out, shutting the door behind themselves.

"Thank God we can finally have some privacy." Umbra fell back onto the couch, laying his sparkly, silver boots on the cushions. "I booked the room for the week, so if the weather gets too harsh, you're invited to bunker down with me. Imagine that: a sleepover."

The wall of windows presented canyons striped with maroon, plum, and bronze sediments, like an abstract painting of colossal scale. Dezi tried to blink the dream away, but found more priceless bronze statues and exotic plants wherever he looked.

He turned to Umbra. "Who are you?"

"One of humble taste and simple needs. I'm no one, really."

"You were at the head seat of the stockholder's table. Do you own the resort? Are you my boss?"

He rolled onto his stomach and swayed his heels. "No, darling, that's not how vested ownership works, but if you must know, I am the single wealthiest individual in Stellaire. I could have this dome bulldozed, or your face carved into that mountain." He rested his chin in his hands, licking his lips. "I can have anything I please."

So what did he want with Dezi? It sent his mind racing to unprofessional places.

Unprompted, Umbra rose from the couch, sauntering to him. "I thought I might chase you around the suite for a bit; dim the lights and stalk you. I'm quite fast, so I hope you're ready to put up a fight."

Umbra wanted to hunt him? Pin him down and—dizzy with nerves, Dezi backstepped to the door.

The vampire halted, and his predatory hunger disappeared behind a childlike head tilt. "Or we could watch a film? I didn't prepare an agenda, so I'm open to suggestions."

With his back against the door, Dezi shook his head. This was way out of hand; they should be in the casino playing games, not alone together in his private suite.

"You are outrageously tense." Umbra retreated to the bar, putting the entire distance of the room between them. "Shall I pour you a drink?"

"I'm definitely in trouble with Ms. Mai for walking out. I-I should get back."

"I can't return you to those vultures in the ballroom; they will tear you apart. Besides, Mai is already aware that I intend to end my evening with you." He peeked over the bar and lifted a bottle of scotch, too damn smug. "So, what will you have?"

Dezi wasn't getting out of this room without risking his job, and the vampire knew it. He felt foolish for letting Umbra's cute face distract him from the asshole he'd always been. A neck-biting, blood-drinking asshole who hadn't finished dinner.

Dezi swallowed his dry tongue. "Water, please."

CHAPTER 15
Pressure

AFTER A FEW SIPS of water and glances at the ceiling to confirm that the vampire had successfully lured him into a cameraless room, Dezi racked his brain for a way out of this trap.

"I've always wondered what the resort's artificial beaches are like. Maybe we could—"

"I don't do pools. I sink." Umbra tossed back a shot and flashed those fangs that sent Dezi's heart racing. "Let's dispense with the niceties. We both know I have you exactly where I want you."

Dezi frowned and reached for the doorknob. "And I have the right to refuse service to any guest, even a VIP. I'm going to the café. You're invited to come with me, but you can't force me to stay here."

That blew the smirk off of Umbra's face. With extraordinary speed, he darted to Dezi's side, placing his hands over the doors. "Wait, darling, we can't speak frankly out there. Don't you want to learn more about me? Aren't you curious about the venom that crone mentioned?"

"Venom?" Dezi crossed his arms. He knew Umbra's game, but he couldn't help himself when immortal secrets were on the table. Info about perennial biology was impossible to find online, almost as if it was forbidden to share. "She said something about a kiss."

"Indeed." Umbra suavely turned back. "A common euphemism for a bite, and mine imparts a potent venom."

Dezi edged back. "Your bite is deadly?"

"What an absurd conjecture. If that were the case, I would have killed every one of my donors." Umbra swabbed two fingers above his fangs and offered them to Dezi. "My venom. Satisfied?"

He approached, examining the faintly blue saliva. "But what does it do?"

"See for yourself." Umbra smeared it on his forearm.

He leaped back, but it was too late.

"You poisoned me!"

"I did no such thing. Poison is ingested, darling; venom is injected."

Dezi wiped the saliva off on his pants, but his wrist was tingly. "It's a painkiller?"

"It contains painwarpers, anticoagulants, digestive aids, and whatever else a vampire has need for. The glands under my tongue produce a coagulant and antiseptic."

Dezi dug his nail into his skin, and it felt...good. Like scratching an itch that was so tender he wanted to make it raw, needed to make it bleed. "Incredible."

"Now imagine the trouble a full dose can cause."

"You could seriously hurt someone..." Dezi pulled his sleeve over his wrist.

"Indeed. Thank God those ill-bred perennials don't possess the gift."

"Are perennials and vampires not the same thing?"

"Obviously not; a perennial can't transform into a fine mist or call thunder. *Thunder!*" Umbra raised his arms, and the room's AI crackled with sound and flickered the lights.

Dezi rolled his eyes. That was the closest he had come to turning into a bat yet.

Umbra laughed. "Maybe our blood carries the same curse, but call a true vampire a *perennial* and you can expect to book an appointment with your surgeon for a new tongue."

"How did you decide that woman wasn't one?"

Umbra tapped the side of his neck. "Our brand identifies our bloodline. Hers is not worthy of the title."

"Hm. And yours is covered."

"Is it?" He playfully tugged his turtleneck.

"I guess it must be a pretty lame bloodline if you're that embarrassed of it."

Umbra blinked once, then reeled back with laughter. "Was that an attempt to goad me? Oh, and how clever you thought yourself."

Furiously blushing, Dezi removed his glove and held up his scar. Umbra had asked about his injury incessantly, so if he had any information worth trading, this story was it.

"If you show me yours, I'll tell you how I got this."

Still chuckling, Umbra crossed his legs, teetering a sparkly boot. "It's impossible."

Dezi shoved his glove into his pocket. "You really can't?"

"No, and you should weigh your curiosity carefully. Some truly dangerous creatures frequent Stellaire."

"Let me guess. You're one of them?"

"The most terrible of all." He smiled, concealing his fang tips behind frost-pink lips.

"I'd be more convinced if I knew your bloodline." Dezi plopped onto the couch and stretched his sore legs. Since Umbra hadn't lept on him yet, he might have genuinely brought Dezi here to get away from the other guests. Without his disguise, he'd draw unwanted attention in every room they entered.

Umbra sat beside him, losing the six inches his stilettos lent him. Although the VIP could evoke a monumental presence when he wanted to, he was actually a good half-foot shorter than Dezi and lithe as an hourglass. In fact, his waist was so narrow that Dezi could easily wrap one arm fully around it. Umbra would look very cute held like that, wrapped up in Dezi's big arms.

He adjusted his posture and reminded himself that he was technically still at work. "It doesn't make my job easy, not even knowing your real name."

"I hate to disappoint, but I'm afraid personal questions must remain off-limits."

"Okay, then what about ichor? You told me it started the *change*, but not what it was."

"Ichor is the blood of an elder. As we age, our blood accumulates artifacts, thickening until we become strong enough to reproduce."

"And artifacts are what, exactly?"

"Demons and ghosts, of course." Umbra flourished his hands. "The demons clog everything up, what with them feasting on our human part, so we introduced the helpful ghosts to transport nutrients, but they began getting lost in our bone marrow's spongy cavities, packing them full. It upsets the demons when blood production falls off, so we supplement it with yours."

Dezi raised an eyebrow. "Wasn't one of the rules of this question game that you tell the truth?"

"No, I don't think it was. But there is another name for the spirits: prions and nanites."

"The immortality treatments make you so sick that you have to take nanite therapy? That sounds counterproductive."

"Not sick, per se, but when one lives forever, the treatments cascade into new symptoms and *abilities*. Those who can't meet the ever-increasing cost to maintain their bodies stagnate in a slow and hideous death, such as the Marztrans."

"Abilities... You mean like how good you are at cards?" Dezi didn't believe in magic, but he had seen immortals do things that weren't easy to explain. For one, the casino didn't allow guests to play traditional dice, because in the hands of an elder immortal, they had a funny habit of beating the odds.

"I thought you'd never ask. Naturally, I can read the thoughts of humans and bend them to my will, but I am also talented in those more eclectic spells, such as mesmerism and fear casting."

"Alright, I'll take the bait." Dezi crossed his arms. "Prove it. Cast a spell on me."

"Are you granting me permission, darling?" His expression darkened, eyes glittering with wicked intentions. "I've been holding back out of respect, but once you invite me in to that cozy little head of yours, I may never leave."

"On second thought, I've changed my mind." Dezi tugged his collar. "Do you have any more physically verifiable powers?"

"Certainly. There is my skin, which is supple to hold, yet hardens against force. There are my claws, fashioned from sapphire glass and sharpened to the nanometer. And, yes, my reflective retinas provide superior vision." Umbra offered his hands. "Humans always ask that one."

Dezi took them. Adorned with pale colored diamonds and dainty platinum bands, his hands were petite enough for Dezi to close his fists around, yet heavier than lead. "Woah. Are your teeth synthetic too?"

"That's quite forward, asking a vampire to show you their fangs." Umbra waggled an eyebrow, curling his fingers into Dezi's. His skin was as soft and cold as freshly fallen snow.

Dezi's ears burned. "Is it? I-I didn't realize."

"Mmm, but I like you, so I'll allow it." He tilted his head and simulated a bite. All four of his canines were classically long and pointed, but the pairs of teeth next to each of them were short fangs as well, making for twelve ice-white blades. "They are composed of zirconia."

Honed finer than ceramic scalpels and coated in his stringy venom, their simple elegance sent a thin shiver down Dezi's spine. Wrapped in those petal-shaped lips, Umbra's bite could shift any pain it caused into a terrible pleasure.

"You want to know how they feel," he said softly, drawing Dezi in. "I'm told they arrive like a whisper, and linger like thunder."

Something odd rippled through Dezi's gut, making him reflexively squeeze Umbra's hands. Sure, he was curious, but in a clinical sense. It had nothing to do with the vampire's heavy gaze, or how his tongue suggestively traced his teeth, or how—oh Mars—he was salivating like a starving wolf.

"You know I would never hurt you." Umbra pressed a kiss to Dezi's knuckles, his devilish smirk revealing the fangs so close to Dezi's skin. "Not unless you begged me to."

Did he mean that? It sounded like a promise, and despite the secrets he kept and lies he told, Dezi wanted to believe him. "T-that's good to know. But don't worry, I won't."

"Ah, well, then the shenanigans continue." Umbra snapped his tongue and theatrically spread his arms. "So, doctor, with your examination complete, tell me, am I undead?"

"Hm..." Dezi rubbed his chin as the funny feeling climbed to his cheeks. "That depends; is a fallen angel alive?"

A flush blossomed in the pointed tips of Umbra's ears. For once, he was quiet, and it sent Dezi's heart pounding loud enough to hear.

Umbra got up and strolled to an ornate door, peering over his shoulder at Dezi. "Your flattery could use some work, love. Come. I'll show you how courting is done."

Dezi followed him to a study packed with paper books, insect displays, and fossils. In the center of the mosaic floor stood a grand wooden device finished in black lacquer. Umbra lifted the hatch covering its ivory key, and Dezi recognized the instrument as a lavishly oversized piano.

"I take it you're not familiar with the acoustic variety." Umbra propped up the piano's back lid, revealing an array of over a hundred steel wires. When he pressed a white key, a red felt hammer within struck a wire, sending a pure tone soaring to the domed ceiling.

Dezi brought his nose down to the archaic device, searching for the stereo output and IR sensors. "There's no way it can get that loud without some electronics."

"Indeed, it can." Umbra dropped his weight-lined coat to the floor with a thud and slid onto its glossy bench. "Have you never experienced a live music performance before?"

"I've listened to the guys who drum on plastic buckets downtown," Dezi offered.

"Well, then let us see how I compare." Umbra lovingly pressed into the keys, creating gentle sounds, but they formed a rendition of a song Vesta had been singing all week.

"You listen to pop music, or did you choose that for me?"

"This isn't *your* pop; this is the original Space Oddity." He slammed the keys discordantly. "The damn Zenimounts must have re-released another AI-butchered version of it."

"Were you alive when the Bowie Estate released the original?" Dezi hastily asked. The thought that his guest was a thousand years old made him dizzy, queasy, and fascinated all at once.

"No, I was born far after Mr. Bowie's time. This was the music my father listened to. He said it embodied the shameless optimism of the last era of exploration, a time when every speck of moon dust was brimming with potential. He often pitied our generations; we have but a handful of living artists, and odds are they're immortals re-releasing their hits the same as the estates do."

Umbra touched his watch fondly, its gold case gleaming against the starry, blue enamel of its dial. Oversized for his wrist, the piece didn't tell time but instead contained a miniature planetarium, with a rainbow of precious stones representing the orbit of each planet. "He was an ancient, unparalleled in his industry. As a result, we had little time to make memories together."

"I didn't know my father well either. We were so close when I was young, but then he just...left."

"He abandoned his child?" Umbra looked aghast. "Did you have your mother, or were you left orphaned?"

"My mom took care of me. She still does, but I can't help but wonder where he went. He used to say we were going to buy our own Hadron and visit every planet together." Dezi scoffed quietly and shook his head. "Guess he got a single seater."

"I lost my father at a young age as well. He was supposed to teach me about what I am, but—" Umbra winced, touching his brow. "I shouldn't overshare; painful memories are forgotten for a reason."

"I didn't mean to kill the mood." Dezi sat beside him on the bench, looking for something to cheer them both up. "Can you sing?"

"No, I'm horrid, but I can play anything you like." He massaged out a mild melody.

"Anything I could sing to?"

He arched an eyebrow. "You sing?"

"Anyone *can* sing, doesn't mean they're good." Dezi tousled his brown hair. "Sing with me so I'm not the only one embarrassing myself."

Umbra fluttered his snowy lashes. "He's making demands now..."

Dezi raised his brows, offering a sheepish smile. "Please?"

"Why can't I seem to deny you?" Umbra murmured. "If they're dancing on Bowie's grave again, they'll be doing this one as well." He played a familiar riff. "On the chorus, they say *under pressure*."

His foot tapped to the beat as his hands danced across the keys, evoking the rhythm, melody, vocals—the entire ensemble at once. Guided by the piano, Dezi sang the lower portion of the duet quietly while Umbra hummed the high end. Dezi elbowed him and enunciated his lyrics, so Umbra raised his chin and sang clearly back. Dezi stole his next verse, letting his voice soar to sweet highs, but when Umbra came behind, he filled the room with a deep song from his chest. Switching between the duet's parts as he pleased, he drowned Dezi out with a shocking range of pitch and breathy tremor, an uncanny mimic of both thousand-years-dead artists. He slammed the keys, threw his hair back, and belted out lyrics proclaiming love on the edge of the night. Eyes shut and sweat beading, he—*they* were rock stars. And as the song came down, their voices melded, they bumped arms, and their eyes met; two kids barreling through a duet for no one but themselves.

Umbra tapped out a few goofy keys, and they fell into the same laughter.

"I hope I haven't put you off live music forever." He pushed his curls back from his face.

"What are you talking about? You're incredible."

He scoffed. "It's a party trick. A strict replication is not art, but it's all I'm capable of; the cost of too much graphene lacing my skull, I suppose."

"Oh... You have that many cerebral augments?"

"Predictive branching circuitry, vasodilation kinesics arrays, neural accelerant matrices—my entire body is peppered with them. Sometimes I wonder how much meat is left in me." He twisted his hand, and as he examined it, the milky crystal of his skin cast flecks of light like an opal. Utterly flawless, he lacked visible pores, body hair, and veins, and by the sculpted edges of his eyebrows, every individual hair on his head appeared intentionally threaded into place.

"But there's something beautiful about that. People designed your augments, so in a way, *you're* a piece of art."

Umbra's laughter caught a few high notes. "Who taught you such flattery? That was far too sweet. Utterly saccharine."

"Oh..." Dezi pressed his mangled hands into his lap. "I won't do it again."

"No, love." He brushed the stubble under Dezi's jaw, lifting his chin. "Never cease being this sweet to me."

It was silent again, terrifyingly so. Should he say something? Touch him back? To a guest, that would appear like an offer to exchange his blood for a better tip, and Dezi didn't want to be seen as a bloodbag, not by Umbra.

"I am rather parched." Umbra rested his hand on Dezi's shoulder, leaning in. He smelled like crème brûlée and wood fire on a winter night. "Would you join me in the reserve?"

The vampire's chilled breath on Dezi's neck swept his mind blank. "T-the reserve?"

"It's one of the rooms I have yet to show you, along with the bedroom." He held one of Dezi's scarred fingers and guided him, glittering with laughter. "But I would need a drink to warm the blood before that."

He approached two gilded doors and pulled the ring-shaped handles, revealing a bar with ebony countertops and wrought iron shelves holding hundreds of vintage wine bottles. He put Dezi's hand on a velvet stool and slid behind the bar. Glass cases embedded in the back wall displayed live animals, including a white python, a pangolin, and a red panda.

When the snake flicked its tongue, Dezi gasped. "Are those holograms?"

"Organics, darling. What use would they be in a reserve otherwise?" Umbra poured a glass of sparkling wine, took a sip, and wrapped around the bar.

Dezi noticed a large, empty box. "There's one missing."

"That one is for Cat. He looked so sad in there, so I let him wander." Umbra handed Dezi the glass and rested a petite, matte-black bottle on the bar for himself. "He's such a charming fellow that I purchased him from Stellaire. If I can't sort out his visa, I may have to smuggle him home."

"I've never had a pet, but I've always wondered what it's like to have someone to hang out with when you don't want to go outside... I don't have many friends." Dezi sipped his prosecco, letting its honeysuckle sweetness bubble on his tongue. "Man, I sound like a loser. Someone like you must have a ton."

"One would think." Umbra pulled the cork from his bottle and took a deep drink. "True friends are rare. Far greater is the number of people who want something."

"So...do you want anything from me? Because if you don't, that makes us friends."

"I'm after something; I simply cannot determine what it is. *You* will have to tell me."

"How am I supposed to know that?" Dezi mumbled.

"Oh, you don't." Umbra smirked and took another sip. "But tonight has brought us closer to the truth, so I thank you nonetheless."

He pondered what truths Umbra could want until he landed on that miserable secret he had carried from Verde Valis. It couldn't be the bounty, because even if Umbra was a Planitr, he probably made several million a night. Actually, he was the only person Dezi knew who had insight into earning that type of money. It felt silly now, keeping this secret from the one person most qualified to help him.

"I think it's time I tell you about this scar."

"Truly?" Umbra's expression brightened. "Someone is looking to secure a historic tip tonight."

"No, this is serious." Dezi laid his hand on the table, presenting his pink scar face up. "I got this in an industrial accident, which my employer framed me for. The truth is, I'm not just a bond skipper. I have a bounty."

If Umbra was familiar with the story, his placid expression didn't offer any tells. "I had my suspicions. May I ask how much and to whom?"

"Two million." Dezi swallowed. "If I tell you who owns the debt, and it's your bloodline, what will you do?"

"Punish you, of course." He feigned a fanged snarl. "No, my family would not expect such an outrageous sum from a mortal—we'd never recover it—but if I am wrong, I promise to personally negotiate a settlement. With any luck, we can have this whole thing written off."

Dezi grabbed onto that spark of hope before he lost his nerve and said, "It's to the Planitrs."

"The Planitrs." Umbra's tone lost every ounce of emotion, yet treated their name with supreme gravity. "You owe to the largest, cruelest family in the system. One which I hold no sway with."

"Yeah...I've heard they're bad. Do you have any advice?"

"There is no escape from them. The Planitrs will stop at nothing to extract every cent of that debt solely on principle." Umbra drew his nail in small circles, forming a ring of sawdust as he scored the countertop. "After working you to death and selling off your flesh, they'll seek a court injunction to take possession of your genetic IP. Future clones will pay off the bulk of what you owe."

"C-clones?"

"You may find it disquieting, but donors from my culture are genetically curated for their role. Catalogs such as Planitr's scout out and edit genomes, and when a patron signs the resulting bond, their genetic IP holder receives a royalty. Planitr would make a handsome profit if your character proved popular." Umbra casually examined his bottle's label, sucking what blood that lingered off his teeth. "I expect it would."

"I've doomed thousands of future mes to be living bloodbags?" Dezi gripped his head while his stomach churned like a rock tumbler filled with spoiled fruit. "That's horrific."

"Not necessarily. You simply need to buy back your debt."

"Two million dollars? Umbra, *two million dollars*? Do you realize—"

"Or I could purchase it." With the steady gaze of a polished negotiator, Umbra said it simply, and silence permeated the room.

"Why?" Dezi's heart oscillated between hopeful flutters and pounding like he was running for his life. "Of all the hosts you could have chosen, why me?"

"It seems I've been dishonest myself..." Umbra chuckled, the sound low and dark. "Truthfully, the moment I met your eyes, I became enamored. I thought it was a fleeting urge, yet it calls to me in dream. Even your scent of sun-dried silt and the salt of man—it's intoxicating. I have no memory of anything as candidly splendid as you."

Umbra cupped Dezi's face in one hand and traced his features with the other, drawing his finger across Dezi's brow, down the well of his eye, then pausing on his lips and parting his own, longingly. "And yet you are so familiar... I want to know you better."

Desire swelled up through Dezi like a tidal wave, washing away his doubts and inhibitions. For so long, he had let his insecurities get between him and every romantic connection, but Umbra didn't care about his lack of education, or unmanly mannerisms, or even his criminal record. Being with him felt natural, and Dezi had never suffered lust this overwhelming before—this raw need to touch someone, to know what they taste like, to hear their voice in the throes of passion; to experience them at their most vulnerable and be vulnerable with them. He wanted to share all of that with Umbra.

He reached for Umbra's cheek, shut his eyes, and leaned in, but the vampire was gone. Like a cloth carried by a gust, he withdrew towards a case filled with songbirds.

Holding his arms at his elbows, he watched the birds frantically beat their wings against the glass. "This is becoming complex. It may not be wise to continue."

"But there's something between us." Dezi approached his back. "And I want to understand it too."

"Yet you do not understand who or what I am. The image you have built of me is a fiction."

"Then show me the truth." Dezi placed his hands on Umbra's shoulders, met his reflection in the glass, and smiled. "You can trust me. I trusted you."

"I wish I could let you go—God, a better man would—but I am selfish." He turned, swept Dezi up by the small of his back, and brought a sweltering kiss to his neck.

Dezi clutched Umbra's shoulders and gasped, but he had been waiting for this. Since they first met, he had dreamt of the shadow slipping through his window at night and pressing him down in all its shameful excellence. He leaned his head to the side, teetering off balance, but Umbra caught his waist and lifted him off the floor. He wrapped Dezi's legs around himself, making Dezi's head go fuzzy when their hips pressed together. With one hand clutching his ass and the other pulling down the back of his collar, Umbra whisked him to the moonlit bedroom.

Umbra slammed him down on the sheets, knocking the air from his lungs. He took Dezi's necklace in both hands, snapped the chain, and threw it aside. Dezi's breath hastened as Umbra nestled himself between his legs, laying their bodies flush to one another. Digging his claws into the mattress, he took a ragged breath by Dezi's nape, and a shiver of anticipation raced between them.

What came next? They had crossed the first line, and now there was no telling how far they might go, but Dezi needed the clothes between them gone and Umbra's bare skin moving against his. He wanted them to make love like it was their last night alive.

Dezi's lips ached to meet his lover's, but the vampire brought his opened mouth to the curve of Dezi's neck, teasing him with the hard edges of his teeth. Dezi grabbed Umbra's belt and threw his other arm around his back, fiercely tugging him down and rocking up to meet him. Equally as ravenous, Umbra ran his blazing touch up Dezi's sides, untucking his shirt and greedily mapping his ribs. Dezi whimpered and strained beneath him, sending Umbra's nuzzling into a fervor. His stomach pressed down on Dezi's, his hips ground into him, and his fangs grazed his jugular like blades of ice. Immobilized under his uncanny weight, Dezi struggled to breathe, but Umbra's affection was relentless—sharp. Umbra was hurting him.

Dezi turned his head, gasping for air, and jolted when he saw the cat napping beside them—a full-grown jaguar, irritatedly flicking its tail.

"U-Umbra."

"Mmh?" he growled, dragging his tongue up the groove of Dezi's throat.

A hot bead of venom slid down Dezi's neck, and he tried to scramble away. "Umbra, the cat!"

He seized Dezi's wrists, pinning him to the bed. "Love…if you struggle, it may cause an accident."

His limbs locked, and he squeaked, "I won't."

As Umbra leaned back, the starlight that filtered through the gauzy curtains illuminated his spectral skin and blood-red eyes. Devastatingly handsome, he carefully rested Dezi's legs over his thighs and wiped the corners of his mouth. "Ignore him and focus on me."

"I-I can't."

He lifted a tart eyebrow, then dismounted. "Cat, you're distracting my company."

Dezi rolled around and clambered off the massive bed.

When Umbra tugged its collar, the leopard moaned and fell over. Dwarfed by the beast, he wrapped his arms around its chest and lifted it upright. "I know, my darling, but you must go."

It yawned and regarded Dezi with intelligent, gray-green eyes. He averted his gaze. "I can't do this."

He wasn't even sure what *this* was. Was he about to become Umbra's dinner, or were they in the middle of a hookup? How did sex with a vampire even work? Did they need protection? He had never told Umbra he was trans. Could he already tell, or would he be disappointed?

"You can't be serious…" Umbra massaged his forehead.

Dezi covered his face, eyes stinging. He was about to be kicked out; he deserved as much for leading Umbra on. He had to fuck this up, didn't he? Why couldn't he be normal for five minutes?

Umbra snapped his tongue and wobbly walked his heels off the mattress, while his cat lumbered behind like an oversized golden retriever. "No, I was overeager. I should have been more cognizant of your limits, but I lose myself around you."

"You're not upset?"

"Oh, bitterly so." He drew Dezi into a loose embrace. "I would take you tonight if you would have me, but I will wait a decade for you if I must."

"Don't say that." Dezi's hands trembled, pinching the cashmere on Umbra's shoulders. "Not if you don't mean it..."

"It bears repeating: You need not rush into intimacy to impress me." He brought his face so close to Dezi's that their noses touched. "We have the week to become acquainted, if you so choose."

Dezi wanted to press his lips to that angel's relaxed smile, but it took all his willpower to stay on his feet. "You're staying the week for me?"

"We're staying together, love. I'm afraid I neglected to mention that they've preemptively closed the tunnel. But you'll forgive me, won't you?" Umbra gave him a fangy smile and then tugged him into a snuggle.

The jaguar rubbed its cheek against Umbra's thigh and circled around to Dezi's leg, pressing into him with its bulk. Purring like a hydrogen combustor, it flopped onto the floor behind them and pawed at the air.

"You tricked me *again*?" Dezi sighed, not pleased with Umbra, but not ready to let him go either. "Wait, Stellaire has never closed the tunnel before. Did you plan this?"

"You give me too much credit. Off the record, the weather is expected to be quite harsh. I came as soon as my informants warned me for fear the worst might befall you." He traced his finger on Dezi's chest, sneaking it between his shirt buttons. "I understand this is sudden, but rest assured that the winds will not disturb us here."

"It's a flash storm, isn't it?" Dezi pushed free, stepping back. "Umbra, why didn't you warn me? I have to tell Vesta."

"Well, dear, I don't even know who that is." Umbra's hands curled closed. "I expected more gratitude for the news that I have likely saved your life."

"What about the other people who might die? Why wasn't there a weather alert? Never mind. You can explain yourself later, but I need to call Vesta now." He turned, accidentally kicking his toe into the jaguar's soft belly.

It grunted and lashed at him, tearing open his pants leg and grazing his calf. Dezi shouted and fell back. He tried to pull in his leg, but the cat's pupils dilated, and it pinned his ankle under its plush paw, caging him with its massive claws. Umbra swiftly grabbed the beast by its neck fat and yanked it up, freeing Dezi's leg.

Dezi scrambled back, but Umbra commanded, "*Be still*. If you crawl about, he may mistake you for prey."

Crouched with the jaguar's thick neck in his hands, Umbra wetted his lips while Dezi clutched his bleeding leg. He was breathing heavier now, inhaling the scent of Dezi's blood. The jaguar jerked and roared guttural thunder, making Umbra slide two inches along his heels, and the floor creaked as it planted its paws back onto the ground. Holding it by the crystals of its collar, Umbra stood and pointed at the door. "That's enough. Out."

It strained against him, snapping its collar to advance on Dezi. The beast bared its fangs, flexing its corded back muscles as it hunched. Hateful eyes locked onto Dezi, it leaped.

Dezi choked on a shriek, but Umbra snatched the beast out of the air by its scruff. It twisted in his grasp, but he dragged the snarling thing on its side. "You are testing my patience, Cat! *Out!*"

The jaguar dug its claws into the floor, peeling the wood veneer, then turned and whipped them against Umbra's chest. They grated like bone on granite, tearing his sweater to ribbons as he gritted his fangs. Umbra hoisted the beast off its front paws while it thrashed and threatened to pull him down. He wrenched its head back and then drove his fangs into its throat, tearing through its tender fur. The cat released an anguished howl, and its writhing slowed. Umbra's pet bellowed, cried, and moaned until it whimpered for mercy. Then he crushed its spine, and blood poured silently over the broken emerald collar clenched in his fist.

The smell of iron and his own sweat—it was too dense to breathe. Dezi stared at Umbra. Eyes shut, the monster was serene as his heaving lungs steadied and his kneading throat swallowed the torrent of blood.

This was wrong. That couldn't be Umbra, the person Dezi had grown so close to, noisily sucking the blood from a corpse. And yet it was.

Eventually, Umbra tossed the cat. It landed with a sick thud, another broken bottle. With blood smearing his chin and porcelain chest, Umbra stepped over the carcass and sighed. "You couldn't just let me have you? Of course not. And now look at this mess."

Blood streamed from the jaguar's neck, crawling towards Dezi as it pooled into the claw marks in the floor. Umbra threw the jeweled collar, sending it clattering across the wood as he ran his sopping fingers through his hair. He exhaled sharply, then shoved the corner of his enormous bed, and the wood creaked as it skidded out of his path to Dezi.

Dezi bolted up and took a step for the doorway, but a rush of dizziness knocked him back.

In a blur, Umbra caught him, ruddy lips and blood-glazed teeth twisted into a scowl. "Stop resisting me, stupid boy."

"No! Please!" Dezi sobbed and struggled. His static-filled limbs screamed as the vampire pushed them down.

"Calm yourself...I'm clearly...for your blood."

The surge in Dezi's ears drowned it out. He slipped as the monster took him off his feet, and his only remaining sense was the smell of fresh death until that, too, perished.

CHAPTER 16

Towers

When a tremor jiggled her bed, Vesta's finger slipped, dropping her video clip into the wrong spot on her timeline. She turned down the opacity on her pod's window in time to see her dorm neighbors bracing themselves against their bunks, all looking around warily. She swung her door up and knocked on the frosted glass of Dezi's bottom bunk. No response. Even if Ms. Mai had made him work a triple, he should have been home by now.

Another tremor rattled the hanging lamps, so Vesta saved her editing progress, put her laptop aside, and climbed out of her pod. While her floormates hastily dressed themselves, she slowly approached the windows. In the swirling murk outside the dome, ropes of lightning struck the metal frame, sending thunder rumbling across the glass. Dimly illuminated by the uranium-orange glow that the dust-choked sunrise cast over the city, the sharp tips of skyscrapers teetered in the clearance space between their neighbors, making Vesta wish she didn't live a thousand feet off the ground. The streets were empty, without a single auto-taxi or drone.

Mingled with murmurs and shuffling, the sand ceaselessly brushed the outer dome. The sound usually put her to sleep, but she wasn't tired. The dome moaned when the wind hit it at the wrong frequency, sending swells of vibrations up to Vesta's soles. Verde's dome didn't do that, but it hadn't survived the brunt of three century-storms like Chryse had. Still, it wouldn't hurt to check with Nikita. She had been a little girl when the last one hit, and her flat was only a few floors up.

Vesta slipped on her boots, ran up the staircase, and knocked on Nikita's door. She bounced on her toes, waiting until a stronger quake threatened her balance and shattered her patience. She searched the plastic garlic flowers on the door for Nikita's spare fob and broke in.

A muffled alarm coming from down the hall greeted her. She jogged to Nikita's sage-scented bedroom and found her rolling out of bed.

Vesta shouted, "What's with the alarm?"

"Alarm? Alarm!" Nikita pounced on the boxy, retro clock on her nightstand. "Was there a—?"

The room shuddered, rattling Nikita's dreamcatchers and knocking Vesta to the floor. Nikita flew into her closet, pulling out a duffle bag and a rolling oxygen tank.

"What's going on?" Vesta asked.

She looped a paper mask over Vesta's ears and threw a musty coat over her shoulders. "Put these on."

"What? Why?" Vesta grabbed the discarded clock and read the screen. "The weather advisory says to stay put."

"Don't listen to that garble. We need to get downtown—to the Hadron Tower if we can make it."

Vesta sighed; Nikita was going full tin-foil-hat mode again, complete with prepper gear. "You're gonna hurt yourself running around with those rickety knees. Why don't you come back with me to my pod and we wait this out together?"

"You're not climbing into one of those coffins." Nikita grabbed her arm. "All that'll do is make it easier for them to dice you up!"

"What in the blood 'n dust are you talking about, lady?"

"The dust is already here! Where's Dezi? We need to get moving, or we'll see the blood, too." Nikita pulled her to the door.

"Ouch! Calm down, ya moonbat."

The room shook violently, shaking flakes of paint off the ceiling and throwing Nikita's crystals across the floor.

Pale as the moth-wing plaster behind her, she rasped, "A domequake is coming."

"Okay—okay, but I need my phone."

"There's no time!" Nikita tugged at her.

Vesta yanked back. "I ain't leaving without my pants or my phone!"

"You don't understand. You've never been through a shake, but I remember—the sand, the screams—and I'll be damned if I let this one take another soul."

The next tremor shook Vesta's resolve, but she glared Nikita down. "Then I need my phone to find Dezi."

Nikita let her go. "You swear to me—swear on your mama's memory that you'll get to the Hadron Tower."

"Fine. I swear I'll go to the damn tower."

"And bring Dezi." Oxygen tank clanging behind her, Nikita wobbled down the hallway without shutting her front door.

Vesta checked the alarm's screen again. *Weather advisory: strong winds. Shelter in place until 11 A.M.*

Bracing against the tremors, she took the stairs to her pod, pulled on some jeans, and tried to call Dezi. If he wasn't home, he had to be at Stellaire—he didn't go anywhere else—but it had been twenty-four hours since she'd last seen him. Could he have fallen asleep in the locker room? That had to be it. He was safely snoozing away at Stellaire. Otherwise, he would have picked up the phone by her fifth call.

Everyone who hadn't left the dorm was locked in their pods. That was probably the safest place to be, because the rumblings were growing and Vesta was likely to hurt herself descending the stairs. Too bad leaky Nikita had forced her to swear on her mother's memory. She didn't have a lick of memory about any mother, but when Nikita had demanded that promise, stormglow eyes with strawberry eyelashes flickered in Vesta's mind. She'd sworn on Mithra's memory, and she'd crack her head on this marsdamned staircase before disrespecting that.

The smell of powdered vitamins and battery acid hit her nose holes when she made it onto the smoggy sidewalks. Coughing and sputtering, the locals were all heading north.

"Where y'all going?" Vesta shouted.

"The Disk. You best get out too," said a man struggling forward with his cane.

"Did the dome crack?" Vesta waved her hand, trying to disperse the acrid fog in her face.

The ground trembled, swelling to a massive quake that rattled the windows in their frames. Warbling loudly, one cracked free and plummeted to the sidewalk. Vesta dashed at the old man, covering his face with her arms, and exploding glass grazed her calves as she fell with him. Street lights bounced against the sidewalks, jumping out of their sockets, while powder lifted off the chalky buildings. They'd already be dead if the dome had cracked; this was the dust they were living in.

After Vesta helped the old man up, she sprinted east, running past families pulling suitcases and baby strollers through the plumes of sand. People realizing the threat too late crowded doorways and flopped onto the packed sidewalks. With her skirt billowing before her socks, a woman ten stories up tossed her weighted boots off her balcony, climbed over the rail, and leaped.

Vesta didn't watch her land. She shoved against the flow of bodies to break onto the road. The ground undulated under her feet as the asphalt pulled apart like damp sand, forcing her to leap between sinkholes. She heard voices wailing in those pits, saw bodies hanging from bent pipes, but fought her way to where three-hundred-year-old buildings stood. The Hadron Tower pierced the sky like a black beacon, ruddy rings of clouds circling its dome-kissing peak.

Squealing and crunching—deep fissures formed in the bases of the powdery buildings on each side of the street. One twisted a quarter turn when its first floor crumpled into itself, squashing its doors to slits. The building sat wrong and jiggled violently in the next tremor, office furniture bouncing and crashing out its windows as it teetered. A few blocks from the Hadron Tower, a stocky woman struggled with her oxygen tank—and in her other hand was the wrist of an eight-year-old boy clasping the mask to his face, his calf jammed between two stones.

Vesta waved her arms. "Nikita! Run! You have to run!"

She couldn't hear her own voice over the crack and slide of the collapsing building. It cast a block-wide shadow as it slid forward on the rubble of its lower floors, leaning over the street. Like a titan's foot, it fell slowly, giving Vesta a split-second choice: turn back or outrun it. She hunched down and sprinted for all her worth, vaulting over toppled billboards and sparking power lines. Just a little further—she could make it. The shadow blocked the purple glow of the Hadron Tower, and the crooked street lamps blinked out. It was dark, but a flash of lightning lit the building's silhouette in crimson.

Not a breath after she heard it, she felt the ending boom. Stinging gravel pelted her back as the ground buckled and threw her. She landed on a jagged pile of stone, and a sudden ceiling pressed her down to her belly. Brick thunder mingled with countless shrieks and slow, wet sounds as the building's carcass settled onto them. Sand under her fingernails, Vesta forced her eyes open through the scorching, smothering darkness in search of life.

"Nikita!" she cried, but no one called back. The dust caking her face sopped up her tears as she scrabbled and screamed until her voice went hoarse. She had been so close, but now there were stone walls wherever she reached out, all black as coal dust.

She was going to die here, like a pill bug under a boot. Panic took over, and she beat on the stone until her hands turned sticky with blood, but a section of the cheap composite crumbled beneath her fists, forming an opening. Vesta forced her way through the gap, tumbling into another dark crevice. She had to get to the Hadron Tower. She had to find that violet star in the dark.

A breeze caressed her cheek, calling her towards a pinhole of light, and she scrambled to it. She clawed at it, tearing away chunks of warped plastic and polyglass until she had dug out a ragged window to the street. She slid through it, falling down the rubble onto the pavement. The dryfog cast the lamp lights and every surface a blood-soaked hue, but she stood at the capitol building. Chunks of its limestone columns had dropped and shattered, revealing rows of rubber-padded beams underneath. Beside it groaned the dark alloy of the Hadron Tower, swaying like a graceful stalk.

She sprinted to the doors and shook the handles, but past the mirrored glass, men in suits pulled against her. Vesta beat on the door and screamed, choking on the frostbitten grit. She screamed for her dreams, to see Dezi again, to hug Pa goodbye—howled like an animal at their moon-wide stares.

They were killing her the same way they had Mithra, four inches from fresh air.

A woman lurking behind the men put her elegant hands on their shoulders, then threw them aside like straw dolls. Vesta slammed into the door, landed on the granite, and gasped succulent air. Dry heaving, she rolled onto her back and stared up at her radiant savior. The gorgeous woman's magenta eyes fell onto her for a single, unreadable blink, then she shut and locked the door.

One of the door closers stumbled to his feet, dusting off his ill-fitting brown suit. "We can't keep letting people in. We don't know how long we'll be trapped!"

"What type of savage would refuse an innocent mortal? Particularly one with such tenacity." The woman knelt to stick a sticker on Vesta's chest, sporting a cartoonishly sweet smile that was somehow emptier than the look she'd given earlier. "Here is your visitor's pass, young one."

When she rose to wipe her hands in a handkerchief, her downy feather earrings tickled the brutal twelve-point scar on her neck. The perennial was petite as a fairy, with a curly blonde bob, skin that glistened like a geode, and a shoulderless dress covered in mirrored disks. From her wrist hung a peculiar charm bracelet ornamented with enamel cakes, puppies, and other girlish things.

Vesta rubbed her eyes, but the young woman nudged her with the toe of her jelly plastic heels. "Don't do that, dear. You'll put sand in them. Can we get some refreshments for the visitors? And someone get the mobile vacs for this dust."

She strutted off, pointing and ordering her staff. Another woman handed Vesta a miniature bottle of water and a bag of low-calorie cookies. One sleeve of her gray blazer was cut short to display a scar on her wrist that matched the sparkly woman's, identifying her as a mortal bound in service to their perennial family.

Vesta curled up against the wall next to baristas, cleaning staff, and secretaries. On the furniture at the other end of the room sat bankers or politicians—she wasn't sure—but they outnumbered the mortals five to one. Two crowds of dust-covered faces, and Nikita's wasn't in either. Vesta gripped her hair, fighting the urge to scream and tear her scalp to bits. What kind of nightmare was this, and why couldn't she wake up? She hated herself for not leaving the second Nikita had warned her. She wanted to blame that poor child for killing Nikita, but she had taken advantage of her kindness too. Saving Vesta had cost Nikita her life.

And suddenly, her emotions withered like petals tossed out on the Martian surface. A dull prickle moved over her skin at the realization of how close she'd come to death. If she had spent one more second helping that old man, that would have been it. Like a toss of the dice, the world just picked who to kill and who to spare.

And Dezi—oh, Dezi—she couldn't lose him too, but there was nothing she could do for him or anyone. She stared at her phone, watching the no-service icon blink in the corner of the screen.

·—⊙—·

The room shook and the lights flickered for hours, but when the quakes finally quieted, the dust only got thicker, sinking from skyscrapers and accumulating in a carpet of brown snow. Each time the debris shifted, it sent up a cloud of the toxic stuff, but inside the Hadron Tower, sweeper drones buzzed up and down the glittering obsidian floors. With its brushed steel beams and indigo LEDs, the lobby was as slick as a luxury cruise shuttle, and probably equipped with just as much emergency oxygen. It was no surprise people had run here for shelter, but they couldn't stay forever. The question was, where would they go? Even if the inner domes weren't destroyed, Vesta couldn't afford rent in Diskos. She'd have to sort out her long-term plans later, because her top priority was finding Dezi, even if all she could do was wait.

Vesta laid her head on her knees and watched the Hadron employees skim up and down the suspended staircase at the far end of the room. The grand feature was grotto-like, with water trickling down the back wall and a gigantic angel statue poised in the middle. The employees didn't smile, but they weren't sweating like their visitors. While the mortals huddling on the floor wept quietly, the perennials hogging the furniture hastily whispered. No one said it out loud, but it was on all their minds; the Hadron employees had offered food and water, but not a drop of blood, real or synthetic.

A perennial with wooden beads and golden wires adorning her hair stood. "Excuse me, may I have everyone's attention?"

The mortals in the room shifted, and the other perennials raised their heads. Several lay back with their eyes closed, sweaty but meditative, while others wrung their hands, their eyes darting between the Hadron employees and Vesta's crowd.

The woman cleared her throat. "I know this has been difficult, especially for our mortal citizens, but we need to address a looming medical issue among the immortals in the room. It's been six hours since we were trapped here, and some of my colleagues haven't taken their medication since last night. For elders, the withdrawal symptoms of missed doses can come on rapidly, and they are fatal."

A heavy silence fell over the room. She was talking about blood—human blood.

Fangless, the perennial woman bit her lip and widened her brown eyes. "If this goes on much longer, we'll need volunteers."

A murmur spread across Vesta's side of the room, and she didn't know whether to laugh or scowl.

She shouted, "Nobody gives their blood away! We sell it!"

The murmur jumped to the perennial's side, gathering in a corner of skeletal-looking suits.

"Blood has to be drawn and tested by an approved distributor to be sold," Ms. Fangless said. "Any human who sold their blood here could get three years in prison, and the immortal who bought it would be unelectable to their constituents. The one loophole is consensual, indirect donations."

A repairman behind Vesta stood. "You've gone senile if you think any of us would put our necks out for you. You campaigned on banning those composite construction drones, and I voted for you, but you let them make those buildings out of sand!" He spat on the floor. "That's the only fluid you're gonna see out of me."

Ms. Fangless cringed, but some of the uppity immortals stood like he had slapped them with a white glove.

"Young one, this may be your first storm, but it isn't ours." A smooth-skinned perennial wearing a satin suit rolled his eyes. "You get what you pay for, and you weren't willing to pay rent in a proper neighborhood."

"Keep smiling. Those wrinkles will set in real nice." The repairman sneered.

"My appetite would get the better of me far before then." Mr. Satin drew a fine claw mark on the lid of a steel trash can, then dented the lid by forcing his palm in. "This will be less painful for us all if you offer a volunteer."

Humans around Vesta gasped and lost color, but others balled their fists and stood with the repairman.

"If you want my blood, you'll have to suck it out of my dead body!" a teen in a maroon apron shouted, his voice cracking. "But marsdammit, I won't make it easy for you!"

Mr. Satin's charming lips curled, and his dead eyes twinkled. "Delicious; now you've gone and piqued my appetite." He glanced at the less-smooth ghouls around him and then nodded toward the kid.

From the feet of the angel statue, the Hadron woman's voice rang through the hall. "Can you not be trusted to wait like civilized vampires?"

"Madame Ambrose." Mr. Satin stood, offering a small bow.

"Ambrose is my father's name. I am Ms. Luminair to you, and the answer is no." She waved as if brushing away an insect. "The Hierarch would cut out my teeth if I let you consume a human in our lobby."

"There are elders here degrading before your eyes." Mr. Satin smiled very hard, displaying two long and narrow fangs. "If you won't allow these humans to uphold their civic duty to sustain us, then you can at least open your reserve to us."

"I'm afraid that isn't possible. Our stockpile is as depleted as the other blood stores across the city."

"But you Ambroses have always preferred your blood fresh…" He eyed the mortal Hadron employees watching the dispute from the staircase. "Do you intend to keep these survivors for yourself? To bleed them until the storm passes? I will not sit idly by, slowly starving until I am too weak to defend my interests. I demand my share now."

"How dare you?" Ms. Luminair touched her collar. "You should be grateful I even allowed you Martian perennials into the building. You are a useful pawn, Santiago, but voice these vulgar demands again, and I will exsanguinate you myself."

Mr. Satin scowled, but his scab-red eyes widened, stressing the dark circles around them. "But I and my caucus won't be much use to you dead, will we?"

"No, but I can always buy out your replacements. If you get too thirsty, why don't you go outside and try some chilled blood? I am told the crunch of a corpse is considered a delicacy on Uranus." Ms. Luminair spread her out-turned hands to the mortals, radiating saintly light with her safranal-gold hair and snow-shimmering skin. "Do not fear, sweet children; love for humankind is an Ambrose founding tenant. We must be patient for a while longer, but have faith that the Hierarch has not forgotten us."

The building shuddered, knocking Ms. Luminair from her feet and swaying the model ships that hung from the ceiling. The lights buzzed and flared brightly. Then, with a pop, they all zapped off.

"Stay calm, everyone. This was expected. Our backup generators will start momentarily," Ms. Luminair said.

Snappy shoes dashed towards them, then a blood-curdling shriek rang out. Machinery below the floor hummed to life, and blue lights dotted around the walls flickered on, one after another, illuminating a slick, black pool forming near Vesta's feet. The aproned boy gasped like a dying fish, bleeding everywhere as Mr. Satin chewed on his throat. Thin as a jackal and hunched over his prey, the crusty chairman sucked great gulps of blood from the boy's opened windpipe.

"You animal!" Ms. Luminair roared. She rushed him like a silver arrow and then lifted him from the ground by his neck, but he clung to the boy with his teeth and claws.

Vesta was locked into place, staring at the bloody goddess as she raised two men in one hand.

Ms. Luminair shouted, "Protect the humans at all costs!"

Hadron employees, both immortals and bonded humans, dashed down the stairs, positioning themselves between the clusters of humans and foreign perennials. Most of the outsiders looked horrified, and many watched on mutely, but a few prowled around the furniture, weaving between their peers, hunting for stragglers.

Ms. Luminair jammed her other hand into Mr. Satin's mouth, pulling his lower jaw with a sickening crack. He released a tongue-less howl, dropping the dying boy into a pool of his own blood, then lashed desperately at Ms. Luminair. He tore off her jingly bracelet, and it skidded across the floor, disappearing into a huddle of children. Her eyes widened, and she dropped the fiend. She didn't seem to notice when he dragged away his kill, still trying to slurp up blood with his broken jaw.

Ms. Luminair dived into the crowd of children, sending them scattering in all directions. "My memento! Someone help me find it."

"No one move!" an Ambrose with silver hair at his temples bellowed, and the room gave him their attention. He ran to Ms. Luminair's side, followed by a pair of bonded humans. "Find the memento, quickly."

And that distraction was the opening the hunting perennials had been waiting for. They leaped at their prey, grabbing who they could and whisking them away while the outnumbered employees struggled to fend them off.

With all the running and screaming, Vesta couldn't tell who was trying to grab her or shove her out of their way. Mind going wild, she abandoned the herd and snuck along the shadowy wall like a rat. There was safety in numbers, but there were elevators behind the stairs. Vesta dashed to the nearest one and slammed on the buttons, but the damn things had ID scanners. She scrambled behind the angel statue and crouched in its shadow, helpless to save anyone—helpless to save herself.

"I'm sorry, Daddy. I'll do better, I promise..." Cowering like a battered child, Ms. Luminair collapsed to her knees as her servants searched around her. Vesta had seen that glassy look in her eyes on another immortal once before: the monster from the train station had worn it after he'd bitten her, when he'd started speaking to people who weren't there.

In the kicking, running riot, a glittery chain slid across the open floor—the charm bracelet. It was too dark to know what waited for her past the shelter of the stairs, but Vesta ran for it. Whatever a memento was, it had to be valuable enough to buy her safety.

Sneakers squeaking on the tile, she grabbed the bracelet, turned hard, and dashed to Ms. Luminair.

"I got it—I got it for you!" she shouted.

The heiress instantly rose to meet her and grasped it, holding it to her breast. "Oh, thank the Lord."

"Let's go. Get her to the elevators." The gray-haired guard pushed Ms. Luminair forward, and her human servants cleared the way ahead of them.

"Hey—hey! What about me?" Vesta followed them, shoving who she had to, desperate not to lose sight of them.

Ms. Luminair turned back and grabbed Vesta's arm. "This one comes with me."

"As you wish, Sire." The guard scanned his wrist at the elevator and waved them in. "Regarding the situation—"

"Prioritize the weak and bring them to the executive offices. I'll try to contact Father." Ms. Luminair touched one of her human servants on the cheek, lingering on her. "If they target our bonds, withdraw."

"Yes, my lady." The guard bowed, and the doors slid shut.

Ms. Luminair suddenly pulled Vesta into a crushing hug. "Oh, thank you, you tenacious thing. This memento holds my most treasured memories, and I couldn't imagine losing them."

"You're welcome." Vesta wheezed, half-terrified she might be suffocated, but also half-terrified she might offend the blood-drinking princess.

"Oop." She released Vesta. "I'm not supposed to touch you. I do hope you'll forgive me for that and...all of this." She gazed out the elevator's glass doors down to the bloodbath below. "Father is going to kill me... No one warned me it would be like this."

Vesta touched her shoulder and hoarsely said, "It wasn't your fault."

Her bottom lip wobbled, but she returned a pained smile. "I'm afraid it is. I have failed his expectations, and I have failed all of you."

Vesta looked at her feet, unsure of the right words to use with someone so important. "Are you going to keep us here?" She was too fearful to voice her real question: *Are you going to eat us?*

"Next, I call on my allies in the city. They will send rotorcraft to the entry port at the peak of the tower, which we can use to evacuate you all to the nearest emergency shelter."

"How long will that take? And when will we get cell signal? There's someone I need to find."

"As soon as I have this situation under control, I will do everything in my power to reunite you with them. You have my word." The elevator bell rang, and Ms. Luminair stepped out. "Until then, you are not to leave my sight."

Vesta followed behind, sniffling as her last bits of energy sputtered out. Sick and numb and drained, a loud noise would be enough to shatter her. "Thank you. You didn't have to save me, but I'll never forget it."

Ms. Luminair frowned. "But I did. A proper vampire pays her debts, and she could never leave a young woman like you behind."

"Like me?"

She clasped Vesta's hands and met her with her beautiful, magenta eyes. "I see the spark of an immortal soul in you. If you can survive this, you were made to be a vampiress."

"How can you say that?" Two tears ran down Vesta's cheeks. "I'm a roach. I made it 'cause the other roaches were slower."

"I was a girl once, too, and I would have been blessed to show half the courage you did." She wiped Vesta's cheek. "Save your tears, child. There is more to come, and you will need strength to face it."

Chapter 17

Pets

Dezi woke with a start, jerking upright in the center of an XXL-king bed, alone. He pushed the comforter off, confirming he still had his uniform on, when a sharp pain shot up his leg.

There was a long scratch on his calf, wrapped in a clear, sensor-embedded medical film, but despite how badly it stung, the wound was nearly healed. His hands slowly traced up his neck, and although he found no punctures, Umbra's greedy kisses had left hairline cuts all across his skin. They, too, were sticky from some type of minty ointment.

The sun hung high in the sky, choked by clouds. It cast the bedsheets crimson, but there wasn't a drop of blood anywhere, not even in the claw marks on the floor. It was as if someone had tried to erase all evidence of what had happened last night, but the image of Umbra slaughtering and devouring his pet was burned into Dezi's memory. A thousand questions roared through his mind, but he had to get out of here before Umbra noticed he was awake. If the vampire caught him, he might never let him leave.

Dezi pulled on his boots and crept out of the bedroom. In the living area, the windows lining the walls displayed an emulation of white beaches and ebbing turquoise waves. Umbra sat at the bar facing them, humming along to the quiet jazz that played from hidden speakers. In his feathery lace and sapphire rings, he clicked away at his keyboard, and his skin was so vivacious that he nearly looked human. Dezi only managed to sneak two steps into the room before Umbra turned his head. "Did you sleep well, love?"

"Y-yes." Dezi straightened his posture, acutely aware that he couldn't outrun Umbra to the exit. Umbra could tear him apart like a tea biscuit if he wanted to.

Umbra shut his laptop and clicked his tongue. "I know things got a little messy last night, but I enjoyed our time together nonetheless. Come, sit with me."

"A little messy?" Dezi would have laughed if the situation weren't so morbid. "You ripped his throat open with your teeth."

Umbra frowned. "Cat struck you. I would have preferred not to finish him all in one go, but I'm sure you are aware he was bred to be fed upon."

Dezi suppressed a shudder. "Fine. You bought him, so I guess you can do what you want with him, but I-I'd like to be dismissed."

Umbra chuckled, tracing a painted nail over his bottom lip. "I'm afraid it's too late for that."

"The storm—" Dezi turned to the nearest window, but he couldn't see through its tropical illusion. "Has it passed yet?"

Umbra waved his hand at the depth screens, and the projections dissolved to reveal the hellish Martian landscape. The soft dunes from the night before were scraped down to ruddy crags, and the wind whipped back and forth across the glass.

"They're still assessing the damages, but it was significantly worse than forecasted. We may be trapped for longer than I anticipated." He switched a window pane to a news broadcast by gesturing at it.

It displayed a map of the city with the southern districts—Southport, Clearair, and Old Chryse—highlighted in red. The screens flickered between aerial footage of trains brushed aside by dunes, shipping-container houses buried in sand, and endless scenes of collapsed buildings, all dead still except for the occasional four-legged drone leaving tracks in the blanket of dust in a futile search for survivors.

Dezi whimpered a meaningless sound and steadied himself on the wall. It was all gone. Wiped away. His home was ash, his community a memory, and Vesta—she was in there! Dezi fumbled his phone out.

"The sand is hindering cellular signals, so you won't have a connection to the main cluster for a while." Umbra picked at the blood-colored tips of his manicure. "You have no choice but to stay here with me. Would you like me to order you something from the café? You look like you could use a coffee, or a stiff drink."

"I don't need fucking coffee!" Dezi shouted. "I have to find Vesta. She's in Old Chryse."

Without a hint of warmth, Umbra looked down at him. "Then she is dead. Your best course of action now is to split open a vein and beg my forgiveness that I spare you her fate."

"You want me to abandon her to what—keep you entertained? Are you out of your mind?"

"Watch your tone with me, mortal. Do you think that because I tolerated your earlier impudence, you had no limit? Your brazenness amused me, but it has since lost its charm." Radiating a cold fury, Umbra strode toward him. "You are here, alive, because you serve me, and if you intend to have my continued support, you will recognize your station."

Dezi's instincts begged him to flee, but the suffocating weight of Umbra's presence pinned him where he stood. He had let himself forget the galaxy of differences between them, but now there was no denying they did not have the relationship he thought they had. Dezi was simply one of the many employees Umbra paid to wait on him hand and foot—one who had grown too accustomed to special treatment.

"T-then I want my favor," Dezi said. "My favor for my service last night."

Umbra's eyes narrowed. "And what favor do you think you have earned?"

"A ride to Chryse."

"To that graveyard? If I knew you'd ask this, I would have let Cat have you and lay with him instead! What does it matter if it all ends the same? Why did I come to this God-forsaken planet if you intend to throw your life away now?" Umbra flexed his clawed hand, and too much muscle moved beneath his skin.

Because we were friends was the pathetic answer that came to mind, but it was clear Dezi was a toy to Umbra; an exotic piece of meat, now rancid. Useless, he was powerless to save Vesta, yet too weak to accept a world without her. He squeezed his eyes shut, biting back tears, but they broke through anyway. "Please, she's my family."

"Family, he says..." Umbra knit his brows and then took a strenuous breath. "I do this on the condition that you return to me. Weigh what the city holds for you against what I offer and see if you don't come pleading for my grace."

Dezi had no intention of becoming Cat's replacement, but this agreement brought him closer to Vesta, so he nodded.

"You will regret this. You cannot fathom what torment waits for you outside these walls." Umbra returned to the bar and quietly called the front desk to reserve a rotorcraft for Dezi. "You go alone. Wait for my pilot in the lobby."

"Thank you." Dezi backed away.

"Call Mai when you realize your mistake." Umbra pointed two fingers at the door, and the bolt unlocked. "I absolutely forbid you from dying before then."

Dezi sprinted to the lobby, passing streams of disheveled guests fighting to get to the front desk. They bickered with the staff, demanding rooms be made available even though the resort was fully booked. Others shouted names, frantically asking if anyone had seen their loved ones.

"Dezi? Is there a Dezi?" asked a man in a navy jumpsuit and nylon body harness.

"Here! I'm here." Dezi ran to him.

The pilot checked his phone. "I got it here that you want me to take you *into* Chryse?"

"Yes, Old Chryse."

"That's not going to happen. It's a disaster zone in there."

"You're paid to fly, aren't you? Follow your damn orders." Dezi's tone bellowed with authority he didn't actually possess, but after facing down Umbra, there was no way he'd let a mortal man get between him and Vesta.

"Alright, alright. But the best I can do is get you in through the top of the Hadron Tower. That was going to be my second stop after dropping you off anyway. You're sure you want to leave, though?" The pilot looked him up and down. "They might not let you back in."

"Dead sure."

The pilot led Dezi to the landing pads crowded with smoking aircraft. Dezi climbed into Umbra's twelve-seater rotorcraft, and his pilot plowed through the burgundy clouds, using his radar and blind skill to bring them over Chryse's bubbles. The pilot pulled up, slowing them, as they reached the top-loading landing pads on the crown of Old Chryse's dome. He lowered them down one of the shafts, and with a final jostle, they came to rest inside the tip of the Hadron Tower.

As the overhead airlock shut and the re-pressurizing system ran, the pilot took a bright-blue satchel from under his feet and offered it to Dezi. "My employer told me to give you one of these."

It was another gift from Umbra, but Dezi wasn't childish enough to reject it at a time like this. He took the emergency crash kit and unzipped it to find a particle mask, a pint of water, a mylar blanket, and three nutrient bars. He donned the thin-as-silk mask and clicked the button on the side. Its straps tightened and its fans whirred, taking the acrid bite from the air.

When the entry doors slid open, a woman in a silver gown walked in, followed closely by a lanky girl. Oversized coat smeared with ash, skinny legs wrapped in bandages, detritus clinging to her poof of tangerine hair—Dezi threw the rotorcraft door open and barreled into her.

"Vesta!"

"Dezi!" She leaped into his arms, letting him swing her around in a hug. He crushed her against his chest and buried his face against the top of her head, laughing and crying and cursing himself for ever letting her out of his sight. Family hardly described what she meant to him. He loved this girl with his whole heart.

"Excuse me." The dazzling woman strode up. "Unhand her this instant. Driver, where did this filthy human come from? You're supposed to be taking them to the shelter, not bringing them here."

"It's alright, Ms. Luminair." Grinning, Vesta let Dezi go. "This is the boy I told you about."

"Well, that makes keeping my promise all the simpler. Now that you have been reunited, have you put any thought into where you will go next, my dear?" Ms. Luminair watched them like they were a pair of canaries ready to have their wings clipped, smiling at Vesta the same way Umbra had at Dezi. Next, she would offer to make Vesta her blood pet.

"We're going to the emergency shelter. We have more people to look for." Dezi took Vesta under his arm and stared Ms. Luminair in the face. He didn't flinch when her unnatural eyes darted to him.

She pursed her lips, raising a brow at the mortal who dared address her out of turn. "Shame. I hope our paths meet again, tenacious girl."

"I'll never forget you." Vesta waved as Dezi ushered her into the rotorcraft. She lowered herself into a seat. "You're gonna have to tell me how the heck you got here so quick."

"It's a long story." Dezi buckled her in, then checked the bruises on her knees. "How badly are you hurt? Was Nikita with you?"

"I'm okay, but the dorm's gone..." Vesta's eyes glazed, sinking to her lap. "Nikita's dead."

The news slammed into Dezi's chest, tightening around his heart like a steel wire. "How?"

"I saw it. Fell on her like she was nothing." Wracked with sobs, Vesta's voice cracked. "Thousands of people—human people. They were like bricks, Dez, falling from the sky. Shattering. I crawled over 'em, and I didn't even think about it."

He wrapped his arms around her. "It's over now. I have you."

She pressed her face into his chest and wailed, but she was so hoarse that her cry was as faint as a wheeze. Dezi took his mask off, looped it around her ears, and wiped the tears from her honey-gold eyes. She was always so unstoppable, always a survivor. Only Vesta could make it through a disaster like this, but now Dezi had to be strong for her too.

The rotorcraft flew out of the Hadron Tower before wrapping back around to the spaceport, where an impromptu emergency checkpoint had been set up on some spare runway normally used for loading private shuttles. With the weather as it was, none of the small ships were likely to be flying anytime soon. Dezi and Vesta were not the first refugees to arrive, and the concrete was already covered in pop-up tents and families huddling under blankets. Dezi registered at the front desk and found Vesta a shady spot to rest for a few hours. The charity service running the shelter couldn't offer much, but the supplies Umbra had provided would be enough to keep them going until the end of the day. Where they would spend the night was still in limbo.

Dezi offered Vesta their last sip of water, but she shot up, nearly knocking it out of his hand to hold her shattered phone in the air. "I'm getting signal."

Dezi jerked out his phone and hastily opened a home-share app.

Vesta huddled back down with him. "Can you get in? Mine's frozen."

Dezi jammed his thumb on the screen, but the app kept spitting out errors. "The servers are crashing. Everybody is probably trying to get on at the same time."

Vesta sighed and pulled their crinkly silver blanket up to her chin. "Half the rentals on there don't exist no more, so we'd have a hell of a time finding a place to stay."

He kept refreshing the app. "I know, but I need to get in before everything is booked."

"Elay messaged me. Said he'd let us sleep on his couch."

"He's a human trafficker. It wouldn't be safe." Dezi dropped his phone on the pavement and then pounded his palms on his forehead. "Damn it—if Umbra had warned me, I could have booked something earlier."

"You mean your guest? Do you think he'd help us? Maybe if we called the front desk—"

"I am not calling him. We can't stay with a marsdamned vampire."

Vesta blinked her worn-out eyes. "Last time I checked, you were pretty smitten with him... Did something happen between you two?"

Dezi dropped his head into his hands, struggling with how to explain last night without sounding like a complete idiot. He didn't even know how he was supposed to feel about Umbra. Had all those tender moments they shared been an act, or was Dezi blowing this out of proportion? It wasn't like Umbra had hurt an actual human, and Dezi was no vegetarian himself, but the cruelty of it...all his lies and secrets. In this moment, with Dezi's heart aching like it did, he never wanted to see Umbra again.

"Dez?" Vesta touched his knee.

He raised his head. "I don't want to talk about it."

She wrinkled her speckled nose. "But you gotta tell me. Did he send you to get me? Can he get us back into Stellaire?"

"He probably wouldn't let you come with me, not unless you agreed to let him drink from you. And that's assuming he likes how you taste." Dezi ground some grit under his boot. "He's apparently pretty picky."

Vesta looked out across the roofless, wall-less, bedless shelter. "This place won't be safe after sundown. If our choice is between a clean eater and the messy ones out there, it's pretty clear what the grown-up option is."

Heat flashed in Dezi's stomach, racing up to his face. "You cannot be suggesting that we let him use us as his personal blood bags."

Haggard and hollow-eyed, Vesta nodded. "You haven't seen what I have, Dez. I'd do just about anything to never see it again."

"If you want to sell your neck to him, try your luck calling Mai, but I'm no blood whore."

Her eyes widened. "Did you just call me a whore?"

He winced. "Mars, no—I didn't mean it like that. I-I got too emotional."

"You know what? If tryin' to keep us safe makes me a whore, then color me red 'cause I'd sell any organ they'd take before I let you go through what happened in that tower. Does that make me a bad person to you?" Tears streamed down her face, drawing channels in the dust on her cheeks. "You don't even know what I did to get you here. You don't even know!"

"Ves—"

"I don't want to hear it!" She snatched her phone off the pavement and stood. "If you got too much ego to even tell me what happened with your VIP, then we're going to Elay's."

He hated it, but she was right; their choice was between Elay, Umbra, or the freezing pavement, and Dezi wasn't eager to spend a night in the open. He gathered their things and stood. "I'm sorry. Let's go."

The walk to Eastdome was long and cold, and when Dezi asked Vesta about what she had been through—why she was hurting so much—she wouldn't say a word.

Vesta hadn't imagined that Elay lived in a neighborhood with crunchy, green turf and a plastic playhouse outside. Eastdome was Chryse's version of a suburb, but with blocky apartment buildings, since the only Martians with their own yards were billionaires. The upper floors of the tan buildings had deep cracks in their facings, but Elay's home was tucked up next to the utility rooms in the basement. Vesta and Dezi took the stairs down to his flat, and she knocked on the door.

Elay opened it, his massive centipede tattoo crawling out from under his tank top and wrapping down his arm. "Glad you made it, Ves, but...didn't realize you two were a package deal."

Vesta worked up her best doe eyes and touched his arm. "You gotta let us stay, at least until we can get our feet under us. Are you really gonna turn a couple of homeless youngsters back onto the street?"

He shrugged her off. "I don't know this kid, and I can't afford an extra set of lungs sucking up my air."

"I'll pay rent," Dezi said.

Elay raised his chin. "Two thousand bucks a day will get you a spot on the floor."

"T-two thousand?" Dezi stammered. He quickly composed himself, lips moving subtly as he worked out mental calculations that probably involved how fast this deal would drain the college fund he had been saving. "The best I can do is seven hundred. I'll need something left over for when the price of food and water spikes."

Elay crossed his arms, frowning with—was that a glimmer of respect? "We'll make it a thousand. You gonna be cool? This house has got rules, and I set 'em."

"I'll be cool."

"I'ght, we got room for you." Elay rubbed Dezi's hair until it looked like a jerboa's nest and let them in.

His flat didn't have windows, but it was kitted out with RGB speakers, a huge depth screen, and three different game consoles. In the trash-scattered kitchen, a pair of scantily clad women wearing aprons worked some type of DIY pharmaceutical project, with one chopping up pills on a cutting board and the other stirring pans full of neon syrups. Two men with their shaved heads covered in insect tattoos watched the Cassini Division 15000 from the synth-leather couches. They pumped their chunky fists when a race ship trying to dodge ice chunks swerved too far and tumbled into the debris field of Saturn's rings.

"Welcome to my castle." Elay coughed and waved at a few women weeping in the back hallway. "You already met my guys when we got you off the Magna, but London and some of the other girls who sling for me are crashing here, too."

London, half of her braids singed short, stopped comforting another dancer to stand behind Elay.

"Hey, London." Vesta smiled weakly. "You alright?"

She kept her head down but nodded.

"Sleep anywhere you want, but don't touch the faucets. For water—" A sharp knock on the door cut Elay's introductions short, and he turned for it, rolling his eyes. "Exactly what I need—more beggars."

"I ain't donating, so you can—" He yanked it open and then shut his mouth real quick.

A well-dressed, strikingly tall man waited in the doorway, looking damn unimpressed.

"S-Sire." Elay sputtered, then half closed the door. "I would have *cleaned up* if you'd told me you were stopping by."

London and the two dome-heads caught his signal and started corralling Dezi and all the homeless dancers into Elay's trashed bedroom. As London quietly shut the door from the other side, she whispered, "Don't come out until we tell you it's safe."

Vesta and Dezi stood in awkward silence while the clammy girls itched the pin-point scabs running down their arms.

"C'mon." Vesta pulled Dezi's arm and claimed a needle-free spot by the door.

He brushed away dirty napkins and empty beer cans to clear her sitting spot. "I'm so sorry for what I said earlier. You didn't deserve that."

"Forget it. We got bigger problems." Vesta crossed her arms and faced the wall. She couldn't care less about being called a whore—she got that at work on the regular—but the way Dezi had said it was like someone had asked him to gargle day-old soda, and she was the soda. Left out, used up, beneath him because of what she'd done to get them here. She'd never even told him about that bloated monster at the train station—hid the scar day and night—but somehow, he smelled the stain on her.

A slam against the wall made them all jump. Vesta scrambled to the door, putting her ear to the bottom.

"Protection fees?" Elay shouted. "The fuck I gotta pay protection for? I paid my tithe—"

With a heavy, Old-World accent, the other man shouted louder, "You want out? There is no out! Your blood is mine."

Elay lowered his voice. "You know how things are right now…"

"I don't give a fuck. My upline is bleeding me, so I bleed you. The city is in ruins, and now I come here to find your home filled with whores? I taught you better!"

"They're working girls—assets. You remember what happened after the crumbling of '08. Skin girls were charging a fortune for an ounce. This time, we'll be ready to capitalize on the shortage."

"You can poach for blood. Ten units from one body."

"Finding men willing to do that work ain't easy. If we're prepared, it won't come down to that."

"Bah—excuses. This is a charity and we have no money for it. You must focus on the family."

"I am, but I ain't forgetting the people who work for me."

He snorted. "Jaxon was right about you. You are baby-fanged. Maybe he is more fit to run this branch."

"I built this house. You ain't taking it from me."

"I am your sire. It and you are my property, and I will organize it how I like."

"Cut the shit, gramps. We both know I cover ninety percent of your tithe. It's got me wondering, the fuck does the boss need you for?"

"You ungrateful child. I brought you up from nothing. I made you!"

Elay chuckled, letting the silence drag out. "The thing about kids is that they grow up. But you're right; it's about time for a change in leadership."

"You think you can replace me? You are dead, Elay. Dead," his sire spat.

BANG!

The hair on Vesta's neck curled, and they all held their breath. Dezi's phone buzzed, and then the idiot answered it.

"What are you doing?" Vesta hissed.

"It's Ms. Mai. It's about our jobs." Dezi's hands jittered as he brought it to his ear.

Vesta crawled over to listen.

Ms. Mai's shrill voice asked, "Dezi? Hello?"

"Yes, ma'am?" he whispered.

"Where are you? Your VIP is *not* happy."

Dezi's jaw flinched. "I'm in Chryse."

"Chryse? How in Nova's good name did you get there? Never mind." She huffed. "Now I'll have to find a pilot willing to risk their life to bring you back in."

"You expect me to work the same day as a natural disaster?"

"No, I expect you to work the night after. Are you telling me you don't want the shift?" Ms. Mai sounded astonished, and Vesta had half a mind to grab the phone and accept it for him. With no idea how long this storm would last, they needed every penny they could get.

"I'll take it," he said quickly.

"Come thirty minutes early to the Egress Cluster, flight pad seven. Let Vesta know she's cut for the week. It's nothing personal, but we're down to essential staff. If you don't want to be cut as well, ensure both your appearance and your attitude are ingratiating to your VIP tonight." Ms. Mai hung up.

The door flew open, and Vesta's stomach dropped. The bald guy in the doorway traded his scowl for a smile that was missing a few of his more important teeth, made a shushing motion, then ushered them back to the living room.

On her hands and knees, London scrubbed purple foam into the carpet while Elay sat back on a recliner with a cig hanging from his lips. Dezi stared at him from across the room, and Elay looked back, daring the kid to say something. Dezi turned for the other side of the living room, but that made Elay scowl harder. He tossed his cig on the floor. "Money's gonna be tight, so I'ma need all of you working one way or another. Rest up. We'll talk more once the dust settles."

Vesta collapsed onto a couch that reeked of chem smoke, and Dezi curled up on the rug below her, using his emergency bag like a pillow. She let her arm fall off the side of the couch, touching Dezi's hair. She wanted to hug him and listen to those sweet promises of his about how he'd take care of her, but he needed rest before his shift. The thought of sending him out there—of being left alone in this drug den—shriveled up her insides, but it was up to Dezi to get them out of here. By some wild stroke of luck, he'd managed to seduce a VIP, so if the two of them could kiss and make up, she and Dezi would be sleeping in a Diskos penthouse by sunrise.

Chapter 18

Stakes

The rotorcraft's blades crunched and whined as it flew Dezi and the other employees lucky enough to get Ms. Mai's call through the muddy clouds. Streaks of crimson lightning crackled around them, but no one flinched. They were too accustomed to being afraid.

When they arrived at Stellaire, they lined up in the staff room for their usual start-of-shift pep talk. Her heels clicking on the hardwood, Ms. Mai stalked into the room.

"Look at the sand you all tracked in. This is unacceptable! Guests come to us to escape their miserable lives. We can't craft a hyper-diamond fantasy covered in dust! Damn it all, it wasn't supposed to be like this…"

The haggard hosts adjusted their collars, the bussers shuffled their feet, and an assistant manager cleared his throat.

Ms. Mai wiped her cheek, smearing her lipstick. "We're taking blood. Line up."

The crowd didn't move. Someone shouted, "Paychecks are at the end of the month!"

She glared at them. "Request an advance. The forms are online."

The crowd mumbled.

"Come on, you stellar superstars, our guests need our top service more than ever. Remember, you are the heroes that keep our city running." Ms. Mai tucked her cheeks into a bleached-toothed smile. "The rate is four dollars a milliliter."

The crowd roared, and a stocky card dealer asked, "What type of shit rate is that?"

Ms. Mai pointed to the door. "If you think you can find a better rate out there, then be my guest, but don't come back looking for shifts here. You should be grateful to be employed at all when there are millions in the city desperate for work."

Dezi had seen this dance at Verde and knew the threats weren't idle, so he shuffled past the headstrong servers into the nurse's queue; it wasn't like rates for tipped staff had ever been good. After giving his quarter unit, he found Ms. Mai finishing transfer papers for a teary-eyed teen host.

"Dezi," Ms. Mai said, "we were expecting a call from you. You left your VIP waiting."

He grimaced. "The phones were out."

Ms. Mai's smile tightened. "I shouldn't have to remind you how critical this guest's satisfaction is to our continued employment. Find him in the café and attend to his every need."

Without giving her a proper response, Dezi gathered some damp paper towels to wipe himself down with and did what he could with his hair. Hosting Umbra was undoubtedly the reason he had gotten this shift, but where did they go from here? He needed to get Vesta out of Elay's place, but staying with Umbra was only marginally better. They'd be at his complete mercy, and Dezi had seen what Umbra did to disobedient pets. If there was any chance of Umbra being violent or coercive to Vesta, Dezi couldn't bring her near him. The only path forward depended on Umbra swearing there would not be a repeat of last night and agreeing to respect Dezi's boundaries. If Umbra valued Dezi's company as much as he had claimed to, it should be a reasonable request.

The casino floor was deserted, with a few pale guests limping between the unmanned games like ghosts mourning a long-dead party. The premier restaurant, however, had a line spilling past the bar, and when Dezi slipped through the kitchen, he noticed that the chefs were not nearly as frantic as the drink staff. He peeked past the final door to the café where a solitary guest sat under the artificial moonlight.

The silvery glow shimmered on the burgundy velvet of Umbra's suit and caught in the curls that fell over his brow. Solemn as a cemetery angel, he concentrated on the contents of a leather-bound journal, drawing deft swirls with his gold-tipped pen. Dezi's heart leaped when he recalled being laid under that breathtaking immortal, but it shamed him that his mind raced to lewd thoughts immediately upon seeing his guest again. He should have known better than to get this attached to someone so unobtainable, but that didn't make it hurt any less. Even if last night hadn't ended in catastrophe, where had Dezi expected this relationship to go? He was probably just another one of Umbra's conquests—a taste of local blood—but he still couldn't let go of the fantasy that this strange thing that had been forming between them was special. Either way, he had more pressing concerns than his bruised ego. He took a deep breath and approached the table.

"Dezi." Umbra lowered his lacquer pen and raised his eyes. "You did not contact me. I assumed you had died."

The VIP's expression was blank, and his voice monotone, but an expectation hung heavy behind each word. He wanted an answer to the challenge he had issued yesterday. Dezi hadn't yet worked up the nerve to deliver his ultimatum, so he evaded.

"I had a lot on my mind."

"What of your family?" Umbra asked.

Dezi took a seat. "Other than a cough and some burns, Vesta's okay. She ran to the Hadron Tower when the quake hit."

Umbra's brows briefly lifted. "Clever girl. Seems the gene for a survival instinct skips the males in your line."

"We're not actually related..."

"It was not a literal statement." Umbra returned to transcribing the loopy, alien script in his notebook.

Dezi couldn't put off this conversation all night, but the atmosphere was too prickly to start demanding handouts. Rubbing his thumb into his palm, he searched for something to make small talk about, when a server approached with a glistening porterhouse steak and accompaniments. Dezi fiddled with his hands in his lap as its richly scented steam wafted over the table. He couldn't remember the last time he'd eaten, but his stomach panged to remind him that it had been a while. It rumbled in protest when the server placed the dish in front of Umbra.

"I hope you don't mind. I tend to take dinner late." The vampire's lips tugged into a mean smile as he took his knife. He cut into the slab and then paused. "Dear me, they've overcooked it."

Dezi swallowed. "The finishing ovens are automated; I'm pretty sure they can't overcook anything."

"Then I must have ordered incorrectly. My stomach doesn't agree with meat that isn't rare." Umbra eyed Dezi slyly, then pushed the steak to him. "I'd hate to see it go to waste. Could I tempt you with it?"

Before the dish was fully in front of him, Dezi snatched the silverware, cut into the medium-rare steak, and took a bite. It melted under his teeth, exploding with salt and luscious juices. He had never eaten red meat before, but it was the most succulent thing he'd ever tasted. His jaw couldn't keep up with his appetite, but as he scarfed it down, he noticed Umbra watching him with voracious interest and then slowed his chewing.

By accepting this meal, Dezi had sent the message that he would be going back with Umbra. That was what he'd hoped to do, but on his own terms—not because he'd been bribed with food.

"Well?" Umbra intertwined his fingers and tilted his head. "I'm waiting for my apology."

Dezi chose to ignore that comment, lowering his utensils. "We need to set some boundaries."

"Indeed, I think you have wandered too far outside your place."

Dezi exhaled, resisting the urge to roll his eyes. "I think you dragged me out of my place."

The corner of Umbra's lip twitched. "Your implication is that last night was my fault?"

"Partially," Dezi said carefully. "I had no business being in your bedroom, but you tricked me into going back with you."

"How else was I to ensure your safety?" Umbra accepted a glass of blood from a passing server. "I couldn't let you waltz back into Chryse."

"You could have told me about the storm." Dezi turned away. "You should have told me."

"So you could chatter about it to the other mortals and start a riot? That was privileged information. It was a mistake to trust you with it at all."

"But why bother coming if I'm just another host to you?" Dezi couldn't stop himself from looking back. "Was your plan for the storm to lock me up in your room and cart me out for entertainment? For sex and blood?"

A faint flush spread across Umbra's white cheeks. "I come here for entertainment. Is that so wrong of me?"

"Yes." Dezi got louder, his own face heating. "I'm a person, not a toy. I won't let you treat me like Cat."

"Like Cat?" Umbra's lip raised, exposing a fang. "He was a priceless, powerful luxury. What are you compared to that? A clueless, conceited, entirely ordinary mortal boy, so underwater in debt he doesn't know what to do with himself. In fact, the one remarkable thing about you is your absolute gall."

"O-ordinary?" Dezi stammered. "That's not what you said last night. Not when you were serenading me and not when you offered to pay those debts."

Umbra scoffed. "You lap up every compliment like a thirsty little puppy, don't you? Did you actually believe I would pay those Planitr philistines two million for an irradiated Martian such as yourself? Laughable! Accepting you as a donor would be an act of charity, and I am in no need of another tax write-off."

"Wait." Dezi's voice wavered, barely holding back an avalanche of contempt. "You said you would help me, not buy me."

Umbra's lips curved cruelly upward. "To have your skin laid bare, I would have told any tale."

"Asshole—I can't believe you! Good thing I'd rather turn myself into the Planitrs than be your bloodbag."

"You are human." Umbra's tone dropped to a frigid growl. "If your blood is not mine, it will be another's."

Dezi's heart shriveled in his chest and his skin prickled as if a thousand needles were digging into his every pore, but the vampire broke the spell when he shut his eyes, tilted his head back, and took a therapeutic breath. "Thankfully, there are certain privileges that come with my status. An extended menu, for example."

Dezi's death grip on his utensils relaxed, but beads of sweat formed on his brow. "What are you talking about?"

With a princely smile, Umbra swirled his wineglass and held the thick fluid to his nose. "Have you ever wondered how you taste?"

"No. Stop." Dezi watched his own blood draw closer to Umbra's lips, fighting the furious urge to reach across the table and do something he'd regret.

"Oh, I'm being a poor tablemate. I've neglected to order you a drink. Here, we can share." Umbra drizzled his glass over Dezi's steak, taking his time to coat even the broccolini with the dark gloss. He locked eyes with Dezi and savored the last sip, proudly violating him. "Ah—tart as a framboise. Are you, perchance, frightened of needles?"

The film of grease on Dezi's tongue soured. He dropped his utensils into the puddle of meat juice mingled with human blood and gagged.

"I'm surprised you haven't asked about your missing collar." Umbra dragged his finger across the steak and licked it. "I so graciously spared you a fine from Mai by returning those favors to her safe in the time between tucking you into *my* bed and lending you *my* rotorcraft, all after slaughtering *my* darling Cat because you couldn't be bothered to put one foot in front of the other properly. Not that you were likely to wear them again, considering how you gleefully raced into the ruination that I wasted my effort sheltering you from! Better to die alone than spend another minute in my company, hm? *Você prefere morrer do que ser meu!*"

That language—it wasn't his native tongue. It was like Earth-Latin, but so archaic that Dezi didn't catch its meaning.

"Sir?" squeaked a busser offering Umbra a bouquet of one hundred black roses. "You ordered these?"

"Ah. Yes." Umbra recovered from his wince with a brilliant smile, then brushed his thumb across the busser's dust-smeared cheek. "*Merci, chérie.* If I startled you, take a seat and allow me to apologize."

The busser dropped into a chair like an obedient child, wide eyes entranced by Umbra's angelic facade.

"This hosting arrangement, I don't enjoy it. Why should I pay for companionship when humans gladly offer it, and their blood, for the pleasure of knowing me?" Umbra took the massive bundle of flowers from the busser and dumped them onto the table. "You are dismissed."

Roses: obscenely expensive with a five percent gratuity. Their densely sweet scent gave Dezi a headache, and every staff member stopped to stare as he carried them to the backrooms. Ms. Mai's tablet slipped from her hand and slapped onto the floor when she saw them.

"What the hell did you do?" she asked.

Dezi wrung the thick bundle of stems between his hands. "We made the mutual decision to end our business relationship."

"You what?" She smacked the bouquet from his hands, scattering petals everywhere. "Did you listen to anything I said?"

"I can't work with him. He wanted things from me that I won't do." That wasn't entirely true; Dezi could have swallowed his pride and apologized, but now that Umbra had admitted to playing with his heart, there was no point in continuing the charade. Dezi would never be fooled by him again, and the dead-hearted vampire would never get whatever it was he had been after.

"Oh, things you won't do. Things he won't do! What the hell do you think you're here for?"

"I'm still a member of the VIP staff. I mean—I'm a top performer."

"You were a top performer because of him." She took out her phone and dialed. "We'll see if he truly has no use for you, because if that's the case, neither do I."

"Wait—" Dezi grabbed for it. "Let me explain what happened."

"Unhand me!" She stabbed her dagger-like heel into his calf, sending him to the floor.

"Vesta and I won't survive without this job. Please, I can serve, I can bus—let me work."

"So can a thousand others. You should have considered that before forgetting your place." Ms. Mai raised her phone to her ear. "Sir, I'll have his termination papers generated immedi—"

She paused. "Will you require his services again? No, he doesn't, but—"

The dial tone interrupted her, and she stared at Dezi, cheeks flushed with rage, but expression dumbfounded.

Dezi stood with his hands clasped over his lap and his head lowered to hide that he was seething. How dare Umbra put him through this? How dare he raise Dezi's hopes so high, only to dash them the moment he asked for a modicum of respect? Umbra wasn't like the other self-obsessed guests; no, he was far worse.

"You're working the VIP section," Ms. Mai said.

"Really?" Dezi's head jerked up. "Thank you—thank you, ma'am. I won't disappoint you again."

She smoothed her frayed bun, leering at Dezi. "I don't know what you think you're playing at, but it would be wise to end this game before we all run out of patience."

Elay's business was open all hours, selling drugs, fake IDs, knock-off sneakers, private time with his displaced guests, and anything else he could get his scummy hands on. Dezi shifted in and out of sleep because of it. He gave up a few hours before his next shift and rose to search the fridge.

Ms. Mai had given Dezi a full shift every day since the storm had started, and each night, he'd spot Umbra lavishing a different host with gifts, but it gave Dezi a small sense of satisfaction that the asshole couldn't find anyone he liked enough to see twice.

Dezi rummaged through aging takeout boxes and flat sodas that smelled like chemicals and cough syrup.

Elay slammed the door shut on him. "What you looking for?"

"Water," Dezi said flatly.

"Water ain't free."

"Is flushing the toilet free?"

"Nah."

"So do you want me to go in the garbage bin, or is anywhere fine?"

"You trying to start shit?" Elay put his chest a millimeter from Dezi's.

"Dezi!" Vesta scrambled off the couch, then pulled him back and hissed in his ear, "What are you doing?"

He glared at Elay over her head. "I'm paying him a thousand dollars a day. I can use the fridge."

Elay crossed his arms. "Rent's getting raised. It's back to two thousand."

"We had a deal. Or are you not a man of your word?"

Elay clicked his tongue and leaned back on the kitchen island. "Situation's changed. The family's gotta elect a new first-line, and I need campaign funds. Mai made you essential staff, so you must be pulling bank."

"He was a top earner thanks to his VIP." London hopped her butt onto the countertop, resting her hips on the dirty laminate. "Heard they broke it off, though. Tough tiddies, Dezi."

"A VIP…" For once, Elay looked like he was thinking about something other than getting drunk or high. "Think you can reel 'em back in?"

When Dezi had first agreed to this deal with Elay, he'd mistakenly assumed he'd still be earning a decent income. Faced with a bitter dose of reality, he realized that he could have tried harder to work something out with Umbra, but compromise was apparently a foreign concept to the VIP.

Dezi tapped his heel on the tile and then sighed. "I've already told him I'll never let him bite me."

"He's a vamp. That's what they're always after." Elay patted Dezi's shoulder. "If you don't wanna put out, you gotta string him along."

He glared at Elay's hand, lip raised in a slight sneer. "That shuttle has launched. A thousand is the best I can do."

Elay squeezed his collar—hard. "Much as I hate to admit it, you're part of the house now, and the house needs money."

Dezi released a dry laugh. "No, we aren't. Me and Vesta are getting out of here as soon as humanly possible."

"I'ght, if you can't find the money, I'll put her to work." Elay flashed his golden fangs at Vesta.

Dezi grabbed Elay's wrist, clenching it in his fist. "Don't look at her like that."

Elay snorted. "You know what? Maybe I can find a job for you instead. Let's talk man-to-man for a minute."

He yanked Dezi by his shoulder, shoving him into the hallway bathroom. Blue smears stained the tile, the torn shower curtain was balled up in the sink, and pitch-black muck with thin purple foam filled the tub. Elay stepped over the wire brushes, shears, and chemical bottles scattering the floor, while the towels lining the floor squelched under his shoes.

He sat on the toilet lid. "You want to be the tough guy? Alright. Do some work for me, and I'll give you two a break on rent."

"What is that?" Dezi covered his nose from the biting, chemical fumes. "It smells like you're cooking drain cleaner."

"Then turn on the fan, dumbass. And put these on." He tossed over a pair of yellow rubber gloves with corroded green fingertips.

Dezi let the gloves slap the floor. "What the hell is in there?"

"If you're so smart, why don't you figure it out?" He grinned.

"I'll pass."

Elay sighed, scratching his scraggly scar. "That girl's been through hell for you, and you ain't going to lift a finger to pay her back? That's cold, kid. Deep-space cold. I guess she'll be paying your rent with her neck."

Dezi snatched the gloves off the ground. "If I clean this, you'll swear not to touch her?"

"Pinky promise." Elay flexed his little finger, grinning like a psychopath. "Now let's see if you can figure out what that shit is."

"You better keep your word this time," Dezi mumbled as he pulled on the sticky gloves. This assignment was more revolting than the time Ms. Mai had ordered him to clean bloody vomit off the restroom mirror, but if he could push through it, it'd get Elay off his back—temporarily, at least.

He knelt by the tub and sank his hand into the bog. A forest of stiff branches blocked him from finding the plug, so he heaved one out, releasing thick bubbles. Smeared with caustic grape jam, it was tough to make out, but the surface was like white granite peppered with metal streaks.

"Rocks in porta-potty fluid?" Dezi wiped the muck off the branch, running his hand over a fleshy knob at its end—gooey cartilage sticking to bone.

He screamed and dropped the femur into the corpse fluid with a viscous plop.

He scrambled back, but Elay grabbed his hair and forced him down, making his bangs graze the foul oil. "You figure it out? What's in my tub? Tell me what's in my tub!"

Dezi scrabbled at the bony hand on the back of his head, but Elay's grip was as strong as a grithead's chem rage.

"Pull the plug or I'll make you drink it!" He cackled.

Dezi shoved both hands into the cold sludge and dug through the lead-weight bones and jelly until he found the chain and yanked it. The fluid drained, leaving an ink-stained skeleton and its scattered porcelain teeth. Strands of undigested hair drooped over the bones like vines, and blackened tissue clumped together like moss in the swampy mess. Dezi threw the gloves off and scrambled to the door right as Vesta opened it.

"Stop it, Elay—" She shrieked. Dezi groped at her bare legs, and she went stiff. "What is that?"

"Vamp corpse." Elay put his bare hand in the tub and pulled out a sternum, its rubbery cartilage carrying a few bouncy ribs. "I was quizzing the smartass. If he guessed, he got another job."

"Give me a question," Vesta said.

He laughed. "Nah, I ain't playing this game with you, honey eyes."

"You don't want us to guess who did it? Maybe I wanna hear how you murdered your own sire." Her little nose twitched.

"London tell you it was me?" Elay shrugged and twisted the dangling sternum, displaying the hole blown in its center.

"B-bullet." Dezi slid up along his back to stand beside Vesta, his eyes and nose still burning from the fumes.

"So you do wanna play." Elay yanked open the countertop drawer, pulled out a handgun, spun it on his finger, then pointed it at Dezi's chest. "*B-b-bullet.* BANG!"

Dezi flinched.

"You think your Earth accent and designer genome makes you worth something, but it don't mean shit when the clouds roll in. I'll still be slinging dope and taking neck by the time your bones are microbe food, 'cause I'm a vamp and you're a bloodbag." Elay lowered the shiny revolver and popped open the cylinder to show him the chambers were empty. "It's been fun, kid, but you're too pussy for the job."

"But where's he gonna go?" Vesta said. "We—"

"Shut the fuck up!" Elay raised his gun like a bludgeon, but then caught himself before he brought it down on her head. "He's probably gonna fucking die. That's what happens to weak men around here, and I ain't signing up to be his new sugar daddy."

Dezi picked up the rubber gloves. "I already said I'd clean it. Just let me get my respirator."

Elay polished his gun with a crusty towel. "You gonna make it sparkle? I want this shit as white as your vamp's teeth. Tomorrow you can help me figure out what to do with the bones."

"Yes, sir."

"I'ght." Elay shoved the gun into his back pocket and held out his hand, fingers decked with rings and long nails. "Welcome to the crew, Dez. Normally, I'd have my guys beat the shit out of you first, but I need you in shape to work."

Dezi gritted his teeth, took the bog monster's hand, and let the slime rub between their fingers. This was the cost of rejecting Umbra; he still had to sell his dignity, but at least this way, it was his choice.

Before Elay pushed her out, Vesta locked her steady, sunshine-gold eyes on Dezi's. She was worth it. Days, weeks, months, however long it took, he wouldn't stop until she was out of this hellhole.

CHAPTER 19

Drinks

With their lights shut off to preserve power, the silent slot machines lined the casino floor like tombstones. Above them hung the VIP lounge, bustling with specters too glitzy for the graveyard below. The spiraling stairs swayed like the tongues of a crystal wind chime as Dezi ascended them, and he couldn't imagine how an immortal twice his weight gathered the nerve to rise a single twist. When he made it to the top, he gripped the glass handrails and avoided the clear sections of the floor. The opposite of private, this lounge presented the VIPs to the commoners below, because spending was a spectator sport. The same gaunt faces occupied these crystalline tables every night, each looking less like they were on vacation and more like they were stranded on this pedestal.

"You could use a rinse, honey." A guest shook a two-thousand-dollar bottle of Bordeaux Sanguinante, then yanked the cork and painted a young host burgundy with the spray of champagne. When the ogre tried to lick her, she slapped him. One of his tablemates grabbed her arm, but she tore her sleeve to get away, tearfully dashing down the stairs.

Dezi cringed as they jeered and threw glasses at her heels, and a group of nearby Venusians raised their noses and promptly left the lounge. Based on their brown-and-yellow centipede tattoos, these Martian perennials were part of the same gang Elay belonged to; the Moroska family was an old bloodline from Earth that had taken root on Mars back when the Ninth Century Recession caused companies to slash their budgets for corporate peacekeepers. Most of them never reinvested in the red planet and, instead, went on to

Venus or to build their own satellite cities, free from regulation and government interference. Elay had talked Dezi's ear off about how his family was royalty in Chryse's criminal underground when they'd smuggled that sack of vampire bones into an industrial waste pulverizer together. Working two jobs, Dezi was physically and mentally exhausted at all times, but at least that made him too tired to keep track of all the laws he'd broken.

"Hey!" The ogre tossed his empty bottle and pointed at Dezi. "We need another round. And make it snappy."

"Right away, sir." Dezi headed for the drink station, though he had no delusions this particular guest was a good tipper.

The bartender placed a bottle on the glacier-themed bar top for Dezi. "This for the locals?"

"Yeah." He sighed and loaded his tray. "Wait until Cormac sees the vintages they're wasting..."

"You didn't hear?" The bartender asked. "Cormac quit. He's booking a shuttle as soon as the skies clear."

"He's leaving the planet? How?"

"One of his moon-shot investments paid off. He bought calls on Ambrose Industries, and after City Council announced they're hiring Stax to re-print the buildings, the price jumped. You should have seen how he left." He laughed. "Told Ms. Mai to *kiss these cheeks* and wouldn't stop slapping his own ass all the way out the door."

Dezi smiled. "That sounds like him. I wish he would have said something. He never messaged back, so I thought...you know."

"Yeah, about that. There's a memorial post for Non, if you have any photos her family might like."

Dezi nodded, but kept his mouth shut. He couldn't count the number of meager condolences he had typed out for people he didn't really know, but Non... He touched the tie she had taught him to knot. How long would it take before he forgot that memory? Before every memory of her was forgotten? Stellaire was already interviewing for her replacement. She had worked her ass off, being a good corporate drone, just to be erased, and Dezi's life was going down the same meaningless path.

"Keep smiling. The tyrant's watching." With a brittle grin, the bartender filled a pitcher of water. "Top the guests up after you handle that bottle service. There's a couple by the band that's been guzzling water."

Dezi placed the pitcher onto his tray and took the long way back, enjoying the swanky piano and bass music; he needed a minute to breathe before he had to serve those pests, and the live band was his favorite part about working this lounge. The musicians could make the same songs sound fresh every night, and the simple pleasure of listening for the differences got Dezi's mind off things.

"Service." A blue-haired guest raised his hand, pointing out the empty glasses in front of him and his associate.

Both of the VIPs wore advanced particle masks and neck-covering scarves, but when Dezi approached, the second vampire raised his crimson eyes and rolled them disdainfully.

"Umbra," Dezi greeted him curtly.

"Dezi." The uppity asshole wrinkled his nose. "You smell like chemical solvent."

Dezi tipped his pitcher over Umbra's glass. "And you smell like burnt pepper." It was simultaneously awful and nostalgic, but Dezi couldn't quite place it.

The vampire plucked an archaic cigarette from an enamel box. "Don't judge me for smoking. It's been a long week."

Dezi stared him down. "It's been nine days."

"Do you count the hours we've been apart as well?" Umbra loudly flipped open his steel lighter.

Water spilled over the edges of the glass.

"It's full, boy." The blue-haired guest took the pitcher from Dezi and placed it on the table. He then offered his hand to Umbra, who dropped the dented lighter into it. "You shouldn't smoke."

"Mmm, and you shouldn't tell me what I should and should not do." Umbra lowered his mask and gestured for his friend to give him a light.

With his chipped nail polish, silver alligator leather jacket, and a spiral headband holding back his mess of curly hair, Umbra looked like a kid from an old movie, smoking the cigarettes he stole from his dad after getting kicked out of his first band. The immortal sparking the lighter looked old enough to be his disappointed father.

"You can stop staring and leave," Umbra murmured between drags of smoke.

Dezi turned away, but with each step, a thread that refused to snap tugged harder on his heart. Why did he let Umbra get to him like this? It was obvious what he had been after. He had tried to trick Dezi into sex so he could bite him in the middle of it for the stupid special flavor it would give him. Dezi had been an idiot to think a vampire would want anything else from someone like him.

Dezi rubbed his itchy eyes, though they were too dry to form tears, and brought the obnoxious perennials their champagne. He froze when he noticed Elay seated with them—and Jaxon beside him, wearing a tacky, patterned suit.

"Elay, Jaxon," the ogreish head of the table asked, "either of you heard from your sire? Igolka's never late…"

Jaxon leaned back in his chair, teetering it like an overactive child. "Last time I saw him, he was dropping by my blood brother's place to check out the homeless shelter he's been running."

Elay shot Jaxon a glare. "Stop spreading that bullshit. I got some of my crew staying with me. Haven't seen our sire since he stopped by. He hasn't been answering my calls either. With the city how it is, he might have tried to scalp one too many bloodbags and ended up on the wrong end of a barrel."

The ogre tapped a hard nail on the foot of his wineglass. "We lose a couple every storm, but it's a shame he went dark before paying tithe. You two'll have to put together what he owes."

Elay nodded. "If you give me a little time, Sire, I can cover it."

"*You* can cover it?" Jaxon snorted and leaned forward, dropping his chair's front legs onto the floor. "Since when? Look at the shit shape we're all in."

Elay exhaled, not bothering to look at Jaxon. "Igolka's been coasting off what I make for the last two decades. I can cover his entire tithe, *alone*."

"When did you get on a first-name basis with our sire?" Jaxon jabbed Elay's shoulder. "Is that a new thing, or are you that sure he's never coming back?"

Elay raised his lip, brandishing his golden fangs. "Touch me again, and I'll break your fuckin' arm."

The ogre smacked his hand on the table. "Enough of that. We're here to celebrate. This storm is an opportunity—blood's never been in higher demand, and overhead's lower than Old Chryse's skyline. Waiter! Where's my damn champagne?"

Jaxon's eyes lit up when he spotted Dezi, but it was too late to turn back. The vamp couldn't touch him while he was in Stellaire, and being a member of Elay's crew had to offer some level of protection, so Dezi approached the table like they were any other guests.

"Here you are, sir." He wrapped a linen over the bottle, squeaked the cork open, and carefully poured the frothing blood wine for the six men at the table.

The ogre smiled at Dezi, flashing a bizarre platinum grill bearing curved fangs emblazoned with diamonds. "Can I get a shot of B positive?"

Dezi couldn't count how many times he had recited the company line about the shortage, but this was the first time he was concerned a guest wouldn't accept it. He cleared his throat. "At Stellaire we pride ourselves in providing the highest level of customer satisfaction, and for that reason, we've had to ration our remaining—"

"You won't even sell me Hemo or fucking pig blood?" He slammed his finger on the table. "Aren't I a VIP? Make an exception."

"Dez." Elay up nodded at him. "Hook us up, would you?"

"They keep everything behind biometric locks, so these specialty bottles are the best I can offer." Dezi wiped the bottle's lip and offered a weak shrug. "You can ask customer services to adjust your ration, but unless you're a stockholder, they'll probably read you the same line they gave me."

The ogre narrowed his eyes and licked his meaty lips, but then Jaxon cut in, sporting a rotten grin. "Sire, he's one of Elay's guys. You can help yourself to his blood."

"Hold up." Elay raised his hands coolly. "He don't do that type of work for me. I got some girls back at my place who—"

"Fuck no." The ogre held his bloated stomach and groaned. "My liver's killing me from that grithead blood you hock. This one actually looks pretty fresh. Hand him over."

Elay grimaced and glanced at Dezi, but then turned his chair away. "Jaxon, help out your greater sire."

"No—wait." Dezi stepped back, but the ogre caught his wrist and yanked him across the table. Jaxon grabbed his legs while another thug covered his mouth, and he stiffened like a piece of roadkill as they dragged him onto the table.

Minutes ago, the entire lounge had been scornfully eyeing this raucous party, but now guests turned their cheeks and staff lowered their heads. Dezi glanced at Umbra from across the room, but when their eyes met, the vampire put his sunglasses on. His vision was blocked by Elay and the other vamps as they formed a privacy screen with their backs.

With drool running down his chin, the ogre smiled, exposing his crooked fangs. "*Relax*, and gimme your arm."

Dezi struggled, but terror sapped the strength from his limbs. With his mouth covered, his muffled pleas didn't rise above the lounge's casual chatter and easy jazz. The ogre wrapped his grimy fingers around his biceps, and Dezi squeezed his eyes shut. He wished he was stronger, strong enough to fight them off, but a human could never win against an immortal.

Hot saliva dripped onto him, but then chairs skidded and glasses shattered. An icy latch closed around his arm—Dezi's eye snapped open, finding a cold-blooded angel standing over him. Umbra covered Dezi's arm in his chill grip as the ogre recoiled.

"Marsdammit, that hurt!" The ogre lowered his hand from his mouth, finding a few dislodged diamonds, then threw them to the floor.

"You motherfucker." Elay grabbed the back of Umbra's jacket.

A flash of blue rushed him—Umbra's friend was on Elay in an instant, gripping him by his collar. "Do not touch them."

Jaxon fumbled in his pocket for a switchblade and then thrust it at the blue-haired vampire. He caught Jaxon's hand in his fist, the blade harmlessly threaded through his fingers. Simultaneously, he spread his gloved hand over Elay's clavicle, and violet lightning jumped from his fingers, tasing Elay and dropping him to the floor. With mechanical efficiency, he wrapped Jaxon's arm behind his back and pressed his wrist out of shape until it made a sickening pop. The brat dropped his knife and squealed, "Letmego-letmego!"

"Silence." He twisted again, raising his sub-zero glare to the other scions. They didn't move, apparently not eager to fight a cybernetically equipped killing machine.

"Careful with the fledgling, Seiyo." Umbra tapped his cigarette ash on an empty glass. "We are not here to offend."

The ogre stood. "Who the hell do you think you are, laying hands on my blood?"

"Simply a concerned bystander. If you drink this one, you will be sick; the boy's a beat away from a heart attack." Umbra placed his hand on Dezi's chest, silently assuring him that he would get him out of here.

The ogre contorted his lips, forming thick wrinkles in the center of his face. "Who the fuck are you?"

Umbra removed his sunglasses, twisting them in his fingers for a moment; then he blew a lungful of smoke into the ogre's face. His eyelids drooped as Umbra batted his snowy lashes and silkily said, "No one at all. But allow me to lend you my ration. I guarantee you will find it more palatable."

The ogre's knotted expression fully slackened. "That sounds nice, babe. This guy smells weird anyway."

"*Parfait*. Charge what you like to the Jupiter suite." Umbra smiled so hard his cheek formed a crease, then he scooped Dezi off the table and turned sharply.

"Collect your sire's teeth." Seiyo kicked in the back of Jaxon's knee and dropped him on top of Elay.

Elay shoved Jaxon off and dragged himself up, watching Dezi with a calculated glare. Dezi wrapped his arms around Umbra as he shoved through the befuddled thugs and carried him away. The sweet scent of his skin, the pepper of tobacco, and the warmth of leather steadied Dezi's racing heart, and he breathed a silent *thank you* into the vampire's shoulder.

Umbra's grip stiffened in response. "I warned that you would become another's, did I not? Do you enjoy your new masters?"

Dezi recognized that he was clinging to Umbra and pulled back. "Put me down."

"Newblood, terrestrial scum!" Umbra dumped Dezi onto the third seat at his table. "I can't believe you associate yourself with those perennial insects."

Dezi caught himself in the seat, mortified that Umbra was lumping him in with Elay's crowd. "No, I'm not—"

"Shut up and sit there until they leave." Umbra plucked out a fresh cigarette, holding it for his friend to light.

Seiyo's hands trembled as he struck the lighter, and his tone dropped another growling octave. "Why did you debase yourself like that?"

Umbra looked at the unmarked back of his hand and nearly smiled. "That's hardly the most embarrassing thing that's happened to me this week."

Seiyo removed his mask and pulled his Neptune-blue hair off his shoulders, triggering Dezi's memory of him from outside the Hadron Tower. He couldn't stop himself from asking, "Are you Umbra's assistant?"

Seiyo finished smoothing his topknot. "Do I look like an assistant to you, mortal?"

Dezi pinched his lips into a thin line. Seiyo lacked fangs, so he didn't wear the typical vampiric markers, though his quartzy skin hinted he had shed much of his human biology.

"There's no need to get snappy with the help, *mon arme adorée*." Umbra winked at him and then turned to Dezi. "He thinks of himself as my bodyguard, but I consider him a beloved friend; we are closer than brothers."

That statement must have caught Seiyo off guard, because he gave Umbra a soft look before regaining his steely composure. With a long face, hooded eyelids, and a pair of stress lines under his eyes that formed his two sole wrinkles, Seiyo didn't appear genetically related to Umbra. Dezi wanted to ask if his accent was Venusian, but his onyx eyes held more disdain than even Umbra's; in fact, the impish vampire's were regaining their normal spark.

Dezi observed the conductive pads on Seiyo's gloves. "I've never seen combat augments on an immortal before. I thought your ability to heal would mess with large implants like that."

Umbra brushed the orange dust off the shoulders of Seiyo's black-on-black suit. "They predate his vampirism. Much like myself, he is an anomaly among our kind; a true feat of engineering."

"That's privileged information, and I think it's time we leave. You're gathering orbiters again." Seiyo eyed Dezi.

"You may take your leave when you please. I'd like to enjoy the music a while longer."

"I apologize for intruding, Mr. Seiyo, but thank you for saving me. Thank you both." Dezi glanced from the table to Umbra. "I didn't think anyone cared enough to help."

"Well"—he squinted and showed his cheek—"if I'm not having you, no dirt-walking Martian is."

That hurt, but Dezi could tell it wasn't fully honest. Umbra had tried to turn away, but something drew him back; something always drew them back to one another.

Seiyo huffed. "So this is the one you had tucked into your bed."

Umbra slumped in his seat. "We are done discussing this."

"Are we? Because as far as I remember we haven't at all. One night you tell me to procure documents for a jaguar, and the next I'm helping you wrap its corpse in my bedsheets."

"I ate him. Is further explanation necessary?"

"You slaughtered an endangered animal, one you seemed very fond of." Seiyo crossed his arms and pointed at Dezi. "Is he the reason for these dramatics? For this ill-advised trip?"

"You press your limits." Umbra stood, threw his cigarette onto the floor, and ground it under his toe. "I will not entertain this line of questioning from you."

"Tell me, boy, what happened between you two?" Seiyo tilted his head toward Dezi. "Has he made you an offer?"

Dezi blinked at him. "I have no idea what you're talking about. I'm just a server."

A wry smile snuck onto Umbra's lips, and he rested his hand on the back of Dezi's chair. "Your insight is worse than usual, Seiyo. Maybe it's time to trade in those servos for an interpolatory chip or two."

"I see enough." Seiyo's nostrils flared as he exhaled, but he turned his chair so he could watch the ogre's table.

Jaxon brandished an overflowing champagne bottle and made an obscene gesture at a table of rough-looking Earthlings while they shouted planetary slurs back. Elay shook his head and poured himself a triple shot while their sire's thunderous laughter egged the shithead on. Jaxon shot Dezi a sour leer and then flung a half-full glass at the Earthlings.

Umbra brushed a hand over his pointed ear as he drifted to Dezi's side. "I suppose it is a bit too noisy to hear the band, but I ought to order something for your time. Do you have your host's menu?"

Dezi picked at his stained nails. "Ms. Mai took it from me."

"Oh, well..." The sounds of shouting and shattering glasses drowned Umbra out. He cleared his throat. "Might we—"

A bottle tumbled through the air directly at Umbra's head. Seiyo dove across the table to catch it, but the glass shattered against his hand, and bloody wine exploded out. Dezi's hands shot up to his face, and he couldn't tell if he was shredded, covered in wine, or both.

Seiyo pulled himself off the table and, as Umbra stared in shock, carefully wiped a napkin over the young vampire's face and hair. "Are you injured?"

"No, of course not." Umbra touched Seiyo's arm, though it seemed he yearned to reach over and clean the wine from the elder vampire as well. "Did they harm you?"

"I'll inform you after I run a diagnostic." Seiyo plucked out a few shards of glass from his torn glove. He flexed his hand, and Umbra's ears reddened at the sight of the black fissures on his bodyguard's stony palm.

Seiyo wiped his hands and then produced an antiseptic pad from his coat pocket. He turned Dezi's head from side to side, dabbing a scratch above his brow. "Do you feel pain anywhere?"

"No, I—Umbra!" Dezi scrambled to get out of his chair.

Pacing towards Jaxon's table, Umbra roared, "Which of you children hurled it?"

Jaxon was gone and Elay stayed in his seat, but the ogre and three other broad-shouldered perennials stood, their laughter lowering to chuckles as they towered over the little vampire; they liked their odds with Seiyo distracted. Dezi sprinted across the section, but

Umbra grabbed the ogre by his throat and groin, hurling him over the balcony. Crashes and screams rang out from below as Umbra grabbed another. Seiyo flew past Dezi and pulled Umbra from the men. Dezi stopped in the middle of the room, mouth as agape as Elay's after seeing how fast real vampires could move.

Seiyo took Umbra's wrists and knelt to his level. He jerked free, but Seiyo held his shoulders and spoke six inches from his face. Umbra turned his cheek and squinted, but he held still. Without reply, he shrugged Seiyo off and walked back to their table, passing Dezi before throwing himself into his chair like that same chain-smoking teen. Drenched with wine, Seiyo straightened his coat and spoke with the remaining perennials, who all kept their distance from him. He eventually asked for signatures on his phone and returned to Umbra's side.

Ms. Mai ascended the stairs, making a droneline for Dezi. "Where is he?"

"Over here, ma'am." Dezi led her to Umbra.

Seiyo dried off a wine-splashed cigarette, lit it, and offered it to Umbra, who tasted the smoke, sneered, then smoked it again.

Ms. Mai pulled a cheek-blistering smile. "Mr.—"

Umbra held up a hand. "Tell me, Mai, what is the point of wearing a disguise if you trounce up and use my goddamn name?"

"My deepest apologies, sir." She bowed all the way down. "We are so, so sorry about the interruptions."

"Mmm." The ember of Umbra's cigarette glowed bright orange as he took a hard draw. "I want the newbloods gone—banned from the lounge."

"Yes, sir. Right away, sir. And please keep Dezi as long as you like." Ms. Mai pressed her fingers together, nodding repeatedly.

"No! All of you go. All I want is to listen to the damn band."

Seiyo dipped his head and left while Ms. Mai hastily retreated to the bar, but Dezi lingered. The fickle vampire looked paler than Dezi had ever seen him, sucking on his cigarette as if it was his only source of oxygen. Umbra had said he only saved Dezi because he wanted him for himself, but he had always been a liar; there was something more going on behind those merlot eyes that Dezi just couldn't puzzle out.

"I told you to leave." Umbra showed Dezi the tip of a fang in a threatening sneer. "The sight of you gives me a migraine."

With a beer can in hand, Elay was waiting on the couch for Dezi when he crept through the door.

He crushed it and tossed it across the room. "You and your star vamp think you're hot shit, huh?"

Dezi sat against the fridge and threw a musty blanket over his shoulders.

"I bet you think getting my greater sire thrown outta the VIP lounge is funny, prick." Elay lumbered over and then prodded Dezi with his toe. "You realize you fucked us, right? I been bribing that fat bastard to put me up for promotion. Guess who the other nominee is."

"Jaxon." Dezi lowered his head; he wasn't going to apologize for something that wasn't his fault, but he understood how hard Elay had been working to maintain control of his house. "If you want me to skip some shifts at Stellaire and do more jobs here, I can."

"Nah, pocket change won't make a difference now. I got some ideas, but it would have been a hell of a lot easier if you took the L and let my greater sire bite you." Elay scratched the ugly scar on his neck. "Shame that VIP dumped your ass. She looked made of money."

"She?" It took Dezi a moment to realize that Elay was talking about Umbra.

"Gotta be honest, I was worried I let a pillow biter join my crew, but if you had yourself a woman like that..." Elay whistled, spitting some beer off his lips. "You're more man than I thought."

Dezi could hardly register the utter bullshit coming out of Elay's mouth, but he could feel his nails digging into his palms. "He's not a woman."

Elay frowned. "Then what's it got in its pants? You laid her, didn't cha?"

"You're clearly too fucking stupid to waste my time explaining this to, but he's neither." Dezi stood and shoved Elay in the chest. "He's a vampire, unlike you and your scum-blooded family."

The room went silent, and Elay and Dezi stared at each other, both processing what he had just done.

Elay grabbed Dezi by the throat, slamming him against the fridge. "The fuck did you say?"

"Stop it! Stop!" Vesta sprinted toward them, but one of his thugs yanked her back.

"Damn ungrateful. You'd be sleeping in a sandbox if it wasn't for my big heart. I told you to man the fuck up and take care of Ves, then she drags you here for my charity? You know she got bit watching out for your bitch ass. I could show you where she hides the scar, but you'd probably cry."

"You swore you wouldn't!" Dezi drove his knee into Elay's stomach. It loosened his grip, so Dezi threw his weight behind his fist and nailed Elay in the center of his face. When he staggered back and touched the dark blood on his nostril, Dezi wound back for another, but Elay backhanded him to the floor.

"Chill, little man. I didn't bite your girl—yet." He kicked Dezi's stomach.

"Elay!" Vesta shouted, then kneed the groin of the man holding her and fought free of him.

She ran for Dezi, but London caught her, struggling to keep the bawling girl back. "Ves—you can't."

"Shut her the fuck up or I will!" Elay hollered over his shoulder and then squatted by Dezi, stinking like blood, beer, and his caustic tub. "I could collect on your bounty and solve all my problems right now, but I like you. You got potential. What you need is respect."

Dezi rolled over, retching, but all that came up was thin bile.

"My sire was a real bastard, you know? Made all types of promises about the money we'd make together, but all he wanted was to leech off me. Bet your woman promised to take you under her wing too; raise you up to be a proper vamp." He patted Dezi's head. "It's better you learn this lesson now, kid. I still got a little bit of human left in me, but past a certain point, the only thing that matters to a vamp is themselves."

"You're a piece of shit…" Dezi swallowed his sour spit.

"Yeah, but I got a plan to keep Jaxon the fuck away from my people. We both know that VIP ain't done with you. In fact, I think she likes you a lot." Elay grabbed Dezi's hair and pulled his face up to his garish smile. "You're gonna get her to bite you. You're gonna set up a camera, let her do whatever the fuck she wants with you, and bring me the video. If we pull this off, I'll blackmail her for enough to save my house and pay off your bounty. Deal?"

"Bounty—?" Dezi shook his head. "He won't do it."

"She will." Elay dropped him, then banged his head with the fridge door as he grabbed another beer. "She better."

CHAPTER 20

Mistakes

Packaged in cherry-red foil and printed with a swarm of bats, the square wrapper looked like a condom, but it was a cauterizing pad. Was it supposed to be cute? Festive? Either way, the cruelty of it pulled a hollow laugh out of Dezi as he faced his reflection in the empty blood cooler's windows.

Elay had let him shave and use the shower to make his appearance more appetizing to their target. He had also given Dezi a bead-size camera to plug deep into his phone's charging port and then ordered him to get a clear shot of the penetration. At least the storm had prevented that vamp from setting up a live feed. Elay was a bastard, but if they pulled this off, he would force Umbra to clear Dezi's debt. This one awful act would set Dezi free.

He checked his reflection to ensure the bruising on his neck wasn't too noticeable and then found Ms. Mai in the security theater. "Can you tell me where Umbra is?"

"So you can pester him for money?" She clicked at her terminal, cycling through a wall of camera feeds crisscrossed with facial recognition prompts. "Absolutely not."

"I'm ready to give him what he wants."

Ms. Mai glanced at him and then pulled her burgundy lips into a narrow smirk. "That took longer than expected. You're lucky he was so patient; I told him you weren't worth the fuel to fly in here every night, but he insisted I kept you employed."

"Of course he did…" Dezi tightened his glove; Stellaire had run out of beige ones, so he had switched to a plain black one. "Where is he?"

"He's enjoying dinner, but be careful; he is *extremely* hungry."

Dezi undid his top shirt buttons and rolled up his sleeves as he approached the premier restaurant. Tucked in a dreary booth with the curtains drawn back and a single holo-candle flickering in the center of the table, Umbra looked small and sickly in his wool overcoat. Instead of its normal shimmer, his skin had the dull cast of weathered marble, and his lips, along with the rings around his eyes, were a dusky lilac. Although Dezi was here to blackmail him, he couldn't deny that, with Umbra in such pitiful shape, he almost wanted to cut open a wrist for him. Giving blood of his own free will didn't revolt Dezi; it was the elements of coercion that made it dehumanizing, but dwelling on that now wouldn't do him any good. He combed back his hair, prepared his sweetest smile, and served himself to the vampire.

"Good evening, Umbra. Is Mr. Seiyo not dining with you?"

"He has been wearing my patience." Umbra cut off a fraction of his veal tartare and brought it to his mouth. "I planned to take dinner alone."

"I know this stay hasn't met your expectations, but maybe I can do something to improve it..." Dezi closed the scarlet curtain and slid into the booth seat.

"I don't want your blood," the vampire said flatly.

"You don't?" Dezi halted, losing the little finesse he had mustered. "But didn't you give your last ration away when you saved me last night?"

"Of course not. I threw that pig off the balcony and kept it for myself." Umbra took a long drink from his glass of water, working his throat to finish it all at once.

"But it wasn't enough..."

He rested his utensils on his plate and finally looked at Dezi. "I have consumed every living animal in my suite's reserve, and it still isn't enough. It feels like my blood has a will of its own, a cancerous hunger eating me alive from the inside. Nicotine can hold off the clawing for a time, but I simply require too much for any mortal here to provide."

Dezi pressed his knees together, trying to stop himself from shivering. "I can give you a full unit of blood right now."

"I don't want it!" Umbra clenched his steak knife, bending the steel like a tin wire. "I don't want anything to do with you. You are the entire reason I'm trapped here. You and my damnable heart."

Dezi hastily backed out of the booth. "Let me talk to Ms. Mai about your ration. I-I'm sure we can find something for you."

Umbra's posture slumped over as he dropped his head into his hands. "If you insist on coming back, bring some of those digestive aids…and water, no ice."

Dezi hurried to the server's station, took out his phone, and dialed Vesta.

"Did he—are you hurt?" she asked.

"I can't do this. He doesn't want my blood. And he's in pain because of me."

"Woah, slow down. What do you mean?"

Dezi pressed on the aching center of his chest, catching his breath. "Umbra came to Mars because he knew a storm would hit and wanted to protect me. He's possessive and manipulative and I'm not sure he even sees mortals as actual people, but it's my fault he's suffering, and I don't want to put him through any more pain."

"We're suffering because of *them*. I should be surprised his type hid this disaster from us, but I ain't. Perennials don't see us as people; we're food."

"You know that's not true. An immortal saved your life at the Hadron Tower, didn't she?"

"She was one of the good ones. If you had been in that tower, you'd understand. It was the law of the jungle in there—eat or be eaten—and if we don't help Elay save the house, we'll be thrown into the wild with those monsters."

"What if I ask Umbra for help? What if I sell him some of my blood?"

Vesta paused for a moment. "Would he give you enough to pay off the Planitrs?"

"I'm not sure..." He hadn't wanted Dezi's blood for free.

"When will you get another chance to call off this bounty, Dez? Think of it. You could get a clean slate. You could get your life back. If anything, this is karmic justice for how he tricked you."

Dezi hated this, and not only because of how it would harm Umbra. He was terrified the vampire might not stop, terrified of how it would feel, and even more terrified he might enjoy it, but everyone kept telling him he had to do this.

Dezi rubbed the bruise Elay had left on his neck. "Is it painful?"

"It hurts, but you just wait for it to be over." She sighed sharply. "If he sucks too much, shove your thumbs into his eyes and scream."

"I'm too scared..." Dezi flexed his gloved hand. His scar still ached, but even in his lowest moments, he was still proud of the day he had earned it. As naive as it had been to believe he would be rewarded for saving Verde, he had never regretted doing it. The scar left after tonight would give him no such pride.

Dezi wiped his nose and cleared his throat. "I mean, he'll sense something's off. He won't go through with it if he can tell I'm forcing myself."

"He won't care. Trust me, when they want something, they don't care how they hurt you."

"Ves..." The words sat in Dezi's stomach, hooked into his guts, and tore at his insides as he dragged them out. "I'm so sorry I let that happen to you. I should have been there. You deserved better."

"It's not your fault things shook out the way they did." She sniffled. "You know I wouldn't ask you for anything I wouldn't do myself, right? I wish I was there instead of you. I already been done like that, gave up that clean piece of me, but you...you had kept out of the grime until I brought you to Elay's."

Hearing her say that shattered Dezi's heart into dry, glassy pieces. "No, Ves. You've done enough. I'll figure something out."

"Is he still whining?" Elay's voice overtook Vesta's, and he snatched the phone. "Look, kid, the vamp's starving. You're doing him a favor here. I'll tell you right now, the only way to get a glass of thick, quality blood is by catching some poor sucker on the street and butchering him like a pig. I know putting up skin ain't the type of work I brought you on for, but sometimes this city brings a man low. Hand to my heart, I ain't proud of every job I've done either."

Dezi clenched his phone, biting his tongue until he tasted iron.

"I'ght, be that way. Just get the fucking money or it's all our necks on the line." And the scum blood hung up.

This was impossible—unfair. He had to make the right choice for Vesta, but there was no marsdamned right choice. There never was! Saving Verde had cost him his future, and now selling out Umbra was the only way to buy it back. Dezi pressed his hands over his eyes and took a shaky breath, trying to get his racing mind to shut up for a second.

They knew the storm was coming. They let this happen, and he's one of them.

It was a dark thought, but it wasn't untrue. Humans in Chryse were fighting over stagnant water while perennials spilled their bloody champagne onto Stellaire's carpets night after night. Millions of dollars down the drain while Dezi couldn't find a safe place for him and Vesta to sleep. This was wrong, but it was the world these monsters had built, and maybe it was karma that they preyed on each other. Dezi was merely the bait meat in Elay's trap, and meat didn't get a choice.

He filled a pitcher of warm water and took a swig straight from the rim, and it didn't matter who saw, because the humans around him felt the same: they were all bloodbags here. Dezi collected the vampire's digestive enzymes, returned to the booth, and poured him his water. Numbly, he rested his phone on the table, hidden camera poised at Umbra, and sat a finger-width away from him.

Umbra sighed deeply. "You haven't given up on this yet?" "You need blood, and I'm the least anemic human in the building. Stop being stubborn and bite me."

"That's rich, coming from you. You think you're so irresistible that I ought to throw myself at your feet? There are plentiful channels through which I could acquire blood, but I *choose* not to. I can stand a little discomfort if it eases the pressure on the humans of this city to provide for us."

It had slipped Dezi's mind that Umbra was one of the wealthiest people in the city. If he was willing to turn to the underground, he could hire a member of Elay's family to murder someone and return with gallons of fresh blood. It was a relief to know he'd rather suffer than resort to that, but it did complicate things. Logical arguments wouldn't work on him; Dezi would have to appeal to his emotions, his bloodlust.

He brazenly put his arm around Umbra, getting so close that his breath wafted the spider-silk curls swirling around his ears. When Umbra's nose twitched, Dezi knew he had his attention.

"You wanted me when we were in bed together, and now here I am. Take me."

"There are a thousand other guests who would pay top dollar for your blood, so this sales pitch is as much a waste of your time as it is mine." Mincing raw veal between his fangs, Umbra reached for his digestive tablet.

Dezi caught his hand and brought it to his chest, pressing his icy palm to the burning skin between his undone buttons. "You're the only one I would let touch me like this."

Umbra's hand flexed, palming Dezi's pounding heart, but then swiftly pulled back. "You throw yourself at me without naming a price. Is this a bid to recover my good graces?"

"Yes. I was stupid and ungrateful, but I understand my place now." Dezi pushed his collar aside, flexing his shoulder to show off all the meat there was to bite. His muscles clenched as he swallowed down his pride. "Make me yours, *please*."

Umbra's gaze traced the teal veins on Dezi's forearm, but he wrenched it away, gritting his fangs. "Liar. If you're going to torture me, at least do me the dignity of being honest about it. You're after my money—that's what they're always after."

It struck Dezi that Umbra could see through him so easily, but he didn't doubt Umbra had experienced deceit before; immortals' lives seemed to be full of it. People like Dezi were the reason he had become so guarded, and it was naive for Dezi to think he had the skill to trick a master of emotional manipulation.

Cold and exposed, he wrapped his arms around himself. "There's really nothing I can say to convince you?"

Umbra's expression softened, and he picked at his plate. "Feeding from you like this would breach legal and ethical boundaries. If you need a meal or a room, I'll provide it so long as you agree to stay out of my sight for the remainder of this storm."

How magnanimous of his knight in shining armor to come riding in at the last moment; any rational person would have been relieved, but Dezi was not in a rational state of mind. Hell, the promises of someone as two-faced as Umbra were worth less than the air he spoke them with. He was as liable to keep this one as he was to snatch it away again. "Why would you offer to help me when you know I came here to exploit how starving you are? It doesn't make any sense."

"I don't take it personally. Most humans would have come to me sooner, or rather, never left at all." He slid the menu to Dezi. "Order what you will, but I still need you to go."

"No, you don't get to act like you care after telling me I'm an ordinary mortal. I'm tired of you treating me like I'm nothing one night and then swooping in to save me the next. Is this some kind of game to you?"

Umbra's eyes widened. "Of course not. If I didn't care what became of you, I would have had you thrown out."

"I assumed you told Mai to put me on the schedule so you could watch me suffer. You've been waiting for this, haven't you? You knew that if I got desperate enough, I'd come crawling back. But now here I am, and I'm still not good enough for you." Dezi laughed dryly. "This is the perfect revenge, isn't it? Making me beg for it so you can remind me how unspecial I am."

"Dezi..." His voice weakened, hoarse and exhausted. "Watching you from afar each night is pure agony."

"What do you mean?" Dezi studied the vampire for signs of dishonesty. "You can't expect me to believe that after all this, you actually like me."

Umbra just looked at him, resigned, but he didn't deny a word. And suddenly, Dezi recognized the cracks in the facade Umbra had erected when their hookup went sideways. He wasn't a jaded billionaire, bitter that his fucktoy had given him attitude. He was the same as Dezi: a twenty-something struggling to get over an extremely inconvenient crush.

Dezi's heart fluttered, but he wanted to kick himself for missing the truth right in front of him. If he had admitted how childish this argument was instead of using it as fuel for his own self-loathing, he could have tried to understand why Umbra was acting out and gotten through to him earlier.

"You like me. You liked me this whole time. Damn it, Umbra, you knew I felt the same. Why have you been pushing me away?"

"Because I don't like you, I'm terrified of you! You don't obey as the other mortals do, and I'm *supposed* to put you back in your place, but whenever you press me, I find myself as flustered as some lovelorn fool. I shouldn't feel this way for a human; the way I let you speak to me, the places I want you to touch me—you bring out a side of me I hardly recognize." His expression tightened, fighting between a thousand conflicting emotions until it burst forth with open confusion. "I feel like I'm in love."

Gravity flipped, rocking Dezi back in his seat; he had heard Umbra correctly, but he still couldn't believe it. "Slow down. L-love is a strong word."

"What else am I to make of this?" Umbra took Dezi's hands and brought them to his chest. It was as still as crystal until suddenly—*thu-dum*—his heart slowly beat to life. He winced each time it pounded, but it beat faster as Dezi's warmth blossomed onto his skin. "I spent this morning pacing my room, fretting whether you ate the night before and whether it was cold where you slept. I hold my breath each evening for fear you won't arrive as I wait by the entrance to watch for you. I cannot explain it, but in these last months, you've taken hold of my heart like no other."

Dezi let his hands move over Umbra's chest, feeling the proof of his affection beating under his palms. They hadn't known each other for very long, and so much of that time had been spent fighting, but Dezi couldn't deny how earnestly his heart beat back. The vampire was moody, and mean, and self-centered, and he had been raised in a culture that treated humans like garbage, but he still saw Dezi as someone worthy of love. Dezi didn't understand it either—why he longed to call Umbra his—but as he thought back to those moments when they'd sung together and lamented about how hard it was to build friendships in this selfish world, something within him stirred. They were both isolated people searching for connection, and this relationship had the potential to grow into something incredible.

"I'm willing to try this again, but you haven't been treating me with respect," Dezi said. "Why did you lie about helping with my debt?"

"Because I can't; the Planitrs are a bitter rival to my family, and if they knew how deeply I cared for you, they'd use you against me. Even without that risk, there are few forms a relationship between us could take, none of which you would accept. That's why this ill-fated romance can't continue." Umbra released Dezi's hands. "I should have sent you away the moment you uttered their name…"

"But you didn't. You saved my life because you don't want this to end."

"You'd like to think that, but I saved you for myself." Umbra turned away. "I planned to do more than bite you that night. I would have hurt you."

Dezi caught his cheek, but he wasn't strong enough to bring him back. "You wouldn't have. You've protected me all this time."

"I'm not so sure, but it doesn't matter now. We have nothing to offer one another but undue danger and heartache." Umbra's expressions traded between a grimace and a smile. "I owe you too many apologies to count, so let me give you this one: I am sorry. I am so terribly sorry that I can never be the companion you deserve."

"What if I don't care?" Dezi curled his fingers into Umbra's hair. "What if I want you anyway?"

"You don't know me well enough to decide that." Umbra let Dezi pull him closer, hands quivering like he might bolt. He was frightened, and Dezi was too, but he'd be damned if he let either of them run from these emotions any longer.

"Then let's make a mistake together." Dezi shut his eyes and moved in.

Umbra brought his mouth crashing down to Dezi's lips. He kissed Dezi like he was starving for him, took his mouth like he already knew its shape, held him like they hadn't touched for a thousand years—like he was terrified of letting him slip away.

He pulled Dezi onto himself, and Dezi readily straddled his lap, gripping Umbra's curls and bringing his entire body into the embrace. Dezi needed this—to feel something other than despair—and Umbra's affection poured into him, washing out the hopelessness that had taken over his life.

Umbra broke away, turning his head. "Dezi—"

Dezi grabbed his face and brought his lips back to Umbra's, softly this time, savoring them. He tasted like ice, spearmint candy, and a whisper of ash. He guarded his fangs from Dezi, so their mouths met as lightly as courting butterflies.

"Dezi..." Umbra groaned, stroking his hands down Dezi's hips. "Tasting you like this...I could cut you so easily."

"It's okay," Dezi whispered in between kisses. "You need this, and I want it."

"Mmm, *muito bem.*" He pushed his hands up Dezi's back, pressing his fingers into his shoulder blades as he kissed and nipped at his chest. "Damn the consequences. I need you right now."

By his nape, he pushed Dezi's neck down to his hungry lips, and Dezi's spine stiffened at the sting of an overeager fang. Umbra sighed when the blood hit his tongue, then he sucked gently on the nick, sending a lethargic pleasure buzzing through Dezi's veins. As Umbra sipped from him, the sensations intensified until the brush of Umbra's breath and tickle of his hair on Dezi's skin were like the lick of flames, but the vampire's aphrodisiac cast all that pain into gut-wrenching ecstasy. In that moment, there was nothing but the warm scent of Umbra's cologne, the smooth touch of his skin, and the motion of his hard body rocking under Dezi's.

Umbra opened his mouth around Dezi's neck, fists tightening in his hair as he tugged his head aside. He made his way around to Dezi's throat, working his venom into his skin, readying him for his fangs. Dezi thought he might die if Umbra gave him any more, but he was desperate to have all of him, and this teasing was agony.

He moaned, weakly lifting his eyelids. His phone rested on the table, with Elay's beady camera lens watching them. Dezi's senses rushed so hard that he clenched Umbra's shoulders. He couldn't go through with this. Fuck Elay and his gang, he would not be their tool.

"Umbra, stop."

With his tongue pressed into the ridges of Dezi's trachea, Umbra held his teeth to the throbbing artery buried in his neck. Trembling, his mouth made a slow, wet sound as it pulled away. With his pupils blown out and saliva trailing down each side of his mouth, he looked downright feral, but Dezi wasn't afraid.

"Are you okay?" he asked.

Umbra rested his forehead on Dezi's shoulder, taking deep gulps of air. "Give it a moment for my heart to settle."

Dezi rubbed his back. "I'm sorry to jerk you around like this, but we can't do it here."

"You're correct. You're entirely correct." Umbra traced his nose up Dezi's neck, dotting his lips with the blood trailing from his cut. "You are not mine to have, so this is terribly inappropriate."

"We can't do that either." He leaned back, but Umbra followed until he had Dezi laid back on the table. Nuzzling his ribs, he wasn't biting, but he wasn't done with him either.

Dezi threw his hand out, groping for the camera. He didn't have a clue how to apologize—and he intended to come clean—but that recording could not leave this booth.

Umbra's body suddenly went stiff. He was like cast bronze, pinning Dezi down, staring at the phone as if he'd spotted a deathstinger. Oh Mars, the lens—his augmented vision couldn't be that good, could it?

Umbra gripped the edges of the table, digging in his claws, and fissures crackled across the granite. "That's all this was? A ploy?"

Dezi scrambled back. "No! Umbra, I—"

"You absolute worm—who set you up to this? How long have you been planning it? Surely months now! Hell, did the Planitrs breed you for it?" He grabbed Dezi's shirt and lifted him by a fistful of the slippery fabric, untucking it, but he gasped when he saw the purple welts scattering Dezi's stomach.

Hot tears rolled down Dezi's cheeks as Umbra lowered him into the booth.

He parted the fabric and faintly touched a bruise, his own eyes glistening. "The insects gave you these?"

Weeping now, Dezi nodded.

"I should slay you where you stand." Umbra smashed his fist on Dezi's phone, shattering it. "I would strike down anyone else for this, even one of my own blood, so why can't I harm you?"

"I-it's not live. I was going to delete it—I was going to tell you."

"Do you think that makes a difference? Seiyo will kill you for this. He'll kill you, your gang leader, your sister, and anyone else you so much as whispered my moniker to."

The blood in Dezi's veins iced over. He knew there were risks to this—star vampires didn't deal with Martian courts, and they certainly didn't leave loose ends—but Vesta had done nothing wrong. It was Dezi who had sexually exploited one of the few people in this world who cared about him, but now Vesta was going to pay the price. His chest tightened, and he managed a single, broken gasp.

Expression muted, Umbra sat. He intertwined his fingers over his mouth and stared across the booth without blinking or breathing. "This is my fault. I was a fool to trust a mortal. Your kind cling to the strong like a swathe of leeches. You cannot help it; weakness is simply your nature."

"Vesta doesn't know anything about you. Please, you can't—"

"*Silence*," Umbra commanded, and Dezi's mouth immediately dried up. Umbra ripped open the cauterizing pad, pressed it against Dezi's cut, and then roughly wiped up the smears of blood on Dezi's chest and his own face. "Seiyo can never hear of this. No one can. Do you understand?"

Dezi nodded, swallowing the sensation that was stuffing his throat. "Let me explain. Let me make this up to you."

"*You are done talking*," Umbra's voice boomed. "Now you follow my commands, human."

He pulled a gold ring from his thumb and dropped it onto the table. Encrusted with more diamonds than there were craters on Phobos and studded with one massive emerald, it looked fit for a museum display case.

Umbra wiped his hands in his handkerchief and stood. "Barter this for shelter in the city. You will not be allowed back onto the premises until the storm has passed, and you are not to seek me out again. We are finished."

Dezi clenched his fists and shook his head. What could he even say? A thousand excuses raced through his mind, but they were just that: excuses. He had known this was wrong, but he'd done it anyway, because Elay had promised to protect him. He was a coward, scum of the lowest class.

"This relationship was fanciful from the start." Umbra returned his handkerchief to his coat, avoiding Dezi's gaze. "It's best if you forget me."

"I can't. I never will." Dezi raised his tearful eyes. This connection they shared—Umbra couldn't walk away from it. He had called it love.

Umbra's brows tensed, pain cracking through his icy mask. "Take care of yourself and take caution with vampires; we are dangerous. *Adieu*, Dezi."

He threw open the curtain and paced out, disappearing into the shadows of Stellaire without a backward glance. Dezi wanted to chase him, but he didn't have a right to. Umbra had already given him more than he deserved. He stared at his last favor sitting on the table, imagining Elay digging through that corpse-filled tub, Umbra's ring like a crown on the head of his putrid centipede tattoo.

Chapter 21

Shelter

Vesta opened the door for Dezi, finding him puffy-eyed and pasty. He was lucky he had gotten sent home early, because he'd have time to rest before Elay could rub sand into his wounds. Elay, London, and his guys were out working or partying—she wasn't sure; they never told her anything.

She hugged Dezi, squeezing as hard as she could, and he collapsed into her.

"I fucked up," he said. "I ruined everything."

"Shh, it'll be okay." She brought him to the couch, trying to give him the comfort he needed, but her own panic was rising. "What happened? Where's your phone?"

"Shattered." Dezi reached into his pocket and produced a dazzling emerald ring. "He didn't bite me. He gave me this instead."

Vesta's jaw dropped. "Bleedin' Mars, what'd he make you do for it?"

"Nothing." Dezi wiped his fresh tears. "Not a damn thing."

"That's good, right? Elay will be pissed, but if we give him this ring and talk him down—"

"Talk him down?" Dezi laughed harshly. "The last time I talked to that vamp, he kicked my stomach into my ribs. I'm not giving him anything."

Vesta looked over her shoulder to confirm the junkies weren't conscious and then whispered, "We can't sell it ourselves. It looks stolen."

"I can't sell it either. I shouldn't have taken it at all." He dropped his face into his hands and sniffled. "I really hurt him, Ves."

She stroked his back. "I'm guessing he caught you? It's alright. We'll find you a new job once this is all over."

"That's the problem; he still didn't tell Ms. Mai to fire me. He honestly cared about me, and I tried to ruin his life. Now he never wants to see me again, and it hurts so much."

Nervous laughter swelled up Vesta's chest. Dezi hadn't even been this torn up when he'd broken up with his high-school sweetheart. "Oh boy, don't tell me you're in love or nothing."

He flexed his tear-damp hands. "I don't know what love feels like…"

Her cheeks flared. "You are not in love with a—a vampire!"

"I didn't say I was. I just have to talk to him again." Dezi held up the antique ring. "Look, this isn't a normal ring. It could be an heirloom. I should at least make sure he doesn't want it back."

The ring looked damn old, but immortals lived a long time; they collected a ton of junk, and Dezi would have a hell of a time getting into the same room with a VIP who didn't want to see him.

"Why'd he give you something so valuable if he didn't get anything out of you?" she asked.

"We have a connection. I can't explain it, but he and I…I need to prove that he can trust me again. And I'm done working for Elay."

Vesta had half a mind to knock the sand out of her ears, because she couldn't believe what she was hearing. "Dez, we need a place to sleep tonight. If that vamp ain't gonna put us up, then the best we got is Elay. I know he's a piece of work, but—"

"Fuck him. Where has following him or these awful managers gotten me? Nearly torn apart over and over, burying bodies, and hurting people. I'm done taking orders and I'm done being used!"

"But if you don't give Elay that ring, Jaxon will take over the house!"

"It won't make a difference; Elay has already lost control of the situation, and this was his last shot. We have to go to a shelter before Jaxon shows up."

"You don't know what it's like out there." Vesta pointed at the door like the thing was radioactive. "The air's filled with poison, the streets are running with ferals, and the sky can come falling down any second. It ain't safe outside."

"Vesta, this place isn't safe!" Dezi shook his hands until his entire body rattled. "Do you know what Elay has made me do? I've seen the inside of immortals' bones, I've smelled melted flesh, I've heard what human livers sound like in a blender, I—"

"He said this was the last job!" She grabbed for the ring.

Dezi guarded it from her, pushing her back. "You know that's a lie! He'll send me after Umbra again, and he's been looking for a reason to add you to his sick blood harem since we got here."

"The blood buffet out there ain't any better!" Vesta kicked his ankles out and wrestled him to the ground, but he clung to his ring like a gold-sick goblin.

The lock on the front door clicked. Dezi kicked Vesta in the pelvis and shoved the ring down his pants right as Elay swaggered into the apartment with London and his dome-headed henchmen.

Elay abruptly stopped laughing and squinted. "The fuck you two doing on my floor?"

Vesta held her sore hip bone and stood. "Ugh. I tripped."

"Sure..." Elay bumped her out of his way to Dezi. "You look like shit. That star vamp suck you good?"

When Elay tried to pat his shoulder, Dezi stepped back. "I quit."

"Too late for that, kid." Elay snorted, grabbed Dezi's face, and jerked it side-to-side. "Where'd she getcha?"

"*He* didn't." Dezi heaved Elay off and tossed his wrecked phone at his feet. "He found the camera."

"Bullshit." Elay squared up to Dezi, scowl twitching like the tail of a scorpion that'd been poked one too many times. "If she saw that, she woulda killed you."

Dezi raised his chin, using his height over Elay. "That would have been as illegal as biting me, and he wasn't interested in breaking the law."

"You expect me to believe a starving vamp wouldn't risk drinking at Mars's finest blood brothel? Vamps don't give a fuck about the law, they care about getting caught."

"Give him a break." London put her hand on Elay's shoulder. "He's pulled his weight as much as any of us."

"It ain't enough. It ain't fucking enough!" Elay paced the room, wringing his hands so his gold bracelets jangled. "The only way this adds up is if that bitch ain't any old satelliter but a real somebody. Somebody who can't afford a speck of exposure, but even then, she woulda drunk her fill and tossed you down a trash compactor."

"He's not a murderer; mystery solved." Dezi delicately tucked his shirt in over his bruised abs.

"Just 'cause she didn't drain you don't mean she ain't a killer. Nah, you must be too valuable to ice..." Elay's eyes widened, wanting to believe Dezi for all the wrong reasons. "Were you telling the truth, Dez? You some Old-World oligarch's long-lost bastard? Or did'ya steal her dead heart?"

"It doesn't matter." Dezi took his emergency bag from beside the fridge. "I'm done."

"If you won't cooperate, I'll cash in your bounty instead." Elay grabbed for him, but Dezi jumped out of the way. "Get back here! You think you got better options than me?"

"A dumpster in Clearair is better than here." Dezi dashed for the door.

Elay pointed. "Walk out and you can kiss your kidneys goodbye. You won't last ten minutes on your own."

Dezi grabbed the doorknob and paused. He peered over his shoulder, locking a hardened emerald eye on Vesta. "I'll find somewhere safe for you. I promise."

When he slammed the door behind himself, Elay kicked a hole in the drywall. "Fucking uppity brat!"

London crossed her arms, fidgeting her toe on the stained rug. "If Dez's vamp is that serious, we might have stepped into something dangerous."

"We're already in deep shit." Elay rattled a cough, dropped onto the couch, and took a swig from a bottle of bathtub-brewed blood substitute. "Need money for blood, need money for tithe, need money for bribes—fuck! FUCK!" He chucked the drained bottle at the TV, splattering it with pink-gray goo. "London, we gotta talk about plan B. Office—now."

He left for the back room, and London gave Vesta a quiet nod before following behind like a good thrall. Not that she was much better after letting Dezi go out there by himself. But what other choice did she have? Trying to make it alone when they barely had enough money left for drinking water was a suicide mission.

Vesta left the flat, went to the end of the hallway, and peeked out the basement door. Dezi was walking down the center of the cracked sidewalk, the lone man braving an evening stroll in this starved city. He'd turn around. Any minute, he'd turn around, and they'd work out a plan. If they had survived this apocalypse, they could survive Jaxon. They could survive anything so long as they were together, but Dezi needed to turn around right now.

After three centuries on Mars and a dozen once-in-a-generation storms, City Council was well-practiced with disaster recovery. The process was the same each time; they dusted off the rubble-pulverizers and released a horde of haz-suited temp workers into the wreckage to reclaim every scrap of rubble for reprocessing. The banks and corporate offices around the Hadron Tower were scrubbed down to their metallic skeletons and prepped for new stone veneers by the time Dezi had picked up a shift, but signing on for the cleanup effort was the only way for an able-bodied adult to get on the waitlist for a shelter. He hadn't realized it when he left Elay's place, but this late into the crisis, every shelter was full.

Braving the ever-shifting debris was a calculated risk, but dirty work paid well, and Dezi had spent the last of his credit on a brick of a phone at a pawnshop. It ran like a microwave trying to compute quantum interpolation, but it got him past the air tolls. And without a phone, he couldn't get Ms. Mai's call when she gave him his next shift. Although he hoped Umbra might change his mind, planning on it was foolish. He'd have to wait until the storm let up enough for Stellaire to re-open and then catch the VIP before he booked a shuttle off planet. Once Umbra was gone, he wasn't likely to visit Stellaire again anytime soon, not unless Dezi could redeem himself. He hadn't worked that part of his plan out yet, but cutting ties with Elay was a good first step. Combine that with returning Umbra's ring and a heartfelt apology, and he might stand a chance.

After finishing his temp shift and turning in his equipment, he trekked across town to his designated emergency shelter. As he approached, the speaker in the shelter door called number four-thousand and ninety-six, then a burly man with a heavy coat exited and a young boy entered. Dezi's number was five-thousand and forty-two, so he picked a spot on the curb to sit.

A dumpster behind him rustled as a white cat with a silver nose crept up through the garbage. The cat's narrow body weaved between the gaps in the cardboard pallets, stalking a roach. When it pounced on the insect, a smile snuck onto Dezi's face, but then a man jumped into the dumpster after it. He reached for the tiny cat, but it deftly jumped onto his back, then when he turned, it vaulted off his balding head. The man struggled to climb out of the huge bin, his limbs tangled in plastic bags.

"Somebody grab it!" he shouted.

Dezi fell onto the cat, snatching it by its scruff. The elegant little guy looked like he belonged in Platinum Plateaus, not outside a shelter on the edge of Simulo. Was he a refugee too, or had he used the chaos as part of an ill-advised escape plan?

The man climbed out of the dumpster, huffing. "How much do you want for it?"

The cat's teal eyes seared into Dezi as the man licked his gray lips. Of course this perennial wanted to eat the poor thing, and while Dezi couldn't hold that against him, it didn't mean the cat deserved to die either. *Deserved*—Mars, neither of them deserved any of this, but could he afford to debate morality right now? Dezi adjusted his grip on the cat, but it bunched its cheeks and swatted him. He dropped it, and it sprinted into a dust gutter drain.

The perennial tried to grab it but fell onto his stomach. "What the hell, man? I was going to pay you."

Dezi threw his mylar blanket over his shoulders, covering the back of his neck. "If you're out here with us, you don't have any money."

"Dick. You're going to regret that." The dying immortal kicked some dust at him and then shuffled down the street.

From the safety of the gutter grate, the cat's eyes shone a predatory light, then disappeared into the gloom in search of more prey. Vesta would have traded that cat for dinner, but Dezi's hesitation had robbed him of a choice.

The queue on the curb shrank as staff called number after number through the speaker in the door, and by the time the sun sank past the burgundy clouds hanging over the jagged skyline, Dezi was completely alone. He moved to sit in the circle of light cast onto the sidewalk by the lamp on the shelter door and curled up, resting his cheek on his knee. The murmur of sand brushing the starless dome overhead was like a lullaby, but his shivering made a constant static sound against his foil blanket. It was so bitterly cold that his limbs stiffened as if setting into ice, and he was so tired that his head spun, startling him like he was suddenly falling, but if he fell asleep now, he might never wake. He needed to be strong, but—sun and stars above—he felt so damn weak.

What did Umbra expect him to do at a time like this? Should he have traded the cat for that perennial man's coat, or would that have been giving in to weakness? Was Elay strong for defending his home at all costs, or was he a coward for exploiting the vulnerable?

Mithra was the strongest person Dezi had ever known. She had raised her younger sister before she was a woman herself. Life had tried to stomp her into the dirt at every turn, but she never became bitter like Dezi—never resorted to cruelty. That was true strength, and it hadn't make a fucking grain of difference when she asphyxiated with her fists pounding on the airlock door.

The strong and the weak, the good and the evil, they all died the same. There was no meaning to be had in it; no point in fighting it. Mithra's eulogy had been beautiful, but the ashes the Edens sent back in her urn were just sand. Sand everywhere, crusted under Dezi's fingernails and caking his lungs. They'd gutted and trimmed Mithra, and after they found Dezi's frozen corpse, they'd harvest his DNA for the next generation of livestock. That would be his afterlife, his immortality: eternal servitude. Fighting only dragged out the inevitable.

"*YEEAOW!*"

"C'mere, you little shit!"

Down the road, a group of flashlight beams scattered and searched the alleyways.

"Forget it," a gruff man said. "We aren't eating rats tonight. You said he was up here?"

"There should be a couple left outside the shelter. There always are." One of them dragged a piece of metal along the storefronts, letting it click and clatter on the stone and glass. "We don't want this to get messy, so come on out!"

Oh, they were looking for Dezi. In another twist of fate, these blood scalpers would decide whether he lived or died tonight. He could have avoided this all if he had agreed to be Umbra's pet from the start, but even now, the thought drove up his blood pressure. Damn it all, he wanted something better. For all the misery in this uncaring world, he wanted more for himself, and he wanted more for Vesta. Dezi rose to his feet, but the trembling of his numb limbs made it clear that he could not outrun either perennials or men.

"I heard something." The lights moved closer, and footsteps clattered.

Dezi wanted to shout at his legs to move, but he had nowhere to go. The shelter was locked, there was no one to call for help, and the darkness down the alleyways was an inky black.

The silver cat dashed past his feet, stopping in front of a graffitied dumpster. It looked back at him, eyes flashing like beads, and climbed into it. Dezi let his blanket fall from his shoulders and limped after it, stumbling and crawling until he had his hands against its grimy steel. He pulled himself up to its lip, lifted the plastic lid, and slid in, falling headfirst into the dumpster's flimsy boxes and stinking bags.

"He's over here." A man ran to the shelter door, loudly rustling the mylar blanket Dezi had left behind. "Shit—come out already! You're going to freeze out here, jackass!"

They banged around and bickered as Dezi held perfectly still, and eventually, they moved down the road.

Warm with rot, the sour, earthy waste squelched around Dezi, and vermin skittered over his head. Roach legs crackling, rat paws padding, snake scales sliding—a furry thing pressed under his elbow. Long whiskers and a dry nose pushed against where his knees and chest met. He made space for it in his lap, and the cat curled against him. It breathed humid air into his face and, eventually, purred. He focused on that sound and gave in to the dark. Whether or not it would be enough, this was the limit of his strength.

Chapter 22
Choices

Vesta dashed into Elay's apartment, slamming the door and taking a deep breath of the sweat-and-chemical-laced air. Dezi was still out there, freezing solid if he wasn't already drained. She had to find him, but when she stepped out under that open sky, her mind went silver and her guts bucked in her stomach. They said the quakes were over, but every rattle of a wind chime made her run for shelter. What was happening to her? She had stared death in the mouth a few days ago, but now a breeze was enough to send her reeling.

"Is that the third time you've come back?" London glanced up from her laptop. "I wouldn't try it again. It's getting dark."

"Shut up." Vesta sat against the wall, tucking in her knees.

"Do you know how many shelters there are in Chryse?"

"Three hundred and eleven," she mumbled.

London nodded slowly, like she was talking to a toddler. "With over a thousand beds each. You're looking at scratch-off odds of finding him."

"So what do you care if I waste my time searching? Why're you always on my case?"

"He's a grown-ass man. He doesn't need you looking after him."

"You don't know him. He spirals. When Mithra passed, he damn near wasted away!"

London raised a partially singed eyebrow. "And what's going to happen to you if you keep going out there?"

"I'm going to find him, that's what." Vesta snatched her plastic bag of supplies and stomped to the door.

"You won't." London put her laptop aside and got up. "You know you won't."

Vesta grabbed the door handle, but her arm shook too hard to turn it. She let go, then gritted her teeth and grabbed it again, but it was no use. For all her talk, she couldn't do one damn thing other than run and hide.

BUHMMM!

A crack of thunder rippled overhead, and she fell back onto the floor.

With her pink flip-flops planted by Vesta's head, London crossed her arms. "Give it up. There's nothing you can do."

"There's always something I can do—there has to be!" Voice cracking, Vesta pounded her fist on the ground. "Otherwise, what's the point of living if it's all out of my control? What did Ms. Luminair save me for? What did Nikita die for? There has to be a reason—a bigger purpose." She curled up on the floor, covering her tear-streaked face in her arms. "Unless I was dumped on this rock to sell cheap lap dances until the next storm catches me in my sleep."

London squatted and stared across the room, gazing over the other girls holed up in this dump. "Why were you after my stage position so bad? It's not worth anything."

"How else could a colony girl bootstrap her way to immortality? I ain't got natural looks or education, but sis always said I had talent. I staked my whole life on a job like that..."

London itched her braids. "It's a display case immortals use to find their next pet. You can have the spot if that's what you're after, but something tells me you're not."

"So the dream I spent all this time chasing was a lie. *Stellar.*" Vesta hugged herself, limply lying on the floor. "Guess I should have known they'd never give us peons a shot at breaking out."

"There's one thing that can get you out of this rat race—money—and it should be all you think about. Forget your friends, forget your creative passion—they're distractions. And, yeah, life isn't fair, but that's why we fight dirty. Hard work doesn't mean shit; it's working smart that will give you a chance."

Vesta pushed herself up. "Then what's the smart way to bring Dezi home?"

"There isn't. All you'll find out there is a meat hook to hang from." London pinched her fingers and pointed her lime-green nails at Vesta. "Open your damn eyes: Chryse is a vampire. You stick your neck out, you get bit, and we don't do that shit for free. Dezi made his choice—he's got a right to live and die on his own terms—but do you want to throw your life away trying to look after a grown-ass man, or do you want to survive? Ask yourself, do you want to make it?"

Vesta buried her cheeks in her cough-wet palms. This was how Nikita had died, wasn't it? Sticking her neck out for someone else and getting it sawed in half with glass and gravel. She was the purest soul Vesta had ever known besides her own kin; it was a miracle she hadn't been snuffed out sooner, but Vesta wanted her death to mean something. She wasn't the only person who'd sacrificed to get her here, either. Mithra had put aside all her ambitions to support Vesta's education. She couldn't waste those gifts—she'd give them meaning, even if it was as small as surviving another day.

She raised her blurry eyes. "I wanna make it."

"Then let's get you a shot of iodine before your thyroid dissolves." London grabbed a rag and offered it. "He's a smart kid. Give him a night to see what you did, and he'll come back."

Vesta shook her head. Dezi was out there looking for punishment, and he wouldn't come back until he'd found enough of it.

Light streamed through the gaps in the dumpster lid, filtering through the garbage. The silver cat lying on Dezi's chest yawned, opening its eyes, then crawled over his shoulder and up through the cardboard. Dezi pushed open the dumpster lid and climbed over the side. He shook the microplastics out of his hair and took his spot on the curb. The cat sat next to him, licking its paws.

Dezi checked the tag on its chartreuse collar. It read *Marble*, with an address in Upper Old Chryse on the back. The little guy's family had certainly been immortals, but they were likely dead. He stroked Marble's head. "I'm sorry. I wish I could do something for you."

Marble scrunched his neck and squinted at Dezi, ambivalent to both his pity and human contact in general. He sneezed, then hopped off the curb and slid into the gutter drain. With no owners to provide food, he had a long day ahead of him, though he seemed to have it under control. Dezi, however, did not.

He examined the yellowed calluses and flaking scars on his garbage-smeared hands; this wasn't the life his parents had planned for him. He was supposed to have a bachelor's degree by now, with interviews lined up at Planitr and Hadron. Those were the families his father had aimed to join, and like any established professional, he'd invested heavily into genetic counseling to give his child the best shot at moving up with him. Even the color of Dezi's eyes had been picked from a swatch to ensure they'd be suitable to turn a robust shade of crimson. His parents had initially ordered a girl, too, and dumped thousands more on stem cell therapy to preserve his shot at joining a reputable bloodline, but it should have been obvious Dezirée was a dud the second she asked why they hadn't made her a boy. If his transition hadn't been disappointing enough, the aftermath of Mithra's death confirmed he would never line up with the blueprint his parents had laid out for him.

That night, after the accident, he hadn't bothered to eat or wash or get out of bed for his exam the next morning. He might have missed the funeral if Vesta hadn't coaxed him out of his room, but by that time, exam week was over and he'd flunked every class. The university would have put him on probation and expelled him if he didn't get perfect grades the next semester. Even then, his GPA would have been permanently stunted unless he could appeal to the admissions committee in Argyre, in person, which required two letters of recommendation and a formal diagnosis that aligned with a registered medical defect. The climb was impossible for someone barely holding on, so he dropped out and signed up to be Verde's next Zero instead.

It was a fitting punishment, and if he got lucky, he wouldn't have to stick around for very long. Dezi didn't want to make it obvious, but the frozen atmosphere had sucked out his desire to live when it took Mithra's last breath. He had been going through the motions, waiting to die the same way she had, until that morning he'd gotten caught in that dustslide. He had thought he was ready for it, but when he finally had an excuse to end it, he saw something. Whether it had been a trick of the light or a ghost from his subconscious, it'd reminded him of all the people his death would hurt. He still owed so much to Verde and Ajax and his mother and, most of all, Vesta. Mithra had been everything to her, and it was Dezi's responsibility to fill the hole she left behind.

To Dezi, the act of living was simply paying down another debt, but something changed when he came to Chryse; he met a vampire who lived for nothing but his own satisfaction. Self-obsessed, maniacal, fantastical, Umbra knew who he was, did what he pleased, and dared anyone to defy him. Unafraid of judgment, he was the first openly trans immortal Dezi had ever seen, and it dared him to hope. When they were alone together and the vampire acted a little immature, Dezi allowed himself to get messy back. He let himself forget that, at twenty-three, his life was already over, and the closest thing he'd see to those rockets from his old posters would be the prison freighter the Planitrs packed him into.

What he had with Umbra wasn't love, and it wasn't healthy, but he couldn't let it go. He recognized the irony of it too; he was doing exactly what Umbra had accused him of by chasing him like a lost dog. What could he even say to Umbra? *I was only going to ruin your life before I knew you actually liked me. Can I have your help now? Thanks.* Umbra had no reason to forgive him; he was as weak as ever. He'd be lucky to survive another night out here.

Dezi placed his phone's solar charger into the sunlight and risked turning it on. Maybe he should call Vesta. Giving up Umbra's ring to Elay would buy them some time before Jaxon showed up. It might even be worth enough to save Elay's house, though that meant little to Dezi. He picked up his phone and, above a hundred missed calls from Vesta, found a single message left by his mother. Oh Mars, she probably thought he was dead. What kind of awful child wouldn't contact their mother after a natural disaster? The dread creeping up his stomach at the thought of speaking to her was only outweighed by the guilt of putting off this call another night. Before he had thought through what he intended to say, he hit the redial button.

His mother picked up instantly. "Dezi, *oh, mi hijo.* Why haven't you called? How many days do I have to wait to get so much as a text from my own son?"

Dezi's mouth dried up, but this was pretty much what he had expected. "S-sorry. Things have been kind of crazy over here."

"Were you hurt? Are you working? I hope you're still employed."

"I've been keeping busy. I'm serving at a pretty nice resort, so you don't need to worry."

"Are you certain you don't need money? Vesta has told me you were staying with a friend."

"Yup, we have lots of friends here." Dezi's voice cracked. "Did I tell you about the college fund I've been saving up?"

"Dezi..."

"Well—I-I have to go help Vesta with something so—"

"Please," she said quietly, "don't go."

Dezi pulled his legs up, cupping his phone to his ear. "I'm here. But I'm fine, really."

"I know it's been difficult for you to be open with others since your father left, but you shouldn't feel the need to lie to your mother."

He passively tugged at his shoelaces. Maybe he was a little anti-social, but that was because he was a nervous wreck, not because of abandonment issues or anything like that. Plenty of kids in Verde had lost family members in worse ways than he had. "I don't want to disappoint you again..."

"Whatever shortcomings you have are my responsibility as well."

"Mom, there wasn't a kid in Verde with as many opportunities as I had. Even Dad did his best to set me up before he left. I can't imagine how much it cost you to help me transition."

"W-we—" His mom caught her stutter. She hated this topic almost as much as Dezi did. "You know your father was elated to have a son, and neither of us wanted recruiters to hold your birth sex against you."

"Recruiters." Dezi rested his forehead on his knees. "I threw any shot at joining a bloodline away when I dropped out of college."

"I shouldn't have pushed you so hard."

"Don't apologize. That was my fault. I dropped out, I flunked my classes, and I sent her out there."

"You can't blame yourself for Mithra's death."

He tilted his head back to the darker half of the sky, and his tears leaked down his temples into his hair. "You're going to say the weather did it. I knew what the weather was like when I handed her that drone. I just thought my grade was more important."

"No. The Edens killed her," his mother said frostily. "They built a plantation on a planet that has no business hosting life and then outfitted it with improper equipment. It's those with the power to make these decisions who should be held responsible, not you. Not us."

"So my actions don't matter? I'm a pawn fumbling around in someone else's game?" Dezi grated his knuckles on the pavement, but it didn't deaden the pain in his chest. "That's how I feel, at least."

"I understand feeling trapped by your past mistakes." His mom chose her words slowly. "In some ways, we all are, but we always have choices moving forward. I was a poor mother when you were young, but I've learned since then. I didn't provide the support you needed, but I'm trying to do better now."

"You haven't made the kinds of mistakes I have. I've done things that can't be forgiven."

"Forgive yourself, Son. You're a different man now; you won't make those mistakes again."

"How do you know that?" Stiff and swollen from the cold, Dezi buried his face in his hands. "What if I'm still weak?"

"You are human, Dezi. Your grandfather, my father, often said, *não existem escolhas perfeitas*. Do you know what that means?"

Dezi struggled with the ancient language, letting his ear guide him. "There are no perfect choices…"

"Sometimes we fail to live up to our ideals, but we can't let our lapses define us. You can strive to be a better man; you already have."

He wanted to tell her she was wrong—to scream that he was worthless—but those were childish thoughts. The truth was that he had been trying, and for each time he stumbled, he fought that much harder. It was time to stop acting like he didn't deserve better—like he didn't want to take control of his life and spit in the face of anyone who tried to steal it away again. He had made the choice to fight when he ran from that dustslide; it'd just taken him until now to realize it.

"I can. I will."

"Show them you're the type of man that I know you are. But remember, through every success and failure, I will always love you."

Dezi's cheeks tingled. "I love you too, Mom."

"Call me again soon and, please, stay safe." Her voice wavered.

"I'll try, I really will. Bye, Mom." Dezi raised his head to the horizon, where a sliver of copper light peeked over the jaws of the city.

The speaker on the shelter door hummed to life. "Five-thousand and forty-two?"

He dashed to the door. "Yes—that's me."

"You're in spot 437." The handle clicked.

Dezi shook his bagged soup to stimulate the heating elements and then tore open the top with his teeth. He took a sip and pressed the grainy noodles against his tongue. He wasn't sure what "noodle flavor" was supposed to taste like, but all he was getting was salt, MSG, and iron supplements. As a connoisseur of instant meals, he'd rate this Nutrosia-brand one as pretty good, but they could have at least given him a spoon. Maybe it was the Earthling in him, but drinking hot soup through a straw was just wrong.

"Mreow." Marble stared at him expectantly. Dezi wasn't sure how the cat had gotten into the shelter, much less found him, but he couldn't deny that he valued the fancy lad's company. He knocked some noodles out of his pouch onto the floor, and Marble scarfed them up, grunting and purring.

After they finished breakfast, he and Marble huddled under the thin towel that had come with his spot on the floor. The shelter was supposed to have given him a green pop-up bed and some hygiene supplies, but someone must have stolen them as soon as the drone placed them out. Without a single live representative from the Ambrose Foundation charity to supervise them, the warehouse-turned-shelter was noisy, lawless, and hardly warmer than outside.

Dezi tied his blanket around his waist and heaved himself up. "We're going to need something to keep us off the floor tonight. Will you help me scavenge?"

Marble turned his back and tucked himself into a loaf. He pretended not to like Dezi, but he'd be back come nightfall. Dezi shrugged. "Suit yourself, but if I find more food, I'm not sharing."

He wove through the rows of beds laid out on the concrete, heading for the industrial recycling bins near the lavatory pods. They'd have cardboard he could fashion into a bed, and if he found some rotten food or anything that the lavatory pods would mistake for organic waste, they'd trade him a water voucher for it. The blood donation terminals offered vouchers too, but he had given what blood he had in exchange for his soup. He heard people saying you could get it to take a little more if you did a lap around the shelter to get your blood pressure up, so if he didn't find anything useful in the garbage, that would be his plan for dinner.

He carefully stepped around a heavily pregnant woman lying in a nest of blankets and old clothing. Her eyelids snapped open, and she pulled her diaper bag to her chest.

"Sorry," Dezi whispered as he crept past.

She huffed, rolled over, and threw her arm over the empty space of her cot, then suddenly sat up. "Pim? Pim!"

Dezi took another step, but she grabbed his leg, howling, "Where did you take him? Give me back my baby!"

He fell onto his ass, trying to pull away without hurting her. "I don't know what you're talking about. Let me go!"

A couple of older white women from a nearby group rushed over. "Zuri, what's going on? Did he hurt you?"

Dezi's stomach drained out; the optics of this situation were getting worse by the second. "I-I was walking by. Ask anyone."

The pregnant woman let Dezi go and stumbled around her cot, unable to keep her attention focused on anything for more than a few seconds. "Pim! Has anyone seen him? I laid down for a nap and now he's gone." Sobbing, she collapsed to her knees.

The gray-haired women surrounded her, promising to help search, while Dezi slipped away. He'd keep an eye out, but he wouldn't give her false hope. A lost child had a slim chance of survival.

Dezi ducked under the hazard tape blocking off the shelter from the inactive factory line and then crept past the unlit machinery, taking it slow to let his eyes adjust. Keeping an eye out for any security drones, he snuck to the aluminum shelves, popped open a crate's plastic lid, and stuck his hand in—purely out of curiosity. He definitely did not intend to steal anything, even if it was water, and he was really thirsty.

The bin was full of slippery little squares with pointy edges. Packaged cookies, possibly? He pulled a handful out, but the red foil packages were cauterizing pads. Dezi sighed and dropped them back in.

He shuffled to the row of recycling bins and worked his way through them, keeping his rustling to a minimum as he leaned over each one's brim. By the time he had searched them all, he had gathered a sturdy cardboard box to sleep on, along with some plastic sheeting to serve as a blanket. He stuck his head under a dumpster, hoping a runaway bottle might have rolled under it, but instead, found a bright yellow crowbar wedged under the bin. Some personal protection would certainly help him sleep better, so he army-crawled to it, grabbed the end, and shimmied it free.

As he slid the crowbar into his belt, a set of hurried footsteps rushed toward him. He hastily tucked his legs under the bin and turned himself around.

"Hurry, he could wake up any second," a raspy woman said.

"Not likely. My venom is more potent than yours," a crisp-sounding man said as their flashlight beam passed Dezi.

The light illuminated an encampment of stolen beds and tents set up deeper in the factory behind a foil-packaging machine.

"You better hope so, or this could give away our location." The raspy woman turned on the camper lantern hanging over their tents, illuminating the group. Composed of two women and two men, the stowaways were finely dressed in their winter coats and checkered scarves.

The second younger woman, wearing a lavender puffer jacket, shivered as she touched her face repeatedly. "Are you sure this is a good idea, Sire? Isn't it better to wait until, like, night?"

"I saw an opportunity and took it. If you take issue with that, spare us your whinging and leave." Her crisp-sounding sire knelt to lay an orange sack on the ground. In his thin cashmere sweater and black slacks, he must have been freezing, but his nose wasn't even red. His face and hands were perfectly white.

Dezi clenched his crowbar, seething silently. Not only had these perennials snuck in and stolen his bed, they were leeching supplies off of the shelter, too. On the bright side, he could steal it all back when they left.

The last parasite, a man with tortoiseshell glasses, slipped into a tent and returned to the circle of light with a needle, tube, and dirty blood bag. "How much are we taking?"

"You tell us, doctor." The sire stood. "You're guaranteed that, unlike the others, he's entirely topped up."

The orange bundle softly cried, "Momma?"

The sire snapped his tongue and stepped back, revealing a child in a winter romper staring wide-eyed at the four gaunt faces looking down at him.

"I can't wait any longer—" The raspy woman dropped to her knees, tore the child's sleeve open, and bit into his arm.

The boy's teddy-bear-brown eyes rolled back, dully falling onto Dezi. It was a scene from a horror film; it couldn't be real. This was too depraved to be real.

The sire hunched down to the child's other arm, but the doctor grabbed his shoulder and pulled him back. "Stop! If we don't measure how much blood we take, he might die."

But the woman did not stop, and the sire's eyes were red with bloodlust. He shoved the doctor aside and lunged for the child. The woman greedily pulled the boy out of his grasp, dragging him back into a stark shadow, while the doctor clung to his sire's legs and pleaded with them both. The younger woman covered her mouth, vomited a little fluid into her hands, and slowly backed into the darkness.

His own stomach turning, Dezi crawled out from under the bin and rushed the feeding ghoul, striking her across the temple with his crowbar. With a wet crack, she fell aside, stringy hair covering her eyes and limp tongue coated in blood. She belonged on the ground, and anyone who would do this to a child belonged there with her. Dezi scooped the boy under his arm and stepped back, panting and trembling.

The sire kicked the doctor off his legs and stood, hands clawed. "He's ours. Find your own."

Staring the monster directly in the teeth, Dezi shakily raised his crowbar. "Take another step, and I'll kill you."

"Aniya?" The doctor nudged the woman's shoulder. She gurgled. When he turned her over and pressed a mess of gauze onto her indented skull, a bottle of water fell from his medical bag and rolled to the sire's feet, diamond-like in how it caught the lantern light.

"Oh. You're human." The sire slowly picked up the bottle. "And you're thirsty, aren't you? We have plenty of food and water."

"Dammit, James, can you cut your shit for one goddamned second?" The doctor scrabbled in his bag, hands painted with black blood. "I need your help."

"If she's not dead, she'll heal." He sneered at his fallen ally, then took a step toward Dezi, offering the water in his skeletal hand. "Say, young one, how would you like to join us? My youngest child has run out on me, but you would make a fine replacement. You're strong; not afraid of a little violence."

"What?" Dezi stepped back. "You can't make a new scion on the spot."

"A family elder can adopt who he pleases. Come now, this is the opportunity of a lifetime. I'll remake you an immortal in my image." The sire smiled, eyeing Dezi's crowbar.

The offer sounded too good to be true because it was. Any vampire with real power would be holed up in Stellaire, paying someone to scalp blood for him rather than doing it himself. This wasted perennial had designed this line to get his fangs into the necks of gullible fools, and Dezi wasn't tempted to become anything like him. He inched towards the shelter's light. "What's your bloodline? It better be a good one if I'm signing up to be an accessory to murder."

"I won't need to kill the child if I have you." He stalked forward, slowly circling to cut off Dezi's exit. "You'll keep me well-fed for the rest of the storm."

Dezi backed up against the dumpster, squeezing Pim to his chest. "So I get my brand now, and you'll blood me after the city opens up?"

He straightened his posture and touched his breast. "Hand to my still heart, I'll blood you tonight if you give me the boy right now."

The wiry fiend looked frail, but he moved with an ancient confidence. Starved or not, he was still Dezi's physical superior in every way. Dezi couldn't take him in a fair fight, but humankind had one advantage over immortals: numbers. He slammed the recycling bin with his crowbar, booming it like a church bell. "Help! Someone help me! HELP!"

The fiend lunged forward, but when Dezi swung his crowbar warningly, he gracefully hopped to the side. He caught Dezi's next swing, wrenching his weapon free, and tossed it aside with a clang. "You're smarter than you look. It almost makes me feel guilty over killing you."

Dezi held his fist at his side, readying it. "I'll make this messy. You won't get more than a mouthful out of either of us before the rest of the shelter shows up."

"You think they're coming for you?" He laughed. "If any human heard you, they're cowering in their sheets. You humans wouldn't brave the dark for a loved one, much less a stranger."

"I did," Dezi said as the clattering of footsteps echoed on the concrete. "Do you hear something?"

The perennial's eyes narrowed. His shoulders hunched, then he dashed for the encampment's bags, whisking them into shadows. The doctor picked up the other injured ghoul and kept his head lowered as he followed behind.

"What's going on?" A portly man leading a mix of survivors raced up, huffing and shining his phone light in Dezi's face.

"They..." Dezi's knees wobbled, and he caught himself on the dumpster as his adrenaline sputtered out. "Perennials. There are perennials preying on the shelter. They went that way."

"Screaming stars." The man's face lost color as he looked over the red blood and black ichor streaked across the floor. "Do you need help? I mean, what can we do?"

"Didn't you hear me? They went that way." Dezi pointed. "Chase them! Destroy their camp! Get them the hell out of here."

"Right—right! Come on!" He grabbed Dezi's crowbar and ran into the factory, heading the charge of those brave enough to follow.

Other survivors focused on the camp, tearing down the tents and carrying the beds back to their assigned placement in the shelter. Dezi stole a cauterizing pad for Pim and brought him to his mother. Weeping and blubbering, she offered him everything she had in thanks. He accepted her apology and a few baby wipes to help with his unpleasant smell. Marble didn't appreciate the wipe down, but he let Dezi handle him without swatting him this time.

They would have to sleep lightly tonight, but every morning the sky got brighter, and there were whispers that the tunnels may open soon.

CHAPTER 23

Lies

Under marmalade-orange clouds, the gondolas brought guests to and from Stellaire for the first time in three weeks. Martians, Earthlings, and Venusians alike crowded the bars, ordering cans of Hemo airdropped from Acidalia that morning. Dezi buffed a bar table in tight circles, with his eyes darting between the exits. He had foolishly hoped Umbra would visit the café for breakfast, but his absence indicated he was taking care to avoid Dezi. The spaceport would open at noon, so his window of time to intercept Umbra was preciously short. He didn't want to press his luck by waltzing up to Umbra's suite in the restricted access area, but he was running out of options. He settled on checking with Ms. Mai first; if she still was under the assumption he and Dezi were bickering, he might be able to trick her into giving the VIP's location away.

He approached the security theater, where Ms. Mai spent most of her day spying on clients. In a scarlet slip dress with a slit up to her hip and a chunky emerald belt trailing down to her ankles, the refined woman's eyes darted between an array of screens in an intense search. She suddenly perked up, then hurried to the bar without pushing in her chair.

Dezi rushed to catch her. "Ma'am, could you help me find my VIP? I think he'd appreciate me bidding him farewell before he returns home."

Her heel caught on the carpet, and she stopped where she stood. "What a brazen lie. I should terminate you for that. He's not protecting you anymore, so I'm free to do it."

Dezi had miscalculated—badly—and bluffing harder wasn't likely to save him. "I-I might have been stretching the truth, but—"

Cormac came jogging up beside the bar, dressed in his street clothes. "Ma'am, ma'am!"

"Oh, Nova, here comes another one." She tried to dodge them both, but Cormac cut her off.

"Please, you gotta give me my job back. It's a ghost town in here. You need me."

"You skipped out on your bond in the middle of a blood shortage." She shoved past him to the drink pickup station.

"But I paid my termination fee." Cormac slid between her and the countertop, cupping his hands. "C'mon, I'll bus, I'll do anything."

"You can get out of my face before I call security." Ms. Mai pointed at his nose, then turned to Dezi. "And you will keep away from my VIP if you don't want to be escorted out with this clown." She collected two martinis from the drink station and paced into the casino.

"Jeez." Cormac scratched the back of his head. "Looks like neither of us can catch a break."

Dezi anxiously tapped his nails on the countertop. "That's an understatement. We have to catch up later, but I need to go."

"Before you head out..." Cormac crossed his arms and glanced to the side. "I heard you were staying with that guy with the centipede tattoo. Think his name was Elay?"

Dezi pressed his tongue to the back of his canine, considering how to reply. He wanted to confide in his friend how miserable working for that vamp had been, but he wasn't sure he could trust anyone with the full truth about the time he had spent as a gang lackey. "I left. I've been trying to get Vesta out too, but she won't stay in a shelter."

Cormac's posture relaxed. "Good. For a minute, I was worried you were in with the Moroskas. So, I've got this new place in Diskos—and they're definitely going to evict me when I miss rent next month—but I could put you all up until then. London, too, if you can convince her to get out of there."

"Really? I mean, thank you. I can ask Vesta to talk to her, but what are you doing back here? I thought you were rich."

"I made some money, but I got into another play that went bust. Easy come easy go, right?" He grinned, but it was a little pained. "I won't keep you from your guest any longer; they're fueling up those long-distance shuttles now."

"Are they? Then I better hurry." Dezi tried to laugh it off, but the thought that Umbra had already left made him want to puke. As he eyed Ms. Mai's abandoned desk in the security theater, a terribly risky idea came to mind. "Hey, could you keep a lookout for Ms. Mai? I'm about to do something stupid."

Cormac checked over each shoulder, then tapped his temple. "Can't get fired if you don't get caught, right? I've got your back."

"Thanks, man." If things went well, he'd have Umbra's protection again, though that was still a big *if*. Dezi had written and rehearsed an excellent apology, but the vampire was fickle at the best of times.

He discreetly approached the surveillance center arranged in the shadow of the crystal lounge. He crept past a couple of gray-suited security professionals watching chips change hands on their monitors, took a seat at a terminal, and cycled through the cameras. After checking the dining areas, casino floor, and cafés, he switched to the private booths, but the system asked for administrator-level access. He raised his chin like he was supposed to be there and scooted to Ms. Mai's favorite computer. She had left her terminal logged in, confirming Dezi's suspicion that she wasn't nearly as good at her job as she thought she was.

He clicked the session she had left up, and it opened to a view looking down on Umbra. Pale as platinum and dressed in a lustrous indigo suit, he was as radiant as a pearly band of stars on a cloudless night. Seiyo sat on the opposite side of the booth, but based on the luggage next to them, Dezi didn't have a minute to waste.

Before he hit the logout key, Ms. Mai parted the curtains and placed a bloodied martini in front of the vampire. It struck Dezi that he had never seen her wearing red before, but the scarlet slip she had on now was as bright as a host's uniform. As she slid into the booth beside Umbra, he put his arm around her, teasing the sliver of bare skin above her long gloves with his sharp nails. When Umbra whispered something in her ear, Dezi grabbed the headset and turned the volume up.

"Are you in need of another favor, my dear?" Umbra brushed his fingers over the emerald studs in her ears. "I'm afraid it may be a while before my next visit, and I don't want to leave you destitute."

"Oh no, sir, your satisfaction is enough." Ms. Mai's smile exaggerated the fine lines beside her eyes.

"I was quite satisfied before you arrived, so you must be here for something."

"Well..." She traced the foot of her martini glass. "Have I not been a loyal servant, my lord?"

Umbra swirled his drink under his nose but then abandoned it on the table. "I am not your lord."

"But I've served your family for decades—my entire life."

"That you have. Is this leading somewhere?"

"You were considering offering your prior host a bond, but a Martian from some storm-torn crater couldn't possibly meet your standards. Someone with more experience would serve you better."

"Pray tell, how might she serve me?" Youthful enough to be her child, Umbra pressed a finger over her lips, then ran it down her chin all the way to her silk scarf.

Ms. Mai's smile brimmed over as she took the invitation to slink closer, sliding her hands onto his shoulders and bringing her legs over his lap. "Allow me to provide a demonstration."

Dezi gripped the headset against his ears as Ms. Mai undid her scarf and turned her head aside. Peppered with pale punctures and stripes, her neck was the texture of tangled lace. Umbra kissed her jugular, letting his lips admire her scars, as he pushed the shoulder of her dress down to unveil the next clean patch in her tapestry of mastications. He licked his teeth, coating them in his venom, and then opened his jaw around her arm. When his lips closed over her skin, a shudder ran down her entire body.

Dezi's heart pounded as Umbra enveloped his prey, tying his arms around her and pressing his nails into her soft flesh. He drank throatful after throatful until Ms. Mai couldn't hold herself up, and then kept going as her head rolled back and her grinning lips limply opened. If he didn't stop now, he'd kill her. Dezi scrambled to his feet, but Umbra released her with a satisfied breath, stretching the threads of bloody saliva webbing his fangs.

"Mmh. *Superbe.*" He dabbed the corner of his mouth, letting Ms. Mai crumple to the bench. "Seiyo, tidy her up, if you would."

Seiyo removed a cauterizing pad from his breast pocket and walked around the booth to Ms. Mai. While Seiyo dressed her gash, Dezi felt dirty, but he couldn't turn away. Had he looked that pathetic when Umbra had his lips against his neck? No, the intimacy they shared hadn't been this callous, but it was still shocking to see Umbra treat a human being as disposable. He was toying with her, stringing the poor woman along on the promise of being picked as one of his dedicated bloodbags. This side of Umbra should have disturbed Dezi, but there was something darkly satisfying about watching the woman who had condescended to him so often be brought to her knees. The type of power the vampire held was intoxicating: dangerous in large doses.

Seiyo propped Ms. Mai up beside Umbra. "Did you intend to leave her alive?"

"Don't be silly." He took her under his arm, brushing her hair back into place. "I intended to leave her conscious, but she was so delectable that I had to catch myself."

Ms. Mai's eyelids fluttered open. Deathly pale, she took labored breaths, staring up at Umbra like he was the light at the end of her tunnel. "Will you sign me?"

"You do such good work at Stellaire. I'd prefer you to stay."

Her eyes widened, and she gripped his lapel, teetering like a drunk. "You promised—you promised to save me."

He peeled her clenched fingers off of his suit. "I have, and I will continue to provide, so long as you don't try my patience."

"Please, I don't want to stay on this hell planet." She raised her hands to his face, too hesitant to touch him, but trembling with the desire to. "Why can't I be with you?"

He sighed and turned away. "I need you to watch over Dezi for me. Without supervision, the boy will surely get himself killed."

Her shoulders sagged, and she leaned into him limply. "You still want him... Why don't you take him already?"

"He and I are not suited for one another." As Umbra stroked her head, his smile betrayed a bitterness. "But it's fine. Maybe it's best to let one go on occasion, hm?"

"Oh no, you deserve the world for what your family has given us. The new planets you brought life to, the shelters you have built for us—" She clung to him like a wet cat, eyes sparkling with venom-induced mania. "Humanity would be lost without the Ambroses' guidance, and you are their treasured prince."

Dezi's hand leaped to his mouth as a harsh breath chilled his lungs. Umbra's paranoia suddenly made sense; he had let slip that his father was an ancient, but to be a prince... Could he be a genetic descendent of the Ambrose hierarch? Being an Ambrose alone made him a member of the most elite bloodline the system had ever known, so it was no wonder he had cut Dezi off after seeing that camera. He was space-age royalty, and likely forbidden from fraternizing with humans not bound under strict contract.

The impracticality of their budding romance crushed Dezi, but it didn't change his mission: return the ring and regain Umbra's trust. Even if a deeper relationship between a runaway human and a vampiric prince was impossible, Dezi could be his host again. He could rebuild their friendship.

The edges of the ring's diamonds cut into Dezi's grip as he approached the booth. He reached for the curtain, but then hesitated and adjusted his tie instead. Umbra saw him as too weak-willed to be trusted, so Dezi had to prove he wasn't the same man who had betrayed him in that booth. He understood why he had made that mistake, but he'd learned from it and come to his own understanding of the difference between strength and power. Strength wasn't about being flawless but, instead, striving for better in an imperfect world.

Dezi knocked on the wall beside the curtain.

"This booth is occupied," Ms. Mai said curtly.

"I know."

"Dezi! How dare you—"

"Hush, Mai," Umbra growled, and they shuffled behind the curtain. "Dezi, I did not ask for much."

"I need to speak to you, and I won't take no for an answer."

Umbra was silent for a moment, and Dezi could imagine how perplexed that response had made him.

The vampire finally said, "You may enter. But you will be brief."

Dezi pulled back the curtain, finding Umbra and Ms. Mai at opposite ends of the table. Ms. Mai wore the glare of a woman caught undressing, and Seiyo watched him expectantly, but Umbra avoided his gaze, wringing a smudged table napkin in his hands.

"I need to apologize"—Dezi's gaze darted between Ms. Mai and Seiyo—"about something private."

Seiyo crossed his arms, and Ms. Mai adjusted her bra strap.

Umbra hid his napkin below the table. "Seiyo and I are departing shortly, so you must state your goodbyes in his presence. However, Mai, you are excused."

"Please call me if you have issues with his *palatability*." Ms. Mai gave Umbra a longing glance, then braced herself on the wall and strutted out with all the grace of a half-eaten chew toy.

"I was expecting this." Umbra intertwined his fingers, adopting a formal posture. "Humans have a habit of growing attached, but it is often to their detriment. I'm afraid I will have to threaten you now."

"Just hear me out. If this doesn't change your mind, I won't bother you again." Dezi took the seat across from Umbra. "I made a mistake, and I'm not here to make excuses, but you need to understand why I did it."

"I am well aware. Human morality becomes quite flexible under strain."

"I did it to survive. With the information I had, it seemed like my only choice." Dezi rested his arms on the table, adopting a pose similar to Umbra's. "As a vampire, you should understand that making ethical compromises to extend your life isn't a sign of weakness."

The immortal's poise broke with an unprofessional lip pucker. "You are presumptuous as ever."

"I might be getting worse." Dezi returned a soft smile. "I cut off Elay. As soon as I left Stellaire, I told him I was done, and I've been surviving on my own ever since."

"Is that meant to impress me?" Umbra crossed his arms. "The ring I gave you was worth enough to pay your living expenses for a decade."

"I didn't sell it." Dezi placed his open hand on the center of the table, presenting the ring. "I'm here to return it."

Umbra's cheeks flushed orchid-pink with Ms. Mai's blood. "You can't be serious."

"I am. I'm serious about us. I know I fucked up, but I'll do whatever it takes to earn your forgiveness. Let me be your host again, and let's go back to how it was before the storm."

"Go back?" Umbra laughed once, far too loudly. "Are you truly so naive to think they would allow that? Allow *us*?"

Seiyo lowered his phone, eyeing Umbra, and Dezi shakily pushed the ring forward. "I didn't say it would be easy, but if you're talking about the Planitrs, I'm sure we can figure something out."

"*They* is *everyone*, you foolish man. I am a vampire; there is no going back for me—only forward—and unless I take you with me now, you'll be lost to me forever." Umbra suddenly gripped his head and exposed his fangs in a ferocious grimace. "And I can't...I can't live without you."

Something was wrong; Umbra wasn't making sense.

Dezi tried to see his eyes past the wild curls falling over his hands. "I-I like you too, but I don't understand. Where do you need me to go?"

"*Além do limite da morte.*" Umbra took the ring from Dezi's hand as dark blue tears trickled from the corners of his eyes. He sobbed and closed his hand around the emerald. "*Mas esse é o único lugar que você não irá seguir, Desidério.*"

"Sire?" Seiyo leaped to Umbra's side, and at his touch, Umbra blinked, as if he didn't recognize the room. Seiyo snatched the ring, scowling at Dezi. "What have you done, boy?"

"Seiyo, the ring is a memento." Umbra wiped away his inky tears. "And Dezi...he is as well."

"That's not possible. The boy is hardly more than twenty years old." Seiyo scrutinized Dezi. "Are you a clone, or an original?"

Dezi's birth certificate had a seal of genetic uniqueness, but he didn't understand how that was relevant. "Umbra, what is he talking about? You called me by a different name, and you were speaking in an Old-Earth language. You've used it with me before, but I never understood you."

Umbra turned to Seiyo. "Don't you see? This explains how my feelings came on so strongly. Desi... I was in love with a man named Desidério, but somehow, I have forgotten him."

"I'm not familiar with the name or the language. If these are truly phantom memories, they are from before my time." Seiyo studied the ring, holding it to the light. "You must have been nearly his age..."

As the vampires ignored him, speaking about Dezi like he wasn't there, he began to feel very small. He never could have predicted that Umbra's love was for another man, one Dezi simply reminded him of, but the news was jet fuel on the embers of the insecurities he had worked so hard to smother. He took a deep breath and decided he could stoke that fire later, when he was alone again. "I'm glad I could help..."

"Oh, darling." Umbra smiled, tilting his head sympathetically, though it still dripped of condescension. "You have given me an invaluable gift, and I intend to express my full gratitude."

"But do you even like me at all? Or were all of those feelings for someone else?"

Something stirred under Umbra's beatific eyes—his walls rising. "You are my memento, and you can rest assured that I will treasure you accordingly."

Dezi watched the velvet curtain, halfway tempted to walk out. He didn't want to be a memento, whatever that meant, but his true desire was too embarrassing to voice.

Seiyo chuckled, shaking his head. "Sire, you have to stop letting humans fall in love with you. You know it's cruel."

"I was never in love," Dezi snapped. "I'm not some heartsick teen."

Seiyo raised a brow. "Fine then, infatuated. Not that it would have changed my sire's intentions for you; if he hadn't torn out his other pet's throat, he would have ground yours between his teeth."

Umbra's jaw flexed. "That was an astonishingly unhelpful comment, and I would be ever so grateful if you allowed me to handle this delicate conversation myself."

Seiyo unlocked his phone. "I'll have someone removed from the shuttle to make space for him, but try to keep this quick. You have a two o'clock in Seoul."

Dezi's face drained of feeling. "He's joking, right? You weren't ever going to kill me."

Umbra's charming laughter filled the booth. "Can we not let our mistakes lie in the past? What matters now is our future, and I intend to spend it exploring the affections between us. They may have originated by chance, but who is to say they can't grow into something more?" Umbra touched his heart with the finesse of a skilled actor. "They may have already, my young love."

"Don't manipulate me. After everything I went through to bring that ring back, it's insulting you can't answer a simple question." Dezi straightened his back, but a prickle traced down his spine. "If we're going to move forward, I need the truth about us and how you knew the storm was coming. I want to know who you really are."

"I suppose you deserve as much, but are you sure you want the whole truth?" Umbra's eyes narrowed, corrupting his smile into something too calculated, too ancient, for a boy's face. "You may regret it."

Dezi didn't hesitate. "Tell me everything."

"You know the story in part, but I omitted a few unsavory details..." Graceful as a feather, Umbra sprang over the table, seating himself before Dezi and extending his legs into the booth to cage him. "Despite your lowly planetary origin, I hoped to accept you as one of my donors, but you owed a debt to a family of charlatans that would sooner spit in my face than accept a fair payment. I was barred from even sampling you, so in my arrogance, I elected to *take* you from them. If I couldn't have you by my side, I would work this puzzling infatuation out of my system by savoring you *completely*."

He drew a claw down Dezi's cheekbone. "I planned to spend the week draining you. I would have ruined your fragile human mind by imparting every pleasure within my power to give. You would know nothing but my touch, think nothing but of me, and in your pursuit to satisfy my desires, offer the decadent climax of your lifeblood. So yes, before I realized your true value, I intended to devour you. You should be flattered; I am a picky eater, and I don't kill often."

With his lips agape and posture frozen, Dezi's shallow breath rattled in his throat. He had worn the same expression when he'd watched Umbra come ounces away from killing Ms. Mai, but what she sold her skin for, Dezi had stumbled into: he'd captured the attention of a genuine monster. Umbra lavished him with jewels and sexual affection, jealously guarding him from the other monsters, because Dezi was special. He'd won the grand prize in this twisted lottery the humans here played, and it made his heart pound so hard he felt it in his fingertips.

"But it doesn't frighten you..." Umbra tilted his head, smiling like a devil. "It thrills you."

Dezi hardened his expression, shielding his reactions from the vampire. "You've killed before? Just for the fun of it?"

"You were audience to one of my more unfortunate cases of overindulgence." Umbra ran a finger across the corner of his pearly jaw, examining Dezi as if recalling his flavor. "Don't feign that my appetites shock you."

"Cat was an animal." Gooseflesh traveled up Dezi's arms as he studied Umbra's pitiless, blood-soaked eyes. "Is that how you see us?"

He clicked his tongue. "I'm afraid you are an animal. Humans struggle to accept this, but your lives flare and fade, as all mortal creatures' do. I would never be so cruel as to attack a mortal for their life, but I have been offered that gift by many an admirer. A polite vampire refuses, but I am not always so polite."

Rage like a balled fist tightened in Dezi's chest. "Is that why you didn't bother to warn us that the storm was coming? You could have saved us, but you didn't give a shit whether we died."

"Saved you? Oh, my sweet thing, it's not so simple; there were greater forces at play."

"Bigger vampires than you? That's a weak excuse and you know it."

"I never said that..." He tapped a finger on his lips, seemingly more amused by Dezi's jabs than insulted. "But if you must know, Chryse's housing market was overdue for a crash. Inflation had surpassed the fixed rates on those intergenerational leases, and suffice it to say, we construct those buildings to fall every few generations. Liken it to the brush fire which keeps a forest healthy."

"W-what?" It seared through Dezi's guard like a bolt of lightning. "No—this can't be intentional. No one would build a city to fall."

"In this age of immortality, every death is intentional. Have you never questioned why so many go hungry when we have the technology to feed all of you tomorrow? The simple fact is that when man came to conquer the natural evils of life, he became its last remaining root." Umbra extended his arms to exhibit himself. "Thus, the vampire was born."

"So we were all just collateral damage?" The corner of Dezi's lips twitched. "I don't know who I thought you were, but it wasn't this."

"I assure you, my heart aches for the sacrifices made, but this is the way of things. The world cannot operate without a measure of evil, and it is my kind's burden to administer it." Umbra brushed a lock of Dezi's hair back, his touch as delicate as the kiss of cold air, sending shivers down Dezi's arms. "I understand it's shocking to learn I might have consumed you, but ethically speaking, what I offered was a humane alternative to the hideous end you would have suffered had I not intervened."

Dezi scoffed in his face. "You're no different from the perennials out there eating children."

Umbra's smile flicked off like a switch. "And you are the paragon of justice? Don't play the innocent, not after what you did to me."

Dezi pressed his tongue to the roof of his mouth, tasting the bitter truth on it. "I was backed into a corner, but I can admit it was wrong."

"It was a necessary evil. Necessary for your personal comfort, of course."

He returned a flat stare. "You tried to kill me to satisfy your vampire fetish. You're sadistic."

"And you are a liar in a class of your own. Admit it: This is the part of me that tempts you the most." Umbra sank his nails into the leather cushion, cutting through it like soft tissue. "There goes your heart racing again. You're drawn to power like a gnat to honey."

"No." Dezi edged back, his breath catching as Umbra pulled his gleaming claws free. "Everyone in this city wants power. They want control over their lives."

"Mortals want security, and that is my offer to you. Whatever it takes, I'll free you from the Planitrs' noose; my price is that you return with me to AZURE."

"Take Ms. Mai. I was never interested in being your bloodbag."

Umbra shook his head pityingly. "Would you rather the Planitrs piece you out to a thousand lesser patrons? The clouds lent you cover, but when they find you, they'll tear away every scrap of human dignity you fight so vehemently for."

"So I should be your pet instead? Let you keep me in a glass case and suck me dry when you get bored?"

"No, my spark of daylight, I intend to fulfill your every dream. I'll commission you a ship and teach you to fly it. I'll write you a letter of recommendation to the Lunar Academy of Sciences. Ask me for anything, and my tender heart will relent."

"How can I believe anything you say?" He turned his head. "You told me you were in love…"

"We left it unspoken, but you and I both knew this relationship would never go the way of fairy tales." Umbra's expression softened, making him more recognizable as the person Dezi had grown to admire. "This is the full truth: A human cannot be my suitor, but I would cherish him as my lover."

But Umbra didn't realize his offer *was* a fairytale to a Martian, and it drained Dezi a little more each time he had to reject it. The vampire's authentic self wasn't pretty, but no part of Dezi's life was. If he went back to Chryse now, he'd have to start from scratch with no savings and no home—no place for Vesta. He'd be alone again, without the chaotic star that had lit up his bleak universe.

"Trust is difficult for you, but I swear I won't abandon you as others have." Umbra took Dezi's hand in his. "I want you as you are, scars and all."

"You think I'm weak. That's why you broke this off the first time."

"This savage world has no mercy for souls as gentle as yours; that's why you need my protection. Please, let me keep you safe. Let me fall in love with you once more."

Dezi's mind raced, but his heartbeat was slowing. He shook his head, thoughts muddled. "I need time to think—I'm scared."

"It's alright." Umbra leaned in, whispering his sweet breath onto Dezi's face. "From here on, my love, you need only fear me."

He clasped Dezi's cheeks and kissed him deeply. It was cloying as a mouthful of chilled syrup as his tongue slid over Dezi's. The vampire's saliva pooled in his mouth and dripped down his chin, forcing him to swallow or drown in it. The rush of his venom hit Dezi like plunging into a depthless pool, and he sank deeper while Umbra explored behind his teeth like a python burrowing into the back of his throat.

Dezi's eyelids sagged and his lungs ached for air, but he didn't fight it. He was a carcass, ravaged by his heavenly little vampire.

CHAPTER 24

SCARS

The door creaked open, and Dezi rushed to hug his dad's pinstriped pants. "Daddy!"

"Woah, squirt. It's nearly midnight. What are you still doing up?" He set his briefcase by the door and lifted Dezi to his bright-toothed smile.

"Mom put me in bed, but you weren't back…" Dezi hugged his neck and glanced across the starlit lawn as his dad shut the door. He smelled like dad cologne and weird eggs.

"The shuttle from Venus was delayed. There was cyclonic turbulence and lightning. The bolts were thick as trains, like—ka-chow," he whispered, but he pitched it as well as the drones he had left Earth to sell.

"If you excite him before bed, he'll have nightmares again." Lit by the swirling animation on the refrigerator's screen, Mom stood in the hallway in her satin pajamas. Dezi shrank into his dad's wool overcoat to hide from his mother's blunt frown.

Dad laughed and patted his gelled, ash-brown hair. "I'm sorry, Renata, but I missed you guys so much. Come here."

She dropped her shoulders and fought a smile as she entered his arms. Sandwiched between them, Dezi decided it was safe to snuggle her too. Dad brushed a hand through Mom's messily bunned, espresso-brown curls and kissed her.

"Yucky!" Dezi covered his eyes.

His dad laughed and bounced him, carrying him down the hall. "It's way past your bedtime, squirt. I have to talk to Mommy, but I'll see you for breakfast, alright?"

"Okay..." Dezi let his dad tuck him into his constellation-patterned blankets, but he had other plans. He'd learned from Grandpa that a lie didn't count if you never got caught, so as soon as his dad closed the door behind himself, Dezi hopped out of bed.

He slowly pulled down the door handle and peeked out in time to catch his mother cross her arms and hiss, "And what about my dissertation?"

"You haven't submitted your proposal yet, and this can't wait." Dad waved his hands like he was signing a secret second language, which he only did when he was really selling something.

"Tell them to send Petyr."

Dad took a deep breath. "They laid off the entire office, but I got a transfer offer. They need one technical rep to lock down the deal with the Edens in Arabia Terra; if I can close, I'll have a shot at regional sales manager."

"*Oh, Lord*—let me talk to Dad."

"No, Renata, this is good news." He brought her knuckles to his lips and widened his water-blue eyes at her. "I've been waiting for a promotion like this, and if Dr. Merlo gets the chance, you know he won't let me have a win of my own."

"He would move heaven and earth for us. If you asked him for a job at the Merlo Institute, he could arrange treatment plans for both of us." She stressed her lips until they lost their strawberry color.

"If we join a stagnating line like the Merlos, we'll be lucky to make it to a second lifetime. Management has already found a facility with an opening for a head doctor."

"But on Mars? Do you hate my father that much?"

"This isn't about liking him, it's about ensuring Dezi gets the treatment he needs, and your father made his opinions on that clear." Dad let her hands go.

"Dezirée is five; she could change her mind."

Quiet tears leaked down Dezi's nose. He had told her he didn't like that name forever ago, but she always used it when he wasn't around.

"But what if she—" Dad caught himself. "He doesn't? What happens when he's twelve and your father won't let him get blockers? What will you tell him when he's twenty and the damage is done?"

Mom crossed her arms and turned to the wall.

"This isn't what we planned for, but things come up. We have to readjust, prepare for any outcome." Dad rubbed her shoulders. "And I know you don't want to spend immortality under your father's thumb any more than I do."

She reluctantly turned back. "How will you explain to Dezi that you expect him to give up the friends he made after the last move? This year has been difficult enough for him…"

Dezi hiccuped and sobbed, triggering his parents to spot him. Now he was caught and losing his new friends? He bawled.

Dad snatched him up and held him tight. "Shh, don't worry. We'll make new friends."

"I don't want to go. Mom doesn't either! Make them send Mr. Petyr."

Dad's brows pinched, but he kept smiling. "Petyr got fired, squirt. They didn't need us both, and Daddy told them he'd do a better job."

Dezi wiped his sticky face. "What if they fire you too? Can't you get a new job here instead?"

"That's a good question." Mom took him from his dad's arms and dotted his tears away.

"I didn't make this decision lightly," Dad said. "This is the best move for my career and our family. There are hundreds of facilities on Mars that need to be modernized; do you know what that means, Dezi?"

"You'll sell lots of whizzers..." Dezi sniffled. "What if I got a job instead? Then I could help you save money for immortality medicine."

"You're still a little short to get into sales, but one day you will." Dad patted his head. "How about I buy you a Hadron with my new raise?"

"A dune bike?" The only thing Dezi wanted more was a speed ship, but he'd have to wait until they were immortal for one of those. "Can we paint it plasma purple?"

"Great idea, Dezi." Dad laughed. "That'll look platinum!"

He giggled and looked at his mom. She was frowning, but she did that a lot anyway.

"Hey there, ya lil' nibble. What's your name?" A grizzly bear of a man leaned down, focusing his peanut-butter-brown eyes on Dezi.

He hid behind his mom's silver slacks. "Mommy, why is he so fat?"

"Dezi!" She shot him a sharp look. "That is not how you introduce yourself."

"Cuz we eat good here, sonny!" The man held his stomach and laughed so hard that spittle landed in his crazy orange beard. "He's a nipper, ain't he? That's alright, you need some fire to handle these crater kids."

Dad jumped at the opportunity to laugh with the local and held out his hand. "That's good to hear. I'm Blaine Marrow. This is my wife, Renata Merlo, and our son, Dezi."

"Ajax." The man took Dad's hand in his sand-smeared fist and shook it hard. "Welcome to Verde, the primest saffron growers on this here red planet. If you need anything at all, Mr. Marrow, you stop by me and Mrs. Dunne's and we'll sort you out. We even got some kitchen equipment, if y'all want to try authentic Martian cuisine. Not everything out here's microbe patties and crickets."

Dad mimicked Ajax's wide grin. "We've got a full kitchen in our suite, and Renata's an excellent cook. We'll host you."

Dezi squinted; Mom could burn a cucumber sandwich.

Dezi's mom stroked his head, smoothing the toss his hair had gotten from the rotorcraft flight. "Ajax, are there many children Dezi's age in this Valis?"

"It's a small facility, but they're always plenty of tots. Let me introduce y'all to a nice little boy named Graycion and his momma."

Ajax bent down and tried to coax Dezi out from behind his mom, but he stared at the sky, watching the whirling blades of the rotorcraft that had dumped him here. It shrank to the size of a fly before disappearing into the mango-mash clouds, abandoning him in a town so dead and dusty it didn't even have flies.

"You have eyes like the people on TV." Graycion stared at Dezi. "Is your dad a TV perennial?"

"My dad isn't immortal, yet." Dezi frowned and turned toward the glass wall separating him from the barren waste of sand that surrounded them. "Your eyes are yellow, and the sky is yellow, and the dirt is all red, and why can't we go outside?"

"There's no air. Duh." Graycion snatched the sleek Hadron rocket out of Dezi's hand and smashed it into another ship model. When they lit up and played antimatter explosion sounds, he dropped them to the rubbery ground in surprise.

Dezi prodded the controls of the robot dinosaur his dad had bought him in exchange for not crying on the shuttle; his dad had ripped him off again. "People never leave? How's Dad going to do his trips?"

"People don't fly in much, so I bet he'd ride the magnet train."

"You mean a maglev?" Dezi didn't realize a place like this had something so high-tech. "Where's that?"

"Near the doctor's office. Since your mom is the new doctor, can you ask her to leave more blood in my mom? She's always tired after."

"I can do that...if you show me the train."

Dezi took two shivering steps into the dark, but Graycion grabbed his arm and said, "Mom says we can't go into the tunnel."

Dezi eyed the glinting rails. "I always see Dad when he gets back from trips, so I need to find where the train stops."

"I'm going to stay here." Graycion stood in the rectangle of light cast by the doorway.

"I'll be back." With a shrug, Dezi left the scaredy big kid and strutted down the tracks.

The tunnel was as dark as the bat cave Mom had taken Dezi to for his last birthday, where he got yelled at for peeing his pants, even though it was only a little, but the luminescent white and yellow paint stripes by the walkway ledge guided him. His balled fists shook, but Dad had told him that if he straightened his back and puffed out his chest, the monsters would be scared of him, and Dad shook hands with vampires every night, so he knew a lot about spookers. He'd tickle Dezi and tell him that monsters can smell fear, but that means they can smell courage too. He said they loved sniffing up courage, so if you were brave, they'd be your friend. And if you wanted to live forever, you needed immortal friends.

Dezi caught the twinkle of gunmetal in the darkness, then ran toward the train. When an LED sign hanging from the ceiling ticked down to 00:00:00, lights along the train's nose pulsed like the spots on a deep-sea eel. It softly whirred, rolled forward, then ejected across the tracks. Wheels clattering, it ripped the wind and fluttered Dezi's clothes as it rushed him. Wide-eyed, he stared at the glittering glass and steel, like he was standing below the belly of a silver dragon flying through the night. Roaring like thunder, it disappeared into the tunnel, and its distant howls left Dezi regretful that Graycion had stalled him at the door.

Before Dezi turned for the exit, he noticed a lumpy shadow hunched on the bench. The train had dropped off a monster! Or maybe the monster had missed the train; it was crying.

Dezi puffed his chest out and shakily strutted up, mustering his deepest voice. "H-hello, my name is Dezi!"

The blob kicked its feet. "We don't talk to strangers."

Dezi wasn't supposed to either, but he didn't have a single immortal friend yet, and he was nearly five. "I told you my name, so we aren't strangers."

"Fine. I'm Mithra." The weeping girl tossed aside her blanket and hopped off the bench. Her face was speckled with Martian clay, and she hugged a bundle close to her chest. "Now leave us alone."

Dezi gasped at the scaly red creature in her arms. "Is that a baby monster?"

"You shut your mash-hole!" Mithra stomped up and smacked him. "This is my momma's baby!"

"Ow!" Dezi stumbled back, rubbing the top of his head. "Doesn't that mean he's your brother?"

"I don't know yet." She plopped onto the pavement and tucked the baby between her stomach and knees, her breath fogging in its silent, wrinkly face. "Momma didn't tell me before she sent me with the stranger-lady."

"Where did the lady go?"

Mithra looked down the tunnel and sniffed. "She told me to wait. Said she'd be back."

Dezi pointed at the timer hanging over the bench. "You're going to wait an entire sol?"

"The heck is a *sol*?"

"A Martian day."

"A Martian day is called a day. You a wet walker or something?" She threw her blanket over her head, and its tassels tickled her button nose.

Dezi frowned. "Can you read?"

She pouted and pulled the blanket down so that it hid her pumpkin-orange eyes.

Dezi crossed his arms like Dad had done when he wore down the toy merchant in the Meridiani Bazaar. "Okay, miss dusty butt, I'm reading level three, and the sign says twenty-four. Your mom left you here for a whole day?"

"You're lying!" Mithra's eyes widened, and the baby started wheezing.

"It has two numbers, so you know it's more than ten." Dezi's own nose was wet and tingly from the chill. "I think you should wait somewhere warmer."

"I ain't goin' nowhere with a stranger. Not again."

"But your mom's baby will get cold, and he's all slimy. My parents have a sink we can wash him in."

Mithra chewed on her split nails, glancing down the pitch-black tunnel. "Promise we won't talk to anyone—especially grown ups. *They'll* punish me if we do."

"I think we should ask for help."

She glared at him, and her blanket fell away from her cheeks, revealing purple marks on her ears and neck. "I won't go if you don't promise."

Dezi met her eyes and nodded. "I promise. I'll tell Graycion to go home and call you when he's gone."

Dezi shuffled down the gray hallway and peered past the concrete door to his new home. "Are you sure you can wash him on your own?"

"I washed myself. How hard can it be?"

Dezi glanced back at her speckled arms and held his tongue; maybe Martians didn't get good soap when they lived so far from the shea and cacao trees. "If I see my mom or dad, I'll talk loud and keep them away."

Mithra pushed past him, went to the kitchen sink, and pulled up a chair to climb on. She put a glass under the faucet and ran the water at a trickle, then snatched a pasta pot and grabbed a towel before testing the water with her finger. When she liked the temperature, she replaced the glass with the pot, put a drop of soap in it, and gingerly unwrapped the baby from his rusty sheets.

Dezi walked up. "How did you lift that pasta pot?"

She chugged the glass of water and turned the faucet off when it covered the baby's feet. "You never lifted a bucket?"

"That's not a bucket..." Dezi rose onto his toes and watched her rub the scaly baby.

The baby opened her eyes, and they were the same nasty yellow as the sky.

Dezi said, "She might be a girl; she doesn't have a dangle."

Mithra nodded as she gently circled her soapy thumbs on the baby's cheeks. "Happy birthday, sister..."

"What's her name?"

Mithra's bottom lip curved up. "She doesn't have one."

The baby opened her mouth wide, but spit and foam came out instead of sound.

"We should call her Volcano," Dezi said. "She's super red, and nobody will bully her with a scary name like that."

Mithra huffed. "You're suppose'ta be my lookout."

"Oh—yeah. I'll check the rooms." Dezi scampered off.

He crept up to each door and pressed his ear to them until he reached his parent's room, where he heard his dad talking quickly. His tone was more serious than when he had told Mom they had to move here. "But we aren't even settled yet. I understand, but—holy shit... How many spots?"

Dad went quiet, but his footsteps paced the room.

"I need three."

It was silent for a long time.

"I understand, ma'am."

Dad opened the door, brown lashes opening wide. "Dezi?"

"Hi, Daddy." Dezi watched his toes.

Dad scooped him up, grimacing. "Did you catch any of that, squirt?"

"You're going on a trip. Can I come?"

"No, not even my manager gets to go, but I might meet Mr. Eden if I get picked."

Dezi squeezed him. "How long will you be gone this time?"

"Stuff like that won't matter when we're immortal." He winked, like the guy in the toothpaste commercials.

"Can't you wait until I'm older? Then I'll be a businessman, too."

Dad's smile fractured, and he pressed the back of his neck. "Dezi, your dad's getting old, and once he gets too many wrinkles, the bosses won't like him as much."

"It's not fair…" Dezi's tears welled.

"You already know it's not…" His father suddenly dropped him onto his feet and held his shoulders. "Dezi, life is like a big mountain, and we don't all start at the same place. If you want to get to the top, you need to climb—climb like hell and don't think about the fingers you step on, because the mountain is sinking. They've only got room for one in a billion at the top, and you need to get there. Do you understand? If you don't want to die, get to the top."

Wrinkles formed around Dad's eyes from all the times he had made them smile when he wasn't happy. He had wrinkles near his mouth just as deep, though Dezi had never seen the frowns that caused them.

He asked, "S-sinking? Why?"

"Because not everyone deserves to be at the top. But if you make it, no one can push you around or send you places you don't want to go. They'll have to do what you say." He wiped Dezi's tears. "That's where I'm going."

"I want to go too. I-I tried to make a monster friend, but I think she's just a sick baby. She's in a pasta pot with a dirty girl in our sink. She told me not to tell anyone, but I think they're lost."

Dad raised an eyebrow. "How about you don't tell Mommy anything you heard, and I promise not to tell either?"

"Hmm..." Dezi held out his hand. "Deal."

His dad took it and then pressed a kiss to his forehead. "Remember I love you, alright? I know you didn't want to come here, but we're paying our dues. When you start at the bottom, you've got to do a lot of climbing. Sometimes you leave people behind."

"I'll climb too, and then I won't let anyone send you away again. I'll climb so high we see stars, and we can all live forever!" Dezi threw his arms around his dad and kissed his face. Underneath the dumb flowers and nose-burning dust, he still smelled like Dad.

He took his briefcase and stood. "I'll see you up there, squirt."

"Yeah! Come look at this baby. She doesn't have a name, but I think we should call her Volcano."

Dezi ran down the hallway and into the kitchen. He heard the door shut and looked back. "Dad?"

CHAPTER 25

Girls

"Lift your tongue." Vesta peered into the vamp's mouth, noting that his top row of teeth was plastic-white, but the naturals on the bottom were yellowed from a century of coffee and wine.

"I hope you check the whores this thoroughly." Sneering, the vamp adjusted his silk neck scarf. He was young in the face, but his cheeks were sallow as a skull's, and his hairline seemed to recede a little more every time he anxiously touched it.

Vesta sighed and filled out the cryptic-cash order on the powder-crusted phone Elay had given her. She didn't understand the technical details, but Elay had told her to scan the customer's cert codes and wait for the green light. "This gets you fifteen minutes of premium time. Knives, needles, and penetration are fair game, but no sucking or hitting. Any *accidents*, and you're speaking with Buff and Buffer over there."

She pointed her thumb at Elay's henchmen, who were sitting in front of the TV with London, watching two muscle-grafted athletes beat each other into pudding in a cyborg cage match. When Spider, the one with the camel spider tattooed on his shiny dome, threw a punch, the grainy muscles on his forearms bulged with more veins than a pornstar's rocket. The other one—his name was Chunk or something—laughed and caught the beer that Spider had tipped with his ghost-boxing.

The vamp scrutinized his phone. "This can't be right. I was here a few days ago, and you charged half as much."

With the city opening back up, she'd have thought Elay would take the prices down, too, but he was holding on to hope that he'd scrape together enough money to put through the right bribes. The rest of the house wasn't as optimistic; Dezi called it when he'd said it was a matter of time until Jaxon showed up to claim his unearned promotion. Vesta pushed Dezi out of her mind before she started panicking over where he was, then crossed her arms. "Price is the price. Leave us a bad review if you don't like it."

"I want to speak to management. This is ridiculous."

"Sounds like we got a customer complaint, Charles," Spider called from the couch, bumping the thug next to him. Spider wasn't in charge, but he did the talking for both Chunk—or Charles—and himself.

Charles cracked his knuckles, sending the centipedes on his biceps rippling with anticipation.

"Forget it. But don't expect my patronage again." The vamp rolled his eyes so hard they could have fallen out of his sunken sockets, then paced to the back room, glossy oxfords losing more polish with each step.

"Watch the time; he looked thirsty." London examined the unraveling tips of her tinsel-woven braids. "By the way, you can't tell if someone has a BTD by looking."

Vesta crossed her arms and pressed them down over her cartwheeling stomach. "I ain't dumb, but I watch how hard they sweat. Elay told me to turn away any shifty-looking ones. Problem is, they all look like vamps."

London tapped at the pink laptop balanced on her thighs. "Looks like you misjudged that one; his cert bounced."

"Ugh—again?" Vesta stomped to the door and banged on it. "C'mon out."

It was oddly silent; normally, the johns double-dipped with biting and bumping nasties. She turned the handle and pushed, but the door wouldn't budge. The vamp had barricaded himself inside!

Vesta hollered, "Boys, we got a problem."

Charles came barreling down the hall, and Vesta jumped out of the way before he rammed his shoulder into the door.

CRACK!

It swung open, wafting the stench of sex and blood out of the dingy room. The vamp sat at the edge of the bed, hunched over a skin girl's neck as she sprawled across his lap. With her eyes rolled back into her head, she arched her back and tensed her limbs as the vamp took a squelching gulp. The scab licker's eyes snapped open, flashing like crimson beads, but he didn't stop sucking. He was dug in like a tick, and Vesta's legs were rooted to the floor.

Charles's confidence immediately evaporated, then London shoved him aside, forcing her way into the room. "Spider! Get him off her!"

He ran in, face like the grim reaper coming to collect due, and slammed his huge fist down on the vamp's head. He tore his fangs from the girl, howling, but Charles was right behind Spider with another swing that rumbled the walls and popped the vamp's nose open like a strawberry.

London grabbed the skin girl and dragged her back, hastily pressing her hands over her throat. "Ves! Get the pads!"

Vesta stopped gaping, grabbed a box of cauterizing pads on the dresser, and started ripping open as many as she could. There was so much blood, caked and sticky, on London's hands as she grabbed for the powdery swatches. Elay was not going to be happy. He was going to absolutely lose his shit.

The girl grabbed London's wrist and tried to say something, choking up blood on her blue lipstick. London's eyes glazed over, and her grip on the pads loosened. Sweet star shine—blood burst from the two ragged gashes across her throat, sopping into her green hair. Vesta moved to press more padding to it, but London caught her hand and hoarsely said, "Don't make her suffer."

The busted door whined as Elay slowly pushed it open. Trying to read his steely expression was like staring down the barrel of a gun and guessing whether there was a bullet in the chamber.

London backed up from the body, and Vesta followed. Spider and Charles stood at attention, their swollen fists shaking.

Elay knelt by the girl, turning her head to get a look at the damage. Spider had fucked up by socking that vamp while he still had his fangs in, but Vesta had fucked up by not picking up on that vamp's red flags sooner. Who was she kidding? This entire operation was the definition of fucked up, and there wasn't a damn good reason Vesta had been picked to cash checks instead of turning out her own neck. That dead girl had come from a colony like Verde. Her name was Mica, and she had stumbled into sex work the same way Vesta had fallen into dealing: desperation and greed.

Vesta's breath caught in her throat, squeaking out a sob, and it took all her will not to loose another for fear it'd make Elay finally snap.

Elay let out a long breath through his teeth, closed the girl's eyelids, and stood. "Where is he?"

Charles dragged out the battered vamp by his shoulders, dumping him on the floor in front of Elay. The vamp spat out a glob of black blood and sat back, smug as a fattened leech.

"Normally, I'd demand compensation for the damages"—he waved at his smashed-up silicone face, looking like a multi-colored lump of clay a kid pressed their hands into—"but considering that blood meal will heal most of it, I think we can call this a wash."

"You an uptown vamp?" Elay took the cig out of his shirt pocket and puffed it. "That's the only way you could think your face is worth one of my girls."

"What, you want my card?" The vamp smirked. "If she had sentimental value, I suppose I could compensate you after my credit lines—"

Elay stomped on the man's groin, grinding in his toe as he snarled. "Shut the fuck up!"

The vamp made less sound than Vesta had expected, but the thing down there must have stopped working ages ago. Elay kicked the vamp in the chin, and he fell back like a wet sack of shit.

He took another drag off his cig, wiping the toe of his boot on the carpet. "I want him out of Eastdome. Dump him in the darkest hole you can find."

Spider picked up the vamp's feet, Charles grabbed his shoulders, and they hauled him out of the flat.

London threw a bedsheet over Mica, then walked over and touched Elay's shoulder. He flinched, but then put his arm around her, lowering his chin to the top of her head. Although Elay hounded after any woman with a pulse, London meant something more to him. She was the one person who could bring him down from a wall-punching rage, and for all London's talk about not caring for others, she had given him shots of her own blood when he'd caught a cold halfway through the storm. Vesta didn't admire what they had, but it wasn't the transactional relationship most vamps operated under. Elay made it no secret that, when he got to pick a scion, he'd choose London first. It must have hurt to miss out on that promotion of his, but Vesta got the feeling the two were used to waiting.

A knock rapped on the front door. Elay shouted, "We're closed."

The knock came again, louder, incessant.

Elay sighed and let London go. "Ves, tell 'em to fuck off."

She nodded and left for the living room, letting her heart tie itself into a hard little knot. She couldn't afford to think about Mica, or Dezi, or anything other than survival right now. Unlike London, she was replaceable, and their friendship was the only reason she wasn't out on the street right now.

Putting on her best resting bitch face, Vesta opened the door. "Business is closed for—"

"Vesta, wow, you look like shit." Jaxon propped his arm up on the doorway, letting his platinum chains slide over his collar. His brassy velour shirt was so shiny, it looked like he hadn't stepped out of Diskos since the storm started, and his gray topcoat had a matching gold label on the hem. "Aren't you going to invite me in?"

Elay came up behind her, gripping the door. "We don't have time for your shit. Go back to Diskos."

He feigned a hurt expression but failed to hold down his cherry-fanged smirk. "Is that any way to talk to your sire?"

Elay hesitated, and Vesta edged back, but that gave Jaxon the chance to push his way in.

"I heard you were running a homeless shelter, but damn, I don't think you could pack another half a whore in here." He laughed, swaggering around.

Elay shut the door. "You think you got the deal stitched? Fine, but don't come at me until you have the contract on paper."

Jaxon pulled a wadded-up folder from his overcoat and dropped it on the breakfast bar. "One hard copy, as ordered. I hope you've got a pen, old man."

Elay stomped up and snatched it, flipping through the wrinkled papers. "The stores don't even have hemo yet, and you managed to push this through? How?"

"You always treated me like a joke, but it looks like the Hierarch's seventy-second grandnephew has got a better handle on family politics than you ever did." Jaxon interwove his fingers and stretched his arms. "With your sire dead and his sire laid up in the hospital, great uncle Moroska realized this branch was falling apart, so Dad told him it was past time to get some new blood into leadership. Speaking of, I have some fresh ideas about how to clean up shop."

Elay clicked his yellowed nails on the countertop, taking this all a hell of a lot more calmly than Vesta had expected, but he was the type of guy who always had ten contingency plans in his back pocket. "Fine, let's talk. I'll give you a rundown of my books, but the first thing you need to understand is that I'm not like the other chumps you're inheriting. I'll be making most of your up-line tithe, so I expect some operating space."

"You don't give me orders, old man; I'm your sire." He jabbed his finger in Elay's chest. "Now, where's Dezi? I want that bounty deposited yesterday. After that, we can round up the other runaways you've been covering for."

"He's not here." London stepped up. "And you aren't cashing out anyone. These people are worth more than your side hustle."

"Your pets are getting mouthy, Elay. You better teach this fat bitch to respect her betters." Jaxon grabbed London's jaw, but as he turned up her chin, she swung her elbow into his face.

He toppled back, catching himself on one of the breakfast-bar stools. "Are you fucking stupid? You can't touch me. I'm a vampire!"

"You're a trust-fund brat with less sense than class." She pointed her acrylics at him. "I don't give a fuck who your daddy is; touch me again and I'll lay you out."

"Blood whore bitch." Jaxon pulled a vintage handgun from his coat, aiming it at her forehead with a slant. "Get on your fucking knees."

Elay calmly stepped into the gun's sights. "This ain't going to work, kid. You weren't made out to be a leader."

"That's fucking rich coming from some scum we picked up off the street. Your sire was an idiot for ever blooding you, but I'll make sure this is where your career ends."

"Everything I have, I earned with my own hands. You're just a kid with a silver spoon shoved so far up your ass, you learned to like the taste of the shit they've fed you." Elay took a step forward, staring him down like a grown centipede facing a baby viper; they both had venom in spades and the intent to eat the other one alive. "You're nothing but a name, and that's all you'll ever be."

"I'm your sire! You can either say it or give back every drop of my family's blood."

Frozen, London's eyes darted to Vesta, trying to tell her something, but what the hell was she supposed to do? She couldn't risk a tackle or the gun might fire. She edged back to the hallway, looking for a weapon.

"You think you can shoot me in my own house and walk out?" Elay raised his chin. "My guys will bury you."

"Your bloodbags are mine." Jaxon pressed his gun muzzle to Elay's scar, grinding it in. "Now that I'm your sire, every drop and dime in here is."

"Their loyalty ain't."

Vesta eyed the front door. She could run for Spider and Charles, but they'd never make it back in time. Or she could just run. This house wasn't safe anymore, so why stick her neck out for Elay? He wouldn't do it for her. The problem was that London already had. London could have kept quiet and let Jaxon turn Vesta in, but she didn't take her own damn advice about forgetting her friends, and now she was paying the price. If Vesta made the wrong move, she'd pay it too.

Chryse killed its heroes—Nikita had taught her that—but Vesta had never aimed to be a hero. She wasn't kind like Mithra or smart like London, but she was tenacious, and she looked out for her friends.

Vesta dashed to the hallway bathroom and threw open the door. The tub was red and chunky and the metallic stink made her gag, but she yanked open the sink drawer, sending loose bullets rolling. She took out Elay's huge handgun and shakily loaded a thumb-sized bullet into the chamber. Gripping the revolver with both hands, she ran back up the hallway, meeting London's wild eyes for a split second.

She raised the barrel, but the nose was so heavy it wanted to dip toward Jaxon's yellow python-leather loafers. "Jaxon! Put it down!"

Jaxon and Elay blinked, like their eyelids could erase the gun.

Elay raised a hand. "Ves—"

Jaxon cackled and lowered his weapon. "Loyalty, huh? Granduncle's going to have you all chopped into bug food for this."

"Shut your mouth and drop the gun—slow-like." Vesta's body shivered as the gunmetal sucked the heat from her arms. Cold and dark as the MagnaLoop, the bullet would be just as fast, and there'd be no going back. "I'll do it!"

Jaxon smirked and stepped towards her, letting his barrel playfully teeter from London to Elay. "You know, I kind of like feisty girls. How about you tell me where Dezi is and I make you my first human bond? I'll even throw in a pair of new tits after I cash my check."

Elay locked eyes with Vesta and pressed his lips until they lost color. The gun sights shivered, and its grip was slick against her palms, but she strained her wrists to raise the sights. She pulled back the hammer—*click*—and Jaxon's smile twisted like a snake with its head wedged under a boot heel.

"Don't you get it? I'm immortal, and you're a meatsack. You can't touch me—none of you can! I—"

She pulled the trigger.

BOOHM!

Ear-splitting, it threw her back against the couch, and the gun smacked her forehead. The bullet hit Jaxon's shoulder, tearing through him like a cannonball. His shredded arm flew out of its socket, and Elay covered his face as viscera and bone shrapnel ejected everywhere. Jaxon hit the ground, lips petrified in an awful grin while his blood pumped into the ratty rug.

Elay held his head, mouthing, *holy shit, holy shit*. No, he was speaking, but Vesta couldn't hear anything. Ears ringing, head banging, she dropped the gun. The lump on her skull throbbed angrily, but her insides were perfectly hollow. She kept her eyes locked on her meat-sprinkled bare feet while Jaxon's corpse burned a hole in the corner of her vision.

London dropped to her knees and touched Vesta's head. Her voice faded in. "Ves, say something."

"I didn't know what else to do..." Vesta tried to wipe her hands on her shorts, but Jaxon's blood was too sticky. It was everywhere.

"Shit, shit! We're so fucked!" Elay grabbed the gun off the floor, then glared at Vesta, bits of flesh caught in the whites of his eyes.

Plum-cheeked, London held back a tearful grimace. "Baby, she had to."

"Right, he had to go." Elay threw his arms around her and pressed his lips to the top of her head. "We'll figure this out."

London and Elay held each other, looking down on Jaxon's corpse like this was the righteous end to a long battle, but Vesta didn't share their vindication. The old part of her wished Elay and Jaxon could have shaken hands and let everyone be friends, but she knew now that wasn't how life worked. Some problems were solved with bullets, and ending this one had made Chryse a little safer for the people she cared about.

She didn't need Dezi to rescue her anymore, because she had saved them both.

Chapter 26

Deals

When Dezi woke, the aftertaste of artificial sweetener lingered in his mouth. His skin tingled, and his head swam with a dull bliss, but as his senses slowly came to, he felt the rumbling of tires on the speedway. Someone was stroking his hair, and they smelled like bourbon and caramel. Lying perfectly still, Dezi peeked open an eye. His head rested on Umbra's warm lap, facing his silk shirt, as they lounged on the ivory couch of a limo.

"We can't walk him into the spaceport," Seiyo said from behind Dezi's back. "He has no papers, and I doubt he's up to date on his vaccinations."

"For the last time, you are not packing him in a crate." Umbra tenderly ran his finger around the shell of Dezi's ear. "I don't want to make this more difficult for him than it must be."

"The Planitrs will take notice. They will demand his return."

"They can bring it to interplanetary court. Once he's on AZURE, he's mine."

"But if they intercept us before then, they'll never sell his debt to you."

"Which is why it is vital this goes smoothly. Ah, I can hear your heart racing, *mon bijou*." Umbra pushed Dezi's bangs aside and smiled down at him. "Eavesdropping is impolite."

Dezi woozily sat up, sliding back from Umbra. "You did something to me..."

"My apologies for putting you out. I did not intend to be so liberal with my venom load, but I had recently fed. In the future, I'll be more cognizant of our incompatible biologies." Umbra scooted towards him. "Now, we need to discuss our strategy for sneaking you through customs."

Past the limo's shaded windows, ad-plastered skyscrapers flickered by, and the dome overhead was black as night despite that it was midday. They were in Diskos, a few minutes from the spaceport.

"Umbra! I didn't agree to this." Dezi unbuckled his seatbelt and stood, brushing his head on the limo's silver ceiling. The spacious interior held couches on each side, but the vehicle handled like a boat, and Dezi nearly fell over when it switched lanes.

"Remain seated." Seiyo pointed at Dezi warningly. "Sire, this illustrates my point. If he attempts to escape, he'll draw too much attention."

"He won't," Umbra said. "Dezi, the surge of shuttle traffic makes today our best opportunity to smuggle you through. We can discuss the terms of this relationship after the Planitrs are no longer a concern."

"Do you think I'm stupid?" Dezi sat on Seiyo's side of the limo and checked his wrists to ensure Umbra hadn't left any surprise marks of ownership. "If I get on that shuttle, you've won. You'll be able to do whatever you want with me."

"I resent the implications of that." Umbra frowned, raising his chin. "I'll have you know that my bloodline's record of humane treatment is sterling. Not one of our donors has ever abandoned their patron."

"I don't care if you're an Ambrose, I'm not going."

Seiyo sighed, pinching his brow. "It's worse than I thought..."

"Let's not do anything rash, *mon arme adorée*," Umbra said. "My name will be on his contract."

"A contract he will refuse to sign." Seiyo tightened his gloves. "You've been ignoring the obvious solution, Sire: We kill him and make a clone."

Dezi's spine went rigid, but he let the panic wash over him like a passing wave, leaving him focused on forming a plan. He wasn't inclined to sell out an unborn clone of himself, but dying wasn't an option, and agreeing to something would give him time to maneuver. If he got Umbra alone, he could appeal to his empathy. The immortal prince may have been taught to believe he was a different species from humankind, but Dezi had seen flashes of kindness sneak through the mask he put on in the company of his fellow immortals.

"What if I give you a DNA sample?" Dezi asked. "Then you can let me go."

Seiyo plucked a hair from Dezi's head, deftly pocketing it. "I agree with my sire that we can't risk you falling into the Planitrs' hands. You know too much, and the camera incident has already proved you are an exposure risk."

And that slammed the coffin shut on any hope of escape. Now that Seiyo had found out about his blackmail attempt, he would never let Dezi go free.

"You read my journal again?" Umbra raised his lip, flashing his fangs. "The sheer insolence. *This* Dezi is my memento. His personality cannot be replicated."

"Don't act so grandiose." Seiyo smiled harshly at his sire, baring his flat teeth. "You like his smell or his taste. If you can't wait for a clone to reach age, I'll find you another mortal who matches his physical appeal."

Umbra's face flushed, his claws digging into the edge of the couch. "As my subordinate, you have no say in the matter. Dezi, come; let us discuss terms without my scion's pestering."

Dezi was skeptical they would reach a compromise, but with Seiyo looming over him like a tombstone, moving closer to Umbra was an appealing option. When he stood to change seats, a gloved hand flew at his face. He twisted away, but Seiyo grabbed a fistful of his hair and hauled him back. Dezi scrabbled at his machine-like grip, kicking wildly at the steely vampire.

"Seiyo!" Umbra leaped up, grabbing his scion's wrists. "Release him! That's an order!"

His hand snapped open, and Dezi scrambled to the back of the limo.

Seiyo rolled his head back, loudly cracking his vertebrae. "I *am* resolving this."

"By murdering him? Are you truly this bloodthirsty?"

"Don't lay the onus on me. If you respected the family protocols for once in your damned life, I wouldn't be forced to soil my hands scrubbing the trail left by your dripping fangs." Seiyo tried to pull free, but Umbra strained the corded tendons in his hands to keep him in place.

"Oh so lucky you wear gloves." Umbra smirked. "You do as I command, scion. Recognize your place."

"My place is as your guardian, and this is for your protection." Seiyo brought his hands across Umbra's wrists and swiftly maneuvered him into an armlock, forcing him to his knees.

"You dare bare your blunted teeth at me?" Umbra growled in a low, warbling tone. With animalistic force, he broke free, lashing his clawed hands at Seiyo's face.

Seiyo caught them. "You are over attached!"

"So what if I am? I will have him!" Umbra bared his teeth like a rearing wolf and drove them both to the floor.

Dezi pressed against the back wall while Umbra's claws cut through the leather seats and Seiyo's elbows knocked dents into the aluminum floor. He checked his pockets for his phone, but one of the vampires must have taken it. If Dezi reached the touch screens mounted at the front, he might be able to stop the limo, but he couldn't build up the nerve to climb over his captors' savage battle. Seiyo wrestled with Umbra like a military drone trying to pin down an enraged viper, careful of his fangs but destroying everything nearby.

Through the windows, the edge of the dome rose in the distance; he could jump when they slowed for the toll, but would the vampires be distracted for that long? He tugged the door, but the vehicle's safety AI beeped loudly, rejecting his attempt.

"Sit down! I don't intend to spend my evening picking your gray matter off the ceiling," Seiyo said as he maneuvered Umbra into a new grapple with his forearm locked around his neck.

"So you can kill me cleanly? I'll pass." Dezi kicked his heel into the door controls, busting open a panel. He didn't have his multi-tool, but that wouldn't stop him from trying to get the thing open.

"Are you both out of your minds?" Seiyo asked. As he looked over his shoulder at Dezi, Umbra seized the opening to sink his fangs into his scion's arm.

Seiyo released him immediately, examining the tar-like blood oozing from his wound. "You bit me. Unbelievable!"

Panting, Umbra wiped the saliva off his chin. "Apologies, but you gave me no choice."

"And you force my hand." Strings of violet plasma arced between Seiyo's fingers, searing his glove. "This affects the entire family. He's seen your face, and it's a matter of time before he discovers your true name."

Umbra retreated, holding an arm out in front of Dezi. "These memories have tangible value to our mission, and the risk he poses on AZURE is small."

"He has no interest in signing a bond." Seiyo advanced. "Either I deal with this now, or it becomes a bloody spectacle for the other families when he inevitably attempts to escape."

Umbra backed into Dezi, pushing him against the door, while wreaths of lightning crackled loudly in Seiyo's hand. Maybe Umbra could survive a weapon like that, but one touch was all it would take to stop Dezi's heart. When Seiyo took another step, the limo jostled, causing him to steady himself on the couch—Umbra's venom was affecting him. If they could stall him a little longer, it might be enough to give Umbra an edge in this fight.

"There's a third option," Dezi said. "Trust me. I've avoided the Planitrs for this long, and I won't betray your secrets."

"You are a coward and a liar," Seiyo spat, closing the distance with his last few unsteady steps. "When the next Martian discomfort strikes, you'll sell this gossip to buy yourself a few more years of life. Your type is all too common."

"I've experienced more *discomfort* in a week than you have in your entire privileged life, and you think you have the right to execute me for one mistake? Fuck you! You have no idea who I am." Dezi desperately jerked the door handle.

"It's irrelevant." Umbra held up his palm to Seiyo, practically daring the vampire to electrocute him. "Dezi holds the key to remembering the night I was blooded. I would risk anything to understand why I was made this way—reborn with blood too thick in a body too young."

Seiyo hesitated, then shook his head groggily. "How can you know? You're saying that to protect him."

"Take it on faith." Umbra flourished his hand, licking Seiyo's blood off his fangs. "Driver, take this exit."

The limo's AI jingled and shifted lanes, knocking Seiyo aside. His plasma-wreathed hand fell to the bar console, exploding with a volley of harsh pops and the stench of burning wire. The lights flickered, sirens blared, and with a rush of wind, both hatch doors swung open. Falling towards the open road, Dezi grabbed the door handle in both hands, letting it lift him over the speeding asphalt of a mid-air overpass.

"Dezi!" Umbra gripped the doorway, reaching out to support Dezi's legs. "Jump to me!"

"I'm not going with you!" He kicked Umbra's hand away. The limo was slowing; if he tucked and rolled, he had good odds of survival, but the faster the car was moving, the more distance it would put between him and Umbra. For this to work, his timing would need to be perfect.

"Please! I only want to protect you. On AZURE, we would be free from this secrecy."

"I would be your property! You say you care about me, but you don't give a damn how I feel." Dezi scoffed quietly. "I was always a plaything to you."

Umbra's gaze hardened, uncompromising. "If you were a toy, I would have torn you apart a thousand times. What I do now is because I care for you. Submitting yourself to me is in your best interest."

"You don't get to decide that." Dezi adjusted his grip, pulled up his legs, and then swung himself at the shoulder of the road.

Weightless, it didn't feel real. The last time he had smelled burning rubber and ozone like this—when he'd crashed his bike—he had been fine with the thought of dying, but this time, he desperately wanted to live. He tucked his head against his chest, squeezed his eyes shut, and waited for the fire.

It didn't come. Umbra leaped out of the limo and wrapped himself around Dezi, rolling under him. Dezi took in a stilted gasp and unbraced, but Umbra had him. He held Dezi's head under his chin, splayed his fingers over the back of his head, and threw out his other arm to anchor himself to the road.

They hit the ground hard, skidding and searing Umbra's suit off like tissue over a flame. Umbra's arm kept them from rolling, but when they collided with a massive strip of discarded tire tread, it sent them tumbling into the ramp barrier. Umbra's side hit it with a crack like crystal against concrete, then Dezi slammed against his stony chest. They bounced off it and fell back together, with Dezi lying over him.

Speeding cars tossed gravel at Dezi's legs, his raw elbows oozed blood, and the world spun around him. When his head finally stopped banging, Dezi rolled off Umbra, and the vampire's arms fell open on the dirty road. His indigo suit was tattered, his opaline skin was scuffed with asphalt, and a wide patch of his nape was scraped clean of hair. With his arms splayed out, he coughed and dully opened his eyes. *"Bordel de merde..."*

"Marsdamn it." Dezi touched Umbra's chest. "Are you okay? Do you need an ambulance?"

Umbra examined the white skin peeking through his torn shirt. Under the flash of headlights from passing cars, it twinkled with an aurora of color. "The damage is cosmetic, but are you alright? You're bleeding…"

"Me? You could have died! What were you thinking?"

Umbra huffed, wiping the gravel off his cheek. "I was thinking that this soft, squishy man was about to be ground down like an eraser on sandpaper."

"I was going to roll…" Dezi tossed a glance down each side of the speedway, though he had no hope of outrunning Umbra. "You're not going to let me go."

Umbra sighed and touched the bald spot on the back of his head. "Do you hate me so much that you would rather die than be together?"

"Yes. I hate you," Dezi bit the words out, but they cut at him as harshly as he'd hoped to cut Umbra. "If you take me, I'll either escape or kill myself trying. I'll make sure you're miserable every moment we're together."

"If that were true, you would have taken off running before checking whether I was injured." Umbra knelt, facing Dezi. "I know how you feel about me. You speak of humanist ideals, but even now, you look at me with admiration. Why not give in? Let yourself be happy."

"I told you that I won't be your pet or your bloodbag." Dezi said quietly, "I won't be anyone's object."

"But why? If blood is the issue, I'll swear to never drink yours. I'll put your entire family in a penthouse. What more could you want?"

Dezi bit his lip. In exchange for his freedom, he could set Vesta up for life, but it still wasn't enough. No payment Umbra could offer would ever be enough. "I don't need your protection; I need you to forgive me."

Umbra's brows furrowed. "Haven't I?"

"No. If you forgave me—if you trusted me—you'd let me stay here where my home and my family are. You wouldn't need to keep me in a silver cage locked away from anyone I might sell you out to. I take responsibility for breaking your trust, but I'm not the same person I was in that booth—I refuse to be." Dezi pressed his palm to his tears. "I've been through so much, but out of everything I survived—sleeping in a rotten dumpster and cracking open a perennial's skull—seeing how I hurt you was the worst of it. Even looking at you hurts, just knowing that you'll never see me as your equal."

Umbra took Dezi's hands, roughly squeezing them in his. "But you have a place with me. One in which a mortal fits."

"That's the problem. I don't want to be a mortal."

"You?" Umbra's lips parted. "You want to become a vampire."

He grimaced and nodded. It was a rotten admission, vile and selfish, but it was the truth. Dezi didn't really care about freedom or the purity of his human soul, but he was done being a tool for others. He saw one way out of this broken system, through the top, and he couldn't trade his shot at it for anything.

"Please, see me as a person; if not as your equal, then at least as your friend." He squeezed Umbra's hands, watching him with desperation brought on by true honesty. He had given Umbra his closest-held secret, the ambition he had thought forgotten, and now he was at the vampire's mercy.

"I am afraid I have not had a friend in a very long time, so I've forgotten what it's like." Umbra avoided Dezi's gaze, absently rubbing a thumb along his scarred wrist. "You may have to teach me."

Dezi laughed, blinking away the tears sticking to his eyelids. "You're serious? This isn't a trick?"

"If I claim to want what is best for you, then I cannot steal your dream away." He met Dezi's eyes in earnest. "And I do truly care."

Dezi threw his arms around Umbra, hugging him tightly. "I won't let you down—I swear. Just be honest with what you need. Talk to me."

He patted Dezi's back, raising his chin to keep his mouth away from his neck. "I'm not sure yet. This arrangement is highly atypical. Seiyo will be a beast to manage."

"Crap—" Dezi pulled back. "He's still going to try to kill me, isn't he?"

Umbra teetered his head from side to side. "I'm quite practiced with maneuvering around his demands, though negotiations would go smoother if I had a few concessions from you. Ownership of your genetic IP, for example. Regular updates on the memories we uncover will be a must."

"Not happening. You can't make a clone of me to keep as a pet."

"Immortals are always one of a kind, darling. I want the right to clone you should you perish. This would serve as my insurance." Umbra formally offered his hand. "If you intend to succeed, you have nothing to fear."

Dezi shook it. "Then I just ripped you off."

Umbra flashed his morbidly masculine smile. "Best of luck, my fledgling hopeful. The clock is ticking and the garden is savage."

Chapter 27

Epilogue

One month later

Dezi kept his hands buried in his coat pockets as he and Vesta walked down their old street together. Every bench was in its proper place; the buildings wore the same ivory moldings and pinkish paint, and the artificial trees had their old maple-shaped leaves, and yet it was all too clean—uncanny. The curbs were glaringly white, and the alleys were absent of graffiti. It was quiet, too. Barren.

They reached the lot where their home had once stood and stopped before a display of electric candles and portraits of the dead. In Nikita's photo, her buzzed hair was auburn instead of gray, and her beaming, ochre eyes had fewer wrinkles around them. Her face was one of a thousand memorialized here. Dezi looked at each one, wishing he could memorize them all, but it was impossible. They were doomed to be forgotten, as all mortals were.

Vesta touched his shoulder. "You alright? We can leave if you need to."

"No. I've been putting this off for too long." He took one of two plastic lilies Vesta had brought and placed it below Nikita's photo.

She put hers down, wiping her tears on her sleeves. It felt wrong not to cry, but Dezi's eyes were dry. They were focused on the cranes assembling the roof of the newly printed apartment building. The freshly printed cement was a lighter gray, sparkling with what might have been the glass from shattered windows. Stax had recycled the old rubble into this new composite, so there wasn't a doubt in Dezi's mind that the buildings would fall again.

Vesta stood, glaring at the assembly drones. "Makes me sick. Makes me wanna register to vote and find out what vamp in city council approved these sandcastles."

"It won't make a difference," Dezi said dryly.

Vesta took his hand in hers. "Everything we do makes a difference, but it takes a lot of small people to make a big change."

He raised his eyes to the Hadron Tower as it glittered like a black diamond in the rosy twilight. "It takes power to make change."

One day, he'd have that power, and he would remember what it had been like to be human.

Vesta wrapped her puffer coat around herself and started walking. "How long do you think we're going to be staying with Cormac? I'm not raring to move out of Diskos, but he's not gonna make rent."

Dezi followed, unsure how to broach this topic. "Umbra offered to buy the flat for me. I told him no, but he sent me a pretty massive favor anyway."

"Hm." Vesta crossed her arms. "Hm... He really likes you, don't he?"

"I would use the term *obsessed*."

A sneaky smile brimmed on Vesta's lips. "And you like him."

"I respect him. I flirt with him because it's my job to, not because I think he'd make a good boyfriend." Dezi ran his fingers through his hair and sighed. "He wouldn't."

"Well, he is probably older than Pa, but some people are into that." Vesta sat down on the bench of an auto-taxi pick-up station.

Dezi rolled his eyes. "Remind me not to tell you about my love life."

Vesta laughed, stretching her thin legs out. "I better call my ride. Got some errands to run before work."

"I hope that doesn't mean you're visiting London again. My debt's been paused, but Jaxon could show up there any day, and he seems like the type to hold a grudge."

"I'm not." Vesta groaned, dropping her shoulders. "Plus, Jaxon hasn't bothered anyone since the storm cleared. Who knows? He might'a got up and left."

"Unlikely." Dezi checked his phone. He hated that Vesta still felt pressured to lie to him, but he didn't have time to coax the truth from her tonight. Umbra arrived on Mars in an hour, and he had no intention of beginning this fresh start of theirs by showing up late. "I've got to go."

Vesta caught his hand. "Be careful. Flings between humans and thousand-year-old immortals can get messy, and we're a lot squishier than they are."

"He's not *that* old." Dezi laughed.

Pursing her lips, Vesta raised a brow. "You telling me he's our age?"

"Alright, he's probably a hundred." Dezi patted her head. "But like I said, he and I are just friends."

She narrowed her eyes. "Sure you are. You tell him that if he breaks your heart again, I'll bust his kneecaps."

Dezi blinked; she sounded like she actually meant that. "I'll let him know. See you after work."

Spider cracked open the door for Vesta, looking mean until he recognized her. He opened it wide and gave her a rough nod that flashed the namesake crawler on his dome, its bug eyes glistening with sweat.

"Can't you put on a hat or something? It's staring at me again," Vesta said.

Spider cracked a smile, but then said under his breath, "The boss stopped by. Keep your cool."

In his dust-stained ivory suit, Elay hurriedly put his arm around Vesta and walked her in. "This is the last one, Sire."

He brought her to a line-up of hookers where a husky vamp leaning on a cane scrutinized them. Elay's greater sire looked worse for wear, with several diamonds missing from his platinum fangs. "You took your time."

"And you got nerve, calling me fifteen minutes before my shift." Vesta popped her hip.

"She's got a mouth." He snorted. "Don't worry, babe. Your manager won't ask questions. Not even if you're a no-show."

Vesta scrunched her nose, but his nasty smirk kept her quiet.

"Jaxon's crew said he left to personally deliver Elay's adoption forms, but no one's seen him since." He hobbled down the line-up. "I'm here to figure out where he disappeared to."

"We don't know," London said. "He never showed up here."

The sire narrowed his eyes, then turned to Elay's men. "How about you two meatsacks? What'd you see?"

"Didn't see him." Spider met his eyes squarely. With his stony poker face, you'd never guess he had snapped Jaxon's joints to help Elay fit him into the tub.

Charles nodded, sweating bullets.

The sire got into his face, slowly turning his head for effect. "You got something you want to tell me?"

Elay cleared his throat. "Charles don't speak much. A dog got ahold of his throat back in his fight pit days."

"Hmph." The sire leered at Vesta.

She put on a doe-eyed look, pretending to be another confused skin doll.

He sighed. "You're pissing me off, Elay. You think I'm stupid? No way both of your sires go missing in the same week on pure coincidence. I know you were pissed he got put up for your spot, but my hands were tied. Bloodlines run deep in this family, and I'm not gonna be able to protect you this time. This is your last chance to cough someone up that I can pin this on to get the legacy vamps off my back."

Elay puffed his cig, looking over his family. His eyes went to London first—she was always his first—then to Spider and Charles; they were his family too, and even if he wasn't close with all the skin girls, he had taken responsibility for them when the storm hit, so there was a slim chance he'd sell any of them out now. And finally, his gaze landed on Vesta. It felt like everyone was looking at her, the outsider, the girl who had pulled the trigger.

Elay shrugged. "People go dark when a storm rolls in. I dunno what to tell you."

His sire shook his head. "Never thought I'd see a vamp too loyal for his own good. You better get your pipes deep cleaned before Jaxon's dad shows up."

"Shit, Victor Moroska's coming himself? I thought he didn't even like the little turd."

"Who did? But that kid had eight percent of the Hierarch's genes in him, and a man don't take an insult like this lying down."

"He won't find jack here." Elay helped his sire to the door.

"Make sure of that, 'cause Victor won't give you the same courtesy I have." He waited for Elay to hold open the door and then hobbled out.

When Elay shut it, Vesta bit her thumb too hard, loosening an acrylic nail. "Did I dust us?"

Elay ran a hand down the back of his neck. "We're in a rough spot, but we've been through worse."

She frowned, trying not to get too emotional in front of the crew. "Y'all covered for me. Not one of you made a peep."

London raised an eyebrow. "You think we'd rat on one of our own?"

Elay nodded, though he didn't share London's cheer. "Running a hit is no joke. Consider yourself officially initiated into the house. You ever need anything, we got your back."

This house was a dump, packed with weirdos, runaways, and girls with nowhere else to call home. It was the kind of place everyone expected a small-colony girl to end up turning tricks, but that wasn't where Vesta's story ended. This was only the beginning, and there was nowhere left to go but up.

"I appreciate it, but I'm aiming for a different career path—non-profit work, maybe," Vesta said. "All of you opened my eyes to what this city's really like. It's ugly and grimy, with cracks people fall into that they never climb back out of, but there's still good in all the bad. There's people doing the little they can to watch out for one another, and of all the blood hustlers I could have fallen in with, I could have done worse than to end up with you guys."

"Alright, leg bone, we don't need a speech." London's glossed lips quirked into a smile.

Spider patted her shoulder, and Charles flashed his gummy grin.

"Stay in touch." Elay took the gun from his back pocket and checked the chamber. "You got potential, Ves, and I got work for people with your kind of steel."

Dezi took his emerald-rimmed watch out of its case and snapped it onto his wrist. It was heavy, and not because of the platinum; this favor had paid the rent on Cormac's luxurious Diskos flat, where Dezi, Vesta, and his newly adopted cat, Marble, had been sleeping on the couch. It had paid for their food, water, and new clothes. Although he and Umbra had agreed to be friends, Dezi questioned whether that was possible between a host and his guest. Any other mortal would have exchanged a liter of blood and an hour in a locked room for a favor like this, but Umbra hadn't even been on the planet when he ordered it. It simply appeared in Ms. Mai's hands the same day she begrudgingly rehired Cormac and promoted Dezi to assistant manager.

As he stood before his locker mirror, rubbing spice-scented pomade between his hands, Ms. Mai entered the locker room in a huff. "Dezi! Do you intend to keep him waiting?"

"I'll be there in a minute." Dezi quickly put a swoosh in his hair and then wiped his hands. He didn't intend to aggravate her, but after seeing her get sucked on like bagged juice, she had lost the ability to intimidate him. He smiled at his reflection, pleased with what he saw, and then shut his locker.

Ms. Mai crossed her arms, standing in the doorway to block him. "If you can't arrive on time, I'll find him a more seasoned host."

"Funny, I thought you wanted to relocate to AZURE." Dezi adjusted his cuffs, flashing his new watch at her. "But I guess blood doesn't age like wine."

"W—who told you that?" she stammered.

"No one in particular."

"The security cameras—that's how you found our booth." She grabbed Dezi's arm and hissed, "Tell me what you saw, you little rat."

"Everything." Dezi yanked free. "And if you can't learn how to log out of a terminal, maybe Stellaire needs a more competent floor manager."

"*Everything?*" Her face turned as pale as chalk, making her pink blush clownishly bright. "You're going to get me killed."

"I could have, but I didn't tell Umbra what I saw." As irritating as Ms. Mai was, he couldn't help but sympathize with her. If someone didn't know better, they'd assume the two of them were a pair of the star vampire's thralls.

"*He's* not the problem, it's Seiyo that's the threat. You can't seriously be this stupid. The moment he loses interest in you, we will both fail Seiyo's next risk assessment."

"He won't get bored of me. I'm not some shiny new toy."

"Dear Nova, you *are* that stupid."

Dezi raised his head, but the seed of uncertainty she had planted in him was taking root. "So what does that make you? Last decade's model?"

She scowled. "Who do you think finds him new hosts to play with? Who helps Seiyo clean up the mess when he's done? Who deletes the recordings? I am useful; that's why I'm still here."

"And you think that makes you special…" Dezi moved for the exit, shouldering her out of his way. "We're all replaceable here. You taught me that yourself."

Dezi paced to the casino entrance, ignoring everyone in his way. He didn't intend to become the next Ms. Mai, but she clearly saw him as a threat, and his situation was too precarious to allow her scheming to go unchecked. It was better to let her think he was a legitimate rival rather than the stupid kid she had initially tried to feed to Umbra. At least that way, she'd have to consider the leverage he had before trying to get rid of him.

Umbra wasn't at the Casino entrance, so Dezi continued to the lobby, searching for the young vampire. A ways past the front desk, a small automated cocktail bar faced the windows overlooking the grand water fountain and valet desk outside. A slender figure sat at the counter alone, his red-bottomed heels tucked onto the stool's footrest.

Dezi licked his lips and approached, struggling with what to say. It had been a month since they had last seen each other—since they had hit the reset on their relationship—and this meeting would determine how they went forward. Would Umbra treat him like a person, or would he revert to seeing him as a possession? Now that they knew his feelings weren't for Dezi at all, but a person from his past, would he even like him anymore? The vampire didn't keep many friends, and at the end of the day, Dezi's use was as a memento.

Standing a little way behind him, Dezi cleared his throat.

"Dezi." Umbra hastily stood to face him. The old Umbra would have taken his host into his arms and kissed his cheek, but now he stood back with his posture as stiff as Dezi's.

"Hi." Dezi smiled weakly. "Am I supposed to bow, or do we shake hands?"

Umbra smiled softly, acknowledging their predicament, then lowered himself in a slight bow, placing his right hand over his chest and turning his head partially aside to display where his family brand would have been if his neck wasn't covered. Immortals did not bow to humans; this was the sign of respect they used with one another.

Dezi mimicked the bow, taking it deeper to show deference.

"I suppose we will make this your first lesson in formal etiquette; it is the younger vampire who should bow first." Umbra sat, gesturing to the stool beside him. "How have you fared since we last met? I heard from my little *sucrerie* that you were promoted to assistant manager."

Dezi took his seat. "I assume you ordered Ms. Mai to do that."

"*Moi?*" Umbra touched his chest. "No love, she nominated you herself. To be fair, she had precious few hosts to choose from and fewer still with the patience to take on trainees."

"Oh." Dezi blinked, half-embarrassed that his first assumption was that this promotion was unearned. "That was surprisingly nice of her."

"I hope you'll make an effort to get along, but I'm sure you are eager to discuss matters of business. You'll be glad to hear I have wrangled those Planitr slugs into a deal. They wouldn't take a direct payment—of course, they had to make it difficult—but I'll be leasing them one of my micro-class ships for the season. They'll finally have their own competitor in the Formula-One division. *Huzzah.*" Umbra rolled his eyes.

Dezi rested his arms on the bar. "Thank you, sincerely. It'd take me a century to explain how much this means to me."

"Oh, do go on. I could listen for a millennium." Umbra propped his elbow on the counter and touched his cheek, absolutely basking in Dezi's praise.

"I think we need to talk about *us*, if that's alright."

Umbra turned his face away slightly. "I don't suppose you've changed your mind about coming back with me. I missed you terribly, and I hate that I had to send spies after you to hear your living arrangements were in jeopardy. You understand that you can come to me when you're in need, don't you?"

"But I can't. It doesn't feel right accepting all this help from you when I'm not giving you anything back."

"You give me your time." Umbra circled his nail on a coaster. "From a mortal, that's a valuable thing."

"But I'm supposed to be giving you memories. I know that you're busy, and you can't visit me every weekend, but I haven't done anything useful for you yet."

"I see your point, though that's easier said than done. I'm not comfortable asking for what recovering these memories entails."

"What do you mean?" Dezi pulled his chair closer. "I want to help you as much as you're helping me."

"Dezi, the person we're talking about was my lover—the first love of my life. To re-walk these memories entails reenacting the intimate moments between us."

Pressure rose up through Dezi's stomach, and he swallowed down hard. Obviously, Umbra and his first love had slept together. Probably lots of time, in all types of ways.

Dezi tugged his shirt, letting out some of the heat building under it. "As long as we communicate and agree to everything ahead of time, I don't think that'll be a problem. I mean, I'm definitely attracted to you."

Umbra's gaze darted back to Dezi, cutting as slivers of ruby. "It is a problem, because I am not comfortable being intimate with you."

His words hit Dezi like a bucket of ice water dumped over his head. Why had he assumed Umbra was automatically down for casual sex? The immortal princeling was already paranoid, so it was ridiculous for Dezi to expect him to be eager to jump into bed with someone who had tried to secretly film him. He had to remember he wasn't entitled to Umbra's trust, and it would take a long time to earn back. "I understand. If you ever want to talk or even vent at me, I'm here for you."

Umbra's jaw flexed, but as he studied Dezi's face, his rigid posture gave out. "It's not so simple. If I don't return to Seiyo with regular progress, he may become impatient. Although he has agreed to allow things to remain as they are, he is quite vexed with us. Though a measure of that irritation stems from abandoning him in a run-away limo. I'm told the wreck was quite a sight."

Dezi grimaced. "Is he alright?"

"Of course. It would take far more than a lithium explosion to kill that man."

"I see he's not with you today. Should I be worried?"

"Oh no, I snuck out. He thinks I'm getting my brows re-threaded." Umbra smirked and waved at the Hadron bike parked beside the walkway outside. It was the same model as Ajax's, but a kitted-out limited-edition Akuma package with a color-shift finish that phased between night black and blood red. It was the type of bike kids dreamed of passing on the highway just to catch a glimpse of.

"Care to take it for a spin?" Umbra asked.

"Oh—I'm not sure. I'd love to, but I wrecked the last one I was on."

"Then we can take it slow, restrict ourselves to the driveways." Umbra offered his hand, wearing a tender expression that promised he would not be offended if Dezi refused.

"Alright, but you can't get upset if I scratch it." Dezi put his hand in Umbra's.

"Give me a moment to register you as a shared owner." He placed his wrist over Dezi's, aligning their chips, and tapped his fingers on his palm, navigating menus displayed on his augmented retinas.

This was the first time they had touched since his last visit, when they'd held each other and kissed. The contact they shared now was as platonic as humanly possible, but it still sent sparks across Dezi's skin. This arrangement was not going to be easy; remaining just friends with Umbra would never be easy.

Umbra released him, tucking a curl behind the flush-pink point of his ear. "There. I leave it on Mars when I'm away, so you can call it anytime you like. You'll need to set up the app to have the auto-pilot ride up to you and all that."

Dezi exhaled, steadying his foolish heart. "You're too generous."

"What fun are all these toys if you have no one to share them with?" Umbra put on his shades and stood. "Shall we?"

Dezi followed him to the bike, then mounted it and took up the kickstand. It was a hell of a lot bigger than his old one, with pillow-like suspension and a gorgeous holo-display. When he gripped the handlebars, the beast of an engine rumbled to life, and ultra-violet lights pulsed along its length.

Umbra climbed on behind him, taking care to keep his hands to himself. "Where will you be taking me, driver?"

Dezi revved the engine, getting a feel for its power. "Let's get out of here. I want to take you to Chryse, to Delta Park."

"Mmm, a walk in the park. If I didn't know better, I'd think you were trying to woo me."

Dezi shrugged, rolling the bike forward. "Romancing you is my job. Can you blame me for trying to enjoy it?"

"I wouldn't want to rob you of that joy." Umbra held Dezi's sides as the Hadron's speed picked up, and from the way his fingers curled into him, Dezi could tell he wanted more.

This film of respectability they had put up was suffocating. It would be so easy for Dezi to poke a hole in it, but if he did, their messy romance would come bleeding through. He'd be inviting Umbra to give in to his man-eating habits and offering himself up as the main course. But—Mars—Dezi wanted him. A vampire unlike any other, Umbra was the unabashed paragon of this age of cruel decadence, and Dezi was morbidly fascinated. As impossible as it sounded, he wanted to make Umbra his, but he wasn't afraid of a challenge. He would climb the mountain, carve his chunk out of the stars, and claim Umbra's heart for himself.

The clock was ticking, but Dezi's immortality had been twenty-three years in the making.

He turned the throttle, sending them roaring into the tunnel. "So we're clear, this is our first date."

Umbra wrapped his arms around Dezi's chest, bringing his lips to his ear. "It's a dangerous game you play, my would-be vampire. It won't end well."

Dezi laughed and checked over his shoulder, meeting Umbra's wicked smile. "How could it? I'm going to end up like you."

Support the Author

Amazon reviews are critical for indie authors, so please consider leaving Bleeding Mars a review!

Eager for more space vampires? You can get a free copy of the novella *Bleeding Mars: Looking Down* by signing up for my email list at **AsherQuazar.com/looking-down**. This story features Umbra, a young vampire down on his luck, and a night to remember at the top of the Hadron Tower.

To get updates on more installments in the Bleeding Mars universe, follow me on my socials:
- www.AsherQuazar.com
- www.tiktok.com/@asherquazar
- https://www.facebook.com/profile.php?id=61559019831921
- www.instagram.com/asherquazar

Playlist

Listen along! Each song is best enjoyed after completing the matching chapter.

1. Rocket Man – Elton John
2. Halcyon age – Vansire
3. Movin' Out – Billy Joel
4. Futuristic Casket – Phantogram
5. Someday – The Strokes
6. Starman – David Bowie
7. Fake ID – Riton
8. Stuck with Me – The Neighborhood
9. Something In The Air Between Us – Sophie Milman
10. Ruthless – The Marías
11. A-Punk – Vampire Weekend
12. Digital Animal – Honey Claws
13. Toi Et Moi – Paradis
14. Animal – Neon Trees
15. Alrighty Aphrodite – Peach Pit
16. Under Pressure – Queen & David Bowie

BLEEDING MARS

17. Money – Widowspeak

18. Naive – The Kooks

19. Back Against the Wall – Cage The Elephant

20. Freakin' Out On the Interstate – Briston Maroney

21. When You Were Young – The Killers

22. Dog Days Are Over – Florence + The Machine

23. Our Love is Easy – Melody Gardot

24. Goodbye Blue – BADBADNOTGOOD

25. Dreams – Fleetwood Mac

26. Human Nature – Babeheaven

27. Cold Heart (PNAU Remix) – Elton John & Dua Lipa

Bonus Novella:
Killer Queen – Queen

For J

Every work of art contains elements of the author's life, but Dezi's journey was inspired by the experiences of my beloved partner of ten years. I began writing this manuscript the same year he re-applied to college after dropping out at nineteen years old. We had met at eighteen, and soon after he'd moved back in with his family, I came out to mine; it was a time when I often felt like he was all I had.

Now the manuscript's final draft is complete, and in two weeks, I'll watch him accept his diploma. We plan to exchange vows at a courthouse later this year.

If you take anything from this story, let it be this: Don't let your mistakes define you. Despite the things outside of your control, you *can* strive for better.

Acknowledgements

Thank you to my family for being my first set of beta readers, to the Critters and Ubergroup communities for being my second, and to my discord friends for being my third. Thank you to my talented editors, Manu Velasco and Anne Casey, and cover artist, Sharlyn Artieda, for helping me bring this project to life. Thank you to the ARC readers who were willing to take a chance on my debut. Each review means the world to me.

Printed in Great Britain
by Amazon

42561102R00212